THE LUCIDITY PROJECT

THE LUCIDITY PROJECT

A NOVEL

ABBEY CAMPBELL COOK

SHE WRITES PRESS

Published 2016
Printed in the United States of America
ISBN: 978-1-63152-032-7
Library of Congress Control Number: 2016930515

For information, address:
She Writes Press
1563 Solano Ave #546
Berkeley, CA 94707

She Writes Press is a division of SparkPoint Studio, LLC.

For Josh, who helps to keep me lucid.

1

"**S**he's lucid," I heard a woman's voice say. "Can you let Dr. Shen know?"

My throat hurt and I felt hot and sweaty, like a child waking from a nap. There was the sound of beeping and people talking somewhere in the distance; it felt like someone had hit me in the head with a sledgehammer. As my surroundings came into focus I saw I was in a hospital bed, in a hospital room, with an IV in my arm and tubes in my nose. My mind began to spin. *How did I get here?* I tried to sit up but my body ached all over. Of course, that was nothing new. My body always hurt lately. All of me did.

There was a nurse in a chair by the door. She had a dirty blond bob, and was eyeing me suspiciously. We stared at each other for a second, then an Asian man with graying temples and a white lab coat walked in. He was followed by another nurse, probably in her fifties, wearing glasses.

"Hello Maxine," said the man. His tone was formal and he didn't try to shake my hand. "I'm Dr. Shen. How are you feeling?"

"My head hurts," I said. This was to be expected. I'd been getting migraines since I was a child, always on the left side of my head, always whenever I was under intense stress. "Where am I?"

Obviously I was in a hospital, I knew that, of course. But how did I get there? My mind was swimming, trying to remember the events from the night before.

"You're at Cedars-Sinai in West Hollywood."

In a flash, pieces of the previous night began to whirl around in my aching head.

"I'm going to ask you a few questions, okay?" he continued.

I nodded reluctantly.

"Do you know what year it is?"

"2016."

"And how old are you?"

"Twenty-five."

"Do you remember what happened last night?"

"No," I lied.

"The paramedics brought you in around 4 a.m. You were unconscious and not responding. You tested positive for benzodiazepine. We had to pump your stomach."

"Benzo-what?" I asked. I didn't remember taking anything that started with a "b."

"Xanax. Do you remember taking Xanax last night?"

Oh yes, I did remember taking that.

"It was an accident," I tried to explain. "The new meds I was trying brought on some sort of panic attack and I was just . . . trying to calm down. So I took a few Xanax."

"I think we both know you took more than a few, Maxine," Dr. Shen said, raising his eyebrows.

"Fine, fine," I said, falling back onto my pillows. "Jeez, you'd think I tried to drown a litter of kittens or something, the way you guys are acting. It's not what it looks like. I had an adverse reaction to the new medication I was trying. That's all."

"I see," was all he said.

I felt the need to explain myself further.

"This isn't supposed to be happening," I said. "I have a good job. I come from a good family." Tears sprang to my eyes, as they're bound to do after waking up from a failed suicide attempt. Still, I didn't feel as emotional as I could have been—probably a side effect from the Xanax. It tends to have a numbing effect. Thank God.

He nodded, then looked back at his chart.

"Who found me last night, exactly?" I asked. It was hard to try and focus in my condition, but I knew someone had to have found me passed out in my apartment and called the paramedics. The question was, who? I barely talked to any of my neighbors. Could it have been the Korean lady next door? I didn't even know her name. And what would she have been doing in my apartment while I was passed out on the floor?

Dr. Shen blinked a few times. "The paramedics brought you in."

"Yes, I understand that. But who called them?" I asked. "I live alone."

He looked down and flipped through a few pages on his chart. "It says here that you did."

"Me?" I asked, my voice cracking. That couldn't be right. How could I call anyone if I was passed out?

"Well, it's a good thing you did," he said, "or you probably wouldn't be here talking to us right now." He glanced over his shoulder toward the hallway. "One of our staff psychiatrists will be coming down to talk to you momentarily. Is there someone we can call for you in the meantime? A family member? A therapist?"

I shook my head no, and began to get out of the bed. This is exactly what I'd been trying to avoid. In California if you do anything that remotely appears like attempted suicide you are automatically 5150ed and thrown into a psych ward against your will. I'd already spent a week at Cedar-Sinai's psych facility two years earlier after a similar mishap with a bottle of Vicodin, and I had no intention of going back. There was nothing these people could do for me. I'd been through all this before.

"I feel better now," I lied. "I'd rather just head home."

Dr. Shen stiffened. "We can't release you before you talk to the staff psychiatrist."

"You can't hold me here against my will," I said to him, my voice rising. "I know my rights." This was also a lie. I had no idea what my rights were. I just knew I couldn't spend the next week in a psychiatric ward. What I needed to do was get back to my therapist and start on a different medication—one that actually didn't make me want to kill myself. This man was a doctor. Didn't he realize that if the psych ward had worked last time I wouldn't be here right now?

I tried to get up again but there was still an IV in my arm. If I wanted to leave I'd have to pull the thing out by myself. This thought was enough to override the numbing effects of the Xanax and practically send me into hysterics.

"I can't stay here!" I practically screamed at Dr. Shen. "You have to take this IV out. Now. "

"Gretchen . . ." Dr. Shen said without changing the tone of his voice.

The nurse in the glasses walked toward me quickly, and then the woman at the end of the bed was on her feet as well. I threw my hands out at them but I was no match against their well-rehearsed offense.

"Five milligrams of Haldol, please," ordered Dr. Shen.

One of the nurses did something to the IV while the other tried to "there-there" me back down onto the pillows. When that didn't work the two of them whipped out restraints and tied me to the bed. Dr. Shen stood back and let the women do the dirty work. Unfortunately for me, they were very good at their jobs.

"Just relax," Dr. Shen said from his safe place, an arm's reach away. "You'll feel better in just a bit."

"Yeah right," I said, laughing, as the scene around me began to slow and darken. "You people have been saying that for years."

●●●

When I woke up sometime later, the lights of the hospital room were dimmed and it was dark outside my window. I looked over at the digital clock next to my bed. It was three o'clock in the morning. Whatever they'd given me had done a good job of knocking me out. They could be counted on for that, at least.

The nurse at the end of the bed was gone, and from what I could see no one was in the hall, which meant it was a good time to get the hell out of there. The IV and breathing tubes were gone. The only problem was the restraints tying me to the bed. I knew if I thrashed around and tried to get free I'd draw attention—so instead I pulled slowly, as hard as I could, and surprisingly the restraint on my left arm began to give. After a few minutes of slow pulling I was able to get the cuff to my mouth. I worked on the buckle with my teeth until the restraint strap pulled free from the cuff around my wrist; then I undid the second one with my free hand. The cuffs themselves were still around my wrists, but they'd have to come off later.

As quietly as possible I made my way over to the door to my room and peeked out. On my left was a hallway lined with hospital room doors; at the end of the hall were double doors below a green Exit sign. That was where I needed to go. To the right, about five doors down, was a nurse's station. A woman was there, but her back was to me and the lights in the hallway were dimmed. Escaping should be relatively easy.

Surprisingly, my headache was gone. Usually after a stressful event like this my head would be screaming in pain like it had been earlier. Perhaps luck was on my side tonight.

It took me only about a minute or two to tiptoe down to the exit doors. My heart pounded the whole way. All the nurse had to do was look to her right and she'd see me sneaking down the hall. She didn't— but as I opened one of the exit doors, a screeching sound cut through the silence.

Oh no! The alarm!

Adrenaline shot through my body. I heard yelling behind me, and I turned to see two large orderlies round the corner of the nurse's station and charge toward me down the hall.

Heart racing, I bolted through the exit door and into an elevator bay. There were three elevators in front of me, and, luckily, one of them was open. I darted inside, spun around, punched the lobby button, and leaned into the button that closed the doors. Just as the two orderlies burst into the room, the elevator doors began to slide shut. In a panic, I pounded repeatedly on the close button, as if that would make a difference. The orderlies lunged at me, their faces flushed with rage, but they weren't fast enough, and I heard their bodies slam against the door a second after it closed.

I sighed a breath of relief, but I wasn't in the clear yet. I still had to get to the bottom floor and out of the hospital before the orderlies caught up to me, and the alarm was still blaring outside the elevator.

"You won't get out of here this way," said a voice to my left.

"Oh God!" I gasped, grabbing my chest. I somehow hadn't noticed that there was someone else with me in the elevator. A man in a purple hat.

"My apologies, I didn't mean to scare you," he said, eyeing my hospital gown. I stared up at him, still surprised I hadn't seen him when I ran into the elevator. He was tall, probably in his thirties, and strikingly handsome, with dark hair, a strong nose, and incredibly light blue eyes that stood out almost unnaturally against his tan skin. He wore a three-piece pinstriped suit with a dark purple hat and matching bow tie. I felt like I'd seen him somewhere before. With looks like his, I figured he had to be an actor.

"Where are you going, exactly?" he asked. His voice was soft but masculine. The stuff movie stars are made of.

"I'm trying to get out of here," I said, unable to break my stare. Where had I seen this man before?

"You tried to hurt yourself." He nodded at the cuffs on my arms. I still hadn't had time to remove them.

My face flushed with embarrassment, and I pushed the lobby button again, impatient to get away. "Not really. I mean, yes, but it was an accident. Honestly, I really don't remember that much of what happened."

"They say those who can't remember the past are doomed to repeat it."

"Yeah," I said with a sigh. "They say a lot of things."

"How long have you been depressed?"

"Why?" I asked, eyeing him suspiciously. "You a doctor or something?"

"Yes," he said. "I am. What's your name?"

"Max," I said hesitantly, wondering if he was going to try to prevent me from escaping. "Why are you asking me all these questions?"

"Because I believe I can help you. I just need some information from you."

"What kind of information?" How could the elevator be taking so long to get to the bottom floor? I smacked the button again.

"Your address, date of birth. That sort of thing."

"I'm not going to tell you my address." What was this guy's deal? I looked him over again—the three-piece suit, the purple hat. *Who wears a three-piece suit these days?* I seriously doubted the guy was really a doctor. But if he wasn't, who was he? And what did he want with me?

He let out a deep sigh. "You're going to make this hard for me, I see. Can you tell me where we are, at least?"

I studied him curiously. "What do you mean, where are we? We're at Cedars-Sinai."

"In Los Angeles?" he asked with an amused smile. "Why am I not surprised? Let me guess: you're a writer."

"Well, yeah, sort of," I said. "How did you know?" It wasn't like I looked like a writer. With my wavy red hair, dark eyes, and thin frame, people always mistook me for an actress. What was going on? The guy was acting as if he knew me. But then I also suspected I knew him from somewhere. Perhaps he was an actor pretending to be a doctor, and that's why he looked so familiar.

As I pondered this, everything around me began to turn hazy and gray, and I had a hard time seeing the man or anything else around me. I froze, afraid to move. But then, just as quickly, the air cleared, and there I was in the elevator once again. Just as I was about to ask the man what was going on, the elevator doors opened and the two order-lies rushed out from the stairwell. They'd beat us to the bottom floor! I tried to push the close button, but it was too slow. I flung myself into the back corner of the elevator and braced myself for some serious manhandling. The man in the purple hat, however, smoothly stepped between the two men and myself and lifted his hand up at them like he was signaling cars to stop. To my total shock, the two men froze in place. It was like someone had shot them with a freeze-ray gun.

Okay, yes, I'm fully aware that freeze-ray guns are things of sci-fi movies and comic books, and not real. But, there they stood: mouths agape, arms reaching toward me, leaning forward in a full sprint, still as statues. Before I could try and comprehend what was going on, the man in the purple hat turned around, laid a hand on my shoulders, and looked straight into my eyes.

"We don't have much time," he said. "What's your last name?"

"What? Dorigan," I said, too frightened to pull away. I glanced at the orderlies, who were still frozen at the door of the elevator. "Who are you?" I asked. "How did you freeze those men like that?"

"We're dreaming, that's all," he answered. "This is a dream, Ms. Dorigan."

"A dream?" I asked. What was he talking about? It was quite obvious I was wide awake.

"If you want me to help you I need more information," he continued.

"What?" I asked again. Then I narrowed my eyes. "Why?"

"So I can find you."

"What do you mean, find me? I'm right here," I said, staring over his shoulder at the orderlies.

"What's your doctor's name? Who can I get in with contact here?"

"Dr. Anne Meade. She's my therapist. Why? What do you want with me?"

"I don't have time to explain that to you right now, and honestly, Ms. Dorigan, you probably aren't going to remember much about this dream anyway." He faded out a little, like he was disappearing, and for a moment I could see through him to the men frozen behind him.

"Of course I'll remember," I said. My fear was starting to be replaced by curiosity. If this man could freeze people in place, curing a young woman of her depression shouldn't be too much of a feat for him. "What's happening to you?"

"I'm waking up, I'm afraid."

"Waking up?" It looked like he was about to disappear. "But you said you could help me! How will I find you again?"

"I'll send someone for you," he said, and he went see-through again.

"Who will you send? How will I know it's you?" I called. I could barely see him now.

"You won't," he said—then everything around me went gray again, as if I were surrounded by a thick fog, and when it dissipated a few seconds later, I found myself on a tropical beach surrounded by what looked like mango trees. The man in the purple hat, the orderlies, and the elevator were gone. But I didn't have too much time to ponder what had happened to them because the ocean was rising up into a massive wave in front of me, unnaturally quickly. I knew there was no use outrunning it—but that didn't mean I couldn't try. I turned and charged up the beach but only got a few feet before the water crashed hard on top of me. I tried to fight it, but it was no use. A freezing cold shock of water filled my lungs, my body revolted, and everything went black.

2

People say that if you die in your dreams you die in real life. That's not true. All you do is wake up. I know—I die in my dreams all the time. Something I just can't manage to pull off in the waking world.

I'd had the recurring tidal wave dream ever since I could remember. It didn't limit itself to the beach, it could happen anywhere: my house, the grocery store, the doctor's office. Sometimes it came out of nowhere. Other times there was a dramatic build-up, like strange noises in the distance. But there were a few things that remained constant: As it got closer, the ground would start to shake and I'd hear buildings or trees crumbling and people screaming. Then I'd look up, out a window, or over the tops of trees, and I'd see it coming for me. Powerlessness would wash over me, and I'd stand there paralyzed, watching it get closer. Sometimes I'd try to run, but it was no use. It always took me under.

I'd been having this dream since I was a little girl. Night terrors— that's what the doctors called them. They said they would stop as I got older, but they never did.

The weirdest thing was that, despite having had this recurring dream many times over the years, when I was in it and the wave appeared, I could never remember that I was dreaming. You'd think seeing that stupid wave would trigger something in my mind, spark some kind of memory, and alert me that the dream wasn't real. But it never did.

The dream that night in the hospital was different, though, because of the man with the purple hat. It all seemed so real. But dreams always seem so real. When you're in them, anyway. Then after you wake up you wonder how your mind could have bought into a reality that made no sense whatsoever. The next morning, I told myself that my unconscious mind was just trying to comfort me by conjuring up the man with the purple hat—a magic Superman who was going to save me from myself. Then reality had come crashing down on top of me in the form of the tidal wave. No symbolism lost on me there. The truth was, there wasn't anyone who could help me. My family and I had spent practically my whole life trying to find a cure to my depression and other health issues. Nothing had worked.

The hospital psychiatrist was waiting in the chair by the door in my room when I woke up. A pinched woman with mousy hair. She said she wanted to admit me to the psych ward on the fourth floor and indicated I didn't really have a choice in the matter. By that point I was exhausted and didn't have much more fight left in me. Where did I think I was going—back to my crappy apartment to hide in my room and cry? That wasn't safe for me. Now that the antidepressant I'd been trying was out of my system I no longer felt like I wanted to die, and I knew if I wanted to find an antidepressant that did work, going down to the psych ward was my only option.

I decided to cooperate. My parents were called, the proper paperwork was filled out, and I was given a robe and some slippers, escorted to the fourth floor, and taken to my room—a sparse, ten-foot-by-ten-foot square with fiber board ceilings and two metal twin beds. The one closest to the opposite wall was occupied by a brunette who appeared to be sleeping. As I entered, she turned over, eyed me for a second, then turned back and faced the wall.

At three I was taken into an office to meet with Dr. Meade and the resident psychiatrist for my psych eval. Dr. Meade had been my therapist for the past four years and had driven all the way from her office in Santa Monica to see me. I liked Dr. Meade. She dressed like an ex-hippie who hadn't quite given up the cause—long, flowy skirts, dangling jewelry, frizzy silver hair—except that she always added something professional looking to the mix. Today it was a blazer, which didn't really go with her gauzy paisley skirt. Of course, I didn't have room to talk: I hadn't showered in a week.

The minute I sat down on the sofa and looked into Dr. Meade's face I burst into tears. We'd been working together for so long, and yet nothing had changed. Nothing! I wanted her to hug me, give me a pat on the back, anything, but instead she sat there and waited quietly. There was sympathy in her eyes, yes, but it was a reserved kind of sympathy—studied, practiced, perfect—and I resented her for it.

The psychiatrist the hospital had assigned to me was voluptuous, had dark hair, and was probably only five or six years older than me. I assumed she wore glasses and her hair pulled back to look more professional, but instead she reminded me of one of those sexy teachers in those old heavy metal videos from the '80s. Like any minute Vince Neil would kick in the door and she'd throw off her glasses and do a striptease on the desk.

"I know this is hard, Maxine," Dr. Meade finally said. "Why don't you tell us what happened." Usually she would stay silent at the beginning of our sessions, forcing me to be the first to talk. Today was a different story.

"What's the point?" I said, not bothering to fight the tears. "No matter what I do, nothing works. I'm so tired of it all."

"I understand," Dr. Meade said. "But if you want help you're going to need to work with us. We need to make a plan."

I sighed. She was right. What I wanted more than anything was to feel better. That's all I'd wanted for as long as I could remember: to be a normal human being who could do normal things like go to work and hang out with her friends without feeling like jumping off a cliff. Plus, Dr. Meade was the one with the prescription pad, so I had no choice but to cooperate.

"It was the medication again, just like last time," I said. My last suicide attempt had also been an adverse reaction to a new medication I'd been trying. "Adverse reaction"—that's what Dr. Meade called it when I freaked out after trying a new antidepressant. According to her I had dysthymia—a chronic, low-grade depression that on its own doesn't usually lead to suicidal thoughts but, when mixed with the wrong medication or a traumatic event, things can go downhill fast.

"This was day two of taking the medication?" she asked.

"Yes, day two," I sniffed, grabbing a few tissues out of the box on a table next to me. "After I took it the first day I started to feel really sad, then when I took it again the next day things got worse. Everything felt so hopeless. I got another migraine, and my body was hurting so much I couldn't get out of bed. I started feeling really anxious, so I took a few Xanax. Then I took a few more. I knew the medication wasn't working, yet again, and I guess I just went into a tailspin. I overreacted, I just couldn't . . . " I shook my head. I was so tired of talking about myself and my depression. When would it end?

Dr. Meade made a few notes on her notepad. "So you think the medication is what led to your suicidal thoughts?" she asked.

"Yes," I said hopelessly. "I don't understand why the medications won't work for me. They work for everyone else."

"They don't work for everyone else, Maxine, and that's what we wanted to talk to you about today," Dr. Meade said.

The sex kitten shifted in her seat.

"I think at this point we need to explore other options besides medication," Dr. Meade said.

"What do you mean?" I asked, wiping my eyes, though I knew what was coming.

"We've tried over fifteen medications. Both of your suicide attempts took place just days after starting two of them, and you've had adverse reactions to at least six of the others. The rest haven't hurt as much, but they haven't helped at all either. You seem to be getting worse with the more medications you try, not better."

"Are you telling me you aren't going to give me any more medication?" I asked, growing frantic.

"I think for now it's time to take another approach."

"But what about my career?"

Dr. Meade lightly pursed her lips together. I knew she hated it when I worried about my "career"—if that's what you could call it. For the past couple of years I'd been a writers' assistant on a TV show called *You Sexy Witch* that was about teen witches who fought demonic crime in low-cut blouses and skin-tight pants. It wasn't a great show, but I didn't have a lot going for me, and my job was the tiny speck of light in the dark stormy night I called my life. My dream was to one day be a full-fledged television writer, and this job felt like the first step toward achieving that dream. But in order to make that happen I needed energy. I needed drive. I needed a goddamn medication that worked. I'd spent the last month of the last season in bed every second I wasn't at work. I couldn't keep it together in front of my coworkers forever; I knew if I didn't find an antidepressant that worked by next season I was going to lose my job—the only thing that was keeping me afloat.

"Let's concentrate on getting better right now," said Dr. Meade. "Getting better comes before career."

"How am I supposed to get better if you're not going to give me any more medication?" I asked, choking back a sob. It was hard to believe that less than forty-eight hours ago I'd tried to kill myself, and now I desperately wanted to live in order to work on a dumb television show about teen witches. Such is the mental and emotional logic of a depressive personality.

"I know it's hard to hear," Dr. Meade said, "but that doesn't mean we can't help you. There are other techniques we can try."

"Like what?" I sniffed.

"Well," she said, pulling out a piece of paper from under the notebook in her lap, "just this morning I received a very interesting phone call from a Dr. Alexandra Luna at the Theta Institute. She and her colleagues there are doing some very interesting research on a new depression treatment that combines hypnosis and dream therapy. She said they're looking for women in their mid-twenties who've had adverse reactions to antidepressants. When I mentioned you, she said you fit the bill perfectly."

"Hypnosis and dream therapy?" I asked. Could those things really help me when science had failed? It felt like a step backward.

"It's a twenty-one-day program at the Theta Institute, a health and wellness resort on a small island in the Caribbean. This might be just the thing you need, Maxine. A peaceful, relaxing vacation with others like yourself. You have been isolating quite a bit since the end of the television season, and it's certainly a much better environment than a psychiatric ward. Dr. Luna is going to be in Los Angeles tomorrow and would like to come and meet with you here at the hospital. How does that sound?"

Was she kidding me?

"I don't even have the energy to get off the couch," I said. "Flying to an island in the Caribbean is out of the question."

Dr. Meade tried again: "The therapy is also paired with a nutritional program that—"

"No," I said again, shaking my head. "Do you really think going on a new diet is going to help? That I'll find out my chemical imbalance has been the result of a gluten allergy or something? I've been down that road before." I'd tried all the depression diets. But when you're depressed, diets are hard to stay on.

"I can't," I said. "I'm too tired. I need to find a treatment here."

"Okay," she said, taking a deep breath. "Well, if you're not willing to go anywhere else, the only other option I'm seeing is electroconvulsive therapy."

We'd talked about electroconvulsive therapy before. Dr. Meade had explained that despite all the scary stuff you see on TV, a lot of people had had success with it. The problem was, there were some major side effects, one of which was short-term memory loss, which could last for weeks at a time.

I was barely able to function properly at work as it was.

"But my job . . ." I said. "It starts back up in a month. I won't be able to keep my job if I can't remember things."

"Maybe you should consider taking some time off from work," Dr. Meade said gently.

"You can't take time off from a television show when you're a writers' assistant," I said, my voice rising. "They just replace you with someone else. It took me two years to get that job. I can't leave now."

I knew I was being unreasonable. Dr. Meade was right: I should be putting my health first. But this job was the only thing keeping me going at the moment. I'd always had this thought that maybe if I made it to being a television writer I'd finally be happy. Like, that level of accomplishment would somehow create more serotonin in my brain, or whatever it was I needed to be normal. The previous year was supposed to be the year I got promoted to staff writer, but I hadn't had the energy to keep up as well as the others, and someone else had gotten the job. My boss Evan had told me I was still in the running for the following season, I just needed to work harder. But in order to do that, I needed to feel better *now*—and it was becoming more and more evident that that wasn't going to happen.

I felt myself starting to shake. I tried to say something else but managed to only get out a strange guttural noise. I sounded like a dying animal. I wanted to back myself into the corner, but there was a ficus there.

"Maxine, remember, it's possible that what you need hasn't been invented yet," Dr. Meade said, leaning forward toward me.

"How do you know that? How?" I knew she was trying to be helpful, but I also knew that what she was really saying was that I had run out of options.

I looked to the sexpot for confirmation.

"A lot of money is going into antidepressants right now," she tried to assure me. "It's just a matter of time."

"For now I'm going to recommend electroconvulsive therapy," Dr. Meade said. "I know, that's disappointing, but it's the only option you have if you want to stay close to home. Your parents are on their way here?"

"Yes. They should be here soon."

"Why don't you discuss it with them and we can all talk together tomorrow."

I nodded. The vamp scribbled something on her pad. Somewhere outside, a bell chimed four o'clock.

Dr. Meade looked down at her watch. "It looks like our time is up."

"Yes," I said. "It certainly seems that way."

••

"What do you mean they aren't going to give you any more medication?" asked my mother. Her eyes were creased with worry; she was frowning her way through visiting hour. I felt so guilty for putting those creases on her face. She and my dad had spent so much time, money, and energy trying to help me get better, and to very little avail.

Dad squinched his pudgy face and burst into tears. This was the third such outburst since we'd started talking ten minutes earlier.

"Bob, stop, please. You're just making it worse," Mom said from behind him. Her short black hair was cropped in a short, pixie-cut kind of thing. She called it her Kris Jenner. Everything she was wearing today, in fact, was inspired by Kris Jenner.

"Jeez, Gale. I'm sorry I'm crying because our daughter tried to kill herself—again! What's wrong with me?" he shot back.

I didn't say my parents were perfect. They had their struggles too. But I couldn't help but wonder if these were just coping mechanisms they'd been forced to develop in their years of dealing with me. Honestly, I was just happy I hadn't driven them to drink.

"Okay, okay," Mom said, putting her hands up defensively and looking back at me. Then she softened and took my hands in hers. "I'm sorry, Max. I'm just so worried about you. Your dad and I, we just don't know what to do. Neither of us has any idea what to do. And now it looks like the doctors don't either? It's very . . . well, it's very frustrating."

Dad started to cry again, which made me feel even worse, so I looked down at my shoes.

"You have to fight this," Mom said, taking my hand and squeezing it hard. "You've been doing so good, Maxine. Look at all you've managed to do, even with the depression. Are you sure you don't want to try Prozac again? My sister Jean's been on it for over fifteen years and it's made such a big difference in her life. She's like a different person."

I shook my head no. "I couldn't eat on the Prozac, remember?"

"That's right. That's right," she said, seeming to have forgotten we'd had this conversation ten times before.

"Why don't you come stay with us for the summer? You can get some rest," Dad said. Mom nodded.

My parents lived up in a small suburban town in Northern California where there was no work for creative types like me. Most of my friends had moved away, and those who hadn't worked at the local Walmart or Applebee's. If I went back there that would be my fate as well.

"But my job—"

"That job is very stressful," Mom said. "You can always get another job."

"Not on a television show," I corrected her. "I can't give up my job, Mom. It keeps me . . . going."

"Maybe you could take a sabbatical from work and come back next year," she tried again.

Clearly the adults in my life didn't understand the cutthroat industry of television writing. There was no coming back. There weren't even any sick days (though I'd taken quite a few). I thought back to the literally hundreds of resumes that had come in for the production assistant position when I had moved up to writers' assistant. The applicants came from Harvard, Brown, Yale—one girl had just been on *Oprah*. They wouldn't boot the girl from *Oprah* out to let me—a girl who barely finished high school and never even went to college—back in. The only reason I'd gotten the job in the first place was because the producer liked my spec script. A new wave of panic swept over me.

"You have no other choice," Mom said, her eyes just short of pleading. "Your life is more important than your job. People like you can't live like the rest of us. I'm sorry, but you can't. You have a disability, Max. You know this. You have to take your health into account."

My mother was the type of person who would call Evan, my executive producer, and tell him that I was suicidal if she thought it would help. And I couldn't fault her for that. She was only trying to help me stay alive. I realized that if I wanted to stay in LA and keep my job, I had to make my parents think that I was going to be okay.

"Dr. Meade suggested electroconvulsive therapy," I said. I didn't want to bring up the dream therapy thing, because as far as I was concerned, it wasn't an option.

"Like in *One Flew Over the Cuckoo's Nest*?" Mom practically shrieked.

She looked at my father, who was staring straight at me, unblinking.

"It's not as bad as you think," I said, but I had to admit the thought of it scared the crap out of me, and I started to cry, which started my dad going again. A few of the other people in the room looked over at us and stared. Could this day get any worse?

"I'm going to go talk to the doctor," Mom said, and before I could stop her she got up and marched out into the hallway.

Oh yes. Yes it could.

I looked over at my dad.

"She's just trying to help," he said.

"I know," I said. I had so many people trying to help. Why wasn't it working?

•••

When my mom talked with Dr. Meade she found out about the dream therapy opportunity and a meeting was set up with Dr. Luna for the next day. I tried to argue with her—said that I didn't have the time or energy to leave the country for a month—but then my dad started crying again and she looked like she was about to as well, so I quickly gave in and agreed to the meeting.

After that enlightening chat it was time for damage control, which meant I had to call Sofia—the closest thing to a best friend I had in LA, and one of the staff writers on *You Sexy Witch*. Crazy people aren't allowed cell phones in psychiatric hospitals, so I waited patiently by the payphone as a woman with pink spiky hair and a large bandage on her neck spoke lasciviously to someone on the other end of the line. When it was finally my turn, I wiped the receiver with the elbow of my robe and dialed Sofia—collect.

"What's going on? Why are you calling me collect?" Sofia shouted into the phone after the operator put me through. I could hear people laughing next to her in the background.

"Because... I'm in rehab," I lied.

"What?!" Sofia screeched through the phone. "What the hell compelled you to go to rehab?"

"My liver," I said. More lies. I couldn't tell her that I was having a major depressive episode and wanted to die. Sofia wasn't friends with people like that.

"But you don't drink any more than any of the rest of us, Max. Half the time you don't drink at all. Shut the hell up, you guys!" she screamed at the people laughing in the background. "I'm on the damn phone!"

"Where are you?" I asked. It never failed to surprise me how different our lives were.

"In Palm Springs," she said, "with Charlie and everyone. I called you to invite you, but I guess you were busy checking into rehab. Jesus, Max."

More than anything in the world I wanted to be more like Sofia. Vivacious and outgoing, she didn't care a bit about what people thought about her. She had energy and drive. A zest for life I wanted so badly. She was often bitchy and short with people on set, and yet everyone still seemed to adore her. It probably helped that she was drop-dead gorgeous with a body to die for.

We'd met at the season opening party. I was bringing Evan, our executive producer, a drink, and Sofia mistook me for someone important. We ended up talking for the next few hours and she did something that was almost impossible to do—made me forget about myself for a little while. This was probably because the conversation was mostly about her. But I didn't mind. She led an incredibly charmed life, had energy to burn, made tons of money, and looked like she belonged on the cover of a magazine—but she worked hard, too. Her parents had come over from Vietnam as refugees after the war and instilled a work ethic in her like none I'd seen before. We didn't have much in common, but I really liked Sofia, and Sofia really liked Sofia, and that seemed to be enough for the two of us.

"I had no idea you were having so much trouble," Sofia continued. "Is that why you're so tired all the time?"

"Yes. I'm sorry—look, don't tell anyone about any of this. It isn't something I want getting around."

"Max, get real. Half the writing team has been to rehab. The other half probably needs to go. It's not that big a deal."

"Still . . . " I said.

"You're right, of course not," she said. "My lips are sealed."

More silence.

"How long do you have to stay in there?"

"I don't know. I don't have all the details yet," I said.

"Well, can I bring you anything? When I get back from Palm Springs, I mean."

"No, I can't have visitors right now. It's very strict here."

"Shut up! I'll be right there!" she screamed at the people in the background. "Listen," she said, returning to a normal volume, "don't even worry about it. Everybody goes to rehab at some point. Evan told me once he doesn't trust writers that don't drink. I know you've been upset that you didn't get promoted to staff writer. Just think of this rehab thing as a little vacay. Pretend you're at the spa, work out like two hours a day, cut out all carbs. Everyone says when you stop drinking alcohol you lose like ten pounds instantly. Think how great you'll look when all this is over. You'll be refreshed and renewed, ready to take next season by storm."

"Yeah."

"We'll have a big party when you get out. I'll just tell everybody you're at your parents' for the month." Her voice rose again. "I know! I'm coming!" She sighed. "Look, I gotta go."

"Yeah."

"Rehab," she said, clearly still stunned. "I mean, Jesus, Max. With the money you're blowing in there you could have bought a Birkin."

3

I slept like a rock that night (thank you, Ambien), but still felt groggy the following morning. I was barely conscious as I dragged myself to my meeting with the dream therapist lady at 10 a.m.

We met in Group Room 2B, a large room used for art and music therapy that consisted of crafts tables and shelves packed with self-help and psychology books.

When I arrived, a woman in her sixties was sitting at one of the long crafts tables in the middle of the room. She wore tortoiseshell glasses, had a shock of silver hair, and was dressed in a very chic navy wrap dress. Her figure was phenomenal for her age—any age, actually—and altogether she had an appearance more becoming of a legendary stage actress than a medical professional.

"Maxine," she said excitedly, standing up from the table to greet me as I walked in. "Come in! Come in! How are you doing today, my darling?"

Her British accent was endearing, but I was thrown off by her enthusiasm. Rather than answering, I stood there feeling confused.

"That's such a ridiculous question," she continued before I could answer. "Obviously you aren't very well or you wouldn't be in the loony, now would you?"

"I'm sorry, I didn't get your name . . ." I muttered.

"Dr. Alexandra Luna, at your service," she said, coming up and giving my hand an enthusiastic shake. "Now, let's have a look at you." She took a step back and began to look me over. I felt like she was x-raying my body with her eyes.

"Hmmm, what's going on here?" she asked, waving her hand around the left side of my head.

"I, uh, I get migraines," I said. "The doctors say once I get my depression under control that should go away."

She looked over her glasses at me. "Yes, they will say that. Although in a way I suppose they're right. There's also some pretty severe fatigue as well?"

"Yes," I answered. "Chronic fatigue. Well, that's what they thought it was until I didn't respond to the medication. Now they don't know what it is. Did they let you read my file?"

"I guess you could say that," she said with a smirk.

I had given Dr. Meade permission to give my information to any researchers or medical professionals she thought might be able to help me, so it wasn't too much of a surprise that Dr. Luna would know so much about me.

"Do you have something for chronic fatigue too?"

"We have something for everything, my dear. Now, hold out your hands, palms up, please," she said.

When I complied, she grabbed an ink brayer from off the table, and before I knew what was happening, began rolling my left hand with ink.

"What's this for?" I asked. "You afraid I'm going to steal something?"

"Steal something? That's a good one! You sure haven't lost your sense of humor, have you?" she laughed, pressing my hand onto a piece of white paper on the desk. "Now, did Dr. Meade tell you anything about our little project?"

"Not much. She just said it had something to do with dreams."

"I see. Well then . . . I'll fill you in," she said, already working on the same inking process with my other hand. "The Theta Institute is a health and wellness resort located on a small island in the Caribbean with a focus on alternative therapies. Our facilities are top notch, providing truly luxurious and personal services. Many people come to us with serious health challenges, others need more . . . emotional and mental support. And some are just looking for some R&R. We have different classes and workshops centered on helping people rejuvenate mind, body, and spirit."

"So this would be like a self-help program?" I asked. "I don't know if Dr. Meade told you, but I'm a little beyond self-help."

Dr. Luna finished with my right handprint and handed me a few wet wipes.

"Yes, I would certainly agree. You are definitely in need of a higher form of assistance. That's where the Lucidity Project comes in to play."

"That's the dream therapy?" I asked as I began to wipe the ink off my hands. To my surprise, it came off rather easily.

"Yes, as well as a full-body eval and nutrition counseling."

"How is dreaming therapeutic?"

"Much like hypnotherapy, dreams give you access to your subconscious. In the dream state you have access to information that many find difficult to access in the waking world. Dr. McMoneagle, the head researcher on the project and the founder of the Theta Institute, has had quite a lot of success with these methods in his practice."

Dr. McMoneagle. The name sounded . . . "familiar" wasn't the right word, but there was something about it that gave me pause. I couldn't help but think of my dream from the night before—the man in the purple hat.

"Dr. McMoneagle?" I asked. "He wouldn't, by chance, be a tall, dark, and handsome man partial to purple hats?"

"No," she said, eying me curiously. Then, after a second or two, she said, "Dr. McMoneagle is blond and prefers much more . . . casual attire."

I relaxed a little. I must be crazy to think that someone in a dream had somehow orchestrated this meeting. Oh, that's right. I *was* crazy. That's why I was in a psych ward at the moment.

I turned and tossed the inky tissues into a small trashcan behind me as Dr. Luna grabbed a loupe from off the desk and began examining the print from my left hand. She seemed to be particularly interested in my thumb.

"What's with the fingerprints?" I asked.

"You can tell a lot by a person's fingerprints, if you know what I mean," she said.

"I don't know what you mean," I said honestly. "I don't really understand what's going on at all."

"What's going on is these people have done all they can do for you here," she said, beginning to pack up her things. "It's time to move on to something new. Something different."

"You think you can help me? But you've barely even asked me any questions." This was by far the shortest assessment I had ever been through.

"Whether we can help you is really up to you," she said.

"Well, if I was going to be under your care it would actually be up to you, wouldn't it?"

"Let's just say it would be a joint effort," she said. "At the Theta Institute, we believe in co-creating your therapy together. Think of us as a Waldorf school of healing."

"So, what . . . you're like, hippies or something?"

She laughed out loud, as if I'd just made a joke. "No, but our techniques are considered experimental by those in our field. Those in other fields as well, actually."

"Experimental?" I asked. Not a word you want to hear while considering treatments in a psych ward. "Does any of it . . . hurt?"

"No, no. Nothing physically painful." She paused. "Well, that's not true. You will need to detox. That can be quite uncomfortable. And how far can you run? When you're feeling better, I mean," she said, stopping her packing to look at me.

"Uh, half a mile, maybe, if I'm being chased by a serial killer. But what does that have to do with—"

"Well, then you're probably going to be in quite a lot of physical pain for the first week or so. But that's not any different than now, is it?"

"Look, you seem to have forgotten. I have chronic fatigue. I can barely get out of bed in morning right now, let alone do any kind of exercise."

"Darling, you were ready to throw yourself off a cliff a few days ago. Would it really hurt you to come to our center and jog a few miles?"

"I don't remember saying anything about wanting to throw myself off—"

"Why don't I leave you our brochure," she said, sliding a colorful pamphlet across the desk to me. I picked it up. On the cover was a picture of a woman being massaged on a white sand beach. Above that it said, "The Theta Institute: dedicated to adventures in health and wellness." Inside were more vivid pictures of healthy, tanned people doing the kinds of things yuppies like to do on vacation: yoga on the beach, lounging by the pool, sipping on coconuts, munching on a plates of fresh, robust-looking vegetables, meditating cross-legged. The place looked like a five-star resort. Even if I wanted to go, there was no way I could afford it.

"This all looks very nice, but I'm afraid it's a little above my price range."

"My dear. You'd be helping us with our research. We will cover all costs, including airfare."

"Oh."

I looked down at the brochure of meditating models and yoga posers, then back at Dr. Luna. "Dr. Meade says that the medication I need hasn't been invented yet. It's just a matter of time."

"No, it's not," she said. "I promise you that there will never be a pill that will take away your depression. Not now, not five years from now, not ever."

I was taken back by her honesty. There was no sympathy in her bright blue eyes, no pity, no sadness, no helplessness. Instead they blazed, wide and glistening, like she thought she had just delivered to me the most important news of my life.

"Who told you that?"

"You did. Right here," she said, holding up the copies of my fingerprints.

"I don't understand," I said.

"Come to the Theta Institute, my dear . . . and you will."

4

Dr. Luna booked me on a red-eye from LA to St. Lucia with a stopover in Miami. I was only able to sleep for half of the trip thanks to a loud snorer sitting next to me on the first flight. By the time I stepped off the plane in St. Lucia I'd been traveling for over ten hours, my body ached with fatigue, and I felt a headache coming on.

The airport was edged by a lush green jungle on one side, ocean on the other, and there was blue sky all around—beautiful. But the heavy, humid air did nothing for my aching head and body. Walking across the tarmac, I felt as if I were moving through pea soup. It didn't help that I was bundled up in leggings, a sweatshirt, and black leather moto boots.

Once inside the airport, I quickly ducked into the bathroom and changed into the oversized grey T-shirt and cut-off jean shorts I had in my carry-on before making my way through the immigration line. I'd forgotten to put flip-flops in my carry-on, so I had to make do with my moto boots.

After getting through customs I found myself outside the arrivals terminal, overwhelmed by the throngs of people rushing around. I stood there dazed, trying to get my bearings, until a small black woman in perhaps her seventies, looking festive in an orange sundress, rushed up to me and grabbed me by the hand.

"Maxine Dorigan," she said in a thick Caribbean accent.

"Yes. Are you from the Theta Institute?" I asked, grateful to have been found. My head was pounding now, and nausea was setting in.

The woman looked up and gave me a big smile. She had large brown eyes and freckles across her nose, and her curly black hair was cropped close to her head.

"I'm Ida, one of de nutritionists at de Theta Institute," she said.

"Oh," I said, surprised a nutritionist would be doubling as an airport chauffeur.

As if she had read my mind she said, "You do not feel well. Traveling is difficult, even on de healthy."

She was right about that.

She reached into her bag and pulled out a glass bottle filled with a green liquid. "Drink dis," she said.

"What is it?" I asked, looking at the bottle skeptically.

"It's green juice mixed wit' some herbs dat should help your headache," she said with a big smile. I couldn't tell if she was joking or serious. "We need to alkalize your body after dat flight."

I didn't remember telling her I had a headache. Perhaps I just looked like I had one. I looked suspiciously at the mud-green concoction, then opened the top and took a sip. To my surprise it tasted like tropical paradise in a bottle.

"Wow, what's in this?" I asked, perking up a bit. "It's delicious."

"I never tell," she said, her forehead creasing.

When I frowned in response, she broke out in a smile and nudged me playfully. "I'm just kidding! It's a mixture of kale, coconut, and pineapple juice, along wit' chlorophyll and some of my special herbs. We've got more of it back on de island."

I smiled. Ida's energy was contagious. I guessed they'd probably sent her to help cheer me up—and despite my debilitated state, it was working.

"Now follow me, please. De shuttle is right over here."

I followed Ida to a van parked at the curb. The side door was open, and inside sat a small girl with shoulder-length lavender hair. She looked to be eighteen or nineteen. Beneath her overgrown lavender bangs I could just make out a pair of large blue-gray eyes. A gray tank dress hung on her skeletal frame, and her skin was white with that blue hue usually reserved for babies and the elderly. She couldn't have looked more out of place in this tropical atmosphere, and by her body language it was clear she felt it. In her hand she also had a bottle of Ida's green juice.

"Dis is Dawn," Ida said. "She's coming wit' us. She's in your program too."

"Max," I said to her, holding out my hand.

As Dawn reached out her hand I noticed she had four or five cuts down her forearm. Had she done that to herself? There was a girl at Cedars-Sinai the last time I'd been there who'd been a cutter; she'd had horizontal scars on her arms. But the cuts on Dawn's arm were vertical and looked more like fingernail scratches. Dawn took my hand limply, avoiding eye contact, and squeaked out a meek hello. Then she noticed me eying her arm and jerked her hand back abruptly.

I didn't take it personally. I was used to unsocial behavior from other psych patients. Most of us had bigger problems to deal with than adhering to social mores.

I sat in the seat behind Dawn so I wouldn't be forced to converse. Neither of us were in any shape to be making small talk.

"De dock is just a few minutes away," Ida said. "Den we take a boat to de island. If eider of you feels seasick, don't worry. I've got more green juice." She got into the driver's seat and pulled away from the curb.

We were headed away from the airport along a rural road lined with shacks and small houses on one side and a mass of jungle foliage on the other. Every now and then we passed a local walking down the street in shorts and flip-flops or riding a bike. I felt like I was in a different world. Everything around us was lush and green. So different from the brown hills of Los Angeles.

Ten minutes later we arrived at a small pier lined with all kinds of boats: sail boats, speedboats, schooners, even a few small yachts. Waving us away, Ida took our suitcases in hand and directed us down a dock toward a whimsical-looking wooden boat with a candy-striped awning that reminded me of the boat Willy Wonka used to ferry his guests through his chocolate factory. I noted the name painted on the side: *Serendipity*.

Ida heaved our suitcases into the boat with the agility of a young dockworker. This woman was probably forty years older than I was and had the strength of an ox. I looked down at my green juice and then finished off the bottle.

After Dawn and I got settled in the back of the boat, Ida made her way to the helm and flipped a few switches on the panel, and off we went. I wasn't looking forward to this part. I'd never been a big fan of the ocean (my recurring tidal wave nightmares had made sure of that), and I was already sick enough as it was without being tossed about on the open sea. I held on to the side of the boat to keep myself steady and looked out at the water over the side—turquoise blue, just like the pictures in the magazines. In some places I could see right to the bottom. How could something so expansive and beautiful have come to be a metaphor for my overwhelming anxiety and depression?

"Where are you from?" Dawn asked from her seat across from me. I could barely hear her voice over the roar of the engine.

"Los Angeles," I called back. "How about you?"

"Lansing, Michigan," she said, staring down at her feet. They were tiny white veined things—so small they looked like a child's—which made her black toenail polish that much more disconcerting.

I wanted to know what Dawn was being treated for at the Theta Institute, but didn't dare ask. That question was considered rude at Cedars. Still, this was a health and wellness center we were headed to, not a psychiatric hospital. Were the rules different? I didn't know.

"Do you know anything about this place?" I asked. I might not be able to ask her why she was here, but maybe she knew more about the Theta Institute than I'd been able to find online. I looked behind me to check if Ida was within hearing distance. She's wasn't.

"No," Dawn said, "but the woman I talked to, Dr. Luna, said they might be able to help me . . ." She looked off in the distance. "Do you think that's where we're going?" she asked suddenly, pointing at a fairly large island ahead of us. It was covered in lush green foliage and studded with pointy mountains, and I could just make out a white building on a bluff at its center. A house? No, a lighthouse.

"I don't know," I said. "I don't know much about this place. But I was referred here by Dr. Luna too."

"Oh?" Dawn asked, looking me in the eyes for the first time. This seemed to be the most interesting thing I'd said so far. "Do you . . . see things too?"

"See things?" I hesitated.

"Like, things other people don't see."

"No," I said slowly. "Not yet, anyway. I'm here for depression." I didn't want to make her feel self-conscious, so I shrugged my shoulders and looked out onto the water. No big deal. Heard it all before.

"Oh," she said. "I see things a lot. Sometimes they hurt me."

I glanced back at her; she was looking down at the cuts on her arms.

"I'm sorry," was all I could say. I figured she had some kind of schizophrenic disorder. Were a few hypnosis sessions and healthy meals really going to help this girl to stop cutting herself and blaming things that weren't there for it? Were they going to suddenly make me happy? Make my mysterious aches and pains go away? I felt my spirits spiraling downward. Not like they'd been that high to begin with.

"It's so beautiful here," Dawn said, obviously wanting to change the subject. "Too beautiful for anything bad to happen, don't you think?"

"I hope so," I said looking back at the island rising ahead of us. "I really do."

5

Sometime later I heard the sound of far-off laughter and realized I had drifted off to sleep. When I opened my eyes I saw that we were heading into a cove. Just a few hundred yards away was a stunning white sand beach peppered with tan, healthy-looking people lying about on white-cushioned lounge chairs under thatched umbrellas. Others swam and snorkeled in the quiet waters. Behind the beach, up on a small bluff, was an oval-shaped swimming pool flanked by white-washed buildings with thatched roofs and canopied patios. Behind that a large expanse of jungle-covered mountains rose up in the background. It was the type of place I was used to seeing on computer desktop screensavers, but never in real life. Besides a trip to Cabo the year before with Sofia, I'd never even been outside of the US.

Standing on a wooden dock to the left of the beach was a tall, thin woman with long black hair. It would have been hard not to notice her. With her tan skin, black maxi dress, and goddess-like physique, she easily stood out against the white sand beach and tropical cheer of her surroundings. And when Ida pulled the boat up alongside the dock, I could see that she was indeed as stunning as I had suspected from far away. She stood patiently as Dawn and I climbed up the ladder and onto the dock, then stepped forward and introduced herself.

"Angelique Ortiz," she said coolly, in a voice deeper than I expected. "Welcome to the Theta Institute."

Angelique was probably in her mid-twenties, with large lips, high cheekbones, and eyes almost as dark as her black hair. Her black tank dress showed off a myriad of tattooed roses winding up both sides of her strong arms. Around her waist hung a man's brown leather belt with an ornate silver dragon on the buckle—the only item that looked out of place on her toned body. Necklaces of quartz and agate were layered around her neck, framed by more tattoos—tiny black stars sprinkled in and around the dip of her left collarbone. She was smiling, but the stiff way she held her body seemed to say, "Please don't touch."

When Dawn failed to reply I answered for the both of us. "I'm Max," I said, trying to not stare. "This is Dawn."

"You all get acquainted," Ida said from behind us as she climbed up the ladder with my bag. I hurried over to help her but she swung it onto the dock like it was filled with air. "I'll take de bags and see you up there."

Before I could object, Ida had both suitcases out of the boat and was rolling them down the dock toward the beach.

"Is she okay taking those on her own?" I asked. I knew Ida was strong for her age (anyone's age, really) but it had been a long trip, and it appeared the hotel was farther inland.

"Don't worry about Ida. She's going to outlive us all," Angelique said, giving me a sideways glance. "Now, I know you've both come a long way, so I'll just give you a quick tour and show you to your rooms so you can get settled before dinner." Her demeanor was cold—or maybe "standoffish" was a better word.

She turned and headed back down the dock. On her back there was another elaborate tattoo of roses and thorny vines. As I got closer, I could see that she had some sort of scarring on her back as well—long, white strips hidden among the roses. The tattoo artist had obviously done his best to cover them up, but they were still visible.

We followed Angelique in silence down a wooden path back behind a whitewashed tiki hut filled with snorkel gear and beach toys, then through a thatched-covered, open-air lounge area with a bar where people in sarongs and bathing attire sipped on smoothies.

"This is the tiki bar. We don't serve or have alcohol anywhere on the island, but you can get smoothies and snacks here during the day. Over there"—Angelique pointed to another thatched, open-air building filled with large round tables and bistro chairs on a terracotta-tiled floor—"is the dining pavilion where we have all our meals. Breakfast is at eight, lunch is at one, and dinner is at seven. A bell will always ring to alert you when it's mealtime."

She turned and walked briskly down the wooden path toward the beach without waiting to see if we were behind her. Dawn and I caught up to her at the beach, where she abruptly stopped and looked out to the cove, which was so clear and blue it barely looked real. Despite my fatigue and headache, it was finally starting to dawn on me that I was at a resort in the middle of the Caribbean that I could never have afforded to visit on my own.

"This is the swimming cove, obviously," Angelique said. "There's a life guard on duty from seven until five. We have meditation on the beach every morning as well. In fact, we have a large selection of classes and activities at the Theta Institute: yoga, qi gong, snorkeling, every kind of fitness class you can think of—even martial arts. That's what I teach."

"You're a martial arts teacher?" I asked. I guess that explained her sculpted arms and fit frame. Not to mention her tough-girl demeanor.

"Yes," Angelique said. "But our self-development classes and workshops are what people really come to Theta for. And we also have a rehab center for people in recovery."

I nodded. I'd read about the rehab center on the Theta Institute website. The psychiatric floor at Cedars-Sinai housed many people struggling with addictions too, and I felt like we shared quite a lot of the same character traits. I may not have ever become dependent on drugs or alcohol, but I had definitely done my share of them. Lately, though, my body had become so weak that it couldn't even tolerate a glass of wine, so I was happy to know there wouldn't be anything on the island to tempt me.

Dawn and I followed Angelique up a small set of cement steps toward the pool, a gorgeous oval oasis surrounded by foliage and palm trees, where more healthy-looking people lounged about in various stages of bliss. They hardly seemed the types to be suffering from any type of mental or emotional disorders. Compared to the halogen-lighted, antiseptic halls of Cedars, this place looked like Shangri-La. Perhaps the people running the Theta Institute knew what they were doing after all. Despite my aches and pains, I felt a wave of hopefulness come over me.

We followed Angelique down a jungle-lined cement path behind the fitness center until we came to a majestic, plantation-style hotel lined with columns, its French doors all flung open. Guests sat and drank iced tea and green juices all along the wraparound patio. It looked like something out of a movie.

"Beautiful, right?" said Angelique.

"Incredible," I said, stopping to take a look at the grand hotel. "How old is it?"

"Almost a hundred years old. This used to be a sugar plantation, up until it was bought by Joseph Harrington, a big steel magnate, during Prohibition. He built it into a posh resort where he could drink legally with his family and friends. After that it fell into the hands of the U.S. government."

"The U.S. government? Why?"

"It was needed as a refueling station for U-boats in World War II. There's still an old military base on the north side of the island. Or what's left of one, I guess."

"Many men died here," Dawn suddenly said. "In the woods there." She was looking to the left of the hotel, where there was a large lawn and, beyond that, the jungle.

Angelique raised an eyebrow. "Yes . . ." she said hesitantly. "I see you've done your homework. During the war, German U-boats and Italian submarines were attempting to disrupt the Allied supply of oil and other supplies. The island was attacked by German soldiers in 1944. Many men were killed."

I had thought Dawn had said she didn't know anything about this place.

"Does the government still own the island?" I asked. I found it strange, a health and wellness resort on a military island. The two just didn't seem to go together.

"No, the Caribbean government owns it now. In the eighties, they sold this part of the island to a popular hotel chain that built it out into one of their resorts. Micah bought it about three years ago and turned it into what you see now."

"Micah?" I asked.

"Dr. McMoneagle," Angelique said. "Around here most of us just call him Micah."

"He's the head of the Lucidity Project?" I asked, remembering Dr. Luna mentioning him in our first meeting at Cedars-Sinai.

"That's right," she said. "He runs quite a few things around here, actually."

"You have horses here too?" asked Dawn. I followed her eyes to an old wood barn peeking out behind the left side of the hotel.

"They did once," Angelique said with a smile. "Now that's been converted into Micah's lab. You'll be spending quite a lot of time in there for the next three weeks. We all will."

"You're in the Lucidity Project too?" I asked, surprised. "I thought you said you worked here." Angelique may come across as a little standoffish, but mentally she appeared quite stable. Not at all like Dawn and me.

"I do work here," she said. "But Micah asked me to participate in the project as well, and I wasn't about to turn him down."

She spun on her heel and headed toward the hotel. Dawn and I exchanged an awkward glance, then continued after her.

"Behind the hotel is the great lawn, which is lined with bungalows. That's where most of the senior staff sleep. All of the participants in the Lucidity Project will be staying in the hotel together, though. In fact, I'm rooming with you, Dawn."

Dawn's eyes widened at this news and I didn't blame her. Angelique didn't seem like she'd be a very fun roommate.

"How do you get a job here?" Dawn asked, changing the subject.

"You just apply." Angelique shrugged. "There's different openings that come up in the kitchen, housekeeping, or guest services. Or, if you're qualified, you can teach classes, like me. You don't get paid all that much, but your room and board is covered, and you can take all the classes you want for free."

"How long have you been here?" I asked.

"Two years."

Two years? I didn't have two years to get better. I had exactly a month before I had to be back at work. I wanted to know so much more about Angelique. Had she been depressed like me when she got here? If so, had the people here helped her? They must have or she wouldn't have stayed. But if she was feeling better, why was she participating in the Lucidity Project? These were quite personal questions, obviously. Questions I knew better than to ask on a first meeting. They would have to wait.

Angelique pointed down another cement path to the right that led back through the jungle.

"If you keep going down that path you'll come to Ida's bungalow. That's where you'll both have your health review tomorrow. It's bright pink. You can't miss it."

I followed Angelique's eyes down the path. Would Ida be able to give me some answers tomorrow? I thought back to how many times I'd gotten my hopes up before. There was so much farther to fall when your expectations were high, and I'd taken that soul-crushing trip many, many times.

●●●

The inside of the hotel was just as stunning as the exterior. Kevita palms, white linen sofas, and rattan tables filled the lobby, and the floor was laid with black-and-white-checked marble. A grand, L-shaped staircase swirled up the right side of the room, and sunlight poured in from the French doors lining the front patio.

There at the giant mahogany reception desk were Dr. Luna and Ida, both of them waiting for us with big smiles. Even though I had only met Dr. Luna once, I felt quite relieved to see her.

"Welcome to The Theta Institute," she said, pulling both Dawn and me in for an enthusiastic double hug. Her friendliness was going to take some getting used to. Out of all the therapists and doctors I had seen over the years, not one of them had ever even squeezed my hand, let alone given me a hug.

Dawn looked over at me and blushed, then quickly looked down at the floor. I guess she felt just as uncomfortable.

Ida took two festive young Thai coconuts off the mahogany reception desk behind them and handed one to Dawn and the other to me. I moved aside the paper umbrella sticking out of the top and took a sip of the sweet juice.

"Now, I'm sure you're both tired from your trip, so I'll make this quick," Dr. Luna said, grabbing two pink folders off the desk. She had traded the sleek wrap dress I'd seen her in before for a loose white embroidered tunic and flip-flops. Her wild silver hair was pulled up in a bun with pieces sticking out here and there as if she'd done it without looking. "Tomorrow you'll both be meeting with Ida and Micah for your health and psychological assessments. In these folders are your appointment times, a map to the grounds, and a schedule of all the classes we have on the island. You'll be busy with the Lucidity Project most of the time, but you can probably squeeze in a class here and there. Now I'll just grab the keys and we'll get you up to your rooms."

As she headed around the other side of the counter to gather our keys, I turned and saw a good-looking surfer type with shaggy blond hair watching us from a corridor that led to what looked like a ballroom at the back of the hotel. He looked to be only a few years old than me, and was wearing blue board shorts, flip-flops, and a sun-drenched T-shirt that read, "This is Where the Magic Happens." There were two watches on each of his wrists, all different colors and sizes, which I found quite odd. He had a bit of a baby face despite half of it being covered by three days' worth of sandy-colored stubble, and by the look of his tan he probably spent most of his days surfing. His unnaturally pale blue eyes quickly caught mine and I got the sudden feeling that I'd seen him somewhere before. I lifted my hand to say hello before realizing I didn't know him at all. Then I jerked my eyes away, totally mortified. I felt my cheeks flush with embarrassment. When I looked back a few seconds later, he was gone.

"Dawn, are you okay?" I heard Angelique say behind me, her voice carrying a tone of concern.

I looked over at Dawn, who was standing stock-still and staring warily at the landing at the turn of the staircase.

"What is it, Dawn?" Dr. Luna asked, looking up from the reception desk.

"They found me," Dawn whispered back.

We all looked up at the landing, but there wasn't anything there.

"Who found you?" Dr. Luna asked, slipping on her glasses and walking over to Dawn.

"The demons," she said, bringing her hands nervously up to the sides of her face. "They followed me here."

A chill went up the back of my spine. Demons? What was she

talking about? I thought back to what she'd said earlier to me on the boat ride over. *"I see things that other people don't see. Sometimes they hurt me."* I looked back up at the landing again but, of course, could see nothing.

Dr. Luna put her hand on Dawn's shoulder. "What do you see, Dawn?"

"One of them," said Dawn, clutching at her head like a crazy person. "He's right there."

"Sit down, honey," Ida said calmly. She and Dr. Luna helped Dawn down onto a bamboo settee, where she began to breathe heavily.

"I thought I'd be safe here. You said I would be," she said to Dr. Luna. She began rocking back and forth on the chair, on the verge of hysterics.

"You are safe here, Dawn," Dr. Luna said gently.

I put my coconut down on the registration desk and looked around. Usually when stuff like this happened, people in white coats appeared with syringes and bottles of pills. But as Dr. Luna had made clear in my interview, this wasn't a psychiatric hospital.

"Should I go get somebody?" I asked Angelique, fidgeting.

"Who would you go get?" she asked.

"Are you going to make them go away?" Dawn asked Dr. Luna, rocking violently back and forth, her hands clutching her chest. "You said you could help me. You said!"

"Maybe you should give her a sedative or something," I said, louder this time, so Dr. Luna could hear.

Angelique shot me a cold look. "Why would we do that? We're trying to wake people up here, not put them to sleep."

Wake people up? From what?

"I want them to go away," Dawn cried as she continued to rock back and forth. "I just want to be normal, like everyone else."

"Normal? Well, that sounds pretty boring," said a voice behind me. I turned around to see the good-looking surfer. He had his hands in the pockets of his board shorts and seemed much too relaxed for the situation.

"You try to live with things haunting you all the time!" Dawn practically spat at him, then continued her frantic rocking.

"Oh, I do," he said, glancing over at me.

Dawn looked up for a second and stopped rocking. "So you believe me?" she asked as a tear slowly ran down her blotched face. "You don't think I'm crazy?"

"No," he said. "Quite the opposite, in fact: I believe you have quite a gift."

Dawn's eyes went wide at this, then narrowed. "How can you call this a gift?" she asked angrily. "Look what they do to me." She held up her arms to show him the scratches.

"Well, then, I guess it's a good thing you're here," he responded.

Dawn sat and contemplated that for a moment, then said, "Why? Do you know how to make them go away?"

"Perhaps, but I have to know what type of entity we're dealing with first. Do you think you could draw one of them for me?" He said this quite matter-of-factly, as if they were discussing a minor rodent problem.

"I guess . . ." Dawn answered. His casual demeanor was having a calming effect on her. Surfer Guy quickly grabbed a piece of paper and pen off the reception desk and handed them to her, and we all stood by quietly as she began to draw her demon.

She was quite a good artist, and within just a couple of minutes she had her monster sketched out on the table. The thing was large and dark, with claws for hands and pointed, shark-like teeth that covered most of its face. It was dressed in battle gear and reminded me of a cross between the orcs from *Lord of the Rings* and Venom in *Spiderman*. The thing was horrifying. I could understand why she was so frightened.

The man, however, didn't seem too concerned. "Just as I thought," he said, examining the drawing and keeping with his nonchalant tone, "an entity from the lower realms. Nasty little buggers, but they can be dealt with. That's something you'll be learning how to do on the Lucidity Project—vanquishing your demons and all that. Until then, you can wear this." He reached down the front of his T-shirt and pulled out a purple crystal hanging by a chain. "It's an amethyst protection amulet blessed by a Mayan shaman I apprenticed with in Guatemala."

Oh brother. Was this guy for real?

"It is very, very powerful," he continued. "Do you understand?"

"Yes," Dawn said, her little face now full of reverence. She stayed very still as he walked forward and clasped the necklace around her neck.

"As long as you are wearing this, these lower entities cannot harm you. To activate it all you have to do is hold it in your hand, imagine yourself surrounded by its protective energy, and let no negative thoughts enter your mind."

I glanced over at Dr. Luna and the others. Was anyone really buying this? From the looks on their faces I could tell that in fact they were. What was the deal with this guy? He was obviously making all of this up. But why? How would encouraging Dawn's delusions help her to get better?

"Go ahead," he said. "Try it."

Dawn looked around at us, nervous and unsure of herself. Then she shut her eyes and grabbed the crystal. After a few seconds she opened her eyes up and looked back up at the landing on the stairs.

"It's gone—you did it!" she said, putting her hands over her mouth like she was witnessing some sort of miracle. "You're the first person who's ever made one of them go away."

Angelique, Dr. Luna, and Ida all broke out into applause. I stood there, mouth agape. I couldn't believe everyone was going along with this nonsense.

"Now remember, Dawn, nothing can stay in your space if you don't want it there. Isn't that right, Ms. Dorigan?" the man asked, turning to me.

"Oh," I said, taken aback that he knew my name. "I, uh . . . I can't see ghosts."

"We all have our demons, though, don't we?" he said. "Whether we can see them or not."

He held my gaze with his cool blue eyes, and I couldn't help but feel that it was a challenge in some way. I supposed it was some therapeutic device, but all it did was make me incredibly angry.

"I think that's enough excitement for today," Dr. Luna interrupted. "Angelique, why don't you show Dawn up to your room. I'll take Maxine to hers."

Angelique nodded. "Let's take the elevator," she said, glancing warily at the stairs before leading Dawn around behind the reception desk to the elevator. Dawn went slowly, turning and staring back at the blond man as if he were some sort of god.

● ● ●

"You're quite a storyteller," I said to the man as soon as they were out of sight.

"Thank you," he replied, his crystalline eyes sparkling. "I hear you are as well."

"I'm sorry, do I know you?" I asked, feeling more annoyed than ever.

"Maxine, this is Dr. Micah McMoneagle, the founder of the Theta Institute and the head of the Lucidity Project," said Dr. Luna.

"*You're* Dr. McMoneagle?" I asked, not bothering to hide the surprise in my voice.

"You were expecting someone better looking," he said. "I apologize."

"No . . ." I said, trying to get used to the smartass responses he was obviously using to throw me off. "I had expected someone a little . . . older." *And by older I mean more mature.* "You can't even be out of your twenties."

"I can be, in fact. I'm thirty," he said. "In this lifetime, anyway."

"What are you a doctor of, exactly?" I asked. I knew I was being rude, but I couldn't help myself. *This lifetime?* This wasn't what I had signed up for.

"I often wonder that myself, to tell you the truth."

The confusion on my face must have been evident. Dr. Luna clarified. "Dr. McMoneagle is being modest. He actually has his Ph.D. in psychology from Stanford."

"Stanford? Is that where you learned how to talk to pretend ghosts, or whatever it was Dawn thought she saw?"

"I take it you don't agree with our methods so far," Dr. McMoneagle said, putting his hands back in his pockets.

"I just don't see how playing along with Dawn's hallucinations is going to help her. Shouldn't you be teaching her how to see through them to what's real?"

"Who I am to say what's real for Dawn—or for anyone, for that matter? I'm not here to get people to stop experiencing things, Ms. Dorigan. I'm here to help them find out why they're experiencing them in the first place."

"By playing along with their crazy stories?"

"Sometimes we have to play along with people's crazy stories to help them tell a new story—to help them transform the one they're telling."

"Well, in the meantime, you're encouraging her delusions."

"Is that what you think we're doing?"

"It seems that way."

"And this worries you?"

"Very much."

"Why?"

"As I'm sure you're aware, I tried to kill myself a week ago. Are you going to tell me to jump off a cliff?"

"That's actually not a bad idea," he said, pretending to mull it over—then he winked at me as if he'd made a funny joke. I looked over to Dr. Luna, who shook her head, trying to repress a smile.

"Excuse me?" I asked, feeling my face turning red with rage.

"You are excused. But just this once," he said.

I couldn't believe the nerve of this man. I'd never been treated this way by any of my therapists. It was beyond unprofessional.

"Okay," Dr. Luna cut in, "let's give Maxine a break. She's only just gotten here."

"We shall leave the witty banter for another time," he said, bowing toward me, hands still in his pockets. "Personally, I look forward to it." And with that he turned and strolled back down the hall.

"That man is not like any therapist I've ever met," I said, watching him go.

"You don't know the half of it, my dear," Dr. Luna said.

6

Dr. Luna led me to a door at the end of a long hallway on the fifth floor papered in a cream damask with mahogany wainscoting. Before she could get her key in the lock, the door flew open to reveal a petite girl in her early twenties with wavy, blond, shoulder-length hair and giant brown eyes.

"I thought I heard talking out here," said the girl in a high-pitched Long Island accent usually reserved for the girlfriend of gangsters in old black-and-white movies. Between her funny voice, the pink lace slip dress she was wearing, and her long, mascara-coated eye-lashes, she reminded me of a blond Betty Boop.

"This is your roommate, Zoe," Dr. Luna said. "Zoe's working in the library for the summer. She's going to make sure you get down to dinner to meet the rest of your group."

"Mi casa es su casa," Zoe said with a sweep of her hand.

"If you have any questions, don't hesitate to give me a call. My number is in the binder on the desk," Dr. Luna said with a smile.

I nodded and shut the door behind her as she left.

"Wow, I like this rock n' roll thing you have going on," Zoe said, checking out my moto boots and ripped cutoffs. "Dr. Luna says you're from LA. Are you an actress? You look like an actress."

"No, I'm a writers' assistant on a television show."

"No way!" she squealed, her eyes going wide. "This is so synchron-icitous. I'm an actress. I've been doing the community theater thing at home, but it's not quite the same as making a go at it in Hollywood. Do you think you could get me an audition on your show?"

I was used to people asking for auditions. I told her what I told everyone else: the truth. "I'm kind of on the low end of the totem pole, if you know what I mean. Maybe in a few years, if I play my cards right."

"Oh, that's so exciting!" she said, clapping, as if I'd just guaranteed her a lead role. "So," she said, switching gears, "your bags are in there"—she pointed behind me at one of two large closets— "and you can take the bed by the French doors if you want."

I followed Zoe past a beautiful white marble bathroom into the main room, which was beautifully decorated with two queen-size beds with tufted beige headboards, expensive white linens, and bright, multicolored Killim throw pillows. On the floor was a jute rug, and the walls were painted a soft white. A dark rattan desk and Chippendale chair sat on the other side of the room. White lacquered French doors opened onto a patio with a breathtaking view of the jungle and ocean in the distance.

Zoe walked over to the French doors and pushed them open even more so I could get a better look at the ocean, which I could see beyond the jungle trees overrunning the island. "How about this view?"

"It's beautiful," I said. I was too tired to express myself as enthusiastically as my new roommate, but I didn't want my mood to ruin this moment. The place was spectacular, and even though I didn't feel good, I was grateful to be there. I attempted to push my negative thoughts aside—for a little while, at least. They would be there for me later. They always were.

"Isn't it?" she replied. "Makes my place back home look like a dump."

"Where's that?" I asked. "Long Island?"

"Born and raised," she said proudly.

"So, what brought you here? Do you have depression too?"

"Depression?" she asked as if she didn't understand the meaning of the word. "No, why—do I look depressed?" She walked over and peered into a small mirror on the desk. "It's probably because I haven't put my bronzer on yet."

"No, sorry. It's just that I thought that the Lucidity Project was for people with uh . . . mental problems and things."

"Yeah, well, I unfortunately didn't qualify for the Lucidity Project," she said with the first sign of a frown I'd seen on her yet. She made her way into the bathroom and I followed.

"How do you qualify for the Lucidity Project, exactly?" I asked.

"I don't know. Dr. McMoneagle decides that. He doesn't seem to think I'm right for it," Zoe said as she began looking through the multiple beauty products strewn across the counter.

"Why not?"

"I don't know. He won't say, the dirty bum," she said playfully. Finally she found what she was looking for—a compact of bronzer. She flipped it open, grabbed a large brush, and began blending it all over her face.

"The whole thing seems very secretive," I said.

"I know, right?" she said, perking back up again. Then, seeing my concerned look, she turned toward me and said, "Look, you don't have to worry. You're in the right place. Dr. McMoneagle knows what he's doing."

"What makes you so sure?"

"Because the man is a genius."

"Yeah, that seems to be the consensus around here," I muttered.

"He's a big celebrity, you know . . . at least in my circles. One of the leading thought leaders on human consciousness. He's been on all the talk shows. *The View*, *Oprah*, *Dr. Oz*, you name it."

"I thought I recognized him from somewhere," I said, thinking back to our strange meeting in the lobby. "That must be it."

"He's pretty hot, right?" she said checking out her lipstick in the mirror.

"No," I said. "In fact, I don't like him at all."

7

The sun was just above the horizon as we came out to the dining pavilion for dinner. Birds and other creatures chirped in the surrounding trees, and bistro lights were strung around the patio, adding a magical element to the already incredible surroundings. The smell of coconut oil and tropical fruit hung in the air. It was almost enough to make me forget I was depressed—almost.

The place was packed with people fresh from yoga, afternoon meditations, and self-help workshops, serene smiles on their sun-kissed faces, bright eyes hinting at newfound bliss.

Zoe and I grabbed some plates and made our way through the buffet, which, as the website promised, was filled with freshly prepared organic food. The offerings tonight were broccoli and fennel soup, braised endives, kale, and quinoa, plus a full salad and fruit bar. At first I thought I was going to be forced to go vegan for the month, but luckily there was fresh red snapper at the end of the bar. If this hadn't been the case I might have run screaming into the sea.

There were no rolls, bread, or pastas of any kind. This is how all the magazines told you to eat: organic, whole, unprocessed foods like healthy proteins, vegetables, fruits, and fats. Even if these people couldn't help me, at the very least I would be giving my body a break from all the junk I'd been eating for the next few weeks.

"There's the Lucidity Project group over there," Zoe said after we finished loading up our plates, pointing toward a table of hip-looking twentysomethings at the edge of the terrace. She headed for the table, and I followed.

I began to feel a little nervous. Back at Cedars I would usually sit with the older people at mealtime because they never expected me to talk to them. Small talk with strangers was not my forte, even when I wasn't feeling depressed. I could do it, but I found it overwhelming. Trying to think up things to say to make you appear happy and normal when you really just want to crawl into bed and hide is exhausting, and I was already dead tired from the trip. With Sofia, I could hide it pretty well, because no one else could usually get a word in while she was around. Unfortunately, she wasn't here to hold up my side of the conversation. I took a deep breath and hoped Zoe would do all the talking.

I noticed Dawn at the table and calmed down a little. I couldn't act any weirder than her, could I? As we got closer, I saw that Angelique was sitting next to her.

"Good evening, everyone," Zoe said theatrically. "May I introduce you to Ms. Max Dorigan?"

"Another beautiful woman!" said a beefy, frat-type boy from behind an iPad mini. "How am I supposed to get anything done around here with all these gorgeous creatures around?" He looked to be in his mid-twenties, and was wearing a University of Miami T-shirt with the sleeves cut off and a cowboy hat over his wavy brown hair. He reminded me of one of the popular jocks who used to ignore me in high school.

"This is Tucker," Zoe said with a twinkle, "our resident ladies' man. Consider yourself warned."

"Don't listen to her," Tucker said, waving Zoe off, his deep blue eyes hinting at mischief. "So, Red, what's your story?"

Zoe sat down next to Angelique and I took the seat next to her.

"Wait, don't say anything!" said a lanky-looking black guy in dark-rimmed hipster glasses who was sitting next to Tucker. He was impeccably dressed in madras shorts and a fitted red polo shirt—and looked like someone had plucked him out of a Tommy Hilfiger catalog.

"Give me your watch," he continued, holding out his hand to me across the table.

"Why?" I asked. I looked down at my chunky gold Michael Kors watch, wondering why he would need it. He was already sporting a very expensive-looking Rolex.

"It helps with the transmission," he said matter-of-factly.

"Brad's psychic," Zoe said, her eyebrows raised with excitement. Then much quieter so only I could hear she whispered, "and gay." She pouted out her lower lip playfully to show she felt this was a great disappointment.

"We're all psychic," Brad said, pushing up his glasses very seriously. "To one degree or another. I'm just more psychic then most people. I have *the gift*."

"Yeah, the gift of gab," said Tucker, going back to his iPad mini.

"Shut it," said Brad. Then he turned back to me and wiggled his fingers and singsonged, "I'm waiting . . ."

"Right . . ." I said. Was this guy really psychic, or was he delusional like Dawn? And did everyone believe him, or were they just playing along? I had been around mentally ill people before, but usually they were unkempt and wearing hospital robes, not Ralph Lauren. This was different. At the same time I wasn't sure I really believed in psychics. Sofia swore by them. Much of Hollywood did, actually. But I wasn't what you'd call a believer, and I didn't feel like becoming one now. Still, I reluctantly reached across the table and handed my watch to Brad.

"Don't tell me anything about yourself," he demanded. He closed his eyes and massaged the watch in his hands for a few moments.

"She's one of us," he finally said, opening his eyes.

"Duh," Zoe said. "She's on the Lucidity Project. Why do you think I brought her over here?"

"I mean . . . she's one of *us*," he said with a conspiratorial whisper to the table. "But she doesn't know it yet."

"I'm quite aware I'm a crazy person, if that's what you mean."

"That's not what I meant," Brad said.

"Would you just let the girl eat?" Angelique said. "She took a red-eye to get here and has been traveling all day. You have plenty of time to show off your talents."

"When can I show off *my* talents?" Tucker asked, wiggling his eyebrows.

"You keep your talents to yourself," Angelique shot back.

"Can I have my watch back now?" I asked.

"Hold on," Brad said, shutting his eyes again. "There's more."

"Of course there is," Angelique said, shaking her head.

Brad closed his eyes and went back to feeling up my watch. I took a bite of the broccoli fennel soup. It was surprisingly quite good.

"You're from the East Coast," Brad said, opening his eyes. "New York, maybe? You come from money—lots of it. I see you're married but, oh . . ." He furrowed his brow. "Let me just say—it's not going to end well."

Everyone looked to me to confirm.

"I'm single, I live in Los Angeles, and I'm practically broke," I said, turning back to my food.

The whole table busted out laughing.

"What?" Brad gasped incredulously. "But I'm never wrong."

"Okay, my turn," said Tucker, holding up his hands. He put his fingers to his temples dramatically and shut his eyes. Then opened them again.

"You're a writers' assistant on the television show *You Sexy Witch*, and you live in LA now but are originally from Windsor, California."

"Wow," I said, genuinely impressed. "That's exactly right. How'd you know that?"

"I just checked your Facebook page," he smirked, turning his iPad around to show everyone my page.

Everyone at the table groaned and a few napkins were thrown.

"What about Dawn?" I asked, attempting to get the attention off me.

"We already did Dawn," Tucker said.

"Dawn sees dead people," Brad said.

The whole table, including Dawn, chuckled affably—then she blushed and looked down, embarrassed, her lavender bangs falling over her eyes. Tucker caught my eye then tipped his hat to me and winked, as if to say, "Welcome to the club."

I was just finishing my meal when I heard a loud noise coming down the road behind the dining pavilion. A few seconds later a gorgeous man in a T-shirt and camo shorts drove up on a dirt bike. He looked to be in his late twenties and was stunningly attractive, with chestnut skin, cropped, wavy black hair, and almond-shaped, dark brown eyes. He was well over six feet tall, and I could see the hint of what was probably a six-pack under his tight black T-shirt. He got off the bike and approached the table.

"Where have you been?" Angelique said sharply to the man as he took the empty seat next to me. "We have guests."

"I apologize," he said. His voice was deep and masculine. "I got caught up at the lab with Micah."

"Meet our new additions," Angelique said, her voice a bit softer. "This is Dawn . . ."

Dawn nodded a silent hello. Then the newcomer's eyes fell onto mine, and I felt something flip in my stomach.

"That means you must be Max. I'm Jeremy Savea," he said. A shot of adrenaline went clear from my heart down to my core, and I breathed out sharply. "Savea?" I asked. His name sounded familiar. No—not his name, exactly. The man himself.

"It's Samoan," Zoe whispered in my ear. But it wasn't his name I was trying to place.

"Have we met before?" I asked Jeremy before I could think about what I was saying. "You look so familiar."

"He gets that all the time," Zoe said with a giggle. "It's because he looks just like The Rock."

"The who?" I asked.

"Dwayne Johnson," Zoe said. "The wrestler-turned-actor?"

Jeremy blushed and shook his head. He did look a little like the actor, except quite a few years younger. I supposed that could be why he felt so familiar. Oh man, just what I needed—a gorgeous hunk to distract me from getting better. The last gorgeous hunk that had crossed my path was a struggling screenwriter with a drinking problem by the name of Zachariah James who I'd met during my first stay at Cedars. He went back to drinking soon after we both got out, and I had to end the relationship. Jeremy, however, didn't seem to have the nervous edge so typical of psych ward hotties. In fact, besides Dawn, the rest of them didn't seem to have it, either. I mean, sure, Brad was a little out there, but I didn't get the impression he was suffering from any sort of mental or emotional disorder. In fact, everyone at the table looked like they took more than good care of themselves. They were all laughing and joking with each other, eating well, and from the looks of their bodies, exercising way too much. Of course, I had to remind myself, I wasn't at a psych ward. This was a health and wellness center, which meant it was possible they weren't sick at all. Perhaps they were here seeking self-actualization or a relaxing vacation like some of the other guests. But if that was the case, what were Dawn and I doing with them?

"Jeremy is helping Micah with the Lucidity Project," Angelique said. "We'll all be going through it together."

"What are we going to be doing, exactly?" I prompted, seeing an opportunity to get some answers to my many questions. "I had a hard time getting much information out of Dr. Luna."

Tucker snorted and went back to his food. Angelique and Brad snickered a little.

"You'll have a hard time getting much information out of anybody here," Tucker said.

"Jeremy's the only one who knows what we'll be doing, but he won't tell," Angelique said. "He started working with Micah on the project when he arrived here a month ago."

Jeremy smiled mysteriously, took a sip of bottled water he had with him, and said nothing. I tried not to stare.

"Good luck if you can get anything out of him either," Zoe said. "Believe me, I've tried."

"So, the rest of you don't know anything about it?" I asked, scanning the table. "Why did you sign up for it?"

"We didn't sign up for it," Angelique said. "We were chosen for it. Besides, you agreed to do the project without having any information about it too, didn't you?"

She had me there.

"When Dr. Micah McMoneagle asks you if you want to be involved in one of his research projects, you say yes," Zoe said. The rest nodded in agreement. They all seemed to share Zoe's opinion that Dr. McMoneagle was some sort of health and wellness super guru or something. After seeing some of his methods earlier that afternoon with Dawn, I begged to differ.

"It's not like we're going in blind," Angelique said. "We're all familiar with Micah's work."

Not all of us, I thought.

"His background is in dream therapy," she continued, "so that's where my money is."

"Yes, and it's called the Lucidity Project," Tucker said. "So it's got to be lucid dreaming."

"Lucid dreaming?" I asked. "What's that?"

"It's knowing that you're dreaming when you're dreaming," Tucker said.

"Is that even possible?" I'd never had a dream where I knew I was dreaming. I always thought I was awake when I was dreaming, but of course I wasn't.

"According to Dr. McMoneagle it is," Tucker said.

"Whatever it is," Brad said, leaning in, "my sources give me good reason to believe Micah's doing a top-secret project for the government. Something with the CIA or the army, I don't know, but I keep seeing army uniforms and getting the feeling of espionage."

"By 'your sources,' do you mean your psychic sources?" Tucker asked with a smirk.

"What other sources are there?" responded Brad.

"Well, you won't have to guess for much longer," Jeremy said, pulling out his iPhone. "Micah wants to meet with us."

"When?" Angelique asked.

Jeremy looked down at his phone, then back up again.

"Right now."

8

Fifteen minutes later, the six of us were sitting in a semicircle of cushy rattan chairs in a large open building on the south side of the beach. With its polished hardwood floors, newly thatched roof, and open-air windows, it resembled a high-end tiki hut.

"Ahoy thar, mateys," said a familiar voice. We turned to see Dr. McMoneagle walking in behind us. He'd added a ship captain's hat to his surfer-dude ensemble from earlier. Strands of blond hair poked out from underneath the hat above his eyebrows, giving him an even more mischievous look than usual. He strolled through the middle of the semicircle, hands in pockets, then turned to face us from the front of the room. Behind him was a panoramic view of the ocean, complete with a gorgeous pink and orange sunset. That, paired with the tiki hut-like quality of the room, gave off the impression that we were at sea, or perhaps marooned on some luxury version of Gilligan's Island. Not a bad place to be, actually. I only wished I was feeling better so I could fully enjoy it.

"Welcome aboard the Lucidity Project," he said with a tip of his hat. "As most of you know, my name is Dr. Micah McMoneagle, but you can call me Micah. I'll be your captain on this journey we're embarking on together." His pale blue eyes twinkled with excitement.

The whole act was a bit over the top, but I couldn't help but admire the effort. None of my other psychiatrists had ever dressed up in costume for our sessions. Hopefully now I'd get some of my questions answered about what exactly we'd be doing here.

"In the next three weeks, things are going to get weird—but they're also going to get wonderful," Micah said. "When you're dealing with the subconscious realms, anything can happen. I've found this approach to therapy does wonders for people like you. *People like us?* you're asking yourselves. *What does that mean? What kind of people are we, exactly?* Well, some of you know. Like you," he said, pointing to Brad. "And you," he said, turning to look at Angelique. He walked over to Dawn, took off his hat, and placed it on her head. "And maybe you," he said.

Dawn blushed and looked down at the floor.

I looked around at Angelique and the others. Did we really have something in common? If we did, I had no idea what.

"Who you are and why you came to be here—that is what we will be exploring with the Lucidity Project," Micah continued. "I know you're all curious about what exactly we're going to be doing, but I'm not going to go into logistics just yet. Our newest guests just arrived this afternoon, and I'm sure they're eager to get some rest. I'll be meeting with them both tomorrow, and the rest of us will have our first group session together the day after that. That will give them plenty of time to settle in. In the meantime, I'd like everyone to go around and introduce themselves. You don't have to go into your whole story. Just briefly tell us what brought you to the Theta Institute and what it is you're looking to accomplish here. We've each come to this island with a question. I intend for you to get that question answered while you're here, and perhaps a few others as well." He nodded to his right. "Jeremy, let's start with you."

Jeremy nodded, looking a little surprised to be called on so quickly. He straightened up in his chair and cleared his throat.

"I'm Jeremy," he said. "I'm a sergeant in the U.S. Army. I came to the Theta Institute a month ago, on the recommendation of an Army psychiatrist, after returning from duty in Iraq. As I'm sure you know, we see some pretty harsh stuff out there. When I came back to the States I was . . . different. I had a hard time eating and sleeping. I was irritable, on edge, having nightmares, and even hallucinations. They diagnosed me with post-traumatic stress syndrome and eventually recommended I come here. I'm here to find out how to cure my PTSD, so I can help others do the same. The military seems to think that this program might be able to help. I hope they're right."

Whoa. I was not expecting Jeremy to be suffering from PTSD. He looked so put together. Perhaps I belonged with this group after all.

Jeremy nodded, indicating he was finished, and turned to Tucker, who uncrossed his legs and perked up once he realized the attention was now on him. "My name is Tucker, and I'm an alcoholic," he said, scratching his chin. Then, as an afterthought, he added, "and a coke-head. I like drugs of all kinds, actually. I'm also possibly a sex addict, but I don't really consider that last one a problem." He briefly paused for our snickers, which we gladly provided. He'd obviously done this intro many times before. "I started drinking at the age of fourteen and just never stopped. I mean, I tried to stop. I tried to stop a lot. By the time I got kicked out of law school last semester I was on my third stint in rehab. That's when I met Dr. Luna, who told me about the Theta Institute and the recovery program they had here. I thought, you know, what the hell—it's on an island in the Caribbean; an island with no alcohol. I figured if it couldn't teach me to be sober on my own, at least it would keep me sober for a few more months. It was only a thirty-day program, but when Micah approached me about the Lucidity Project, I decided to extend my stay. I'm here to find out how to stay clean, I guess. If that's even possible. Who knows . . ."

Tucker looked out at the room, which had gone silent, then shrugged his shoulders and stretched out in his chair. "Plus, you know, it gives me extra time to work on my tan."

Again, I was in complete shock. You'd never guess by looking at him that Tucker was an alcoholic. Then again, I'd known quite a few addicts in my day, and they were often the most charming people in the room.

Next up was Dawn, who was still wearing Micah's hat. She used it to hide under as she spoke. "I'm here because I see things other people can't. Bad things. I'm hoping that I can learn how to make them go away here. Thank you."

She tilted her head down, prompting the hat to fall forward and cover the top half of her face completely. This seemed to be all we were going to get out of her for tonight.

Angelique crossed her arms over her chest when it came to her turn, as if she was being questioned against her will. "You all know who I am," she said. "I teach martial arts here on the island"—she paused and then took a deep breath—"which I became interested in after running away from home in my teens. I saw it as a good way to protect myself on the streets. Two years ago I met Dr. Luna while teaching a women's defense class in Seattle, and she told me they were looking for a martial arts teacher here on the island. I came here three days later and haven't left since. When Micah approached me about the Lucidity Project I jumped at the chance."

"And what are you hoping to get out of this project?" Micah asked.

Angelique took a deep breath and held Micah's gaze for a few seconds. The whole room was silent. It was clearly unlike Angelique to open up in this way.

Finally, she carefully said, "To move beyond my . . . past. Despite all the work I've been doing here on the island, all the workshops and meditating and self-help classes, I still feel very angry a lot of the time."

There was obviously a whole lot more to Angelique's story—to all of our stories. Something told me that much more of them would be revealed before these three weeks were through.

Next to share was Brad, who was from New York. A third-generation psychic, he'd come to the island three months earlier for one of Micah's workshops, after which Micah had asked him to participate in the Lucidity Project. On leaving the island, his plans were to (in this order): become a psychic spy for the U.S. government, write a bestselling book, get his own television show, become famous, and make millions from his psychic empire. His big question was how to make this all happen as fast as possible. I'd heard a lot of this kind of talk in my therapy groups at Cedars. People with emotional problems are often delusional and obsessed with becoming rich and famous. But honestly, what was wrong with that? I'd choose Brad's delusions of grandeur over my depression any day.

Then it was my turn. I shrugged off the nervous feeling I always got in my stomach whenever I had to speak in a group and began: "My name is Max. For most of my life, I've struggled with depression. The many doctors I've seen think it's a chemical imbalance, but I've had adverse reactions to almost every medication I've ever tried. The rest just haven't worked. Last week my therapist told me she wasn't going to give me any more medication. I guess I'm here because . . . I'm out of options." I tried to fight back the tears as I said this, but it was no use. Everyone else had managed to get through their stories without falling to pieces, and some of them were much worse than mine. I covered my face with my hands so they couldn't see me cry.

A few seconds later I heard someone walk over and kneel at my side, then felt a warm hand on my shoulder.

"Ms. Dorigan," Micah said—quietly, but loud enough for everyone to hear—"I know it doesn't feel like it now, but the truth is you have infinite options. You've only forgotten what they are."

I pulled my hands away from my face and looked into his eyes, which I was surprised to see were filled not with sympathy but excitement, just as Dr. Luna's had been a few days earlier when she'd told me antidepressants wouldn't be able to help me. The sadness I'd felt moments before seemed to dissipate.

"How do I remember?" I said, not really understanding what I was asking.

"That's what we're here to help you with. Healing is a process, Ms. Dorigan. Sometimes a long one, especially when you have forgotten who you are and what you've come here to do. Of course, there are a few things you can do to help it along. Exercise, for instance, is extremely crucial to this work. Monday through Friday we go on a mandatory run up to the lighthouse, so please meet us on the great lawn tomorrow morning at 10 a.m. sharp, hydrated and ready to go."

I inwardly groaned. Dr. Luna had warned me about the running, but I hadn't thought they'd make me start right out of the gate. Ugh.

"We've got a lot of deep psychological baggage to work through," Micah said, "and it's going to be scary, and it's going to be hard, and it's going to be heartbreaking at times. But we're on a tropical island in the Caribbean where all our basic needs are being provided for. We have access to some of the most healing modalities in the world, and more important than that, we have each other."

I looked around at the other people in the room. What was he talking about? How did we have each other? We didn't even know each other.

"I know my methods might seem strange, and I'm in no way attempting to gloss over the seriousness of anything we're going to be working on while you're here, but there is fun to be found in this. If you don't believe me, stick around. Things are about to get very interesting."

9

By the time I made it to the dining pavilion the next morning, it was nine thirty and the breakfast crowd had come and gone. There were a few stragglers, but no one from the Lucidity Project. I imagined most of them had already headed off to their respective jobs or whatever New Agey self-help workshop they had signed up for that day.

I checked out the buffet, dreaming of pancakes, French toast, or anything else I could pour syrup on. No such luck. Besides scrambled eggs and bacon, the rest of the buffet was filled with vegetables. There was some sort of sautéed vegetable and quinoa dish, which resembled Chinese fried rice; another green soup; sautéed spinach; and green smoothies. The fruit bar was also open, which made sense, but so was the salad bar, which I noticed a few people had taken advantage of. *Salad for breakfast? No thank you.* I grabbed some scrambled eggs and fresh fruit and gobbled it down.

As I was finishing up I saw Tucker and Jeremy jog by. I looked down at my watch and saw that it was five minutes to ten, which meant they were heading out to go running—the mandatory run that I was also supposed to go on with the team. But in this heat? It had to be at least 85 degrees out, not counting the humidity, and it wasn't even noon. Not only that, but my body was more achy and fatigued than usual, probably due to all the travel. I quickly ducked under the table and waited until they passed. Then, when I was sure they had put enough distance between us, I made my way back to my room. I was in no shape to go running, today or any day. I hoped that Ida would give me a free pass from any and all exercise after my health assessment.

●●●

Ida's bungalow was one of a handful of colorfully painted little structures tucked between banana trees, palms, and flowery foliage. Hers was bright pink, just as Angelique had said, with an ornate white woodcut trim.

Ida welcomed me in with a big smile. Today she was wearing a blue peasant dress embroidered with flowers and leather sandals. She had the air conditioning on—not so high that I felt like I was walking into a refrigerator, just enough to provide a nice reprieve from the heat outside. She led me through a comfy-looking living room filled with rattan furniture and brightly colored textiles, down a hall, and into her office, which actually looked more like an old apothecary's shop. The entire wall opposite the door was filled with shelves loaded with little brown glass bottles that were all hand labeled. I tried to read them, but they were just beyond my field of vision.

Ida led me to the middle of the room. "Okay," she said, peering at me, "I need you to stand here and put your right arm out in front of you at a ninety-degree angle, parallel to de floor."

Okay, well this was something I hadn't seen before. Despite my reservations, I did as I was told.

"Now, when I push down on your arm, you try to hold it up. Dat is all you have to do. You ready?"

"Uh, sure," I said.

We tried it once and I was able to keep it in place without any problems. Then she took one of the bottles from the wall and waved it over my abdomen while pushing on my arm again. I tried hard to keep it up, but it went right down with very little effort on her part.

"What are you doing?" I asked.

"I'm testing to see what supplements you need," she said.

"How do you know which supplements I need?"

"Your body tells me."

"Right," I said. Of course. That wasn't weird or anything. Clearly, my doctors at home had been doing it all wrong by using science to figure out what medications I needed.

Keep an open mind, I reminded myself. Maybe if I continued to repeat that to myself I wouldn't feel so judgmental. I looked around at Ida's unconventional office. The little brown bottles lining the shelves behind her. The bamboo chairs upholstered in vibrant fabrics. The posters of strange geometric shapes on the wall. This clearly wasn't going to be like any of my normal doctor visits.

She picked up another bottle and waved it over my head, behind my ears, and in front of my abdomen. My arm stayed up this time.

"Dis one you need very badly," she said.

"What is it?" I asked.

"Enzymes. Dey help you digest your food."

She turned and jotted some notes down on a chart she had on the desk. We went on like this for some time, Ida holding medicine bottles up to me, touching different points on my body, and my arm staying up or going down. It was all very, very weird. Finally, Ida returned all the bottles to the shelves and asked me to take a seat in front of the large desk next to us.

"Tell me something," she said, circling around behind the desk and settling down in her chair. "You find your life in danger a lot back in Los Angeles?"

"In danger?"

"People dere make threats on your life? You have to fight for food and shelter?"

"No. Not at all," I said, thinking this was a strange line of questioning. "I have an apartment in West Hollywood. It's pretty safe."

"Really? Das not what your body tell me. Your body tell me you live in constant fight or flight. Your adrenals? Dey shot. Your body is spending all its time trying to keep you alive; it has nothing left for digestion, nothing left for immunity, nothing left for anyting else. If your life is not in danger, what is it dat you fear so much in West Hollywood?"

The truth was I had a lot of fears. I feared I would lose my job and have to move back in with my parents, and that I would sink into a dangerous depression again if that happened. I feared I wasn't smart or strong enough to make it as a television writer. I feared I didn't have the energy to take care of myself or live life normally. The list went on and on.

"A lot, I guess," I said. "So that's what you think is wrong with me? I'm constantly in fight or flight? That would make sense. But I've already tried cognitive therapy, which I think would—"

"No," she said. "De fear is not de cause of de problem. It's just a symptom."

"Oh," I said, surprised. "You know the cause of my problems? My depression?" No one had offered me a definitive cause to my depression and health issues before. I sat up straighter in my chair.

"Yes. De problem is," she said, folding her hands on her desk, "you don't listen to your soul."

"My soul?" I asked. My heart sank. I was expecting a medical explanation of some kind—a disease perhaps, or a new DSM-IV diagnosis. Something I could take a pill for and cure.

"De mind, de body, de soul, dey're all connected. Dey all affect each odder. You've come to de island to work on dese tings. I'll help you wit de body, but if you don't also work wit de mind and de soul, tings won't change much. You see?"

"I'm sorry, I don't see. I'm not really religious . . ."

"Dis has noting to do wit religion," Ida said, raising her voice and pointing at me. "Dis has to do wit your soul. It is your guidance system, but you don't listen to it."

I sighed. I was hoping for a cure to my depression, not a bunch of New Age mumbo jumbo. But I'd told myself I would try and keep an open mind, and the fight or flight stuff did make sense—plus, I respected Ida. She was probably three times my age and yet she had more strength and vitality than I'd had in my entire life. She was obviously doing something right.

"Wit de soul," Ida went on, "dere are two ways to learn: de hard way and de easy way. You have chosen de hard way."

"Great," I said, sinking down in my chair. Even though I didn't really get what she was saying, it didn't sound encouraging.

"Dat's okay," she said cheerfully. "Because now you can tell de soul, 'I prefer de easy way, please.'"

"And . . . how do I do that?"

"You start to listen."

"Well, I don't know how to listen to my soul."

"Honey, you sure don't," she said, shaking her head and laughing. "But your soul knows how to talk to you. And you're just 'bout killing yourself trying to ignore her." She turned around and grabbed a few of the brown bottles off the shelf behind her. "Now, I can give you some supplements to help de body, but if you don't do de work, dey're not going to help much. Herbs need energy to work, and your energy is stuck. You got to exercise, you got to meditate, you got to move de energy. You work on listening to de soul, and I'll work on helping de body. With helping de body we tell de soul, 'You don't have to make me sick anymore. I'll listen now.'" She squinted at me. "Between de herbs and de healthy food you'll be eating here, your body is going to start to detox. The next few days you may not be very comfortable."

"More uncomfortable than I am now?" I asked. "I can barely walk up a flight of stairs as it is without feeling exhausted."

"'Fraid so. But it will give you an excuse to rest—both de mind and de body."

"Does that mean I'm excused from Dr. McMoneagle's morning runs?" I asked hopefully.

"Absolutely not," she said. "De running will be good for you—help you get de blood circulating and sweat de toxins out. But de other twenty-three and a half hours you can relax. Swim in de ocean. Read some good books. Do some new activities. You'll find some pretty interesting stuff on dis island."

"Yeah," I sighed. "That's what everyone keeps telling me."

10

To say I was frustrated as I left Ida's office would be an understatement. All this stuff about listening to the soul. Living in Hollywood, I heard talk like that all the time, but I usually checked out or left the conversation when things got too *woo woo*. We all have our place in this world. Some are meant to be spiritual people, some are meant to write sub-par television shows and hang out with Hollywood types. I was the latter. Ida clearly didn't understand the seriousness of my depression. I had a major chemical imbalance. I had just tried to kill myself. Jogging around the island and meditating was not going to change my brain chemistry. All I could do was hope that Micah would have some better answers for me.

After lunch, I headed over to his house, which was on the south side of the cove, right on the beach. For the owner of a posh health and wellness resort he lived quite modestly, in a white one-story bungalow not much larger than Ida's.

He answered the door in a T-shirt, striped board shorts, and fuzzy bunny slippers. On his head was some sort of headband, or headset, which had black earbuds and a few wires hanging down the sides of it. His blond hair was sticking out in all different directions, and judging by the sleepy look on his face, he had been napping until I knocked.

"I'm sorry," I said. "Did I wake you?"

"Not exactly," he said, wiping his eyes like a drowsy toddler. "Come on in."

I would have thought his house would be messy and unkempt, like his appearance, but it was neat and elegantly decorated, with beautiful crown molding, rustic wood floors, and natural woven rugs. A tan leather Chesterfield sofa and two linen lounge chairs sat around a stacked stone fireplace, over which hung a surfboard. Two more leaned against the wall by the French doors on the far side of the room, which led out to a backyard with a lawn and patio area, and beyond that, the beach. The only thing that seemed out of place in the room was a large machine next to one of the lounge chairs. The thing looked like a stereo system from the eighties, except much more high tech, with lots of knobs and buttons. Micah took the headset off his head and placed it on top of the machine.

"What's that thing?" I asked, nodding at the machine.

"That thing," he said, "is the Lucidity Project."

I followed him down a hall into a very masculine-looking office, painted a cool grey. Built-in bookshelves lined three of the four walls, including the one opposite the door, which also included a large picture window that looked out onto the backyard and had a beautiful view of the ocean. In front of the window was a large leather-top desk that looked like something out of the oval office. A red Victorian sofa sat against the wall to the right of me next to the door.

"We missed you on our run to the lighthouse this morning. I do hope you'll join us tomorrow," Micah said. There didn't seem to be any sort of reprimand in his voice, but I couldn't be sure.

I wanted to explain to him that I was too tired to try to participate in any sort of exercise schedule, but instead I just nodded, feeling the same uneasiness I'd had when I'd first met him the day before. What was it I was picking up on? Despite his unconventional views, he didn't seem like a bad person. Sure he was eccentric and a little full of himself, but he seemed like a good guy. So what was this strange feeling I was getting about him? And why, despite all my hesitations, did I still have a strong desire to work with him? It was as if I was attracted to and repelled by him at the same time—an experience I couldn't remember having with anyone ever before.

I sat in the chair on the other side of the desk and Micah went silent, as psychologists are apt to do at the beginning of a session as they wait for you to start complaining.

"So, what's the plan? Should I tell you about my mother?" I asked, trying unsuccessfully to keep the sarcasm at a minimum.

He leaned back in his chair, put his fuzzy-slippered feet up on his desk, and gave me an amused smile. "Do you want to tell me about your mother?"

"No." I sighed. "I've already been down that road. Many times. I'd rather discuss my treatment."

"Your treatment?" he said. "You shouldn't think of the Theta Institute as a treatment center."

"What should I think of it as, then? A hippie commune?"

He laughed. "More like a school."

"A school," I repeated. "You think you can teach me how to be happy?"

"Of course not. That's ridiculous," he said, waving that idea off with his hand. "You already know how to be happy. I'm just here to help you to remember."

"You think I've forgotten how to be happy?" I asked skeptically. I wanted to believe what he was saying was true, because that would be an easy fix, but it just wasn't logical. Of course, nothing I'd heard him say so far had really been logical.

"I think you've forgotten who you are. Your true, authentic self, not the self you're trying so unsuccessfully to be—this Hollywood television writer, or whatever you want to call it. We need to move you out of your intellectual identity and into your soul identity—the truth of who you are really are. I'm talking the divine nature of your expanded self. That disconnection between who you really are and who you are trying to be is what's making you so unhappy. Well, that and you eat a lot of junk food."

"I'm sorry," I said, wondering how he and Ida both knew about my poor diet. "I don't get the New Age lingo you all speak here. The psychiatrists I've seen say I have a chemical imbalance. Then I come here and Ida says I'm sick because I don't listen to my soul. Now you're saying I've forgotten who I am. Which is it?"

"It's all of those things," Micah said. "You've forgotten who you are because you've forgotten how to listen to your soul. Possibly that you even have a soul—*are* a soul. That's what's causing the chemical imbalance."

"Really? Because from what I've heard, bad genetics are what cause chemical imbalances. But what do I know. It's only science, after all."

"But you've already tried science and it didn't work for you, did it?" Micah said. "So let's not worry about science right now."

"What should I worry about?"

"Getting comfortable on that couch over there," he said, standing up. "I'd like to do a hypnotherapy session with you."

"You think you can hypnotize me into being happy?" I asked with a smirk.

"No," he said. "One hypnosis treatment is most likely not going to cure your depression."

"What is it going to do, then?"

"Perhaps bring some pieces of the puzzle to the surface."

"Like a repressed memory from my childhood or something?"

"Yes, or perhaps something traumatic from another lifetime."

"Another lifetime?"

"Yes."

"You mean like a past life?"

"That is correct."

I sighed. This was getting to a level of weird I just wasn't comfortable with. Past lives were something that Buddhists and hippies believed in, not me. I'd never been able to wrap my head around concepts like that, and I wasn't about to now.

"Can we just stick with this life?" I asked. "That's all I can really handle at the moment."

"Oh, it's not up to me," he said. "Your subconscious mind will go where it wants to go, and you will bring back whatever we need to know at this moment in time. Now, let's go. Chop chop," he said, clapping his hands.

I'd never in all my life had a psychologist who was so damn pushy.

I moved to the couch, lay down, and got settled in. Micah grabbed the Chippendale chair from in front of his desk, pulled it up next to me, and sat down. I shut my eyes, tried to get comfortable, and failed. I opened my eyes and looked up at Micah.

"I want you to know I think all this stuff is really weird," I said.

"Yes, I get that."

"I'm only going along with it because I have exhausted all other options. And by 'all other options' I mean the reputable, scientifically proven ones."

"Understood," he said. He waited as I grabbed a chenille throw from a basket next to the couch and tossed it over myself. Then I shut my eyes again, and he began.

"Okay, just get nice and comfortable, Ms. Dorigan," he said. "Take a deep, slow breath in, then exhale slowly and completely."

I snuggled my shoulders into the sofa, took a deep breath, and exhaled.

"Take another deep breath in, slowly and completely," he continued quietly.

I could hear the ticking of the clock on the wall and birds chirping outside the window. Micah's voice came again.

"Allow a peaceful wave of energy to move over your entire body from head to toe. If any thoughts come, let them come and let them go like clouds floating away through the sky. As you continue to settle in you may feel your eyes becoming a little heavier."

Indeed my eyes did feel heavier. The room was warm and comfortable, and I found Micah's voice surprisingly relaxing.

"Your jaw relaxes . . . your throat relaxes . . . your neck and shoulders relax . . ."

He continued on in this way down through every part of my body, very slowly, until I started to weave in and out of consciousness. At some point as I was falling into sleep I began to see bluish-white sparks swirling around me in my mind's eye, almost as if I were falling through space. It was all very surreal and dreamlike, and soon I found myself dozing off.

What felt like a few seconds later, I woke out of my dream state to hear Micah counting.

"Five . . . four . . ." he said, "three, you're feeling very grounded . . . two, you are feeling relaxed but energetic . . . one, you can open your eyes now feeling relaxed and refreshed."

I opened my eyes and looked around the room, blinking my eyes. Micah was still quietly sitting in the chair across from me. The energy in the air was intense, like when you walk into a room where people have just been arguing.

I sat up. My whole body felt feverish, as if I were waking up from a nightmare, but I could remember nothing. I reached up and felt my face was wet, and I could tell I had been crying. But how could that be? I'd only been out for a few seconds.

"You did very well, Ms. Dorigan," Micah said gently. His face was calm and relaxed. "I do believe I can help you."

"What happened?" I asked. It was as if I'd been through some terrible ordeal. I tried to remember, but like a dream that slips away soon after you wake up, the only thing I had to hold on to was a feeling—a feeling of deep and utter sadness.

When Micah didn't respond to my question, I looked into his eyes. "You know something," I said. "You know what's wrong with me. I can tell by your face. What did I say?"

"I'm sorry," he said. "I can't tell you."

"What? Why *not*?"

"Because you're not ready to know."

"Who told you that?"

"You did. Just now."

"While I was under hypnosis? Well that's very convenient," I said. "You've got to be kidding me. You hold all the answers to what's wrong with me and you're going to keep them from me?"

"That's the thing," he said, impassive. "I don't hold all the answers; you do. Another, higher part of yourself understands that. It's just waiting for you to catch up."

"A higher part of me?"

"It's not a conscious part of you that makes this decision. It's another part. Some call this the subconscious, some call it the higher self. Others call it—"

"The soul," I said, finishing for him.

"That's right."

"Well, I don't care what my soul says. I would like you to tell me the information anyway."

"You want to go against the wishes of your soul?" he asked with a incredulous look on his face.

"Yes," I said stubbornly.

He shook his head, then got up and walked to his desk.

"You want to know why you're depressed, Ms. Dorigan? There's your reason right there."

11

After leaving Micah's, I felt a headache coming on. I dealt with it the only way I knew how: by going back to bed. I stayed there for the rest of the afternoon, running over different possibilities in my mind and, as usual, getting nowhere.

By the time I came down to the dining pavilion for dinner, I felt exhausted and hopeless, completely strung out from worrying all afternoon. The last thing I wanted to do was leave my room and interact with people, but I was hungry.

Everyone from the Lucidity Project was already at our regular table when I arrived. I grabbed a baked chicken thigh, garlic green beans, and a green salad before heading over.

"All I'm saying is," Brad said as I approached the table, pointing his fork at Dawn, "I don't think it's coincidental that you saw that strange entity at the hotel when you got here. It's a sign from the universe."

"You think everything is a sign from the universe," Tucker said between bites of his food.

"That's because everything *is* a sign from the universe," Brad shot back.

"Do you really think so?" asked Dawn, considering whatever it was Brad was proposing.

"Well, yeah," Brad said. "You got proof that these demons, or whatever they are, can be gotten rid of. You just have to practice."

Curiosity got the best of me. "What are you talking about?" I asked, taking the empty seat between Jeremy and Dawn.

"We're so glad you asked," said Brad with a sly smile.

"Brad's heading up a paranormal investigation at the lighthouse tonight," explained Angelique. "We're trying to convince Dawn here to go with us."

"Why?"

"Because she can see dead people—duh!" said Brad.

"You're going to look for ghosts?" I asked. God, these people were so weird!

"Well, I haven't found any spirits up there yet, per se. More like impressions of the past. But that doesn't mean they aren't there."

"Impressions of the past? What does that mean?" I tried to keep the exasperation out of my voice but wasn't very successful.

"Strongly charged events in the past can leave an energy imprint on certain places in the present. Sensitives like Dawn and myself can pick up on these energies and are able to get a glimpse into the past. I thought the lighthouse would be a good place for Dawn to start. I feel a lot of residual energy up there."

"Yeah, but you could just be picking up on the energy of an argument someone had fifty years ago, not necessarily a ghost," Tucker said before shoving a bite of salad into his mouth.

I took a bite of my green beans, which had been sautéed in a perfect combination of butter, garlic, and salt. The people on this island might be crazy, but at least they knew how to cook.

"Well, that's why I want to take Dawn up there, to make sure," Brad said.

I looked over at Dawn, who looked less terrified than I would have imagined.

"Look, Dawn, it's no big deal," Brad said. "Tucker, Angelique, and I went up there a few nights ago and did a full investigation."

"What did you find, exactly?" I couldn't help but ask.

"Nothing," Tucker said. "A big fat zero. And we're not going to find anything tonight, either, because there's nothing up there."

"I'm telling you, there's something up there," Brad said.

"A spooky feeling does not count as *something*," Tucker said.

"Fine," Brad said. "Then it should be a perfectly safe place for Dawn to start working with her gift."

"Agreed," Angelique said.

Tucker sat back with a sigh.

"Why don't you come with us, Max?" Jeremy asked. Tonight he was wearing green khaki shorts and a tight grey T-shirt that showed the outline of every muscle.

"Oh, I would, but I can't tonight," I said weakly.

"Why, you got big plans?" Brad asked with a smirk. "Lying in bed sulking doesn't count."

I couldn't figure out what annoyed me more—his comment or the fact he knew I'd been hiding out in my room all day.

"You really should come with us," Angelique said with a stern look. "It'll be good for you to get out." By the tone of her voice I could tell this wasn't a request.

The last thing I wanted to do was go wander around some creepy lighthouse on a delusional self-help ghost hunting expedition. I looked at Dawn. If I could talk her out of it, maybe I wouldn't have to go. "I thought you were trying to get away from these ghost things, Dawn. What if they come back? Seems like you're asking for trouble."

Angelique shot me a look so dirty I was glad we were in a public space.

"Dawn needs to learn how to use her gift if she wants to be able to control it," Brad said in a much nicer tone than I imagine Angelique would have used.

"Well," Dawn said, glancing over at me timidly and grabbing at the purple amethyst around her neck. "I have Micah's amulet, so I'm protected now. If you go, Max, I'll go."

Oh, great. Thanks a lot, Dawn! Everyone looked to me expectantly—except for Angelique, who was still giving me the evil eye.

Jeremy leaned over. "Don't try and fight it," he whispered. "You'll just make it worse."

I had just met these people. Why were they acting like we were the Scooby Doo gang or something?

"I mean . . . if you really need me there . . ." I said, looking over at Angelique.

"Perfect," Angelique snapped back, smiling triumphantly. "We'll meet outside the hotel at nine."

12

A full moon was just peeking out above the jungle as I headed out to meet the team on the hotel porch. Despite the late hour it was still in the seventies, and I'd dressed casually in a pair of tribal shorts, Vans, and an oversized T-shirt. Tucker looked equally casual in swim trunks, a tank top, and an old pair of Nikes, but the rest of the team looked like they were going on some sort of top-secret military op. Jeremy was in camo pants and a black T-shirt, and Angelique looked like the spitting image of Lara Croft in khaki shorts, a black tank top, and the dragon belt she never seemed to be without. Brad and Dawn were both in head-to-toe black and looked like they were about to run a marathon or scale a large building.

"Wow, you guys really take this ghost hunting thing seriously," I said as I joined them. "Should I go back and get my proton pack? I left it in my room."

"Very funny," Angelique said as she tossed me a flashlight. "You won't be laughing when you try to get up the trail in those shoes." She pushed past me toward the great lawn.

"I'll be fine," I snapped, but as I looked down at my beat-up Vans, I realized she probably had a point. Oh well. It was too late to go back and change them now.

As we headed across the great lawn and toward the jungle, Jeremy fell in line next to me.

"I'm surprised to see you here," he said as we started down a path at the edge of the jungle. Next to it was a wooden sign that read DASHEEN PASS. "We weren't sure you were actually going to come."

"Yeah, well, I didn't want to but I was afraid Angelique would pulverize me if I didn't."

He smiled knowingly and looked down.

"What about you? Is ghost hunting a hobby of yours?"

"No," he said with a playful smile. "I'm afraid of Angelique as well."

I looked up into his dark eyes and felt a surge of electricity run through me. You'd have to be crazy not to be attracted to him. I tried to remind myself to keep a safe distance. The last thing I wanted was a romantic entanglement on top of everything else.

"So you've never gone on any of these ghost expeditions before?" I asked.

"Ghosts aren't really my thing," he said. "I prefer the living."

"Yeah, me too. You guys sure do have some really weird methods here."

"Definitely. These are literally the strangest people I've ever met in my life," he said with a smile.

I laughed. At least there was one other person here who thought this stuff was bizarre, even if he did enjoy it.

"I try to stay open-minded," he said. "But it's not easy sometimes."

"You seem . . . more grounded than everyone else."

"Yeah, well, that wasn't always the case."

"What do you mean?" I asked.

"You don't want to hear my whole story, do you?" he said playfully. "I gotta warn you. It's pretty sad."

"Does it involve two suicide attempts and a lifetime of depression?"

"That it does not."

"Then I think I've got you beat."

"That remains to be seen."

"Okay, how about this: I'll go first," I said. I briefly told him about my struggle with depression, suicide attempts, and mystery illness. It was nice to talk to someone who wasn't a therapist. I hid everything from Sofia and my other friends in LA. At Cedars I shared my problems in group, but those people were usually worse off than me, or at least I perceived them to be. Jeremy was different. Despite his association with the Lucidity Project and this island, he came off as a normal guy. He was so easy to talk to.

Jeremy listened quietly as our feet crunched on the leaves littering the jungle floor. But when I was done he said, "That's it?"

"What do you mean, that's it?" I said. "Did you hear the part where I tried to kill myself—twice?"

"I just mean . . . you don't see things?" His eyes searched mine in the moonlight.

"See things?" I asked. That was the second time I'd been asked that question this week. "No. Do you?" Maybe he wasn't so different from the rest of them after all.

"Sometimes," he said, looking up at the sky between the trees as we walked. The large moon peeked through overhead, giving us enough light to see without flashlights. "I didn't used to, but after being deployed to Iraq, something in me changed. I saw a lot of bad things there."

I nodded. Jeremy looked like such a tough guy. It was refreshing to see he was actually a tough guy with a brain . . . and a heart. Not like a lot of the guys I met back home.

"Needless to say, it really messed me up," he said. "When I came back to the States I was different. I couldn't sleep. I couldn't eat. I was paranoid all the time. And then I started seeing things. Things other people couldn't see."

"What kinds of things?"

"People in trouble. Crying out to me for help. There's this one woman who I see a lot. She's blindfolded and looks like she's been beaten." He took a deep breath and shook his head.

"Where do you see these people?" I asked.

"They're like hallucinations," he said. "But I see them in my dreams too. One night it got so bad I ended up in the hospital. That's when I was finally diagnosed with PTSD. But the pills the doctors gave me didn't work. In fact, they seemed to make things worse."

I nodded. "Tell me about it."

"I was working with an Army psychiatrist at the vet hospital," Jeremy continued. "She put me in touch with Dr. Luna. Next thing I knew, I was here."

"And you've already started the Lucidity Project," I said, thinking back to the big machine in Micah's living room.

"Yes."

"So what does that machine do, exactly?" I asked casually.

"I'm sworn to secrecy," Jeremy said. "But if you can wait for one more day, you'll find out for yourself."

●●●

The path narrowed as we navigated up a sharp turn marked by a wooden sign that read DEVIL'S BEND and I fell in line behind Jeremy. I could hear Brad chattering away to Angelique up ahead of us as they hiked up the path, which was now beginning to get quite steep. Every now and then Tucker would say something funny and Dawn would giggle. Jeremy treated me as if I were a princess he was chaperoning through the forest—holding branches aside for me, pointing out places where I should watch my step, and helping me up the steep parts. He hardly seemed the type to see things that weren't there. Perhaps his treatment was already working.

"So is Micah helping you?" I asked Jeremy after we'd walked in silence for a while. "Are the hallucinations going away?"

He was walking ahead of me, up a steep incline. He turned back to face me. It had gotten darker now, so I couldn't see his face very clearly, but his voice was intense. "No," he said, "quite the opposite. Since I started the program they've begun to progress."

"Oh no, I'm sorry," I said. My heart sank. That didn't bode well for me.

"I'm not sure 'sorry' is in order," he said, pointing to a protruding rock on the path as he continued on.

I stepped around it. "What do you mean?"

"I know this sounds crazy, but I'm starting to think my hallucinations aren't hallucinations at all."

"Well, what would they be, then?"

"I think they're people reaching out to me for help."

"You mean like ghosts?"

"No, living people. Living people that are in some sort of trouble. I'm not sure. They don't communicate like you and me."

No, of course they don't. I have the same problem when imaginary people come to visit me for help. What!?

I stayed quiet. What could I say? *You sure were cute until you started talking like a crazy person.*

Jeremy stopped walking again. "You really don't believe in any of this stuff, do you?"

"It's a bit of a stretch for me," I admitted. "It's just—how do you know it's just not the PTSD tricking you into thinking these people are real and not imaginary?"

"I don't know how to explain it. I just know," he said, and he started walking again.

"Hurry up, you slow pokes, we're here!" Brad yelled out ahead of us.

"Keep your pants on!" Tucker, who was just a few yards ahead of us on the path, shouted back. "Except for you, Red," he said, turning back toward me. "Feel free to remove yours at any time."

I gave him a sneer he probably couldn't see in the dark, and Jeremy stepped forward and gave him a playful shove. Tucker laughed and jogged up the steep path until he reached Angelique, Brad, and Dawn, who were disappearing through an opening in the foliage up ahead.

A few moments later I found myself coming out into a clearing. The light from the full moon easily reached us now that we were out of the trees, so we all turned off our flashlights. In front of us was a white lighthouse on a grassy bluff overlooking the ocean. It wasn't a traditional cylindrical turret lighthouse but a small colonial-style home with the lighthouse portion on top—like someone had just come along and added it as an afterthought. I recognized it as the one I'd seen on our trip over in the boat with Ida.

If I had to pick a haunted lighthouse out for a scary movie, this wouldn't be the one I would choose. The house was in pretty good condition. No boarded up windows. No broken glass. Sure it was old and a bit weathered, but it was well taken care of. Two pillared columns held up the white awning over the door, and whitewashed steps led up to a wraparound porch. Still, as I looked up at the place, a strange feeling crept over me. I wasn't exactly sure why, but I suddenly felt nervous to go inside.

"What's the story with this place?" I asked, trying to shake off the ominous feeling.

"It was built in 1888," Jeremy said. "Micah has been working on restoring it. It's been difficult, though. There's no road to bring supplies up here. He's had to do it all by hand."

"Dasheen Pass is the only way up?"

"There's a small path down to Mango Beach, below, but it's much steeper," he said.

"How did the house get built, then?" I asked.

"There evidently used to be a road at some point, back there behind the house"—he pointed to the left of the house where there was now nothing but dark, dense forest—"but it obviously grew over many years ago."

Everyone else was already waiting on the porch. Brad was fiddling with some sort of device that looked like a walkie-talkie.

"What's that?" I asked as Jeremy and I walked up the steps.

"An EMF detector," Brad said, flipping a switch on the side. A red light on the top of the gadget went on.

"A what?" I asked.

"It detects fields emitted when electrically charged objects move."

"I don't understand."

"It's a ghost detector," Tucker said, walking to the front door. "If there's a ghost near you, the light on it turns green. That means run." He twisted the doorknob and disappeared inside.

"It does not mean run," Brad said, following him in. "It means *investigate.*"

"How do you investigate a ghost?" I asked, heading in behind him.

"You ask it questions, see if it will make a noise for you. Spirits are quite apt at making noises, like knocking or the sound of footsteps. Even moving things. Once I had one shut a door right in front of me." He paused. "Though I guess it could have been the wind."

Ironically, the lights in the lighthouse didn't work, so we turned our flashlights back on. I inspected my surroundings. The inside was sparsely furnished, and the few pieces present were covered in heavy canvas. There was a dining room to the left and sitting room on the right and stairs that went up to what I assumed was the turret where the light was stored.

"Now," Brad said, turning to face us in the hallway. "Just walk around the house. If you sense something—anything at all—just call it out."

"What sort of things should we be . . . sensing, exactly?" I asked.

"Spirits don't communicate the way you and I do," Brad answered, pushing his glasses up on his nose. "They're not just going to start up a conversation. Instead they might show you pictures in your mind. You might hear a sound or suddenly feel a sensation, like a cold or warm spot. Or you might feel one of them touch you."

"Touch me?" I asked with a shudder. If ghosts did exist, I certainly didn't want any physical contact with them.

"Fine by me," said Tucker, "as long as it's a hot girl ghost."

Brad let out a sigh then walked into the sitting room. We all followed. Tucker plopped down on the covered sofa and put his feet up on what looked like a coffee table. He obviously took this ghost hunting stuff about as seriously as I did.

"Are you picking anything up here, Dawn?" Brad asked, turning toward her. She was keeping close to Angelique and looked only moderately freaked out, considering it was dark outside and we were in a supposedly haunted lighthouse in the middle of the jungle.

"Ye-yes," Dawn stuttered. She looked back toward the entryway. "There's something . . . over there."

A chill went up my back.

"Well now we're getting somewhere," Tucker said, sitting up and slamming his feet back down on the hard floor. The sound made me jump.

Brad shushed him. "Keep going," he said, holding out the EMF detector, which still showed red. "Is someone here with us?"

"I . . . I'm scared," Dawn said. Her voice was shaking. I figured we probably had about three seconds before she ran screaming from the lighthouse. At least then I could go home and go to bed.

"Remember your crystal," Angelique said. "Nothing can hurt you when you have it on."

Dawn nodded bravely, grabbed the piece of amethyst around her neck, and shut her eyes. A few seconds later she opened them again. "Something very bad happened here," she said. "Very bad."

My incredulity began to waver, and I couldn't help but feel a little freaked out. Dawn's wide eyes, hunched shoulders, and creepy demeanor were very convincing.

"What else can you tell us?" Brad asked, taking a few steps toward her. "Use all your senses."

"I feel a woman. She's very . . . upset." Keeping one hand clutched around the crystal on her neck, Dawn held her other hand in front of her, palm out, like she was pulling her observations from the air. She walked back toward the front hall. "It started here. I think she was running from someone."

"Who was it?" Brad asked. "See if you can get a name."

I looked down at Brad's EMF reader. It was still red. If there was an actual ghost in the room, it should have turned green. Was Dawn making this all up? From the way she was acting, I certainly didn't think so. Perhaps it was another delusion, like the demon she'd seen when we first arrived. Regardless, I was starting to get seriously scared.

"I'm not sure," Dawn said, shaking her head. "She was hurt." She clutched at her chest and scrunched up her face in pain. "Here, in her heart. It feels like there's a knife going through it."

She spun around, as if someone had called to her, and darted through the entryway to the front door. The rest of the team headed out behind her. I reluctantly followed as well. I wasn't sure what was going on, and I wasn't sure I wanted to find out.

"She ran out here to get away from someone," Dawn said, opening the front door—then, without giving us any warning whatsoever, she took off at a full sprint toward the cliff.

The rest of glanced quickly at each other then took off down the steps after her.

As we ran across the grassy bluff towards the cliff, I couldn't help but doubt my decision to come to this crazy island. Chasing a so-called ghost around the jungle in the middle of the night? What was I doing?

Dawn came to a stop next to a wooden bench just a few yards away from the edge of the cliff and the rest of us stopped beside her. The ocean stretched out before us in the moonlight.

"Someone was chasing her. I'm sure of it. She was trying to get away but there was nowhere to go, and then . . ." Dawn took a few more steps toward the cliff.

"Whoa there, little lady," Tucker said, grabbing Dawn's shoulder to keep her from going any closer to the edge. "Don't get ahead of yourself."

Dawn stared down at the water below. We waited in silence.

"I think she might have gone over, but I'm not sure. I lost it," Dawn said. Her hands, which she'd been holding out in front of her, fell to her sides. Her shoulders slumped in disappointment.

We gave her a few minutes as she looked around, trying to get the feelings back.

"Maybe we should go back to the lighthouse," Brad finally suggested. "You seemed to have a stronger sense of things there. We didn't get to go through the whole house anyway."

"Yes, I suppose," Dawn said, not sounding convinced.

The last thing I wanted to do was go back inside that creepy lighthouse and be scared out of my wits in the name of self-help. This ghost hunting stuff was not for me. If Dawn was suffering from some kind of psychosis, encouraging her just seemed to be making it worse. And if she really was sensing a ghost, I wanted no part of it. My body was aching and fatigued from the trek up, and I felt another headache coming on. What I really needed was to go to bed. I couldn't believe we still had a two-mile hike ahead of us. At least it was all downhill.

"I'm going to wait for you guys out here," I said.

"You okay?" Jeremy asked, coming over to me.

"I just have a little bit of a headache," I said, looking up into his dark eyes. "The fresh air helps. Go ahead. I'm fine here."

"We shouldn't be too much longer," Jeremy said.

I nodded and took a seat on the bench as they walked back toward the house.

It felt good to finally sit down. From the bench I could see up the northwest side of the island in the moonlight, and the lights of St. Lucia in the distance. The waves crashed softly at the base of the bluff. After a few minutes of resting there, I found I was having a hard time keeping my eyes open. But just as I started to doze off, I thought heard a small movement on the other side of the cliff.

Oh great, now I'm going to get eaten by a wild animal? I thought. But what kind of wild animals were able to climb cliffs? Monkeys? Sloths? Did they have sloths in the Caribbean? Did sloths bite? I had no idea. I stayed still and waited, hoping it was a lizard or a bird.

The noise came again, louder this time—it sounded like rocks and dirt were dislodging and falling into the ocean below. There was something large moving around on the underside of the cliff. I froze, staring hard at where the noise was coming from. Suddenly, an arm appeared over the ledge of the cliff. I gasped as another arm came up, and then a head. In the moonlit shadows I could see what looked like the outline of a woman in heels and a dress crawling over the edge of the cliff.

She stood, then took a crooked step toward me as adrenaline ripped through my body. I was right. It was a woman—or at least it had been once. Her skin was moldy and falling off her bones in places, as if she had spent the past fifty years at the bottom of a lake. Her body was mangled and hunched over, making her look inhuman. There was a gaping hole on the side of her head, and where her eyes and mouth should be there were only dark pits. The dress she wore was a tattered drop waist evening gown; the few beads and sequins left on it glistened in the moonlight.

A ghost, just like they'd said. Even petrified by fear, I didn't miss the irony. What they had been saying was true. All of it.

I sat there frozen on the bench, unable to move or scream. She took another labored step toward me, her left foot dragging behind her. From the way it turned unnaturally to the left, it was obvious it was broken.

She tilted her head as if she recognized me, then growled out something—a word. "*You.*" But it wasn't a woman's voice that came out; it was something monstrous. My heart leapt, and I let out a terrified scream and turned to run—but as soon as I did, the thing appeared directly in front of me.

For a brief second I stared into her eyes. They were completely black and seemed to be leaking down her face. As I stared, she lifted her hand, and before I could register what was happening she struck me hard across the face. The blow landed on the left side of my nose, and I fell backward onto the grass, stunned.

I screamed again, hoping someone in the lighthouse would hear me. She came toward me again and I saw she had something in her hand: a rock. Not a big one—it was only a bit bigger than her palm— but big enough to do some damage. I tried to get up, but before I could she slammed it down against my left temple. Pain surged through my head once again. She gnashed her teeth as if she wanted to eat me alive; the pits where her eyes had once been were dripping with black fluid. She hauled back to hit me a third time and I desperately grabbed on to both her forearms, which were dripping wet and cold as ice. Her rotting flesh seemed to fall away in my fingers.

I continued to scream. In response to, or perhaps in spite of, my screams, she let out a blood-curdling wail and tried to smash my head with the rock in her hand again.

Then there were more hands on me, shadows of figures in the moonlight. I couldn't see their faces, and didn't know if they were from our group or were more of her kind coming to finish me off, so I just continued to scream and swing at anything that came near me.

"Max! Max! Stop!" I finally heard a familiar voice yelling. It was Angelique. I looked around. The demon woman was gone.

"Where did she go?" I cried, pulling away from them and scooting backward on the grass. I could feel blood on my face and taste it in my mouth.

"It's okay now, Max. Tell us what happened," Jeremy said, kneeling in the grass in front of me. Dawn, Brad, and Tucker stood behind him, looking completely freaked out.

"Something . . . attacked me," I said, twisting to look toward the cliff. There was nothing there. "Didn't you see her? She was right here."

"It was dark. We couldn't see anything," Angelique said, exchanging a wary glance with Jeremy.

"You must have scared her off," I said, trying to catch my breath. The side of my nose throbbed from where I'd been hit, and the left side of my forehead felt even worse.

Tucker shone his flashlight on my face and assessed the damage.

"Oh man," Angelique said.

"Is it bad?" I asked, reaching up and feeling my nose, which was where the blood seemed to be coming from. So much adrenaline was pumping through my body I couldn't tell how badly I was hurt.

"You'll be okay," Jeremy said. He grabbed a tissue out of his pocket and wiped my face, then grabbed another and folded it into a small rectangle. "Put this under your top lip. It should stop the bleeding."

Brad knelt down next to me. "What attacked you, Max?"

"I don't know," I said. "But it wasn't human. Not anymore, anyway."

I couldn't believe the words that were coming out of my mouth. I sounded like—well, just like one of them.

"I thought you said it was safe here!" Dawn cried out, turning to Brad. She looked on the verge of hysterics.

"I thought it was," Brad said. "Nothing has ever happened up here before. I'm sorry, Max. I never would have brought you here if I thought it was dangerous." He then took his EFT reader and ran it over my body, then waved it around in the air near me. The light stayed red. "Whatever it was, it's gone now," he said. "I'm not picking up anything. Dawn, how about you?"

"I can't be receptive right now," Dawn said, clutching at the amethyst around her neck. "I want to leave. I want to leave now."

"Well then, let's get the hell out of here," Tucker said. Not even he had a joke to break the tension.

Jeremy turned to me. "Can you run?"

"You bet your ass I can," I said. Only a few minutes earlier I'd been wondering how I was going to walk the two miles back to the hotel, but now I felt as if I had enough energy to run all night—whatever it took to get me away from this place and that thing.

Jeremy held out his hand and helped me up. "Okay, I've got Max," he said, holding my hand protectively. "Everyone else grab a partner."

We all flew—away from the cliff, past the lighthouse, and back down Dasheen Pass into the jungle.

I stayed close to Jeremy—as close as you can when you're running for your life through the jungle in the middle of the night—the whole way back. He had to let go of my hand at a certain point so we could run faster, but he made sure to go ahead of me, and Angelique closed in protectively behind me. The only sounds I could hear were our breath and the pounding of our feet hitting the dirt path. It was as if all the creatures in the forest had gone silent.

"Head to Ida's," Angelique said as we exited the jungle and spilled onto the great lawn. "She'll have something for your injuries."

A few minutes later we were pounding on the door of Ida's bungalow on the other side of the great lawn. She opened the door a few minutes later in a blue robe and slippers, and despite the late hour and the blood that was all over my face, she didn't appear too surprised.

"I . . . I got attacked by something up at the lighthouse," I said, stepping forward.

She looked into my face in the porchlight and calmly shook her head. "Yes," she said, opening up the door to allow us in, "dis is what happens when you choose to do tings de hard way."

13

Ida dabbed a foul-smelling liquid on my face from one of her little brown bottles. Angelique stood next to me, watching Ida work, while the rest of the team looked on tensely.

"Is my nose broken?" I asked as Ida turned my head from side to side.

"No, just bloody, and you gonna have a bruise on de side of your head tomorrow. Odder den dat, you're just fine."

I glanced over at a mirror on the wall and caught my reflection. Ida was right. Once the blood from my nose had been wiped away, my injuries didn't seem so bad. My nose was red but intact, and the cut on my left temple wasn't big enough for stitches. Ida put a bandage on it, then handed me an ice pack she had made.

I heard the front door open and tensed. I was still convinced that the ghost was going to come back. But a few seconds later, Micah appeared in Ida's office doorway. It was the first time I'd seen him without his signature smirk. Jeremy stood behind him with an equally serious look on his face. In my confusion I hadn't even noticed that he'd left at some point.

"Good evening," Micah said calmly. He approached me, lips pursed, then touched his hand to my chin, examining my face. He'd obviously been pulled out of bed: he was wearing blue pajama pants and a white T-shirt. Salt crystals and sand speckled his tan face, probably from an early-evening surf outing, and he was standing so close I could feel the heat coming off his skin.

"She was attacked by something," Ida said, looking over her glasses at him. "Up at de lighthouse."

"I see," he said sternly as he continued to inspect my injuries. His eyes were such a light shade of blue they looked more unnatural than normal.

Ida put her hands on her hips. "You've got to tell de girl about what happened up on dat cliff, Doctor Micah. It doesn't matter what she believes or doesn't believe."

"I knew it!" Brad said, jumping up from where he was sitting in one of the chairs opposite Ida's desk. "I knew something happened up there. I could feel it."

The look on Micah's face was even more serious now. "The woman who attacked you. Did you see what she looked like?"

"Sure," I said, holding my hand at shoulder level. "About yea tall, bashed-in head, moldy skin, black dripping eyes, really frickin' scary. Why, do you know her?"

Ignoring my sarcasm, Micah put his hands together and touched his lips with the tips of his fingers. "I guess you could say something like that."

This wasn't the answer I'd been expecting, and I decided I should probably answer his question seriously. "It was dark and her body was badly decomposed," I said. "But from what I could make out, she was maybe in her twenties or thirties with short, dark hair. She had on a black evening dress, and her left leg was broken."

I could see a spark of something in Micah's eyes as I spoke. "I see," he said, leaning back like I'd given him some very interesting news. Then he walked to the window and stared out into the moonlit night.

"What happened up there?" I asked. "Did someone die?"

The room was dead silent. Micah didn't answer for a long time, and I thought perhaps he hadn't heard me, but then he spoke.

"Yes," he said. "Three people, in fact. It was a very long time ago—in the twenties. They fell off the cliff during a storm and drowned. It was quite a terrible tragedy."

I thought back to the ghost that had attacked me. The black drop waist dress she was wearing definitely could have been from the twenties.

"So, what you're saying is that you think the woman who attacked me was the ghost of one of those people?" This felt like a line from *You Sexy Witch*. I couldn't believe I'd said it out loud.

"Ghosts can't do dis," interrupted Ida, waving her hand at my temple. "Dey don't have dat kind of power."

"Whatever it was, has anyone seen it up there before?" I asked.

"No," said Micah shaking his head. "I've never heard of anyone seeing anything up there. I mean, intuitives like Brad and Dawn have picked up on the residual energy left over from the accident, but nothing beyond that." He looked over at Ida, who nodded her head in agreement.

"Perhaps it's something else," Brad said. "A lower entity, like Dawn saw on the stairs when she first got here."

"No, that's not what it was," said Dawn. "This was a woman. A human woman."

"Well whatever or whoever she is, she obviously needs our help," Micah said, turning back to us from the window, still deep in thought. He looked at me and rephrased. "*Your* help."

"I'm sorry?" I said, a feeling of indignation rising in me. "You must have missed the part where she tried to brain me with a rock."

"Energies of these sorts are tricky," Micah said, unruffled. "They seem to gravitate toward those they believe can help them. That means she found some sort of connection to you. It's your job to find out what that connection is."

"Are you crazy?" I gasped. "I'm not the Ghost Whisperer. That's Dawn's job. I want to get as far away from that thing as possible."

"Don't worry," Micah said calmly, like we were discussing a homework assignment. "I can help you. This is the type of stuff we do here."

I looked around the room. Everyone was staring at me with earnest looks on their faces.

"It is what you do here, isn't it?" I said with a sigh. "This whole time I thought you all were just having delusions of some sort, or trying to make yourselves feel special with stories of ghosts and psychic powers. But that's not what's going on. Brad, you aren't here because you think you're psychic. You *are* psychic. I mean, you're not a very *good* psychic, but still. And Dawn, you aren't psychotic. You really can see ghosts— or demons, or whatever."

"Well, yeah," Dawn said with a shrug. "I mean, we weren't trying to hide that from you or anything."

"If you'd been taking this seriously you wouldn't be so surprised right now," added Angelique.

"So what are you guys—like, the Ghostbusters or something?" I asked, only half joking.

"This has very little to do with ghosts, actually," Micah said. "That's not really . . . my specialty."

"What *is* your specialty, exactly?" I said. "And more important, what does it have to do with me?"

"Quite a lot, as it turns out," said Micah.

"Enlighten me, please."

Micah took a breath. "I'm here to help people access those parts of themselves they for one reason or another have shut down or forgotten about. In doing so, many of my clients find that they have abilities they weren't aware of before."

After what had just happened I couldn't deny that there were things in this world that were beyond me—things that I didn't understand and couldn't explain. Still, that didn't mean I had to be a part of it. All I'd ever wanted was to be a normal person with a normal job and normal friends. I had no desire to be a psychic ghostbuster.

"I'm sorry," I said. "I'm just not into this hocus pocus stuff. I don't get up in the morning wanting to do psychic readings or run around after ghosts. I barely have the energy to do normal stuff like take a shower or go to work. I'm exhausted all the time. I'm depressed all the time. You just don't understand what I'm going through right now."

"We all came here just like you," Angelique said. "Some much worse off than you are now. You think we don't understand sadness? You think the path here was easy for any of us? Depression and desperation drove us here, just like you. The only difference with us is that we're trying to do something about it."

"Well, I guess I'm just not as strong as you are," I shot back. "I'm sure if you were in my situation you would have just turned around and karate chopped the crap out of that thing that attacked me. But I'd rather just leave this place and sidestep any more demonic ghost attacks, thank you. I don't need to be psychic to know that."

"Please don't fight," Dawn pleaded, shrinking down in her chair. "Please."

"At least not until we can find some mud to dip you both in first," Tucker said.

The room went quiet for a moment—then everyone, including me, broke out in nervous giggles. I didn't want to laugh, but I couldn't help it. Tucker's timing couldn't have been more inappropriate and he knew it. After the giggles died down I was able to relax somewhat and respond less defensively.

"Look, you guys, I'm sorry," I said, sliding off the desk. "I can't stay here. I just can't. I can't risk that thing coming back and attacking me again."

I looked over at Micah, who pursed his lips, then nodded. "If that's what you want," he finally said. "I can have a plane ticket sent over to you in the morning."

"Thank you," I said as I slid off the table and headed out the door. "The sooner I get off this island, the better."

14

Zoe was asleep when I got back to our room. I dragged myself over to my bed and crawled under the covers. The room was warm, but I still couldn't stop shaking. My last-ditch effort at a normal life had been a total failure. Not only was I still depressed and sick but I'd also somehow opened a door to a horrific world that, up until tonight, I had never believed existed. All I could hope for was that the ghost woman would stay on the island when I left, which hopefully would be tomorrow. I didn't know much about spirits, but if all the horror films I'd seen were correct, they usually haunted the places where they'd died. Hopefully Micah was wrong about the ghost attaching herself to me, and as soon as I left this crazy place I'd never have to deal with anything like that again.

Of course, that wasn't the worst of my problems. I would now have to go back to LA without a cure for my depression, which meant I'd probably get fired at some point in the next few months. Everything I'd worked so hard for, gone. And how was I going to take care of myself? The side of my temple where I'd been hit ached. It was all too much to try to process, so I did what any clinical depressive just attacked by a deadly ghost woman would do: popped a Xanax and went to sleep.

●●

I was awoken by music—old-timey jazz music, coming from somewhere outside my room. The song sounded familiar, but I couldn't place it, partially due to the fact that I couldn't hear very well over the rain that was pelting the window next to me. I sat up and looked out the window. It was so filled with water, I could barely see the palms below bending against the wind. An unexpected summer storm, and from the looks of it, a big one.

I sat up, wondering who would be playing such loud music in the middle of the night. As I strained to listen, I heard the sounds of voices and laughing as well. It sounded like a party.

I glanced over at Zoe's bed; she wasn't in it. I got up and walked out into the hall, where the music and chatter were even louder. It *was* a party. Somewhere downstairs. Why hadn't anyone told me about it? I walked to the elevator and took it to the bottom floor to investigate.

As the elevator opened I saw the whole downstairs was packed with people who were dancing, talking and laughing. It was a costume party. Not just any costume party, but something straight out of *The Great Gatsby*. The men wore tuxedos with coattails and top hats, the women slinky dresses covered in beads and sequins—not the cheap kind with rows of fringe that you get at costume stores for Halloween, but the real thing.

I could barely hear anything over the music. Ragtime now, I was pretty sure. I walked into the packed ballroom, where I found a stage complete with chorus girls, a brass band, and people dancing the Charleston. Silver balloons and streamers hung from the ceiling between a half-dozen crystal chandeliers.

Looking around, I didn't recognize anyone from the resort. I hadn't exactly met anyone other than the Lucidity Project team in the past few days, but I'd gotten used to seeing many of the same faces—and none of them were here.

"Would you like a drink, miss?" asked a familiar voice. I looked down. It was Dawn, dressed in an old-fashioned maid's uniform, complete with white ruffled apron and collar. She held a tray of champagne out to me, her lavender bangs peeking out of a frilly white cap. I laughed at how cute she looked and played along.

"Thank you," I curtsied, then took a glass off the tray. "I'm afraid I'm a little underdressed." I glanced bashfully at my dirty T-shirt and shorts, which I'd failed to take off when I went to bed that night. "Why didn't anyone tell me about this party?"

Dawn's eyes fell on something toward the back of the room, and her already pale face went even whiter. "You're about to find out, I'm afraid," she whispered, and then scurried away into the crowd.

I turned around, anxious to see what had spooked her. My heart jumped. The ghost woman from the lighthouse was coming toward me. In the light of the room I could more easily see how absolutely frightening she was. Her short, wet hair was matted and falling away from her skull where the side of her head had been crushed, and her face was a moldy green, almost completely decomposed.

I turned and pushed my way through the crowd, desperately trying to get away from her, but the place was packed, and no one else seemed to notice the horrifying ghost in the room. Ahead of me I spotted Micah, dressed in a tuxedo and talking closely with a young blonde in a silky, cream-colored dress.

"Micah!" I screamed out, but he didn't hear me. No one seemed to. When I grabbed at the people around me, they only laughed and went back to their conversations, or shot me annoyed looks for interrupting their good time.

I was still trying to make my way through the crowd when I felt the ghost's wet, icy hands rake at me, her nails clawing into my arm. I screamed out, struggling to get free, but still no one noticed, opting instead to dance around me like I was a chair or a cocktail table. The ghost opened her gaping black mouth at me, then struck me in the side of my face. I fell to the floor, and panic took over—I felt paralyzed. The ghost grabbed me by the hair and began dragging me toward the front of the room. Terror filled my body, and I kicked and screamed, fighting her, but she was too strong.

As she hauled me across the room, someone stepped out of the crowd and blocked her path. Her grip on my hair loosened just a little and I yanked my head forward and broke free. Turning, I saw that the person blocking the ghost was Micah. I ran and hid behind him, clinging to his jacket for dear life.

Micah just stood there. The ghost closed her horrible mouth and cocked her head as if contemplating this new turn of events. Micah held nothing in his hands, but it was clear she considered him a threat, and after a few seconds she took a step backward. They were communicating in some other way, I realized. I kept cowering behind Micah, and the ghost glared at me hatefully, like all she wanted to do was tear me to pieces but he was somehow forbidding it. He clearly had some sort of power over her.

Defeated, she looked up to the ceiling and screamed at the top of her lungs. More black liquid came oozing out of her eyes and splashed onto the checkered floor around her. Instinctively I buried my face in Micah's back and braced myself for another attack, but then the screaming stopped, and when I opened my eyes she was gone. The party continued around us like nothing had ever happened.

"How did you do that?" I asked as Micah turned to face me.

"Do you really want to know?" he asked with an incredulous smile.

"Yes, I do."

The band started up a new song. This one I did recognize—it was "West End Blues" by Louis Armstrong, a slower song with a sleepy tempo. Instead of answering, Micah opened his arms, and before I knew what was happening he was waltzing me slowly around the dance floor.

"How did you get her to go away?" I asked him again.

"If you haven't noticed, I'm quite good with the ladies." He smirked and twirled me around gently.

"What are you?" I asked. "A witch or something?" I knew a thing or two about witches; I worked on a television show about them, after all.

"I'm a man who understands universal laws. Not all of them, but definitely more than you. I have to say, though, you're beginning to show some potential."

"So you're able to fight off something like that with just your mind?"

"Not just my mind, but yes."

"Can you teach me?" I asked.

"Of course. That's what the Lucidity Project is all about. It's what you came to the island to learn. The first class is tomorrow. You should come."

"I can't," I said. "I have to get off this island. If I stay here, that thing is going to attack me again."

He shook his head and smiled as we glided across the dance floor. "Leaving here won't help; wherever you go, she'll find you. Your best option is to come to my class tomorrow."

"I don't want to come to your stupid class!" I said, a little louder than I intended. I was frustrated that he wasn't listening to me. I struggled to remember another person who had made me this angry while doing so little.

"Why not?"

"Because." I paused. "I don't like you."

"Why do you think that is?" he mused, appearing more curious than offended.

"I don't know." I tried to think of what it could be but drew a blank. He hadn't really done much besides act like a bit of a show-off. All I felt was frustration, but I wasn't sure why it was there. "I'm sure I have a good reason."

"I'm sure you do," he agreed, and twirled me around again.

God, he could be so patronizing. Everything the man said and did seemed to trigger a wave of negative emotions in me. Why did he think this was all a game? Didn't he see I was in real danger? That ghost was going to come back soon and finish me off.

As Micah continued to whirl me around the room, I felt something cold touch my feet and I looked down. Water was flowing onto the dance floor. A deep foreboding crept into the pit of my stomach. I turned to look out the front window, where, despite the time of night and the storm, I could see the beginning of a very large wave rising way off in the distance. My heart sank.

Micah saw it too, and we stopped dancing.

"I believe that's yours," he said.

"Yes," I said, staring at the wave. "We have to get out of here."

Before he could respond, I grabbed his hand and yanked him toward the exit at the far end of the room.

Micah stood his ground. "You really think that's the best idea?"

"Can you think of a better option?" I asked, panic rising in my voice. Was this guy for real? The wave tumbling toward us was taller than the trees.

"Like I've said before, we have infinite options," Micah said, looking down at the watches on his wrist. "We always do. The easiest one right now is probably just to wake up."

"Wake up?" I asked. My mind was reeling with confusion. "What are you talking about?"

Micah looked back at me with a hint of a smile. "Haven't you figured it out by now, Ms. Dorigan? You're dreaming."

His eyes danced as he watched me try to comprehend what he'd just said. Was he trying to trick me? I looked around at the partygoers, who were dancing around in two inches of water and carrying on as if nothing were wrong. It was odd that they didn't notice the water or the loud crashing of the wave heading toward us, but they were very drunk and the music and storm together were quite loud. I looked down at my hand in Micah's and squeezed, looking for some proof that I was dreaming, but could find none. It was solid—corporeal. I felt my arm; it felt just as it always did. Nothing felt different. This wasn't a dream. I was awake.

The wave was getting closer now. I could hear the trees and buildings crashing under its weight in the distance.

"You're full of it," I challenged, dropping Micah's hand. "I'm getting out of here."

"I wouldn't do that if I were you," Micah said with a shake of his head. "Running or movement of any kind only keeps you in the dream. Your physical body, which is not the one you see here but the one that's in your bed, is in sleep paralysis. If you want to wake up, it's best to stay very, very still. This is all stuff you'll learn if you come to my class."

I froze, not sure whether to believe him or not. I felt as awake as awake could be. "Stop screwing around, Micah," I said, getting frantic. "We're all going to die if we don't get out of here. All these people are going to die."

"These people have been dead for many, many years," he said.

I looked around at the people dancing through the rising water. Dead? All of them?

"Tell me something, Ms. Dorigan," Micah said. The evenness of his tone was putting me even more on edge. "That tidal wave out there. Do you ever see it when you're awake?"

"When I'm awake?" I asked. I looked back at the white water crashing over the trees, and something clicked. The wave only came in my nightmares. Micah was right—I was dreaming! How had I not noticed it before?

I breathed a sigh of relief—and then promptly realized that just because we were dreaming didn't mean we were out of danger. Maybe we wouldn't die in real life, but drowning in a massive tidal wave, even in a dream, is incredibly painful. I should know; I'd experienced it many times.

"Okay, so we're dreaming," I said. "What do we do?" It was taking every last bit of my willpower to stop myself from running for my life. I was so scared, I felt like I was going to climb out of my skin.

"We wake ourselves up," Micah answered, putting his hands in his pockets like I had just asked him what he'd like for lunch.

"How?"

"Just like you do anything else in life: you decide to do something and then do it. It's really that easy, and yet few people know how to do it."

The wave slammed closer, shaking the ground and causing the chandeliers to sway overhead. It was only about fifty yards away now. We didn't have much time.

"Show me how to wake up then, damn it!" I cried.

Micah looked casually down at his toes, then back up at me. "Will you come to my class tomorrow?"

"Yes! I will do anything you ask. Just show me. Please!" I begged.

"Like I said, it's simple. You just set your intention and then command it to happen. Like this"—he shut his eyes then very loudly commanded, "Wake up, now!" while snapping his fingers. To my complete astonishment, he then disappeared right before my eyes.

I gasped. I couldn't believe he'd just abandoned me there on my own. Tears of fear sprang into my eyes, only to be quickly replaced by tears of panic. The giant wave was seconds away. I didn't have time to pontificate on what a Grade-A jerk Micah was; I had to get out of there.

I shut my eyes like Micah had only a few seconds before and pleaded desperately, "Wake up. Wake up, damn it! Please!"

Nothing happened. I shut my eyes to try again and heard an evil cackle to my right. My eyes flew open to find the ghost woman standing next to me, her disintegrating face just inches from mine.

"You can't get away from me," she hissed through her dark mouth.

Before I could react, the window shattered and the wave slammed down on top of us. My neck snapped back, and my head hit something hard behind me as the ice-cold water swallowed me up. Terror screamed through my body as I tumbled through the darkness and cold. Clawing and flailing, I tried to make it to the surface, but the strength of the water was too much for me. I held my breath for as long as possible, but the pain was unbearable. Having no choice, I gasped for breath—and my lungs seized in agony as the water rushed in. I tumbled helplessly in the icy darkness. And then there was nothing.

15

For the first time in quite a while I actually woke up feeling grateful to be alive. Zoe's bed was empty—she'd already left for the day. I gulped in a deep breath of the warm island air and tried to shake off the intense nightmare—but it wasn't easy. My nose was sore, and there was now a large bump on the side of my forehead where the ghost had smacked me with the rock. I went into the bathroom and took off the bandage. The cut wasn't as bad as it had looked last night. Strangely, though, it was in the exact place where I always had my migraines.

Ever since I'd come to the Theta Institute my life had just gotten progressively worse. Not only had I awakened some psychic ability that allowed me to be physically attacked by ghosts, I'd just found out they could terrorize me in my dreams as well. It was imperative that I get off the island as soon as possible. I'd had quite enough of psychics, paranormal investigations, and ghosts.

I headed over to the desk to grab the phone, and I found an envelope with my name on it next to my laptop. Inside was a plane ticket for a flight back to Los Angeles leaving at eight o'clock that night.

Relief swept over me. Micah may be a lot of things (smug, secretive, and quite full of himself), but at least he kept his word. A note inside said someone would be coming to retrieve me at four. That gave me enough time to eat, pack, and write Zoe a short note explaining my hasty departure.

Hoping to avoid any awkward run-ins with the Lucidity Project team, I skipped lunch at the dining pavilion and grabbed a to-go salad from the bar lounge before heading back upstairs to pack.

●●●

I was just finishing up when the phone rang at 3:15 that afternoon. It was Micah.

"Ms. Dorigan," he said.

"Yes?" I hesitated. The last thing I wanted was for him to try and talk me out of leaving.

"Did you forget something today?"

"Forget something?"

"Yes, you have class today. Right now, in fact."

"I told you I was leaving last night at Ida's. You sent over a plane ticket."

"Yes, but then later you changed your mind and agreed to come to my class. Don't you remember?"

I thought back to the conversation I'd had with Micah in my dream. That couldn't be what he was referring to.

"I never said that . . ."

"You did. We made a deal: I'd show you how to wake up from your dream, and you'd come to my class."

"What?" I couldn't believe what I was hearing. I don't know why anything that happened on this island surprised me anymore, but it did. I sat there dumbstruck, racking my brain for a logical explanation and coming up with nothing.

"We're in the lab," he said. "It's in the barn next to the hotel."

I paused. *Damn it.* "Okay, I'll be right there."

"And Ms. Dorigan?"

"Yes."

"Don't forget your watch."

●●●

A few minutes later I slowly pushed open the door to the barn and was quite surprised by what I saw. The entire inside had been renovated into what looked like a modern loft. There was a small, rustic kitchen area to my right as I walked in the door, and a living room area beyond that where, in the middle of the room, Micah, Angelique, Dawn, Brad, Tucker, and Jeremy were sitting in a circle of mismatched recliners on top of vintage Persian rugs. Most of the wall opposite me was filled by a huge picture window that looked onto the great lawn. Bookshelves filled with books and various curiosities lined the wall to my left. If it weren't for the rafters overhead, you might forget you were even in a barn.

The same large machine that I'd seen at Micah's house, along with a large brass gong, was sitting next to the group.

Despite my behavior the night before, everyone smiled as I walked toward them.

"Ms. Dorigan. It's so nice of you to join us," Micah said. I felt like a teenager who was tardy for class. He patted the one empty recliner between him and Angelique, and I noticed he had two watches on each of his arms again today. "We saved this seat just for you."

I sat down and looked over at Angelique, who was back in her Lara Croft outfit, complete with braid and dragon belt. In fact, everyone was wearing something similar to what they'd worn on our excursion the night before, like we were heading out for a ten-mile hike in the forest instead of an afternoon of New Age dream therapy.

I looked down at my burnout tee, jean shorts, and moto boots, which I'd put on to keep my feet warm on the plane. "I'm sorry," I said. "Are we going somewhere?"

"In fact," Micah said, sitting up in his chair, "we are—and now that you're here, we can begin." He reached over and rang the big brass gong. Leave it to Micah to turn this all into a show.

After the sound died down, he cleared his throat dramatically. "As most of you know, I've had quite a lot of success helping people work through their emotional issues using dream therapy techniques I created and researched at Stanford. In the last few years, however, I've been working on a new interactive healing therapy that combines hypnotherapy with lucid dreaming."

"So it *is* lucid dreaming we'll be doing, then!" Tucker crowed, slapping a hand on his knee triumphantly. "Ha! I knew it!"

"Yes," Micah said, "but more specifically, astral projection."

"I'm sorry," I said, "I didn't grow up in a commune. What's astral projection?"

Micah glanced sideways at me, that familiar smirk on his face. "Astral projection is the ability of the spirit to leave the physical body. Whenever you're dreaming or lucid dreaming, you are astral projecting, or out of body. Astral projection is also what's enabled me to visit you all in your dreams the last couple nights."

I squinted my eyes and pursed my lips. No one else in the room so much as blinked at Micah's last statement. Visit us in our dreams? How could that be?

"Ms. Dorigan, you look confused," Micah said. "More confused than usual, that is."

"I'm sorry, you've lost me," I said. "You came into our dreams? But that's impossible."

"How can you say it's impossible when you've already experienced it?"

"But . . . I haven't," I stammered.

But I had. It was the only way to explain how Micah had known about my dream last night. He had been in the dream with me.

"So what exactly are you doing in our dreams, then?" I asked. My mind spinning. "I mean, isn't that an invasion of privacy?"

"I'm trying to help you," he answered.

"Help us to do what?"

"To wake up," he said.

I supposed what he said was true. He had tried to help me wake up and escape the tidal wave—kind of. But something told me that wasn't exactly what he was talking about.

"I just don't understand how it's possible," I said shaking my head in disbelief. "Isn't dreaming a solitary experience created by the mind?"

"No," Micah said, "as you will come to see, it is not. When you dream, your spirit leaves your physical body and travels on the astral plane, a non-physical dimension layered on top of the earth plane that's almost identical to our waking world. What you saw last night was my astral body. My physical body was still asleep in bed. When you go into REM sleep, your subconscious mind projects images onto the astral plane, creating a world of illusion you've come to know as dreaming. Kind of like if you were to put a transparency over a drawing and then draw another picture on top of it. Our astral bodies are not bound by the same rules of time and space as our physical bodies."

"This all sounds really cool, but how is running around a dream world supposed to help cure my depression?" I asked. "Or help anyone else do what they came here to do?"

"Astral projection is an exceptional tool for emotional and spiritual growth. Instead of discussing your issues in talk therapy you can symbolically work through them in your dreams. Repressed emotional traumas that were previously hidden from you can be brought to light, giving you an opportunity to address them directly. You'll be exploring your psyche as if it were a virtual reality of sorts."

"A virtual reality world that's created by your own subconscious," Brad added excitedly.

"Not just your subconscious—" Micah began.

"The collective unconscious," Angelique said.

Micah nodded. "And also the superconscious."

"What's the difference?" I asked. All of this spiritual and psychological lingo was way over my head. Angelique, Dawn, and Brad were nodding along excitedly like they had understood every word. Meanwhile, I was having a difficult time following along. Superconscious? Collective unconscious? Astral projection? What was this, the Twilight Zone?

"The 'collective unconscious' is a term coined by Carl Jung that refers to the idea that all human beings share a universal consciousness," Micah said. "The superconscious is the consciousness of transcendental reality, a higher consciousness—the highest consciousness—that we're all a part of but not consciously aware of at all times."

"Are you talking about God?" I asked, then turned to the rest of the group. "Is he talking about God?"

Micah gave me what could best be described as an enigmatic smile, and continued.

"You do not control the astral plane all yourself—not consciously, anyway. That is the realm of the superconscious; however, your thoughts do directly inform your experience, and you do have an immense amount of, shall we say, creative input. Think of yourselves as co-creators. You have much more power there than you realize, and it's most easily accessible when you remember it is. But the dream world is a highly emotional realm, and it's easy to get caught up in its drama and forget that you're dreaming. You therefore need to stay lucid, not only to perceive the meaning behind the drama but also to reach your goal."

"What goal?" I asked.

"To get to the lighthouse," Micah said.

"The one where I was just almost killed by a bloodthirsty ghost?" I asked. He had to be kidding. I couldn't go back up there. "What if that thing comes after me again?"

"Then you will have to face it," Micah said. "That's what the Lucidity Project is all about."

Great, I thought. But at least it would be in a dream—not real. Although, thinking back to last night, dreams sure did feel real when you were in them.

"What's at the lighthouse that's so important, anyway?" Tucker asked.

"The reason you came to this island," Micah said. "The answer to your big question."

"The big question we talked about the other night?" Tucker asked. I thought back to two nights earlier, when we'd gone around the room and told the group what we had come to Theta in search of.

"Hold on a second," I said, putting up a hand again. I knew I was asking a lot of questions, but I didn't care. I was new to this stuff, and I wanted to know what I was dealing with. "You're telling me that if I get to that lighthouse I'll find the cure to my depression?"

"That's right," Micah said.

"And Jeremy will find a cure to his PTSD? And Tucker will find a cure to his alcoholism?"

"And I'll find out how to be a psychic spy?" Brad piped in.

"That is correct," Micah answered.

This was getting more unbelievable by the minute, and I didn't understand any of it. I rubbed my sore temple in frustration as I tried to process the information he was giving us. In all honesty, I didn't want to believe Micah, and I would be walking out of the room right now if I hadn't experienced him coming into my dream the previous night. He obviously had knowledge of the astral plane, or whatever it was, that somehow translated to this plane as well. I had no choice but to go along with him.

I had another question: "Who, exactly, is going to be answering our questions?"

Micah smiled again. "I guess you'll just have to get to the light-house and find out."

"Isn't this kind of cheating?" Angelique asked. "I mean, people spend lifetimes trying to answer the big questions in their lives. They give up everything, leave their jobs and families, sit in meditation for years at a time. All we have to do is run up to the lighthouse in our dreams? That doesn't seem fair."

"I didn't say it won't be without its obstacles," Micah said.

"What do you mean, 'obstacles'?" I asked, detecting something a bit ominous in his tone.

Micah smiled. "That depends on you. The astral plane is a place of mystical happenings. There are repressed feelings that may need to be released, energies that may need to be acknowledged and worked through, and battles that may or may not need to be fought. Everyone you meet in there is important, whether they are a spirit or a dream figure."

"What's a dream figure?" I asked.

"A symbolic creation of your mind or someone else's. What you should understand is that most of the energies involved are ultimately working toward your greatest good. Unfortunately, this assistance isn't always pleasant. The spirit world values spiritual lessons over physical comfort. Many of you will be encountering your deepest, darkest fears."

"What if we die on the astral plane?" Dawn asked, her voice a little shaky. "Will we die in real life?"

Micah looked up at the ceiling, contemplating the question. "I can't say it's impossible, but it's unlikely."

"Wait a minute, you're saying we could die doing this stuff?" I sput-tered. I don't know why this was so disturbing to me; I had just tried to kill myself a week ago. But things had changed.

"I haven't lost anyone yet," Micah said.

"Who else has gone through the Lucidity Project?" I asked.

"Well, let's see," Micah said, tapping his lips thoughtfully. "So far it's been Dr. Luna, Jeremy, and me, I guess."

"Three people? You've only tried this on three people?" I practically snorted. "That's very encouraging, thank you."

"Look," Micah said, leaning forward. "I understand this is extremely challenging work. If you want to opt out, this would be the time to do it, and there's no shame in that. If you do decide to stay and go through the program, though, I can tell you that the benefits that await you are beyond your wildest imaginations."

We all looked around at each other, waiting to see if anyone would take Micah up on his offer and leave. Dawn was sitting on the edge of her seat, looking ready to bolt for the door, but she made no effort to move. The others were showing everything from nervous excitement to steadfast resolve.

In the last twenty-four hours I'd experienced a violent ghost, psychic phenomena, and shared dreaming, or what Micah was calling "astral travel." Despite my residual skepticism, I had to admit Micah's work fascinated me. And the truth was, a lifetime of depression was much scarier than anything I could imagine facing on the astral plane. There was no going back now.

When it was clear no one was going to leave, Micah stood up, grabbed a handful of headsets from the top of the Lucidity Project machine, and passed them around. They were the same as the one he'd had on the other day when I'd visited him at his house. They were made of neoprene, and had earbuds, two little black nodes in the front, and looked like fancy sweatbands.

Micah went over and pulled down the shade on the window overlooking the great lawn.

"Okay," he said, sitting back down in his chair and grabbing his headset. "Now, before we go forward I would like to request that you not discuss anything that happens here with anyone outside this group. Everyone okay with that?"

We all nodded our agreement.

"Wonderful." Micah smiled. "Now, please put on your headsets so that the black nodules are pressed firmly against your foreheads, and place the earbuds in your ears."

"What do these things do, exactly?" I asked.

"They use binaural beats and small electrical pulses to put you into REM sleep much more quickly than you could on your own."

Oh, is that all? That seems totally safe.

"Don't worry," he said, chuckling. "The chances of brain damage are very slim."

Great.

He put on his headset as he had suggested, and we followed suit. The headband was soft and comfortable. I could barely feel the two rubbery black nodes on my forehead.

Micah flipped the footrest out from under his chair, grabbed a remote off the machine, and lay back in his chair.

"You're coming with us?" I asked.

"In a way," he said, shutting his eyes. "I'll explain when we get into the astral. Now just sit back, relax, and I'll see you on the other side."

I reclined my chair, shut my eyes, and settled in—for what, I had no idea. Within seconds Tibetan singing bowls began to play through my earbuds, and then a young woman's voice joined in, using the same hypnosis technique Micah had used on me in our session together.

I had a difficult time relaxing at first, but after a few minutes, I suddenly felt an influx of exhaustion, as if I were being put under anesthesia, and I began to fade out of consciousness. Then a loud buzzing sound came from near my left ear, like an airplane was taking off right behind me. My body jerked violently, and my eyes shot open.

●●●

Looking around the lab, it was obvious that Micah's little experiment hadn't worked. Everyone was sitting up in their chairs and had their eyes open, except for Tucker, who was cramming his shut like a little kid pretending to be asleep.

"It didn't work," I said, pulling the earbuds out of my ears.

"Shhh . . . you're taking me out of it," Tucker said, his eyes still closed.

"How do you know it didn't work?" Micah asked, looking down at the watches on his right wrist.

"I mean, it's pretty obvious," I replied, looking around at everyone in the circle. "We're all wide awake."

"That's exactly what you said last night when you were dreaming," Micah said, taking off his headset and placing it on the arm of his chair. The rest of us did the same. "That's the thing about dreams," he continued. "While in them we have a tendency to believe that whatever we're experiencing is reality."

"Yeah," Tucker said. "But c'mon, it's obvious we aren't dreaming. Everything's the same."

"Is it?" Micah asked, standing up. "Tell me then, how is it that I'm able to do this?"

And with that, he levitated three feet into the air.

16

Micah hung suspended in midair, hands on hips, chest out, like a comic book hero—nothing but air between his feet and the floor. We all jumped out of our chairs to get a better look.

"H-how are you doing that?" I stammered, staring down at his feet. Tucker was waving his hands around, checking for invisible strings.

"Don't you see?" Angelique said, her eyes wide with excitement. "It worked. We're in the astral! We're dreaming!"

I looked around, trying to see if anything around me appeared dreamlike, but from what I could tell everything was exactly the same. I studied my hands, my cuticles, the length of my nails. They looked and felt just like they did in real life. I pinched myself hard on the arm until the pain was so bad I had to stop. I felt totally, 100 percent wide awake. And yet there Micah was, floating in the air right in front of my face.

Jeremy was the only one who didn't appear wowed by Micah's gravity-defying stunt. He stood there, arms crossed, as if he'd seen this trick of Micah's before—which I imagined he had.

Micah lowered himself back down to the ground.

"So if you hadn't just done that, how would we know we were dreaming?" Dawn asked, looking around the room for other evidence. "Everything looks and feels exactly the same, as if we were awake, just like Tucker said."

Micah shrugged playfully. He was enjoying this way too much. "Look around. The astral plane changes in response to your thoughts and feelings. It's in constant flux, changing, morphing, transforming. Sometimes it's a little thing," he said, picking up a book on a small table. He held it in his hand and stared at it intently for a second—until it transformed into a small black bird and flew into the rafters.

We all gasped.

"Other times it's much more obvious." Micah waved his hand at the bookshelf behind him, and all the books on the shelf turned into a flock of black birds. They flew into the air in a beautiful black mass and soared around the room, cawing and chirping above us. Dawn screamed in delight as they did a loop above our heads, then headed back to the bookcase and became books once again.

I looked at Micah in complete awe. The rest of the team broke out in applause.

"Everything looks basically like it does on the earth plane," Dawn said. "Except . . . where, exactly, are our physical bodies?"

"They're right where you left them," Micah said.

I glanced back at my recliner and started. Micah was right. There I was, lying asleep with my headset still on, along with Micah, Angelique, Jeremy, and the rest of the team. How had we all failed to notice our bodies just lying there like that? But even more disturbing was the fact that I had what looked like a silver cord coming out of my stomach. All of us did. I traced the path the cord took, and quickly realized that mine linked around behind my astral body. When I reached around to find its end, I found it was going right into my back.

"What the hell is this thing?" Tucker asked grabbing on to his cord. He looked just as freaked out as I felt.

"The sutratma," Micah said. "Also known as the thread of antahkarana."

"English please!" I said, touching my cord again. It felt alive, cold to the touch, almost like a snake.

"It's the cord that connects your astral body to your physical one," Brad said, pushing up his glasses.

"Your lifeline to your physical body," Micah clarified. "Without it, you wouldn't be able to get back into your body."

"How are we supposed to get anywhere with these stuck to our backs?" I asked. I pulled on the thing again, but it was part of me.

Stuck tight, like an appendage. I couldn't believe I hadn't noticed it before.

"The silver cord is etheric, infinite—it can go wherever your astral body can go. As soon as you stop thinking about it, you won't even feel or see it anymore. That's how it took you this long to notice it in the first place."

"So if we don't think about it, it disappears?" Dawn asked.

"Let's just say it will appear to disappear," Micah said.

"Well, that makes absolutely no sense," I said.

"The astral plane is a dimension driven by thoughts and feelings," Micah said. "What you think about here, you will experience almost instantaneously."

"So that means we can do anything we can think about here?" Tucker asked, stepping onto a nearby side table. "Anything we want? Even fly?"

"Technically yes," Micah said, taking a few steps toward Tucker. "But you see—"

"Well then, check this out!" Tucker yelled, and before any of us could move to stop him, he flung himself off the table. Instead of soaring off into the rafters, however, he belly flopped right onto the floor below, landing with a loud crash. He let out a soft "ow" as we all rushed over to see if he was all right.

Angelique got to him first and turned him over. Lucky for him, he'd landed on one of the plush rugs, which had softened his fall.

"Flying is very advanced," Micah said, kneeling down next to him.

Tucker let out a pained sigh. "So if we get hurt in here, we really get hurt, huh?" he asked, holding his nose.

"Your physical body won't be hurt, not technically," Micah said. "But if you believe that you will get hurt then yes, your astral body will experience pain."

"But if our thoughts create our reality in here then why wasn't Tucker able to fly?" I asked.

"Because Tucker didn't really expect to fly," Micah said. "He expected to fall."

"I think I broke my face," Tucker said. He sat up and rubbed his nose.

"Now remember," Micah said, "as you get deeper into the dream your mind will start to accept what you see in front of you as real. You'll forget things you knew were true only moments before. Your brain has been trained not to question reality, or what it perceives as reality. I intend to help to break you of that habit. That's why it's important to try to stay as lucid as possible. When you forget you're dreaming, that's when you get into trouble."

"So how do we remember we're dreaming?" I asked.

"That's what these are for," Micah said, holding his hands up in front of him.

"Our fingers?" Tucker asked.

"Our watches," I said. "Look at your watch." It was the only thing Micah had asked me to bring to class that day, and they were the only things on his wrists.

I looked down at my gold Michael Kors; nothing different there.

"It's four," Tucker said. "So what?"

"Keep looking," Jeremy said.

I kept looking at my watch. It said four, then slowly all the numbers began stacking themselves on top of one another. For the tenth time that day, I couldn't believe what I was seeing.

"The numbers . . . they're moving all around!" Dawn said.

"Incredible!" Tucker said, running his fingers through his hair.

"In dreams, words and numbers aren't static," Micah explained. "When you look at a watch in a dream, the face changes after a few seconds."

"So all we have to do is look at our watches to see if we're dreaming?" Brad asked.

"That's the best way to do what's called a 'reality check' in the lucid dreaming community," Micah said. "For most of you, however, the biggest problem will not be trying to do a reality check to figure out if you're dreaming—it will be remembering to question whether you're even dreaming in the first place. Your brain will do everything it can to keep you in the drama of your dream. It will try to make you believe that things like levitating are normal. And that's where remembering your goal comes in. This will help you to stay focused and lucid. Does anyone remember what that goal is?"

"To get to the lighthouse," Dawn said.

"That's right," Micah said, suddenly serious. "Now, you should go. You have less than ninety minutes."

"Why ninety minutes?" Angelique asked.

"You've been induced into an REM cycle, and one cycle lasts only ninety minutes. After that, you wake up." He opened the door to the great lawn and made a sweeping gesture. "Out you go, then."

"You aren't coming with us?" Dawn asked nervously.

"I'll be going," Micah said, "but only as an observer. In fact, when I snap my fingers in a few seconds you won't be able to see me at all." He raised his fingers in front of him. "Stay lucid, my friends," he said, then snapped his fingers and disappeared. One minute he was there, the next he wasn't, just like in my dream the night before.

I blinked my eyes in shock. It was going to take me awhile to get accustomed to the astral plane.

●●●

"How'd he do that?" Tucker asked, staring at the place where Micah had stood only seconds earlier.

"Just like he said, everything here is highly suggestible," Jeremy said, stepping toward the door. "We believe we can't see him because he told us we can't see him. But I imagine he's probably still here somewhere."

Tucker shook his head and looked around. "The man is like a frickin' Jedi!"

"Okay, we should go," Jeremy continued, not missing a beat. "We don't have much time to get to the lighthouse."

"Dude," Tucker said. "We run there every day. It'll take us half an hour, max. Why don't we look around a little and have some fun?"

"That's the absolutely last thing we should do," Jeremy said. "The longer you spend in the dream, the easier it is to get distracted and forget you're dreaming. The best thing we can do is try to get to the lighthouse as fast as possible. We'll have enough to deal with just trying to do that."

"What do you mean?" I asked. "How long does it usually take to get there?"

"I don't know," Jeremy said, looking out and scanning the great lawn. "I've never made it there before."

The rest of us exchanged "Oh crap" looks. If Jeremy, a trained soldier who'd been working with Micah on this project for the past month, couldn't reach the goal, how were the rest of us supposed to?

"Everyone grab a partner," Jeremy continued before we could ask any more questions. "Tucker, go with Angelique. Brad, you take Dawn. I've got Max."

I breathed a sigh of relief. I didn't know what we were up against in here, but I felt my best bet was to stick with Jeremy.

"Now, if you get lost or separated from your partner, just head to the lighthouse," he said. "Better that one of us makes it than none. Got it?"

We all nodded nervously.

"On the count of three," Jeremy said, taking a deep breath. "One, two . . ."

"Three!" Tucker yelled, bolting out the door so fast he scared a large raven on the grass up into the trees. Clearly he'd learned nothing about using caution from his little flying fiasco.

The rest of us followed. The next thing I knew we were running across the great lawn toward Dasheen Pass. Despite having to run in my moto boots, I noticed that I had no aches or fatigue. My head no longer hurt, and the soreness usually present in my body was nowhere to be found. Even my mood was highly elevated. It was like I had borrowed someone else's body. I hadn't felt this healthy and strong since I was . . . I couldn't remember. But the feeling was so wonderfully familiar, like this lightness was my natural state. Like this was how I should always feel. Light, empowered, and free.

We made it to the end of the great lawn and headed up Dasheen Pass into the jungle, which also pulsed with a new kind of energy I'd never seen or felt before. The colors were so incredibly vibrant that I had to squint at times to keep them from hurting my eyes. I reminded myself to focus, not to get caught up in the dream, but it wasn't easy. It was like I was on some sort of drug—like nothing I'd ever experienced before. I felt more alive than I ever had when I was awake. I wanted to stay there forever, get lost in the forest and never look back.

"You still with me, Max?" Jeremy yelled next to me. I looked over, surprised to be pulled out of my reverie. Jeremy looked back at me, his dark brown eyes sharp and clear. I shook my head yes, attempted to focus, and sped back up.

We continued to run as a group for a few more minutes, and then I saw a movement to my left and turned just in time to see someone, or something, duck behind a tree.

I grabbed at Jeremy's arm and began to slow down. "There's someone in the forest," I whispered. "To the left."

"Keep running," he said, pushing me forward, his voice urgent.

A second later a loud bang rang out to our left. Pieces of bark exploded on a tree only a few feet away from us. Behind me, Dawn let out a scream. It took me a few seconds to realize that someone was shooting at us.

"Cut to the right! Into the forest!" Jeremy shouted back to the others. To the left of me I saw a man, or what looked like a man, in tattered old army fatigues and a large helmet step out from behind a tree about twenty yards away from us in the jungle. I held back a scream and slowed. His face was inhumanly white and gaunt, and it appeared he'd been shot multiple times in the chest. There was blood all over his jacket, and his eyes were grey and vacant. As I tried to comprehend what was happening, more soldiers came into view.

"Zombies!" Tucker yelled, tearing into the forest. "We're being attacked by zombies! Run for your lives!"

Zombies? Was that what they were? My heart jumped at the thought, but I didn't have to time to contemplate the matter, as Jeremy was pulling me into the forest after him.

We continued running as fast as possible, my legs getting scraped and scratched as we jumped and tore through the tangle of heavy brush and foliage covering the forest floor. I realized then that everyone was much better equipped at running for their lives than I was in my cut-off shorts and moto boots. At least I wasn't in flip-flops.

Another bullet whizzed by me, and my heart jumped again. I looked behind us. There were more zombie soldiers moving through the forest toward us. They were well camouflaged by their army fatigues, but even so I could see we were greatly outnumbered.

Jeremy grabbed me by the arm and yanked me back behind a large tree, then covered my body with his. Under normal circumstances I'd be quite thrilled to be pressed up against a tree in the jungle by a guy like Jeremy, but these were not normal circumstances.

"Are those really zombies?" I whispered into his ear as he held me pinned against the tree.

"No," he whispered back while attempting to peer around the tree. "They're spirits of U.S. soldiers that were killed here in World War II."

I remembered the story Angelique had told Dawn and me on the day we first arrived. Army men ambushed and massacred by German Nazis in the jungle. *This jungle.* I guess that explained why their uniforms looked so dated.

"What should we do?" I asked, trying not to panic. Having Jeremy pressed up against me helped to ease my anxiety somewhat, but not by much.

Jeremy put his finger up to his lips. We could hear them coming— dead men trained to hunt and kill, tromping through the forest toward us. By the sound of all the crunching there were many more of them than there were of us.

Angelique edged around the tree next to us as the footsteps got closer and gestured silently that one was coming up on the other side of us. Before I had the chance to even react, Jeremy struck out and hit the thing hard the face with his fist. I saw a flash of green and the man fell backward onto the ground. Jeremy swooped in, grabbed the gun out of his hand, and shot him in the chest. The man lay on the ground, still as a stone.

I reeled back, horrified. I'd never seen anyone shot before.

Next to us, another soldier grabbed Angelique by the neck. She elbowed him hard in the gut, then whirled around and kicked him in the head, grabbing his gun as he fell and smashing him over the head with it, knocking him out. Her martial arts training was serving her well. I made a mental note to take a lesson from her if we got out of this alive.

"Where the hell is Tucker?" Jeremy yelled as a splattering of bullets exploded the bark off the trees around us.

I looked over at Angelique, who was braced against the tree by herself. Tucker was nowhere to be found.

"I don't know, I looked over and he was just gone!'" Angelique yelled back as she elbowed another soldier in the face and threw him to the ground. I was seriously out of my element here. If Tucker were smart, he would have stayed as close to Angelique as possible.

"Damn it," Jeremy said. I could tell by the look on his face that we were in serious trouble.

"What do we do now?" I asked him, my heart pounding in my chest.

"Now," he answered, taking a deep breath, "we run."

He pushed off the tree and pulled me forward with him, using the momentum to push me ahead.

"Go!" he yelled. "Angelique and I will hold them off!" He turned and fired off a few rounds into the oncoming soldiers. "Go! Go! Get to the lighthouse! I'm right behind you."

I tore off up through the jungle, away from the oncoming bullets, so full of fear I could barely see where I was going. The lighthouse? What was at the lighthouse? It seemed there was a reason I needed to go there, but I couldn't remember what it was. The underbrush below my feet was thick, reaching up to my calves in some places, making it that much harder to run. My heart thumped wildly as I found my way back onto Dasheen Pass. There was something I was supposed to remember. What was it? I couldn't, for the life of me, think what it was.

After a few minutes of frantic running, I turned to look behind me and saw that I was all alone. There was no sign of Jeremy, Brad, Angelique, Dawn, Tucker, or the army men anywhere. The forest had become eerily quiet. I slowed down for a second to catch my breath and get my bearings.

That's when I heard a familiar growl behind me. I whipped around and there was the ghost from the night before, still in her torn evening gown, the blacks of her eyes still dripping down her moldy face, her head tilted awkwardly to the side. She took a step toward me, dragging her injured foot behind her.

I let out a scream and tried to run, but my left leg went out from underneath me and I hit the ground hard on my back. The impact knocked the wind out of my lungs, and before I could catch my breath I felt an icy hand clamp around my ankle and begin to drag me along the ground, as fast as if I were tied to a runaway horse. I tried to reach up to release my foot, but her grasp was too strong. Gravel and sticks cut and scraped into my back. I screamed out again, but it was no use.

The jungle sped past me in a blur, and within a matter of minutes a familiar scene came into view—the clearing where the lighthouse stood. I had a flash of hope that the ghost was taking me to the lighthouse, but instead she picked up the pace and charged full speed ahead toward the end of the bluff.

Oh my God, I thought, realization dawning. *She's going over the cliff, and she plans to take me with her!*

I thrashed and fought as hard as I could, clawing at the ground whizzing by beneath me and trying to get my leg free, but her fingers were locked on my ankle like a vise. As the edge of the cliff drew closer, the fear became almost unbearable, and I knew if I didn't do something fast I was going to suffer the same horrific fate as my doomed captor. At the very last second, I made a desperate lunge for a large boulder jutting out at the edge of the cliff—the very same boulder I'd first seen the ghost climb over the night before—wrapped my arms around it, and hung on for dear life.

The ghost plunged over the edge cliff, still holding on to my ankle, and as she fell I felt the weight of her jerk so hard on my body I thought my arms were going to rip out of their sockets. Pain shot through my back and up my neck as she dangled there, yanking on me and screeching, intent on taking me with her. I clutched at the rock with everything I had.

Below us the ocean rose and churned in an unnatural way. The waves were so large, they seemed to be attempting to reach up to grab us. I knew what that meant: Soon, a larger wave would be coming. A tidal wave.

I struggled to hold on to the rock, but I knew I couldn't hang on much longer. Of course, once that wave came, it wouldn't matter anyway.

"Let go!" I screamed down at the woman, trying kick her off with my other foot, but she only held on tighter and laughed.

Just then I heard a loud caw and a black raven landed on the boulder just a foot or two from my head. It edged toward me, looking at my hands. *My God!* Could things get any worse? It wasn't bad enough that I was dangling off the edge of a cliff; now a damn bird was going to attack me as well? I leaned away from it, hoping it wouldn't peck me.

The bird hopped forward, bent down and tapped its beak on my watch, then cocked its head at me—and suddenly I remembered why I was wearing my watch in the first place: to check if I was dreaming! This certainly didn't feel like a dream, but as I looked up at my watch, sure enough, the numbers began to move all around. I *was* dreaming. In all the fear and chaos, I had forgotten.

A euphoria unlike anything I had ever felt before overtook me. This was a dream—and that meant neither the wave nor the ghost could kill me. No matter what happened, I would wake up safe and sound in the lab.

Power surged through me, every cell in my body magnetized to its full potential.

As the waves beneath me rose higher, I realized there was a chance I could wake myself up, just like Micah had done the night before. I hadn't been able to do it then, but I knew so much more now. What had Micah said? *Don't get caught up in the drama of the dream.* That's what I had been doing all along: identifying with the fear instead of identifying with what was real—that I was only dreaming. Now that I was aware of what was possible, perhaps I was no longer at the mercy of this dream.

The tidal wave made its appearance now, and it rose up above the cliff until it towered high above me. Apparently natural disasters didn't have to follow the laws of physics on the astral plane. I knew I only had a few more seconds before the wave hit, so despite the wall of water hovering over me, I shut my eyes, set my intention to wake up, and snapped my fingers as I'd seen Micah do the previous night.

The moment I snapped my fingers, I felt myself being yanked backward as if by a string. I closed my eyes as I whooshed down through a gray nothingness—and when I opened them again, I was sitting in my recliner in the lab, safe and sound.

The rest of the team were still fast asleep in their chairs, even Micah. I sat there for a few seconds, attempting to process what had just happened. I'd woken myself up from the dream. I'd done it! And for the first time in my life I'd also managed to get away from my nightmarish tidal wave before it could drown me.

I was about to jump up and dance around the room when something hit me: if the team was still in the astral, it was quite possible that they were about to get pummeled by my tidal wave. Hadn't Micah said that what affected one of us in there affected us all?

I had to wake them up, and do it fast. I ripped of my headset, jumped up, grabbed at the nearest thing to me I could find—the brass gong next to Micah—and threw it as hard as I could onto the floor. It made a horribly loud crash that reverberated throughout the room. To my relief, everyone's eyes flew open at the sound.

I stood there in the middle of the circle as they all stared at me, glassy-eyed, trying to get a handle on what had just happened. Micah was the only one who didn't have a look of utter shock and relief on his face.

"You saved us," Brad said, looking up at me. "You saved us from that huge wave."

So I was right—it had continued in the dream even after I had woken up.

"That was so close," Dawn said, leaning over and rubbing her hands down her face.

"I didn't know what to do," Angelique said, shaking her head, looking equally relieved. "You can't fight a tidal wave."

"Well, Ms. Dorigan," Micah said, getting up and stretching. "Looks like you do have a psychic power after all."

"I do?" I asked, confused. "What psychic power do I have?"

"The power to remember," Micah said, as if it were quite obvious.

"The power to remember what?" I asked.

A clock chimed in the distance. Micah glanced at his watches, then turned back to the class and clapped his hands together. "Okay everyone, let's take a break for dinner then meet back in the great room at the top of the hotel for debrief and discussion at eight o'clock."

The group began collecting their things quietly—still, I assumed, attempting to process the intense experience.

"The power to remember what?" I repeated as Micah headed for the door. "What does that mean?"

"It means," Jeremy said, "that you have a flight to cancel."

17

After the session I went straight up to my room to cancel my flight. As soon as I opened the door, Zoe flew out of the bathroom wearing only a towel. She had a lipstick tube in her hand but tossed it onto the nightstand and hopped onto her bed.

"How was it? Tell me everything!"

"I can't," I said, feeling a little guilty. She had wanted to be a part of the Lucidity Project so badly. "We've kind of been sworn to secrecy. I'm sorry . . ."

"Oh," she said, not letting my response deflate her in the least. "What happened to your forehead?"

"I got attacked last night," I said, reflexively reaching up to touch the bump there. I realized I hadn't talked to Zoe since before I'd gone up to the cliff the day prior. After everything that had happened, it seemed like such a long time ago.

"Attacked? By who?"

"I know this is going to sound crazy, but I'm pretty sure it was a ghost."

Zoe's eyebrows shot up. "What?"

I took a seat on my bed and told her the terrifying story of what happened up at the lighthouse and the dream I'd had after that. I didn't mention that the ghost had also shown up in our astral session, because I had promised to keep the project a secret.

"Wow," Zoe said when I was finished. "Well, you know what this means, don't you?"

"No, I don't, actually."

"It means you have to help her, Max!" she said. "I watch a lot of those ghost shows on TV. If she's an earthbound spirit it means she has unfinished business here, and it's up to you to find out what it is."

"You sound just like Micah. If she wants my help she needs to stop trying to kill me first," I said, rubbing the bump on my temple.

"I guess it's good to set some boundaries. From what I understand, ghosts can be really pushy when they want something," Zoe said. She grabbed her lipstick and headed back to the bathroom to finish her makeup.

"Tell me about it," I muttered.

"You better figure something out though," she called from her station at the mirror. "Ghosts don't go away on their own!"

"Yeah, I'm starting to realize that," I said.

After a few seconds, Zoe smacked her lips together and said, "I heard a rumor you were leaving the island. Is that true?"

"No," I said. "I'm not going anywhere."

●●●

Later that night the team met in the great room as planned to discuss the day's events in private. The great room was—as suggested by its name—a large room at the top of the hotel, with thirteen-foot ceilings, crystal chandeliers, arched, floor-to-ceiling windows that looked out onto the ocean, and two sets of sitting areas filled with plush sofas and lounge chairs. It had started raining outside, so we took the sitting area near the fireplace, and Jeremy built a fire. Angelique made a pot of hibiscus tea and placed it on the gilded glass coffee table, along with some cups and stirrers. Then we sat back, listening to the water fall against the windows and trees outside, and waited for Micah.

"Well," Micah said when he finally walked in at five pase eight. His hair was damp from the rain, but still managed to stick out in all different directions. "I take from the fact that you're all here that you plan to stay on with the project." He sat down in a chair with his back to the fire and began to pour himself some tea.

"That depends," Angelique said. "Are we going to get shot at every time we go in there?" She was only half joking.

"That's up to you," Micah said nonchalantly, like we'd just been playing a harmless video game instead of getting attacked by an army of ghosts and almost swept away by a tidal wave.

"What do you mean, that's up to us?" Angelique said, her eyes flaring. "You think we can stop a bunch of dead soldiers from shooting at us?"

"It's not that we don't appreciate this opportunity," Dawn said before Angelique could spring across the table and strangle Micah, "but, um, being attacked like that was really scary. Is that really what it takes to make it to the lighthouse?"

"Not at all," Micah said, taking a sip of his tea. "You should try and remember that the next time you go in there."

Now it was my turn to get angry. "What is that supposed to mean?"

"It means," Micah said, holding up his hand, "that today's exercise was probably a little more challenging than you expected, but I promise you that if you stick with it, all the pain and suffering will be worth it. The truth is, there's really only one small obstacle you need to overcome to get to the lighthouse."

"Only you would call the ghosts of an army of soldiers 'one small obstacle,'" Angelique snapped. "Thanks for the warning on those guys, by the way, Jeremy."

"I asked Jeremy not to tell you about the soldiers in the jungle," Micah interjected. "And I did that for your own benefit. The astral plane responds quickly to your expectations. I wanted you all going in clean."

"Forget about the soldiers; what about that tidal wave?" Brad asked. "That's a much larger obstacle than the ghosts. At least we can run from them. You can't run from a tidal wave."

"Just for the record, I've never seen a wave like that in my sessions before," Jeremy said. "That's new."

"That's because it's mine," I said. All eyes turned to me. "It's a recurring nightmare of mine. I've been having it for as long as I can remember. Today was the first time I've ever been able to get away from it." I permitted myself a small smile. I was still pretty excited that I'd managed to wake myself up.

"Well this is just great," Angelique said, smacking her teacup down on the coffee table. "Not only do we have ghosts to deal with but we bring in our own nightmare elements too?"

"Yes," Micah said. "The astral is the nesting place of both fantasies and fears. But the reality is that none of these perceived obstacles are truly keeping you from the lighthouse. Not really. No army, no natural disaster, no amount of men or monsters can prevent you from doing what you're supposed to do in there, or out here for that matter. You're the only ones holding yourselves back. In fact, the things that you view as obstacles might even hold the key to you reaching the lighthouse. Embrace your challenges with open arms, my friends. Ask yourselves, 'What is the real obstacle here?'" He looked at me expectantly, as if I should know the answer.

Suddenly I flashed on the part of the dream where I'd become lucid on the cliff. Remembering that I was dreaming, had made me realize that I wasn't really in danger; that I wasn't really about to die; that everything that I'd been worried and frightened about was just an illusion. When that happened, the fear I'd felt had fallen away, and I'd been inundated with a sweet sense that anything was possible. That was the feeling I'd taken back with me when I woke up—and that was the key to getting to the lighthouse. I was sure of it.

"We have to remember we're dreaming," I said.

"That's right," said Micah, pointing at me. He sat up, his eyes intense. "If you can stay aware and remember you're dreaming, you can see the dream world for what it is: an illusion."

"What about those ghost soldiers?" Angelique asked. "Are you telling me they aren't real?"

"I'm telling you they don't have the power you think they have over you. Nothing does. That's why it's important to stay lucid. Staying lucid opens you up to higher options, higher energies, and higher possibilities. The key to this work is awareness, people. Once you understand that, the world is yours."

Micah gulped down the last of his tea then looked down at the two watches on his right arm. "That's all I've got for tonight, folks. I'll be joining you for your run to the lighthouse in the morning at 10 a.m. Ms. Dorigan, I expect to see you there."

●●●

Micah's speech was passionate and inspiring, but after he left, the question still remained: How could we stay lucid while we were dreaming? The only reason I'd even been able to remember I was dreaming in our session was because that raven had tapped on my watch. Had my subconscious created the raven, or was someone—or something—else behind its appearance? Either way, I couldn't expect the thing to come back and remind me every time I forgot I was dreaming, could I?

"What about dream signs?" Angelique suggested. She had been flipping through a book titled *Lucid Dreaming*, and she now plopped it down on the coffee table open to a chapter called "Lucid Dream Inducers."

"What are dream signs?" I asked, leaning forward and glancing over at the page.

"They're signs to alert your conscious mind that you're dreaming," she said. "Dreams are often filled with repetitive themes and events, like how you see a tidal wave in your dreams all the time. So the idea is, if you can train yourself to check your watch whenever you see or think of a tidal wave, then when you see it in a dream, you'll remember to do a reality check to see if you're dreaming. And we could do the same thing with the soldiers."

"That's a good idea, but it could take weeks to implement a dream sign," Brad said. "In the meantime, we need a backup plan."

"Like what?" Tucker asked.

"Like maybe you not running off into the woods and leaving your partner to fend for herself," Angelique said.

"Oh please," Tucker said. "Like you need me to defend you. Those soldiers were lucky you didn't karate chop them all to death."

"They're already dead, genius," she shot back. "And it's pretty hard to fight people when they're shooting at you. You would have known that if you had stuck around."

"Can we focus, please?" Jeremy said, glancing over at me with a slight smirk.

"Sorry everyone, it's hard for Angelique and me to concentrate with all the sexual tension between us," Tucker said.

Angelique rolled her eyes and Jeremy continued.

"We can work on trying to stay lucid," he said, "but we should also try to figure out how to get around those soldiers."

"Why don't we just go the long way to the lighthouse, through the north woods?" Brad asked.

"I've tried that way too," Jeremy said. "It's too long. I always lose lucidity and end up wandering through the jungle the whole time."

"Yeah, but now that we're all in there together, we can remind each other to stay lucid," Tucker said.

"Not necessarily," Brad said. "The minute we saw the soldiers and got scared, we all instantly forgot we were dreaming."

"What about taking the *Serendipity* around the bluff to Mango Beach and climbing up the cliff path to the lighthouse that way?" Tucker asked.

Jeremy shook his head again. "I've tried that too. Same thing. I can't stay lucid long enough. Look, you guys, Max almost made it to the lighthouse today. She actually made it to the bluff. I've never gotten that far on my own."

I wanted to tell him the only reason I'd made it to the bluff was because I was dragged there kicking and screaming by a crazy she-demon, but I didn't want to be a downer.

"I think we should do the same thing we did today," he continued. "Angelique and I can get the soldiers' weapons from them and hold them off while the rest of you try to make a run for the lighthouse."

"No!" Dawn said suddenly. She spoke so infrequently that it was quite a surprise to all of us.

"What's the matter, Dawn?" Angelique asked.

"I think shooting at them is . . . bad," she said.

"Bad?" Tucker said, incredulous.

"It's just that . . . you have to see things from their point of view," Dawn said. "They suffered a terrible death. They were taken out to the woods and shot. It's cruel to shoot at them even more."

"In my business, when people shoot at you, you shoot back," Jeremy said.

"I'm with Jeremy on this one," Angelique said. "Besides, what's the big deal? It's not even real. They're already dead."

"It *is* real . . . to them," Dawn said.

"Why are they attacking us, anyway?" I asked. "We aren't the enemy."

"Because they don't know they're dead," said Dawn. "They're still in that battle back in 1945 or whenever it happened. They probably see us as the Nazi soldiers who killed them. It's like they're on autopilot, just replaying that last battle over and over again, trying to work it out, not realizing that they're dead and stuck between worlds."

"Dawn's right. What we should be doing is helping them to cross over," Brad said.

"Maybe . . ." Jeremy said, mulling it over. "But I don't know anything about how to do that kind of stuff."

"Well," Brad said, looking over to Dawn, "Dawn and I sort of do."

Dawn's eyes went wide. I could tell she was not fully on board with this new plan.

"Have either of you ever helped a spirit cross over?" Angelique asked. "Like, actually done it?"

Brad shook his head and Dawn's face fell.

"Usually," Dawn said, "when I see ghosts I run away or hide under my covers and cry."

"That doesn't mean we couldn't learn," Brad said. "We just need a way to get through to the soldiers. Break them out of their spell so they can move on."

"Move on to where?" I asked.

"To the higher realms," he said. "The spirit world."

"Aren't they already in the spirit world?"

"No, they're on the astral plane, which is more like a weigh station for souls. Where they stay until they cross over into the higher realms. Like Dawn said, some spirits get stuck there."

I realized that my ghost woman was probably stuck on the astral plane too. Perhaps I just happened to be in the wrong place at the wrong time up on that cliff when she first attacked me, and in her confusion she mistook me for someone else. But who? Micah had mentioned that two other people had died with her. And Dawn had said she thought she'd been running from someone. Had one of them been responsible for her death?

"You guys, the soldiers aren't the biggest problem," Angelique said. "The tidal wave is. Max can't wake us all up every time it appears, we'll never get to the lighthouse that way."

"How do we even know it will show up again?" Brad asked. "Each dream is different, right?"

"That's true," Jeremy said, "but some things stay the same. Those soldiers attack every time I go up Dasheen Pass, and if the wave is a recurring theme in Max's dreams, I think we can count on seeing it again too."

I tried not to get frustrated, but I could feel my energy buzz fading as we talked about the seemingly impossible hurdles in our path. "The wave doesn't usually come in until the very end of my dreams," I said. "That will give us some time at least."

"Okay, good," Jeremy said. "Then maybe what we need to do is find a way to get to the lighthouse faster, before the wave appears."

"But we took the shortest possible route there this time, and that didn't work," Brad said.

For the next half hour or so we brainstormed more ideas, none of which were very good, before finally calling it a night. I was heading out the door after the others when I noticed that Jeremy was still on the sofa staring into the fire, deep in thought.

I waited until everyone left, then went back and took a seat next to him. "You okay?"

He looked over at me, smiled, then rubbed his hands over his face and sighed. "Yeah. I just . . . you have to understand, I've been doing this for a month longer than you guys, and I haven't been able to figure out how to get to the lighthouse. Maybe only certain people are able to navigate the astral plane. I think that's what Micah's really trying to find out. We may just not have what it takes."

"Maybe we just need to get a little more creative," I said.

"Look at you, Ms. Positive," he said with a smile. "If only we had a helicopter or something to take us over the jungle to the lighthouse."

An idea popped into my head, and the euphoric feeling I'd had earlier that day coursed through my body again.

"Okay," I said, feeling my heart start to race. "I think I might have an idea."

18

I spent the hour after breakfast the next morning catching up on my e-mails, which I'd neglected to answer for two days, then met the team at the entrance to Dasheen Pass for my first morning run to the lighthouse. It wasn't even noon yet and it was already almost 80 degrees, not counting the humidity. This run wasn't going to be easy.

As I approached, everyone turned with surprised looks on their faces. Luckily for me, none of the guys were wearing shirts. At least I'd have something nice to look at on the way up.

"Well, look who decided to join us today," Micah said, adjusting the water belt around his waist. I noticed that everyone else had one too; I hoped they'd be up for sharing, because I hadn't brought my own. Then again, maybe I'd get lucky and get sent back early to the beach to recuperate if I started to dehydrate.

"It didn't seem I had much of a choice," I said.

"Well we're quite happy to have you along," Micah said. His tan chest was already wet with sweat. I found it all a little distracting. "Do try your best to keep up," he said, and with that he turned and took off up Dasheen Pass.

I was surprised to see that Micah had two massive black wings tattooed on his back. They were folded, as if in rest, and reached from his shoulders down to his waist. They were delicate—the type of wings you might normally see on a woman—but on his back they looked quite masculine, making me think of a dark angel. Why someone would want to put something so audacious on their back was beyond me. One drunken night at the age of eighteen I'd stupidly thought it would be a good idea to get a dolphin tattooed on my left ankle. It had taken me five rounds of laser treatment to get the thing taken off and it still didn't look quite right. Something told me, however, that Micah's dark wings weren't the result of a wild night out on the town.

The rest of the team took off after him, and I followed reluctantly behind. Exercise had always seemed like a luxury that only normal, healthy people got to enjoy. At the end of the day I barely had enough energy to feed myself dinner or take a shower, let alone go to the gym.

Beneath the shade of the jungle canopy the heat wasn't quite as stifling, but I was even more out of shape than I thought. When we'd run back from the lighthouse two nights earlier, we'd been going downhill and I'd been all pumped with adrenaline. Going uphill in the heat of the day was a whole other ballgame. By the time we hit the halfway mark, I was dragging and the rest of the team was long gone. I was perfectly fine to be left alone to gasp and wheeze up the hill at my own leisure.

When I got to the clearing at the bluff about a half an hour later, I was soaked from head to toe in sweat, out of breath, and pretty near tears. I found the team on the lighthouse porch, stretching and drinking from their water bottles like they'd just done a quick lap.

"Tag the door," Micah said as I shuffled over to them.

"Why?" I asked, trying not to wheeze.

"We're training your brains to go to the lighthouse," he said.

"Of course you are," I said, shuffling over to the door and placing my hand on it, more for support than anything else. Jeremy handed me his water bottle, and I took a few gulps then leaned on a beam, pretending to stretch while really just trying not to pass out.

"I'm not sure which run was harder," I gasped between gulps of air. "This one or the one in the astral with the killer ghosts."

"You'll get used to it," Jeremy said, clapping me on the back. "Give it a few days."

"So, can we go now?" Angelique asked, turning to Micah excitedly, bouncing up and down on her heels. I couldn't believe she had so much energy after that insane run.

"You want to go somewhere else?" I gasped. "But we just got here."

"Yeah, go ahead," Micah answered.

"Last one down's a rotten mango," Tucker yelled in a singsong before he kicked off his shoes and bolted barefoot off the porch, heading toward the cliff. Jeremy, Angelique, Brad, and Dawn tore of their shoes as well, then took off after Tucker, leaving Micah and me staring after them on the porch.

"What are they doing?" I asked, feeling a little concerned as they continued to run full steam ahead towards the cliff. The same cliff I'd almost been pulled off the day before in the astral.

"You'll see in a second," Micah said with a wry smile.

I watched incredulously as they increased their speed. I was expecting them to cut quickly to the right but instead they jumped right off the cliff, one after another—like lemmings! Even Dawn, who was the last of the bunch, paused only briefly before jumping.

"Are they nuts? That has to be at least a forty-foot drop!" I yelled. I didn't wait for Micah to answer; I sprang off the porch and ran after them. I'd seen what that fall had done to the body of my crazy ghost lady. I dashed to the edge and peered over, half expecting to see the dead and broken bodies of my friends dashed against the rocky cliffs below—but instead they were swimming around a quiet cove in the turquoise ocean below, totally unharmed, hooting and hollering at the thrill of their jumps. Farther in was a beautiful white sand beach, totally devoid of people and surrounded by palm and mango trees. It must be Mango Beach, the place the team had mentioned last night.

"Come on in, the water's fine!" Tucker yelled. I waved him away like he was nuts. Micah walked up next to me, hands in his pockets and trademark smirk on his face.

"That's why you run up here? To jump off this cliff?" I said, still finding it hard to believe that they had all gone over with no hesitation at all—even little Dawn, who was afraid of her own shadow.

"No, we run up here as part of the training. Jumping off the cliff is just for fun."

"But it was your idea originally, wasn't it?" I asked accusingly. He'd probably have us walking across hot coals and skydiving next—all in the name of spiritual growth.

"Yes, it was. What makes you ask that?" He squinted his eyes at me, and I felt strangely like I was being psychoanalyzed.

"Because it sounds like you," I said. "You're reckless with other people's lives. You sent us into the astral yesterday with no warning of what dangers to expect. You act like this is all a game."

"What's wrong with that?" he asked.

His cocky self-assuredness infuriated me. "People have died jumping off that cliff!"

"That happened in the middle of a storm, and they were very drunk," Micah said. "It's about jumping under the right conditions."

Drunk? I didn't remember him mentioning that fact when he told us the story.

"What are you waiting for, Red?" Tucker yelled up from below. "C'mon!"

I looked down at the long drop below me. Just the thought of it sent fear through my entire body. Then a picture flashed into my mind's eye: My ghost woman falling over the cliff. The scene was dark and I couldn't make out any details, but it looked as if there were someone chasing her. My stomach fell and the view pulsed and swirled before me. I stumbled backward.

"Whoa there," Micah said, reaching out to balance me.

"I don't . . ." I suddenly got so light-headed I thought for sure I was going to faint. My knees felt like jelly, and everything around me began to fade. Micah caught me as I was going down. He pulled me away from the cliff and we tumbled down onto the grass.

"Just breathe," he whispered as I bent over and gripped the grass in front of me. As long as there was grass in between my fingers it meant I wasn't going over that cliff.

"What's going on?" he said urgently, putting his hand on my back. "Talk to me, Ms. Dorigan."

I had the sudden feeling that Micah was trying to manipulate me somehow. Trying to get me to jump off the cliff—but not for the reason he was saying.

"Why are you doing this, Micah?"

"I'm trying to help you," he said. His voice was quiet.

"Help me what? Have a panic attack?" I asked, pulling away from him.

"You don't have to jump if you don't want to."

"But if I don't jump I'm not one of you. Is that it?"

"Ms. Dorigan," he said, cocking his head to the side, "you're one of us whether you like it or not."

For some reason this was more upsetting to me than if Micah had told me I had to jump. I covered my face with my hands to keep the tears from coming, but it didn't work. I felt the heat of his body as he came closer, then both hands pulling me gently into him. I didn't fight him this time.

"I don't want to jump," I sobbed. I wasn't really talking about jumping off the cliff anymore, but whatever it was I was afraid of, I couldn't put into words. I got the sudden feeling that my life was about to change dramatically, and the thought sent a horrible fear through me. I clung to Micah even harder. We were both hot and wet from the run, and my tears mixed with the sweat on his bare chest. Everything was a blur of heat and emotion.

"It's okay," he whispered, brushing my hair out of my face. "I'm sorry if you feel I'm pushing you too hard. This work we're doing, it's not just about becoming lucid in dreams, it's about becoming lucid in your waking life as well. That's the ultimate goal. To accomplish that sometimes you have to . . . jump."

"Well, I can't," I said, pulling back from him. My hair was wet and plastered to my face. I wiped at it in an attempt to regain my composure. I felt embarrassed about my outburst and wanted to leave. "I'm sorry, I'm not ready. You go ahead and jump. I'm going back to the resort."

"Don't," he said grabbing my hand gently. "Come with me."

Before I could object he helped me to my feet. Then he turned and, with my hand still in his, led me back toward the jungle. I watched how the black wings on his back shimmered under his sweat. The tattoos were intricately detailed; you could see almost every strand in every feather. They looked like they could spring to life at any moment.

Micah stopped in front of an outgrowth of palms and bushy foliage to the right of the cliff.

"Where are we going?" I asked.

"There's another way down," he said.

"Another way?"

"For now," he said. He pushed aside a tangle of palm leaves, revealing a path that wound down the side of the bluff to Mango Beach below. Now I remembered. Jeremy had mentioned there was a trail.

Micah turned back to me. "At some point, though, you're going to have to jump, Ms Dorigan. We all do, whether we want to or not."

19

"Okay," Micah said, clapping his hands together. "Today we're going to talk more about how your thoughts create your reality."

It was a little after three, and we were back in the lab again. I was dead tired after the morning's run, but I perked up a little at Micah's words. For once, a New Age concept I was actually familiar with.

"You're talking about the Law of Attraction," I said.

He nodded. "I am."

The Law of Attraction had been all the rage in LA a few years earlier. For a while everyone was making vision boards and trying to "think positive" in order to manifest the things they wanted into their lives. I'd made a vision board and added all the things I wanted to it: an antidepressant that actually worked, a big house, a boyfriend, and, most importantly, a job as a television writer. None of it had come to fruition, and I'd quickly dropped it.

"If the Law of Attraction really worked wouldn't everyone be living in mansions and driving Porsches right now?" I asked.

Micah shook his head. "People assume the Law of Attraction works with only your conscious thoughts. But it works with your subconscious thoughts as well—the ones you don't know you're having. And those are thoughts you can't directly control. Not at the consciousness levels we're at most of the time, anyway."

"Thoughts like what?" Tucker asked.

"Limiting beliefs and toxic emotions deeply ingrained from your childhood, your past lives, ancestral lines, Karma, soul contracts you made before incarnating here on earth, et cetera," Micah said. "So consciously you may be telling yourself one thing, but subconsciously you believe the opposite. Our goal here is to locate those limiting beliefs and clear some of them out, at least the ones that are ready to go."

"And how do we know which ones are ready to go?" Angelique asked.

"Because those will be the ones that are presented to you."

I felt my brow furrow at how *woo woo* this was all getting once again. Discussing esoteric spiritual theories was not my favorite pastime. But something Micah was saying did make sense to me. It did feel like no matter what positive action I took in my life—talk therapy, antidepressants, positive thinking techniques—there was something working against me, some program running that, despite my best efforts, I felt compelled to play out. The negative self-talk, the self-sabotage, the incessant worrying and future-tripping, the health problems—no matter how hard I tried, I couldn't seem to stop any of it. Could the Lucidity Project be what I needed to break the cycle?

● ● ●

Knowing what to expect made it much easier to relax the second time around, and just a few minutes after the singing bowls started playing I slipped into a deep sleep. At some point I began to hear that same buzzing I'd experienced the day before, but when I tried to open my eyes this time, it was difficult—like my sight was obstructed somehow. The buzzing continued, and I tried to stand up but I felt like I was glued to the back of the seat. Finally, after struggling for some time, I heard a loud popping sound and found myself on my hands and knees on the floor. I blinked my eyes and could see clearly once again. Turning around, I saw my physical body still asleep in the chair.

The rest of the team were already out of their bodies and standing by the door waiting for me—everyone except for Micah. By the looks of it, he'd already come and gone.

As we stepped out onto the great lawn I saw a large raven making its way across the grass a few yards in front of us. It stopped to consider us and I couldn't help but wonder about the raven that had helped me during our last session. Was it the same one?

"Okay, what's the plan here, guys?" Angelique asked, bringing me back to the task at hand.

"I'm going to try to talk to the soldiers in the west woods," Brad said. "Try to convince them that they're dead so they can move on."

"Easier said then done," Jeremy said.

"Just try not to shoot at them as I attempt to convince them we're friendly. Okay, Rambo?" Brad said, marching ahead of everyone.

Jeremy and I looked at each other, and Jeremy shrugged. Did Brad really think this could work? If those soldiers had been here for years, the idea that we could get through to them with just a few words seemed unlikely. And a few words were all he'd be able to get out before they started shooting at us again.

We headed up Dasheen Pass and into the west woods, just like the day before except feeling much more on edge. We weren't in the jungle two minutes before the first shot rang out.

"Okay, Brad, you're up," Jeremy said ducking behind a tree and pulling me with him. "Show us what you got."

The rest of the team took cover behind adjacent trees as Brad nervously stepped forward toward the oncoming throng of dead soldiers slinking towards us in the woods.

"I command you to stop!" he said suddenly, throwing out his hand. "We are here to help you. The truth of the matter is that all of you are dead. You died over fifty years ago at the hands of Nazi—"

A bullet exploded on a tree next to him, narrowly missing his head.

"What now?" Brad asked, ducking for cover behind our tree.

"Now, it's time for Plan B," said Jeremy. "Follow me!"

Jeremy once again took off into the jungle, and the rest of us followed. We bounded around trees and over the thick underbrush as bullets flew by us. A few minutes later he skidded to a stop in front of a pile of sticks and leaves, which he quickly tossed aside, revealing three dirt bikes.

"Where'd these come from?" Angelique asked.

"Max and I put them here last night after you guys went to bed," Jeremy said, lifting one and gesturing for Angelique to grab the handlebars. "It was Max's idea. We were hoping to get to them before the soldiers attacked. We didn't want to tell you in case it didn't work."

Jeremy picked up the second bike and rolled it over to Brad.

"Wait, where the hell is Tucker?" Angelique cried. We all stopped and looked around. He had disappeared again.

"Dammit!" she said. "He was just here!"

A flurry of bullets splintered the trees around us. The soldiers were catching up.

"We can't wait around for him," Jeremy said, throwing a leg over the last bike. "We have to go! Get on, Max!"

I did as I was told, jumping onto the bike behind him and wrapping my arms around his waist.

Angelique shook her head angrily, then jumped on her bike. Dawn got on the back of Brad's and we sped off into the jungle with the soldiers following close behind.

Jeremy gunned it up the hill and into the jungle while I clung on to him for dear life. My heart pounded in my chest as he dodged and wove through the trees until we finally made it back onto the jungle path. The bikes were so loud I couldn't hear anything else going on around me. We passed Devil's Bend, and I began to think we might actually make it to the lighthouse. Wait—but why did we need to get to the lighthouse? I couldn't seem to remember.

As I continued to rack my brain for an answer, a soldier stepped onto the path directly in front of us with his gun pointed directly at our heads. Jeremy quickly swerved to the right and into the jungle, once again magically dodging trees like they were traffic cones, with Angelique, and Brad and Dawn close behind.

I turned to look back, and saw another soldier step out from behind a tree, right in front of Angelique. It all happened so fast, she had no time to even react—she crashed into him head-on. Time seemed to go into slow motion as she flew forward off her bike, slammed headfirst into a tree, and fell to the ground in a heap.

Dawn and I both screamed. I couldn't believe what I was seeing. Brad and Jeremy skidded to a stop, and we all jumped off the bikes and ran toward Angelique, who lay face down on the ground, her neck bent backward in an unnatural position. Dawn and Brad reached her first, and by the time I got there, Brad was feeling for her pulse. He looked up at us and shook his head. She was gone.

Then a shot rang out, and I turned just as Dawn collapsed to the ground. The soldier who'd been run over by Angelique was now sitting back up, his gun pointed in our direction. He was a brawny, middle-aged man with a mustache and the air of a high-ranking officer. But the light was gone from his eyes. He was completely lost to his own nightmare.

Brad whipped out what looked like a crucifix, threw it in front of him, and began chanting, "Ashes to ashes, spirit to spirit. Take this soul. Banish this evil."

The soldier stood and took a step backward, staring at Brad with a somewhat confused expression. Then he raised his gun again and shot Brad in the chest.

I stood there in complete shock as Brad fell to the ground and the soldier turned his gun on me.

"Run, Max!" Jeremy yelled. I did as I was told and took off back into the woods. But when I heard another shot I turned—only to see Jeremy lying on the ground, blood everywhere, a piece missing from the side of his head. The soldier looked down at him, then turned his eyes back to me.

I didn't have time to cry for Jeremy or the others. Fear surged through my body once again and I took off in a blind run, my mind a blur of panic and despair. Under the fear, there was a strange feeling pulling at me—the sense that there was something I was supposed to remember. Something that could save us all. But what?

I could hear the soldier following close behind, his feet hitting the soft underbrush hard and fast. Another shot rang out and I felt something rip through my calf. Hot, searing pain shot up my leg, and I crumbled to the ground. I looked down: blood was beginning to pour out of a small hole in my calf. I'd been shot! The pain was unlike anything I'd ever felt before. I tried to get up, but I was too late. I heard the sound of the soldier's feet crunching in the underbrush toward me, and I looked up to find him standing over me, his gun trained right at my head.

"No! Don't!" I screamed, shutting my eyes and holding up my hand as if that could stop a bullet. I sat there waiting for a few seconds, bracing myself for impact, but the bullet never came. When I opened my eyes the man was still standing in front of me, but his head was tilted at an unnatural angle and his face was slack. He slumped forward onto the ground. Behind him—with her tattered sequin dress, moldy skin, and matted black hair—stood my ghost.

Before I could react, she lurched forward and grabbed my wrists. I struggled against her but she was too strong for me. Grabbing tightly onto my hands, she flipped them around so that my palms were face up and pushed them roughly in front of my face. I continued to try to pull away until I looked down and saw that my hands were glowing. I looked closer, and saw that there was a map on my palms—a shining, moving, vibrating, pulsing, beautiful, multidimensional matrix of symbols and algorithms, peaks and valleys, rivers and deserts, oceans, stars, and solar systems that never began and never ended. As I stared in awe a euphoric rush filled my body and everything flooded back to me.

Suddenly I felt an immense expansion that encompassed all of who I was, and I remembered that I was dreaming. My friends hadn't really been killed by those soldiers. They would all be back in the lab once I woke up. Not only that, but life on the earth plane was but a dream—a tiny fraction of the true experience of all I really was. God, how could I have forgotten where I came from or what I came here to do?

I looked back up at my ghost woman, shocked at this turn of events. She stared back at me fixedly, and the black liquid that had filled her eyes began to recede and reveal her actual eyes. They were brown, with gold flecks that shimmered in the light. Her hair and skin were also transforming. If I didn't know any better I'd think she was . . . healing. *Here I thought she was trying to kill me, and really she was trying to help me.* If anyone had told me that an hour earlier, I never would have believed them, but I was sure of it now.

I tried to reach out to thank her, but everything around me began to fade to gray. I could feel the dream slipping away from me. *No!* I didn't want it to end. I wanted to stay here in the remembrance of who I was—an infinite being of love and light here to help the world. I knew that once I woke up it was likely I'd forget. I reached out to the ghost, thinking that perhaps she could make the dream stay—but the grayness enveloped her like a thick fog. The last thing I saw was a black raven taking flight into the trees above me. Then I felt myself being pulled backward, whooshed through time and space, and in a matter of seconds I was back in my physical body in the lab with Brad, Dawn, Jeremy, Tucker, and Angelique, who were staring at me anxiously.

"Did you make it? Did you make it to the lighthouse?" Angelique asked as soon as I opened my eyes. Everyone from the team was literally on the edge of their seats, except for Micah, who was just waking up in his chair next to me.

I blinked, trying to readjust to this quick change of reality. "No," I said, pulling off my headset.

Their faces fell. I looked down at the palms of my hands. The map was gone, but the feeling that had come with it—something that could only be described as pure bliss—was not. I tried to grasp at what had happened, the information I'd been given when I'd looked at the map, before it faded from memory, but it was like it had been erased from my mind. I'd had this experience before, not being able to remember my dreams on waking, but this had been so important. Why couldn't I remember?

I looked around at my friends' shell-shocked faces and realized they hadn't had quite the same transcendent experience I'd had in the astral. In all the excitement that had followed, I'd forgotten they'd all been killed.

"Are you guys okay?" I asked.

"Well, we're all still here, if that's what you mean," said Angelique looking accusingly at Micah.

That wasn't what I had meant. I looked over at Micah. Where had he been while everyone was getting shot down? Of course, if he had come and helped us, I never would have seen the map on my hands, or had the experience that came along with it.

"What happened to you?" Dawn asked, looking over at me from the other side of Angelique. There were tears in her eyes, which was understandable considering she'd just been shot to death. The energy in the room was thick with emotion. "I wanted to wake you up, but Angelique and Jeremy wouldn't let me. Did you get killed too?"

I thanked my lucky stars they hadn't woken me up.

"No. I ran into my ghost, and she gave me a map."

The energy in the room shifted suddenly as everyone considered this new information.

"A map to what?" Dawn asked.

"I'm not sure," I said, staring down at my palms, as if doing so could bring the memory back. "I think it was to my life."

20

"**I** need to go back in," I said, looking at Micah. We were still sitting in our chairs in the lab, trying to process everything we'd just been through.

"And you can," he said. "Tomorrow. But don't be disappointed if you can't find your map again."

"What do you mean?"

"I mean we're often given information in dreams that we're then supposed to follow up on in our waking life," he said. "Most likely the map was a symbol of something. Consider seeking not the map itself, but what it represents."

"But I don't even remember enough to figure out what it might represent!" I looked down at my hands yet again, frustrated with myself for not remembering better, and with Micah for giving me yet another vague answer to a straightforward question.

"Well this is just great," Jeremy said, standing up. "We're getting killed. We're given important information and then can't remember it when we get back. These sessions aren't helping us get any closer to the lighthouse or doing anything other than traumatizing us more. What's the point?"

"And where the hell were you?" Angelique rounded on Tucker. "You disappeared—again!"

"I don't know," Tucker said with a sigh, looking up at the ceiling in frustration. "I keep getting lost."

"How hard is it to stay with the group?" Angelique said, crossing her arms over her chest and leaning forward. "The rest of us manage to do it."

"Listen," Micah said, putting his hands out to calm us down. "You had a rough time in there today, I get it. But you're just starting out with this. Like anything you do in life, you'll get better with practice. Until then, you're going to have good days and bad days, just like any with other type of therapy."

"Yeah, but you don't get shot in regular therapy." Dawn sniffed, and a big tear rolled down her cheek.

She had that right. And I noticed that the after-effects of these past two sessions had stayed with me longer than normal dreams did—and they took longer to process emotionally, too, probably because they were so intense. Luckily for me, the euphoric feeling I'd gotten from seeing the map had overpowered most of the trauma I'd experienced that day—but the rest of the team hadn't had been so lucky.

"We need more help in there from you, man," Jeremy said to Micah. "It's like you're just sending us on one suicide mission after another. We don't have time for this mystical *woo woo* stuff. We need you to come with us and show us how it's done."

"Showing you how it's done defeats the exercise—defeats the whole project. It's not just about getting to the lighthouse, it's about learning *how* to get there. Learning how to work with the energy there. You know this, Jeremy."

"Yeah, well, in the meantime there are people going missing here in the real world. People we could be helping to find."

Missing people? *Oh.* I had forgotten. Those people who talked to Jeremy—the ones he thought he was supposed to save. Could that be real?

"You need to be able to find yourself first," Micah said.

"How can that be true?" Jeremy asked, throwing his hands open in frustration. "If we all ran around trying to find ourselves all the time, nothing would ever get done."

Before Micah could answer, Jeremy stormed out of the room.

Micah took a breath. "Okay, you guys. Let's take the night off tonight. We'll have our debrief before our session tomorrow in the lab. In the meantime, get some rest. You're going to need it."

●●●

When I arrived at our table for dinner, Brad and Angelique were the only ones there, and they didn't look happy.

"Where is everyone?" I asked, putting my tray down next to Brad. On the menu tonight was a delicious-smelling seafood chowder and fresh salad.

He looked up frowning, and shook his head.

"Jeremy went for a walk to blow off some steam," Angelique said, her tone wary. "Dawn said she wasn't hungry. I'm going to bring dinner up for her after this. I don't know where Tucker is, but what else is new?"

"It was pretty brutal in there today," I said cautiously. Since my experience in the astral today had ended on high note, I wasn't feeling the frustration and despair the rest of the group was experiencing.

"Like Micah said, it's only our second session. I don't think we should let ourselves get too discouraged," Brad said.

"It might have only been our second session, but Jeremy's been doing this for a month and he's clearly getting pretty frustrated," Angelique said, pushing her salad around on her plate.

"If Micah's able to move around the astral plane so easily then there's obviously something that we're missing," Brad said.

"Well yeah," I said, "but it sounds like he's been doing this for years. We don't have that kind of time."

"No, we don't," Angelique said. "Why don't you tell us about this map you saw, Max."

"The map?" The mere mention of it made my palms tingle. "I don't remember much of it now, except that it was on my hands."

Angelique and Brad both stopped eating and looked up from their plates.

"On your hands?" Brad repeated. "Does Micah know that?"

"I don't know," I said, wondering why Brad looked so interested all of a sudden. "Didn't I say that earlier?"

Brad and Angelique exchanged a look.

"Have you ever had your handprints read?" Brad asked.

"You mean like by a palm reader? Uh, no," I scoffed.

"I mean by a hand analyst," Brad said, ignoring my tone.

"Is that a fancy name for a palm reader?" I took a bite of my seafood chowder, which was, not surprisingly, amazing. It was going to be hard to go back to eating takeout when I went home to LA.

"Hand analysis is a modern form of palmistry," Angelique said. "Palmistry uses the lines in your palm to foretell the future. Hand analysis uses your fingerprints to reveal your life purpose."

"By life purpose you mean . . ."

"We all come to earth with a purpose, something we're supposed to work on and share with the world," Brad said. "But sometimes we need help figuring out what that is."

"Okay." I sighed and rubbed the bump on my forehead. I was beginning to feel a little overwhelmed. "So say I'm willing to give this hand analysis thing a try. Where do I find someone who knows how to do it?"

"You're in luck . . . there just happens to be an expert right on this island," Angelique said, shooting an amused glance towards Brad.

"Oh," I said, wondering what she suddenly found so funny. "Who?"

"Micah," Brad said with a smirk.

"Micah!" I said, and my heart skipped a beat. Why did everything on this island seem to lead back to him?

●●●

Fifteen minutes later I knocked on the door of Micah's house. He answered wearing only his board shorts, no shirt. I wasn't quite sure I would ever get used to the island dress code—or lack of one, I should say.

"Hello, Ms. Dorigan," he said. "Fancy seeing you here. I've just put on some tea. Would you like some?"

"This isn't exactly a social visit," I said, trying to look anywhere but his bare chest. I didn't want him getting the wrong idea, especially after the intimate moment we'd had earlier up at the lighthouse.

"That's too bad," he said opening up the door to let me in. I walked past him and into the living room. "Let me guess: this is about your map."

"Yes," I said. "It was on my hands. Brad and Angelique told me you were a palm reader, and you might be able to help me figure out what it means." I stopped for a second to ponder what I just said. "I can't believe that actually came out of my mouth."

"That's nothing." He smiled, grabbed a T-shirt off the couch, and threw it on. "Wait until I get done with you."

He led me back to his office and I sat down once again on the red Victorian sofa while he rifled through a filing cabinet behind his desk.

"So, do you need me to hold your crystal ball for you while you call on the dark spirits?" I teased.

"I used to charge $350 an hour for this back in the States, you know," he said.

"I guess that explains how you can afford this resort."

He looked up at me with an amused look on his face. "I didn't get this resort by reading people's hands."

"No? How did you get it, exactly?" I asked, looking out his giant window at the beach. The sun had already gone down behind the water, lighting up the horizon with an orange and pink glow.

"I manifested it," he said matter-of-factly, going back to his files.

"You manifested it," I repeated, turning my attention back to him. "Okay, I'll bite. How did you manage that?"

"When you need things for what you're supposed to do here, the universe provides," he said.

"You just happened to need a resort on a tropical island?"

"I needed a place to help people. The powers that be thought the best place for that would be this island. I happened to agree."

"So you just woke up one day and someone gave you this resort?" I asked.

"Nope, I won the lottery. Then I bought the resort." He grabbed a large manila folder out of the file then headed towards me, dragging the rolly chair from his desk behind him.

"You're kidding." My mouth dropped open. "Maybe after the palm-reading thing you can teach me about manifesting."

"What do you think I've been trying to do this whole time?"

"Honestly, Micah, I have no idea." I sighed. "You aren't exactly forthcoming about it."

He gave me a big, mysterious smile that indicated that for once we were in perfect agreement, then scooted his chair directly in front of me and sat down so close to me our faces were just a foot apart. I was used to therapists being on the other side of the room, not practically between my legs. Of course, I knew by now that Micah wasn't a normal therapist. Micah wasn't a normal anything.

"Here's the deal." He gently grabbed my wrist and brushed his fingers across my palm. Tingles traveled up my arm, reminding me of the attraction I'd felt toward him on our run. I pursed my lips and tried to concentrate on the current task instead of the palpable energy I felt between us.

If Micah was feeling it as well, he didn't let on. "Your fingerprints form on your hands five months prior to birth," he said. "These unique patterns represent our soul's agenda: what we came to earth to learn, what we came here to do. We call this our life lesson and our life purpose." He paused, his pale eyes checking in with mine to see if I was following along. "There are many types of fingerprint patterns, and where they are on your fingers determines your life purpose and life lesson. For instance, your highest ranking mark is here, on your pinky finger."

"How do you know that? You haven't even looked at my hands."

"Actually, I have." He grabbed the manila envelope off the sofa next to me and pulled two pieces of paper out of it—the copies of my handprints that Dr. Luna had made at Cedars-Sinai. They were all marked up in what I assumed was Micah's handwriting.

"You've had these this whole time and you didn't tell me? Why not?"

"Because even now you're going to have a hard time believing what I have to tell you."

"You've got that right." I sighed and looked back at the papers. At the top of the page with my left handprint on it, "The Messenger" was written in big, bold letters.

"What's this mean?" I asked, pointing to the words.

"Each finger symbolizes a life purpose theme represented by an archetype: The Leader, The Mentor, The Innovator, etc."

"So there are only ten types of people in the world?" I asked, assuming each finger accounted for a personality type.

"No, you can have a mix of many high-ranking prints. For instance I'm a Leader-Mentor archetype."

"Why doesn't that surprise me?"

"And you—you are a Messenger."

"But what does that mean?"

"It means, Ms. Dorigan, that you've come here with a message for the world."

21

"A message for the world," I stammered. "From who?"

"From you," Micah replied. "It's your message."

"I don't have any messages for anyone."

"That's not what it says here."

"Maybe you should check my toes."

"It doesn't work like that," he smiled.

"Why would I be sent here with a message for the world and then not be told what it is? And why would a woman who died almost a hundred years ago care about it at all?"

"That's what you're here to find out."

I didn't like that answer.

"Perhaps my ghost was pointing at my hands to tell me that *she* has a message, and I'm supposed to get *her* message to someone. Ghosts are always trying to get a message to someone, right?"

"Either way, your objective is the same. To find out what the message is and convey it to the world."

"But I don't have time to get a message out to the world. I have to be back in LA ready to break twenty-two episodes of a television show in less than three weeks."

He stared back at me, unsympathetically.

"Okay, fine. Fine! Let's say hypothetically that I have a message for the world and I figure out what it is. What would be an acceptable way of getting it out there? Do I have to announce it on the ten o'clock news, or will a Facebook status update do?"

"That's for you to decide."

"But I couldn't possibly be here with a message," I argued back. "I'm not an outgoing person. I like being behind the scenes. That's why I'm a writer."

"You don't have to stand at a podium and preach to the masses. There's myriads of ways to share your message. You could give it to one person at a time, or perhaps write it all down, in, say, a book."

"But I don't have anything meaningful to tell anyone. I work on a television show about teen witches. The biggest topic we tackled last year was how keep your demonic ex-boyfriend from crashing your prom."

"Well, perhaps it's time for a change."

"To what? The stuff we're doing here is really weird, Micah. With my emotional issues and depression, I'm already weird enough as it is. I came here to try to find out a way to be normal. You're not helping things with all this messenger stuff."

"Well, that's tough, because The Messenger has to share her truth whether it's weird or not, and it isn't always what other people agree with or want to hear. But that's how it goes. You see, when pursuing your life purpose you always come into conflict with its opposite. As a result you'll be attracted to it and repelled by it at the same time. The fact that you're having such a knee-jerk reaction to this only proves more that this is your destiny."

"Destiny? What is this? *Star Wars?*"

He laughed. "Think of it more like a star *game*. You're a star-being that's come here to the earth plane to learn and expand your awareness. The game is to face your fears and express your true self to the world."

Express my true self? I'd spent so much time trying to be more like Sofia or the writers at work—a charismatic and successful television writer with an active social life—that I didn't have much of a concept of who my true self might be. I knew one thing, though: I didn't want to be some hippie, New Age messenger girl. If Sofia knew all the weird stuff we were doing here she would laugh me right out of the writers' room. They all would.

"And what if I decide I don't want to share this message?" I challenged. "What if I don't want anything to do with any of this?"

"I think you already know the answer to that question. Up until last week, you've been living it."

"So basically you're saying I won't be happy until I find out this message?"

"I think you won't be happy unless you are at least pursuing it."

"But how do I pursue it?" I said, feeling more frustrated by the second.

"This ghost was the one who pointed the map out to you on your hands," he said peering into my eyes intensely. "Maybe you should start there."

***

My head was reeling when I left Micah's. Why would anyone in their right mind give me a message for the world? I barely had the energy to take a shower most mornings. Getting a message out to the world was a serious long shot.

Still, despite all my reservations, I was lit up with energy once again. Every cell in my body was screaming that Micah was right—that I was here for some purpose, that we all were. It was like my heart was telling me one thing and my head was telling me another. Which one was I supposed to listen to in this situation?

If I was going to search for this message—if I was going to follow my heart in spite of how crazy that seemed—I needed to do it now. Once I got back to LA I wouldn't have the energy or the time. That meant I had less than three weeks to find out what the message was and who I needed to get it to. I hoped by then I'd be feeling better and I could go back to LA and finally live a normal life—something that didn't feel unrealistic anymore. My depression and fatigue were lifting bit by bit every day. Each time I visited the astral, I came back with more of myself, despite how frightening it was in there at times. Maybe when this was all over I could go back to my job and have the energy to finally get promoted to staff writer and live the life I'd always dreamed.

It was time to get proactive. My ghost was the one who'd shown me the map, so the first thing to do was find out more about her—who she was, what happened the night she died up on that cliff, and what, if anything, I needed to do about it.

I returned to my room to find Zoe reading in bed.

"You're out late," she said. Her hair was all tied up in little rags all around her head—to ensure effortless-looking, beachy waves for the next day, no doubt.

"Zoe, it's not even nine o'clock."

"Nine island time is like 2 a.m. in the States. So, who were you with? Jeremy? Not Tucker, I hope."

"I was at Micah's," I said, and regretted it as soon as it came out of my mouth.

"What?" Zoe practically jumped out of bed with excitement. "You little minx! Sit down. Tell me everything!"

"Would you stop it?" I laughed as I went over to the closet and began changing for bed. "I was there talking to him about my ghost. Get this: He thinks she has a message for me. Or I have a message for someone. It's not all that clear. Either way, he says I need to find out more about her."

"I told you!" Zoe said. "This ghost is obviously trying to reach out to you. The dead can be relentless when they want something."

"What do you know about the dead, exactly?" I asked.

"I've seen practically every episode of *Ghost Adventures* and *Paranormal State*," she said. "That's got to count for something."

"So basically, everything you know about ghosts you learned from reality TV?"

"What's wrong with that?" she asked. She didn't wait for me to answer. "I can't believe you have a real live ghost haunting you. It's so cool! Well, I mean, except for the fact that she keeps trying to kill you and everything."

"Yeah, that part is kind of a bummer."

"So, how much do you know about her, exactly?"

"Only what Micah has told me. She fell off the cliff up at the lighthouse during a storm. Two other people died with her. They were drunk, evidently. That's what Micah said. But it happened so long ago. I wonder how he found out that information." I'd been trying to keep such a distance from the whole thing, I'd failed to ask him.

"I think I might know," Zoe said, puckering her lips thoughtfully.

"Really?" I asked, surprised.

"There's hotel archives in the library. They're not much—just a bunch of old newspaper clippings and pictures in scrapbooks from throughout the years—but if there's anything on three deaths up at the lighthouse, it would probably be there."

●●●

First thing the next morning, Zoe and I headed down to the library, which was at the back of the hotel next to the ballroom. She let us in with her key and snapped on the lights.

The library itself was quite grand. It had thirteen-foot ceilings and floor-to-ceiling bookshelves on three walls. The fourth was lined with tall, arched windows—the same ones that were in the great room at the top of the hotel. As I scanned the shelves I noticed the majority of the books were quite old and had been there for some time. But there was a section of new books too—mostly spiritual and self-help, and I was pleased to see they had a fiction and mystery section as well.

"Okay, all the historical stuff from the hotel is over here," Zoe said, grabbing my hand and yanking me over to a large bookshelf at the back on the room. On the bottom of the shelf was a row of large photo albums with dates on the bindings starting in the early 1900s.

"Do you know what time period your ghost is from?" Zoe asked, crouching down.

"Micah said the accident happened in the twenties," I said. "And the ghost woman's dress looked like something from that period."

"Well, that means anything on her would probably be in here," Zoe said, grabbing the album labeled 1920–1930.

I plopped down next to her on the floor and opened the cover. The first few pages were old brochures about the resort and its former owner—Joseph Harrington, the steel magnate who'd opened the Avalon Hotel on the island during Prohibition. We continued to flip through more pictures: the resort under construction, Micah's house, which apparently used to be maids' quarters, and multiple shots of the sugar fields, which no longer existed—at least, as far as I had seen.

We continued flipping through pictures of the resort until we came to one of Harrington standing with three women in front of the main hotel. Below it, *The Harrington Family* was written in cursive. The older woman was, I assumed, his wife. She had a pinched look on her face and wore a gray dress that looked like it belonged more in the Victorian age than the twenties. Next to her was a young woman in her mid-twenties. She was round and somewhat matronly looking, with brown hair pulled back into a tight bun. Standing next to her, in a fashionable-for-the-time, white drop waist dress, was a taller woman that I recognized immediately.

"That's her," I said, pointing to the woman in white. "That's my ghost." A chill went up my back as I held the picture closer to get a better look. As a non-dead person my ghost was actually quite pretty—tall and thin, with dark hair cut into a bob.

"She must have been one of Joseph Harrington's daughters," Zoe said. "Boy, they don't look too happy, do they?"

"They sure don't," I agreed. There was a sadness about the family. Back then people didn't smile in pictures, but even given that, the Harringtons looked overly serious.

We continued looking through the albums and scouring newspaper clippings, most of which were about the hotel. It had been renovated quite a few times since those years, but I recognized the black-and-white-checked floor and L-shaped staircase of the lobby—those were still just as they had been then.

I could see from the next few clippings and photographs that the Avalon had been quite a success in its day. It appeared the clientele had mostly been New York high society types and celebrities who wanted a few weeks to rub elbows with each other and drink in peace.

I was almost to the end of the album when I finally found what I'd been looking for—a small clipping of an article from *The New York Times*.

"Look at this," I said to Zoe after seeing the title. She leaned over, and we read the article in silence.

Three Killed in Storm on Caribbean Island

New York socialite Millicent Harrington Last, her husband, stage actor Roald Powers Last, and her brother-in-law, Charles Miller Last of Manhattan, were killed last Saturday after being swept into the sea during a storm while vacationing in the Caribbean. The three were celebrating New Year's Eve at a party with friends and family while on holiday at the posh Avalon Hotel, a resort on a small island off St. Lucia owned by Mrs. Last's father, Joseph Harrington. Witnesses say the three disappeared sometime after midnight. Their bodies were found the next morning in a small cove in the northern part of the island. All three had drowned.

Millicent made headlines ten years ago when she married actor and former playboy Roald Last. The two were active in New York's social scene.

Charles Last was a sergeant in the U.S. military, and a veteran of The Great War. A private memorial service will be held for close friends and family.

"Millicent Harrington Last," I said. I finally had her name. "But now what?"

"Now we Google her!" Zoe said, as if that were the obvious thing to do. "See if we can find a relative of hers or something."

"You really think there'll be a record of her somewhere on the Internet?" I asked. "She died almost a hundred years ago."

"It said she was a socialite, didn't it? Married to a famous actor," Zoe said. "C'mon!" She grabbed my hand once again and tugged me over to the laptop at the checkout desk. I waited as she typed "Millicent Harrington Last" into Google and pressed return—and sure enough, she got a hit. The first result on the screen was a list of Millicent Harrington Last's closest relatives.

"Bingo! Thank you, Ancestry dot com," Zoe sang, Broadway musical–style.

"You know, if this whole acting thing doesn't work out, maybe you should go into ghost detecting," I said, peering over her shoulder at the screen. "You seem to have quite a knack for it."

"You know, I was thinking that too," she said, nodding her head as if that were the greatest idea in the world. "That might be a good way to support myself before my acting career takes off. I hear Hollywood is just swarming with ghosts!"

She looked back to the computer screen. "Okay, here we go. Millicent Harrington Last, daughter of Joseph Ellsworth Harrington. Spouse: Roald Powers Last. Looks like she didn't have any children, but her sister, Margaret Dorothy Duncan, had one child, Frances

Marjorie Duncan, and there's no death date for her, which means she might still be alive."

Before I knew what was happening, Zoe had pulled up a Facebook page belonging to a Frances Marjorie Duncan. "How in the world did people research the ghosts haunting them before the Internet?" she asked.

From Mrs. Duncan's Facebook profile picture I guessed her to be in her late eighties or early nineties—old enough that I was surprised she was even on Facebook. She had white hair, pale skin, and a kind smile, and looked like your typical grandmother. According to her profile she lived in New York, and, from what I could tell, rarely used Facebook. Her last post was from three months earlier, when she'd commented on a picture of her great grandchild.

"That's got to be her, don't you think?" I asked.

"Absolutely," Zoe said. "How many Frances Marjorie Duncans are there, do you think? We're lucky she kept her maiden name."

"So now what?" I asked.

"What do you mean, now what?" Zoe asked. "Now you send her a message!"

"And what am I supposed to say, exactly?" I asked. "'Hi, you don't know me, but I'm being haunted by the ghost of your dead aunt. She was trying to kill me at first, but now it looks like she has a message for someone, possibly the world. Any idea what it might be?'"

"I think you need to be a little more tactful than that," Zoe said, ignoring my attempt at a joke. "Leave it to me. I'm really good with this kind of stuff. What's your Facebook sign-in?"

I leaned over her and signed in, and Zoe went back to Frances Marjorie's page, clicked the "message" button, and got to typing.

"Dear Mrs. Duncan," she read out loud as she typed. "My name is Maxine Dorigan. You don't know me but I'm currently a guest at the Theta Institute, a small resort in the Caribbean islands previously called the Avalon—the same resort once owned by your family, and where your aunt, Millicent Last, met with a most tragic death. I know this is going to sound strange, but please just stay with me. I've had a few—I guess you could call them 'visits,' from your aunt's ghost. It's been quite traumatic, to say the least. I was hoping you might be able to shed some light on what happened to her. She obviously has some unfinished business here on earth that she needs to deal with before she can cross over into the spirit world. I promise you I am not looking for money, only information that might finally help put your dear aunt to rest. Sincerely, Maxine Dorigan."

"I don't know," I said. I felt like I needed to think up a better plan, or at the very least finesse the letter a bit more. "Let me think about—"

"You think too much," Zoe said, and she hit the "send" button.

22

I didn't do all that much better than I had the day before on our run to the lighthouse later that morning, and once there I opted to take the rocky path down to Mango Beach again instead of jumping off the cliff with the rest of the group. I wasn't anywhere near ready to make the jump—and despite what Micah had said the day before, I doubted I ever would be.

We swam and lounged around on the beach until a little after noon, then headed back down to lunch at the resort, where I filled the team in on my discovery in the library, as well as Micah's thoughts on my map.

"A message for the world . . . that's a pretty tall order," Tucker said with a snort.

"Of course, that's just Micah's opinion," I said, realizing I must sound like I thought quite a lot of myself.

"Don't listen to Tucker. Micah is absolutely right," Brad said. "You do have a message, and you'll get it out soon enough, through your writing."

"How do you know that?" I asked.

"I'm psychic, remember? It's part of my gift to know what people are here to do. I know Micah's right about you the same way I know Dawn's here to communicate with nonphysical entities and help them cross over."

"But that's not what I want to do," Dawn objected.

"Too bad for you," Brad said. "The Universe doesn't just change its mind on these things."

"Well, I don't need a psychic to tell me what my life purpose is," Tucker said. "I already know it's to keep as many of the ladies on this fine planet as sexually fulfilled as possible."

"Don't you have a meeting to get to?" Angelique snapped, throwing down her fork. Tensions had been high between the two of them over the last few days. Angelique was seriously pissed that Tucker kept disappearing in the astral. I was beginning to worry for his safety.

"A meeting?" Tucker asked, feigning confusion.

"Your twelve-step meeting? The one you're supposed to go to every day? Dr. Luna said you'll be put on probation if you miss another one."

"This whole place just feels like one long meeting," Tucker said. He got up, snatched his plate and glass off the table, and walked away.

Jeremy got up and went after him. Brad shrugged, then continued arguing with Dawn about her life purpose. Angelique, meanwhile, suddenly found something on her plate very interesting.

"You okay?" I asked.

"Yeah." She sighed. "I think I overreacted there a little bit. I'm just worried that Tucker's not taking any of this seriously. He's disappearing in our sessions. He hasn't been going to his meetings. Those are all signs of a relapse."

"Are you an alcoholic too?" I asked. I knew the question was rude, but I was curious and she seemed comfortable enough with the subject.

"No but my father was. He didn't like going to his meetings either," she said, looking down and lightly touching the dragon belt she never seemed to be without.

"Was that his?" I asked.

"Yes." Her demeanor darkened. "After a big night of drinking he liked to come home and hit me with it . . . among other things."

Her words hung in the air between us as she turned and looked out at the ocean.

"Why do you wear it?" Her father sounded like a monster. Why would she want to keep a symbol of him on her body?

"As a reminder," she said, "that I'm a survivor. That there's nothing this world can throw at me that I can't handle." She looked down at the belt again, then gave me a half-hearted smile. "Obviously I need to be reminded of that a lot."

I nodded. "You and me both," I said. I was surprised Angelique was opening up to me in this way. She seemed so guarded all the time. We didn't always see eye to eye, but I wanted her to know I was there for her, regardless.

"Don't get me wrong," she said. "I want to be able to let go of what he did to me and move on. And they say the way to peace is through forgiveness. But I just can't seem to get there—anywhere close to it, really."

"I think you're being too hard on yourself," I said. "It doesn't sound like your father deserves your forgiveness."

"No," she said. "He doesn't. But it's not really about him, is it? After I ran away from home I spent so many years fantasizing about how I was going to get back at him. Punish him for what he did to me. It's a good thing Dr. Luna found me and brought me to this island or I don't know where I'd be right now. Probably in jail."

That must have been what all those martial arts lessons were for—preparing for a battle that would never come.

"It wasn't until I came here that I began to understand that the only person I was hurting by holding on to all that hate was me. But no matter how many workshops I do or books I read, I can't seem to get beyond the anger." She turned back to me, her eyes shining and intense. "That's why we have to get to the lighthouse, Max. The truth, is this is my last hope. I've tried everything else. I have to find out how to let this go and move on. If I don't, I'm afraid this anger is going to eat me alive."

●●●

I arrived at the lab a few minutes early, eager to start our next session. When I walked into the barn Micah was already sitting in his old leather recliner, cross-legged.

I took my seat next to him. The leather felt pleasantly cool against my body. I self-consciously felt my hair, which had only just finished drying from our swim and was an untamed mess of bushy waves. I started to brush at it with my fingers, but made myself stop. I wasn't there to look pretty for Micah, or for anyone, for that matter. I had serious business to attend to. Like Millicent Last.

"I found out the name of my ghost," I said, dropping my hands to my lap.

"Ah yes," he said, his eyes meeting mine. "Ms. Harrington."

"Millicent Harrington Last, actually," I corrected him. Of course he'd known her name all along. He had access to the albums in the library and had probably read them over many times. How else would he have known about the accident in the first place? But why hadn't he just told me her name and whatever else he knew about her? I supposed that was the modus operandi of most therapists—wanting you to do everything on your own, with as little input as possible—but still.

"You could have just told me," I said. "It would have made things a lot easier."

"Others can always give you the answers, Ms. Dorigan," he said, "but the ones that have the most impact are those we discover ourselves."

Before I could respond, the door opened and Angelique and Tucker walked in, talking loudly. It sounded like they were in the middle of an argument, and Angelique looked more annoyed than usual.

"I don't want to talk about it any more, Tucker," she snapped at him. "Put your money where your mouth is."

"I'd rather put your money where my mouth is," he said. "I'd like to put anything of yours where my mouth is, actually."

Angelique gave him the dirtiest look I'd seen from her so far and sat down stiffly in the chair next to me. Tension filled the room. I was happy when Dawn, Brad, and Jeremy filed in soon afterwards and got settled into their respective seats.

"Okay, we're all here," Micah began. "Now that we've all gotten some time to process, let's talk a little more about what happened in our session yesterday."

"We all got killed, that's what happened," Angelique said, pushing back one side of her long black hair with a flick of her wrist.

"You certainly did," said Micah, looking more amused than sympathetic. "And why do you think that is?"

I couldn't believe he found this funny. The rest of us did not share his sentiment.

"Because you're enjoying watching us fail," Angelique shot back with a scowl.

"No," Micah said, pointing at her sharply. "It's because you are stuck in victim consciousness. "

Angelique's eyes flared, but she closed her mouth, and the room went silent.

"Listen and listen closely, my friends," Micah said, placing his hands on his knees and leaning forward. "You are not totally power-less over all the things that happen in your life. Maybe we all start off helpless as infants and children, but you don't have to stay there if you don't want to. I am giving you the chance to rise into a new level of awareness. It's time to get out of victim consciousness and take back your power."

"But how?" I asked.

Realizing we weren't going to fight him on this one, Micah relaxed back into his chair and continued. "What many of you are experienc-ing is caused by what in the shamanic tradition is called Soul Loss. Many shamanic cultures teach that everything has its own spirit, or soul essence. When we experience any sort of trauma, a piece of ourselves can break off and move into nonphysical reality as a way of trying to protect itself and escape from the pain. The shaman's job is to work on the client's behalf to go into nonphysical reality and bring those pieces back. With the Lucidity Project you are being given the opportunity to do this for yourself. You're getting the chance to sym-bolically pull back the curtains on your subconscious programming and gain more awareness of yourself and your limiting beliefs."

"And how are we supposed to do that?" Angelique asked.

"By staying lucid," Micah said. "When something frightening or disturbing presents itself, don't run from the pain and discomfort; get curious. See what it has to offer you. As Rumi so elegantly put it thou-sands of years ago, 'The cure for the pain is in the pain.'"

"But the soldiers kill us whenever they see us!" Dawn cried.

"Do they, though?" Micah asked, cocking his head to the side. "You don't look dead to me. Get out of victim consciousness, people. You are powerful manifesters. Co-creators of your experience. If you need help, stop and ask for guidance."

"Guidance from who?" I asked.

Micah's eyes squinted and he puckered his lips together. "Consider that part of your assignment as well."

●●●

The transition into the astral was much easier this time around. After coming to, I quickly checked my palms to see if the map was still there, but it wasn't. I shut my eyes and tried to will it back with my mind. Still nothing. *So much for your thoughts creating your reality.*

Once we were all in, we gathered in the middle of the room. Everyone except for Micah, that is, who promptly stood up from his chair and disappeared into thin air.

"Man, he's got to teach me how to do that," Tucker said.

"I think you're already a pro at the disappearing act," Angelique said.

"Ha, ha. Very funny," Tucker said, shooting her an annoyed look. "So what's the plan?"

"I think we should take the dirt bikes again, but this time go the long way to the lighthouse—through the north woods and then back to Mango Beach," Jeremy said. "I moved the bikes back to the garage so we won't even have to go into the west woods with the soldiers."

"Sounds good to me," Angelique said.

"I really don't feel like getting shot and killed today," Brad agreed. "It's worth a try."

"Wait, you guys," I said. "Micah just finished giving us a lecture on how we need to face our fears and not run from them."

"Yeah, well, Micah didn't get his head blown off yesterday," Jeremy said, his dark eyes fixed on mine.

He had me there.

"Plus, those soldiers are ghosts," Tucker said. "How could they be part of our subconscious programming?"

"We can go back in and face the soldiers once we've figured out how to help them cross over," Brad said. "Until then, I say we do it Jeremy's way."

I wanted to argue the point more, but I could see I was outnumbered.

"Okay, it's settled then," Angelique said. She then turned, reached underneath her recliner, and pulled out what appeared to be two long swords in black leather sheaths. We all stared at her, open mouthed, as she strapped the swords in an X to her back.

"What are those for?" Brad asked.

"Not getting killed again," Angelique said as she adjusted them on her back. "I have something for you too, Tucker." She reached into her back pocket and pulled out a pair of handcuffs, which she quickly cuffed to one of his wrists, and then to one of her own, before he registered what was happening. "It's for your own good," she said in response to his shocked look.

"Where'd you get all this stuff?" Tucker asked, looking dumbfounded.

"I brought them from home," she said with a shrug, like swords and handcuffs were household items everyone had tucked away in their sock drawers.

Tucker sighed dramatically. "A woman after my own heart."

●●●

Once we got the dirt bikes out of the garage we headed down a dirt path and through a meadow before turning north into the jungle. On the bikes we moved much faster in the astral than on the earth plane. As we drove through the jungle, the landscape transformed from one scene to the next in the blink of an eye—from a meadow to a valley with a river to back in the jungle. Then we emerged from the jungle and into another clearing, where what looked like an abandoned compound of old stone and brick buildings sat surrounded by a broken chain-link fence topped with rusty barbed wire. I guessed it was the old military base Angelique had mentioned.

The asphalt road leading into the base was cracked and worn, and the whole place was overgrown with foliage. The windows in the building closest to us, a large warehouse of some sort, were broken in many places, and there were vines growing up the side and in through the cracks in the windows. It was clear this place hadn't been occupied for a very long time.

"Dammit!" I heard Angelique yell over the sound of the bikes. Jeremy and I turned toward her. She was sitting on the bike by herself, looking at the empty handcuff hanging from her wrist. Tucker had disappeared again.

Jeremy stopped and turned off our bike, and Angelique and Brad followed suit.

"Where did he go?" Jeremy asked.

"I don't know!" Angelique said, her face red with anger. "But he's going to frickin' get it when I see him."

"I guess handcuffs don't work the same way here as they do in the waking world," I said.

"You think?" Angelique snapped.

Jeremy shook his head and was about to start up our bike again when a terrifying sound echoed through the jungle. I'd never heard anything quite like it before, but it sounded like a roar. A flock of birds flew up into the air, and I felt all the muscles of Jeremy's body tighten. Around us, the jungle became eerily quiet.

"What was that?" Brad whispered. His eyes were wide, and so were Dawn's. We looked toward the direction of the sound but saw nothing.

"Are there tigers on this island?" Dawn asked, her voice wavering.

The sound erupted again, cutting through the silence of the jungle. It was definitely a roar, and it sounded like it was coming from something much larger than a tiger. We all looked beyond the military base, in the direction of the roar. As we stared, the trees began to shake as if something very big and very strong were pushing through them toward us.

"That's no tiger," Brad said.

That's when I saw it coming through the trees in the distance—first just a flash of silver, then a long, sinuous shape. We continued to stare, frozen in place, as it stepped out into the clearing. It was a silver dragon, just like the one on Angelique's belt. Two giant horns stuck out from its large, scaly head, along with a crown of smaller spikes. Its mouth was beaked and pointed at the tip—one strike from that thing and you'd be torn in two, or maybe even three or four. It turned its head to the side to reveal its profile, and a red eye. Nothing good ever had red eyes. I was sure of that.

The minute the dragon spotted us it roared again and charged. There was no time to tell the others that the dragon on Angelique's belt had somehow come to life.

"Go! Go! Go!" Jeremy yelled as he started up the bike again, and I tightened my grip around him as we took off into the forest, back the way we had come.

The fear the dragon inspired was overwhelming, and even though

I continued to repeat to myself that I was dreaming, I found myself losing lucidity for a few seconds at a time. I shook my head, attempting to focus on the task ahead. Behind us I could hear the dragon roaring and crashing toward us, even over the loud motors of the bikes.

I turned around. The dragon was getting closer, barreling around the trees after Jeremy and me. Angelique, Brad, and Dawn had cut to the right and were disappearing through the trees. At least they were safe—for now.

I glanced back at the dragon again, heart in my throat, just in time to see it rear back and shoot a massive stream of fire out of its mouth at us. I screamed out a warning and Jeremy cut fast to the left. I felt heat grazing my side; then I found myself airborne. Jeremy had swerved too quickly and I had been thrown from the bike. I flailed helplessly in the air before hitting the ground hard and rolling to a stop against a tree.

I was dizzy and disoriented, but by some miracle I wasn't hurt. I sat up quickly, and when I looked around, found I was no longer in the jungle but in the middle of a long mahogany hallway. Jeremy and the others were nowhere to be seen. How I'd gotten there, I didn't know— but what I did know was that the dragon was about twenty yards away and charging right toward me. Heart pumping, I scrambled up and ran toward the other end of the hall as fast as I could. I didn't know how close the dragon was getting, but I could hear the pounding of its feet behind me and the heat from the fire on its breath.

I threw myself into a door at the end of the hall, yanking frantically at the handle, only to find it was locked. I spun around to see the dragon closing in fast. In desperation I kicked and pounded at the door, screaming for whoever was on the other side to open up.

"I say, dear girl. You'll never get anywhere that way," a voice said. "Can't you see that door is locked?" I jerked my head to the right, and I saw the man with the purple hat standing inside an open doorway just a few feet away. He looked exactly the way he had in my dream at Cedars-Sinai.

How had I not seen him or the second door before? Had they appeared magically, out of nowhere, or had they been there all along and I had just failed to see them? I didn't have time to ponder the situation. The dragon screeched again and a trail of fire shot down the hall toward us. I lunged toward the man with the purple hat and the open door. He deftly stepped aside, then pulled the door shut behind me as I fell hard onto the wood floor and scuttled backward, expecting the dragon to come bursting through the door any second.

"It can't get you now," the man with the purple hat said. "This door was a portal, but the portal is closed now. See?" He opened the door as I got to my feet, and I flinched until I saw it was now a closet filled with women's dresses. Looking around, I saw I was in a Victorian-era bedroom, complete with a four-poster bed, sitting area, and vanity. I looked out the window to see the island's swimming cove and what should have been the rest of the resort, except that most of the buildings that made up the resort were missing. I was back at the hotel, but in the past.

I was about to ask him what was going on when another door on the opposite side of the room opened and in walked Millicent Last. She looked fresh-faced and healthy, and was wearing a burgundy lace dress with gloves and pearls. Her short, dark hair was styled in soft waves, and she had an air of excitement about her. In her hand she clutched a letter.

I quickly scooted behind the bed to hide myself.

"That's not necessary," said the man with the purple hat, gesturing over at Millicent. "She can't see you, or me for that matter."

"And who are you, exactly?" I asked.

"You mean, you don't know?" He smiled at me mischievously.

"No!" I said. Then I thought again. "I do know you, from my dream at the hospital. You were in the elevator with me."

"That's good," he said. "That's very good." Then turned on his heel and walked out the bedroom door. As he did, a young blond woman in a maid's uniform rushed in. She was small and thin, and much of her hair was tucked up into a maid's cap.

"Is that what I think it is?" the maid whispered.

"Yes," Millicent said, "it's a letter from Charles. Shut the door, Alice. I don't want Mother to see!"

The maid did as she was told and then rushed over to Millicent to inspect the letter. The Charles that Millicent was talking about must be her brother-in-law, the one who'd died with her up at the lighthouse. I wondered what he was doing sending her a letter. It seemed inappropriate, especially back in those days.

"Oh, how exciting. Do open it!" Alice clapped and giggled.

Millicent opened the letter and began to read it, relaying the information as she went.

"He's still with the spiritualists in Los Angeles. He says they want me to write a book for them about what they're doing. Can you imagine? Me, writing a book about spiritualism? Mother would have a heart attack."

"Why not?" Alice said. "You used to write for the papers."

"Yes, until Mother put a stop to that," Millicent said with a scowl. "She doesn't approve of anything I do. But spiritualists don't care about 'shoulds' and 'supposed tos.' They could care less about social etiquette. They're the strangest people, and yet ever since we met them, I feel like I belong with them somehow."

"I feel the same way," Alice said.

They looked at each other for minute.

"Maybe we could visit them in Los Angeles!" Alice said. "Get to know them better, like Charles is doing. Roald wouldn't need too much convincing to go to LA, and then we could sneak away for the day and see them."

Millicent's eyes widened with interest, but she shook her head. "I can't just go sneaking off with fortune tellers and conjurers. What would people think?"

"Why couldn't you do it in secret?" Alice asked.

"I'm so tired of doing everything in secret, Alice. I've got so many secrets I can't keep them all straight these days. Oh, how I dream of the day when I don't have to abide by everyone else's rules."

"But what about the nightmares you've been having? The ones about Roald, up on the cliff? What if they're some sort of premonition and you're in danger?"

"In danger from Roald? Don't be silly. He may be a drunk and a poor excuse for a husband, but he'd never hurt me. Not like he does in my dreams, anyway."

"Yeah, I think you're wrong on that one," I said in response, despite the fact that I knew Millicent couldn't hear. I was obviously being shown this scene for a reason. Perhaps Millicent was trying to tell me that Roald had been the one to push her and Charles off that cliff. If they'd been having an affair it would have been a strong motive.

"The dreams have got to mean something," Alice said. "Perhaps the spiritualists might be able to help."

The two continued to argue, but they began to fade away into a gray fog. As I tried to adjust my eyes, I realized that the gray fog was actually smoke. After a few seconds it cleared somewhat and I saw that I was now back in the forest—and the whole place was on fire.

I looked around and felt panic rise in me once again. Hot smoke was swirling all around me. I could still see several yards in front of me, but it wouldn't be that way for long. I started through the forest, but the smoke caught in my lungs, causing me to choke and cough. I pulled my shirt up over my mouth, and that helped; I could still breathe for now. But for how long?

I heard familiar voices yelling up ahead, and then the terrible roar of the dragon. I was back on the astral plane, in the present. My friends were still alive—and still in trouble.

"Jeremy! Angelique!" I called out. The smoke burned my eyes, and I still couldn't see more than a few yards ahead of me.

I was starting to make my way toward the voices when I saw a shadow coming toward me through the smoke. I froze, scared out of my wits, not sure whether to scream or run. I opted for neither. Instead, I stayed perfectly still as the shadow got closer, until finally a little girl in a white nightgown stepped out of the smoke in front of me. Her face was smudged with soot and stained with tears. When her eyes met mine, they filled with relief.

"Help me!" she said, running toward me. She couldn't have been more than four or five years old and had long black hair and big brown eyes. Her face was filled with panic. "He's going to get me."

I paused. This was a dream, after all; even a little girl could be dangerous. But looking at the tears running down her face and considering a dragon was on the loose and setting the whole jungle on fire, I decided she was most likely an innocent and needed my help.

"It's okay," I said, reaching out to the girl. As she looked up at me I saw she had a splattering of tattooed stars across her neck. They were just like Angelique's.

The monster roared again and the child jumped into my arms.

"Please don't let it get me. Please!" she cried, burrowing into me. "Please!"

I held her tight. "I won't," I said. "I promise."

My mind whirled as I tried to understand how Angelique had reverted to her child self—if that was indeed what had happened.

The forest was continuing to fill with smoke, and behind us a tree crashed to the ground. I spun around to see a large, dark shadow moving toward us through the flames and smoke. Angelique's dragon.

With the child still in my arms, and my heart beating a mile a minute, I turned and ran as fast as I could. But even though the little girl was small, she was heavy; I knew I wouldn't be able to get very far. How was I supposed to keep her safe? I was nothing against a fire-breathing dragon—lucid or not.

The little girl screamed again and I whipped my head around to see the dragon breaking through the smoke behind us. My blood ran cold.

Then out of the smoke sprang Angelique. The adult version of Angelique, swinging her swords. She sliced the dragon broadside across the face, and it reared back and screamed out in pain.

Then I felt hands on me, and I turned defensively, ready to fight off whatever it was—but it was only Jeremy, pulling us to safety behind a tree where Brad and Dawn were already hiding.

"We thought we lost you," Jeremy said as we all huddled against the large tree for safety. His face was sweaty and smudged with soot.

"What's going on?" I asked. I could explain my foray into Millicent's past later.

"Angelique," Jeremy said. "She's going after that dragon like she has some personal vendetta against it."

"She's lost lucidity," Brad said. "Has anyone else noticed that this dragon is identical to the one on that belt she wears every day?"

I nodded.

"Do you know what it represents?" he asked.

"We were just talking about it earlier, at lunch," I said. "That belt was her father's. He was very abusive. He used to . . ." I didn't know how to finish without betraying Angelique's confidence. "Hurt her."

"Okay." Brad said, nodding that he understood. "So the dragon most likely symbolizes Angelique's father, and a deep-seated betrayal. That explains why she's going after it."

"We tried to help her, but she said it wasn't ours to fight," Jeremy said. He turned his attention to the little girl in my arms, who was still clinging to me like her life depended on it. "Who is this?"

"I think," I said, pulling the girl's hair aside to show him the stars across her neck, "that it's Angelique as a little girl."

Jeremy's eyes went wide. I looked over to Brad, who didn't miss a beat.

"This is the soul loss Micah was talking about earlier today," Brad said, studying the girl. "How pieces of us can break off and seek refuge in nonphysical reality. Well, guess where we are."

"We need to get this child out of here," Jeremy said. "Away from the dragon."

"No," Brad argued. "What we need to do is get her back where she belongs. Reunited with the adult version of herself. Soul loss occurs when a piece of yourself breaks off because of some sort of trauma. The abuse that Angelique suffered as child must have been too much for her to bear, so part of her broke off and came here."

"I thought Micah was speaking symbolically," I said. "I didn't know these pieces of us were real."

"It's not real," Brad said. "Everything on the astral plane is symbolic."

I didn't have time to get into a metaphysical debate. Besides, Brad was right. We had to get Angelique back together again.

"But how?" I asked.

"Jeremy and I can try to distract the dragon while you get Angelique's attention and help her reunite with this lost part of herself," Brad said.

"Wait, you want *me* to try to get through to her?" I asked. "I don't know anything about soul loss or any of this stuff, Brad. This is your domain."

"The girl came to you, Max. And Angelique confided in you," he said. "This is for you to do."

Something in me knew Brad was right. I'd made this little girl a promise that I'd keep her safe, and if the safest place for her was back with Angelique, then that was where she needed to go.

I looked out into the clearing next to us, where Angelique was still battling the dragon. She was burned badly on her arms and chest, and her face was singed and covered in soot, but she wasn't letting that slow her down in the least. All the martial arts training she had done had paid off; she was working those samurai swords like a master.

I took a deep breath, and Jeremy looked over at me expectantly.

"You ready?" he asked.

I nodded, and he grabbed an orange flare gun out of the back of his pants.

"Where'd you get that?" I asked.

"Angelique wasn't the only one who thought about bringing a weapon," Jeremy said. "This was the closest thing to a gun I could find on the island."

"But how much damage can you do with a flare gun?"

"Look, I know it won't kill it," Jeremy explained, "but if I can hit the dragon in the right place it may give you enough time to get through to Angelique."

"Okay. Do your worst," I said. *And please don't get toasted*, I added silently.

Jeremy nodded, took a deep breath, then ran out to the clearing. Luckily, the dragon was busy with Angelique and didn't notice him. Jeremy snuck up alongside the dragon and fired, striking it in the side of the neck, and it reared back, screeching in pain. It turned on Jeremy, and I thought for a moment it was going to attack—but instead it flew off into the smoke.

"What are you doing!" Angelique screamed at Jeremy as she watched the dragon fly away. "This is my battle to fight! Not yours!"

She was about to take off after the dragon when I hurried out into the clearing with the little girl in my arms. "Angelique," I cried. "Wait!"

She spun around, and as I approached her I saw that her eyes had a glazed-over look to them—she was lost to the dream.

"Please stop," I said, speaking more calmly as I walked toward her. The little girl trembled in my arms, burying her face in my neck.

"Stop what?" Angelique hissed back at me. She continued to hold her samurai swords in each of her hands, poised and ready to fight me if necessary.

"Stop fighting. That dragon isn't real. It's a personification of your anger at your father. We're dreaming. Remember?"

"How dare you tell me what happened to me wasn't real!" she cried. "You weren't there. You don't know. I'm going to make him pay, and no one is going to stop me!"

Her need for revenge was stronger than her fear of pain or death, and it was keeping her obscured in a nightmare, just like the soldiers in the west woods.

"No, Angelique," I said. "That's not the way."

"Look what he did to me," she cried, looking down at the burns on her body, which were now quite bad. "He's destroyed me, Max. He has to pay!"

"He didn't destroy you," I said. "You're still here. You're all here. Look." I glanced down at the little girl in my arms, who still had her face buried in my chest.

Angelique eyed the little girl and paused for a moment. I had her attention.

"Part of you had to leave for a while, but she's safe. She's right here. And she's ready to come home." I pulled the girl's hair aside to reveal the side of her face.

Angelique's forehead wrinkled and she took a step closer. The little girl turned slightly and studied Angelique quietly.

The dragon's roar filled the clearing. I couldn't see through all the smoke, but it sounded like it was close.

Angelique, however, seemed to have forgotten the dragon for the moment. She was in some sort of a trance, staring at the little girl intently. She blinked and I could see a faint recognition in her eyes.

"I think I . . ." Angelique said slowly, her face softening. "I *do* remember."

"Is this the kind of home you want her to come back to?" I asked, looking around at the burning forest.

The dragon roared again. I could see almost nothing through the canopy of smoke, but I knew we only had a few seconds before it would be on us again.

Angelique looked down at her hands and back up at me, and the clarity returned to her eyes. "No," she said. "No it's not." She dropped the swords onto the ground then stepped forward and reached toward the child, who smiled shyly and stretched toward her. Angelique caught her up in her arms. "I'm so sorry, little one," she said. "I thought I needed to fight, but I don't, do I? Not like this."

Light emanated from where the two were touching, creating a glow that surrounded them both. Instantly Angelique's burns began to heal, the singed, bloodied skin regenerating into caramel flesh, until she was beautiful Angelique once again.

"I'm so sorry," she said to the child. "I thought he had destroyed you, but you'd only run away. You don't have to hide anymore. And you shouldn't. You're so . . . beautiful. Everyone should be able to see you. Isn't she beautiful, Max?"

Her teary eyes met mine and I nodded.

"So beautiful," I agreed, trying to keep from sobbing. I'd never truly seen another person actually witnessing their own inner beauty before—not like this.

Suddenly the dragon screamed out again, and I looked up to see a massive black shadow coming at us through the smoke from directly overhead. Before I could act, it broke through the haze, almost upon us. Jeremy dove for the swords on the ground, but it wasn't necessary.

Without taking her eyes away from the little girl, Angelique put her hand up toward the dragon, and just like that it came to a complete stop, frozen in the air just inches from us, like she had pushed pause on a remote control. It hovered there for a few seconds; then it exploded.

I threw up my arms, convinced we were all about to be engulfed in a fireball, but instead I felt light touches of warmth land on my face and body, and when I opened my eyes I saw a shower of golden sparks and white light raining down on us all. The sparks of light landed in our hair and eyelashes like fiery snowflakes, and dreamland ecstasy surged through my body once again. I allowed the feelings of bliss to flow through me. Each time another speck of light landed on my skin, I shivered with delight, feeling more calm, more peace, more safe than I ever had in my entire life.

23

"So," said Micah. "Today you experienced firsthand the way that painful emotions and past traumas reveal themselves in the astral. But they do it out here in the waking world as well, just not in the same way. What manifests as dragons and monsters in there shows up as limiting beliefs, negative thought patterns, and addictive behaviors out here. You ever wonder why you keep repeating the same kind of destructive patterns over and over again? It's because there's something inside you that's ready to be looked at and transformed."

It was eight o'clock, and the seven of us were sitting in the common room for our debrief. Though our session today in the astral had had a happy ending, there was an air of confusion in the room.

"We all have our own unique journey on the road toward higher consciousness," Micah said. "For most of us, it's not a direct route, and it's not always easy, or pretty—in fact, oftentimes it is incredibly painful. But as you continue to trust the process you will begin to shift out of fear and into love—into your authentic self. You will find parts of yourself that perhaps you've neglected, hidden, or forgotten about along the way. That's what happened with you today, wasn't it, Angelique?"

Angelique nodded. "Yes," she said. "I definitely found something today that I thought I had lost."

"And what was that, if you wouldn't mind sharing?" Micah asked.

"The power to heal," she said, tears pooling in her eyes.

Micah nodded in agreement. The rest of sat quietly.

"I also have the power to forgive," Angelique said, "but I'm not ready to do that yet."

"One thing at a time," Micah said.

She gave him a tiny smile and wiped the tears from her eyes with a balled fist, reminding me of the child version of her we'd seen in the astral.

"I want to thank you, Max," she said, turning to me.

I sat up a little on the couch at the mention of my name.

"Micah was right," she said. "You do have the power to remember—and it's a very important power. It may not be as obvious as Brad or Dawn's, but after experiencing what I did today, I think it may be the most important power of all."

I didn't quite know what to say. I couldn't take responsibility for what Angelique had experienced any more than anyone else could. I was still trying to figure out what had even happened.

Angelique looked back at Micah and said, "If you don't mind, I think I'd like to turn in early tonight. I have a lot to process."

"Of course," Micah said. Angelique gave the group another smile, then headed out.

Micah then turned his attention to Tucker. "Why don't we talk about you next. You seem to keep losing yourself in our sessions. Not just a piece, like Angelique had, but all of you."

All eyes turned to Tucker, who slunk down lower in his seat on the sofa across from Jeremy and me, his eyes focused intently on something on the floor.

"Where do you end up when you disappear from the group? Where do you go?" Micah asked, taking a sip of his tea. His voice held no hint of blame, but Tucker still appeared agitated.

"Like I said before, I get lost, man," he said looking up, his tone defensive. "I don't know." He held Micah's gaze for a few seconds, then turned away and said nothing else.

"Is there anything you'd like to share with the group today?" Micah asked after a long, awkward silence.

Tucker took a deep breath. "No," he said finally, placing his hands on his knees. "I'm going to head to bed as well. It's been a long week."

Jeremy and I exchanged a worried glance. Whatever was going on with Tucker wasn't good.

Micah nodded. "Okay, you guys. You've done great work this week. I know it might not feel like it but you have. Enjoy your weekend. Relax, get some sun and some exercise, and I will see you all on Monday."

●●●

"Have any of you guys talked to Tucker?" Jeremy asked after Micah had left the room. "Brad? He's your roommate. Has he said anything about where he goes during our sessions?"

"He won't talk to me," Brad said, shaking his head. "You've seen him. He's been getting more and more withdrawn. Whenever I ask him, he says he can't remember and changes the subject."

"Yeah, he says the same to me," Jeremy said. "I think one of us should follow him during our session on Monday. See where he goes."

"He's Angelique's partner," Dawn said. "Shouldn't she be the one to do it?"

"Angelique has enough to deal with right now," Jeremy said, rubbing his chin in thought. "Max, I think you should do it."

"Me?" I frowned.

"Yeah. Just like Angelique said, you seem to get the astral plane a little better than the rest of us."

"I don't know about that," I said. I was flattered Jeremy had that kind of confidence in me, but I still had a lot of doubts about my ability in the astral.

"It's possible that Tucker just loses lucidity and he really can't remember where he goes or what he does," Brad said. "Max, you disappeared for a while today. Do you remember what happened to you?"

"I do, actually," I said. "I found myself in a moment from my ghost's past."

"What kind of moment?" Brad asked eagerly.

"It was in the hotel—a conversation between her and her maid. It looked like she might have been having an affair with her husband's brother. They'd both been corresponding with some sort of religious sect in Los Angeles. She called them spiritualists." I shrugged. "Are any of you familiar with that term?"

"Absolutely," Brad said, sitting forward. "Spiritualists were quite popular in the twenties and are still around today. The church was founded on the belief that the spirits of the dead can communicate with the living, and many of their practices involve communing with the dead."

"So these spiritualists, they sit around and have séances and stuff?" I asked.

"Kind of," Brad said. "But they use their abilities to do awesome stuff too—predict the future, heal the sick, find missing people, things like that."

"So they're basically like us," Dawn said.

Brad chuckled. "Yeah, I guess so." He looked at me again. "What else did your ghost say?"

"Millicent mentioned that she was having this recurring dream about being with her husband up on the lighthouse cliff. It sounded somewhat ominous."

"Do you think he might have had a hand in her death?" Dawn asked, peering out from underneath her lavender bangs.

"I can't say it hasn't crossed my mind, but I don't have any proof either way. At this point, all I can do is wait for her to show me more in the astral or hope her niece will get back to me soon."

"Something tells me you won't have to wait for long," Brad said.

24

It was nice to take a break from all the ghosts, dragons, and other strange entities lurking around on the astral plane. I slept in on both Saturday and Sunday, went to Zumba and yoga classes with Zoe and Dawn, and even had time to relax and lie by the pool. For the first time since I'd gotten to the island, I actually felt like I was on vacation. Perhaps even Millicent Last sensed my exhaustion, because she left me alone the entire weekend.

By the time I arrived at the lab at three on Monday afternoon I was feeling refreshed from the weekend and ready for another session. Even our run to the lighthouse that morning hadn't seemed so bad.

Micah hooked us right up to the lucidity machine and sent us into the astral without much preamble. When I woke up on the other side, everyone else was already in, so we gathered our things and headed out.

"What's the plan today?" Angelique asked as we walked across the great lawn. A new softness had entered her face since Friday's events, and for the first time since I'd met her she was without her dragon belt. Dawn told me that over the weekend the two of them had gone up to the lighthouse together and tossed it into the ocean.

"Let's head north again," Jeremy said. "If it hadn't been for the dragon, I think we would have made it to Mango Beach the other day."

"I agree, but this time let's skip the bikes and take our time," Brad said. "When we're zipping around at high speeds it's difficult to pay attention to what's going on around us."

I kept an eye on Tucker as we walked north, feeling for the flare gun in my back pocket that Jeremy had given me earlier in the day. The idea was that once Tucker and I got to wherever it was he was going, I could shoot off the flare to alert the rest of the team.

We'd only been in the north woods about ten minutes before I noticed that Tucker was starting to flicker, like he was a hologram in a sci-fi movie—like he was about to disappear.

That's how he's been getting away from us so quickly, I realized. *He hasn't been running away from us at all; he has literally been disappearing!*

He flickered again, this time more dramatically.

"No, Tucker, wait!" I yelled and ran toward him. I attempted to tackle him, but instead of making contact with his body I went right through him, like he was made of air. Suddenly I was falling through nothingness in slow motion, and the air around me was swirling in blurry blues and grays. I flailed around in a panic, trying to grab on to something—anything—but there was nothing there.

After a few seconds the grayness began to clear, and I fell onto what felt like sand. I wasn't hurt, but I stayed where I fell for a moment—flat on my stomach, propped up on my elbows—and tried to get my bearings as the grayness dissipated. When I felt steady enough to stand, I got to my feet and looked around.

I was on the beach down by the swimming cove of the resort, probably a good mile away from where we'd been in the north woods. But how had I gotten there? And where was Tucker?

That last question was answered as soon as I turned around: he was walking up the beach toward the tiki bar lounge.

"Tucker!" I yelled, but he ignored me and continued walking. I brushed the sand off my clothes and watched him go. Was he conscious that he'd just teleported here? He'd gone from the north woods to the beach in a flash, and I'd gone with him. His body had acted as some sort of portal.

I was about to follow him when I heard the pounding of feet against wood to my right. I looked toward the sound and saw a black-haired woman in a knee-length white dress running down the pier toward a wooden boat that was pulling up to the dock. It was Millicent Last! This must be another flashback. Tucker would have to wait.

As I sprinted through the sand toward the dock I saw there was a man in the boat Millicent was running toward.

I reached the end of the dock just a hair behind Millicent and got a better look at the man in the boat. He was probably in his late twenties, tall and broad-shouldered, with wavy brown hair and green eyes. He was quite handsome, and was dressed in a cream suit with a baby blue tie.

As the green-eyed man tossed a small suitcase onto the dock, Millicent opened the parasol she'd been holding at her side and began to swirl it over her head.

"Why hello, Millie. To what do I owe this honor?" the green-eyed man asked with a grin as he climbed up onto the dock.

"Oh, don't be coy, Charles," Millicent said with a flirtatious smile. "You know I've been waiting here all day for you."

So this was the infamous Charles Last, Millicent's brother-in-law. But what was Millicent doing meeting him down here on the beach by herself? And where was Roald?

Evidently Charles was wondering the same thing, because his smile faded and he asked, "Where is that charming husband of yours?"

"You mean your charming brother? He's occupied with a young blonde at the moment, I'm afraid," Millicent said, suddenly finding something interesting to stare at by her feet.

"She wouldn't happen to be Myrna Banks, the actress, would she?" Charles asked, his tone sober.

"Yes." Millicent's eyes appeared to darken as she looked back up at him. "How did you know?"

"It's been in the papers," Charles said. "I can't believe he brought her to the island."

A shadow fell over Millicent's bright face. She looked past Charles out into the cove and became very still. "He used to at least have the decency to hide his affairs from me. I'm afraid I don't even merit that respect anymore."

"Millie, it's *your* respect he doesn't deserve. Not the other way around. I don't understand why you can't understand that."

"Mother says—"

"I told you not to listen to your mother. She's very old fashioned."

"Yes," Millicent said, looking down at her toes. "I suppose she is.

The truth is, I think she's secretly happy that he's turned out exactly the way she warned me he would."

"Well, I have something that's certain to cheer you up," Charles said, pulling an envelope out of his pocket and handing it to her. "It's a letter for you from our spiritualist friends."

She took it and smiled at him like he'd just handed her a deed to a house. "Thank you, Charles. Did you get to know them well while you were in Los Angeles? Do you think they'll be able to help you with your visions?"

"I believe so," he said, offering his arm to her. She took it and the two of them began to walk back down the dock together. I followed close behind, hanging on every word.

"What did they say?"

"They told me that I shouldn't try to stop the visions—that I can use them to help people."

"But how?"

"They said they could teach me. They want me to move to Los Angeles and work with them."

"But Charles," Millicent said, her voice plaintive, "you can't leave me here by myself. Not with Roald and my family. I'll fall apart without you."

"I'm quite aware of that fact," he said as they both came to a stop at the end of the dock. "That's why I want you to come with me."

"To Los Angeles? To live with the spiritualists?" Millicent's voice rose a whole octave. "Are you *crazy*?"

"We don't have to live with them, Millie," Charles said. "We can get our own place."

"Oh Charles, you can't be serious. I've caused enough scandal for my family as it is."

"I know it sounds strange," he persisted, "but I have the strongest feeling about this. Like I belong with these people—and you belong with them too. That's why you must come with me."

"Charles, you know that if I left Roald, my parents would disown me. I'd have nothing."

"You'd have me," he said, hurt in his voice. "Sure, we wouldn't be living in the style you're accustomed to, but at least we could be together. Plus we'd have a group of supportive people around us. And you know almost all of them already. You've been corresponding with them ever since we met them in New York."

"A pen pal does not a true friend make," Millicent said dismissively.

"What about this book they want you to write for them?" Charles said, all earnestness. "It will pay well, and they'll be wanting more books after that. And once I'm trained I'll be working for them too."

"Doing what?"

"Helping to change the world. Don't you want to be a part of the movement?"

"Oh Charles." Millicent sighed. "I do, but I'm just not as brave as you."

Charles reached out and took her gently by the shoulders. "You're being given a chance for a new life, Millicent—a life where you get to make your own rules instead of being shackled to the ones others have created for you. The world is changing, faster than you think. And now you have a choice to make. Are you going to stay with your family and be miserable? Or are you going to take a chance and go out and create a new life for yourself?"

Charles and I stood there and stared at Millicent. Her eyes were wide, and she was clutching at the handle of her parasol like she was holding on to it for dear life.

Just then a loud cheer went up at the tiki bar. I'd thought we were alone on the beach, but I was obviously wrong. I turned to see that the bar was filled with people—and they were all cheering as Tucker sat at the bar pouring a bottle of tequila down his throat. When I turned back to Charles and Millicent, they were gone.

I sighed and wondered if Millicent had decided to go with Charles to Los Angeles. They were definitely having an affair, regardless; perhaps Roald had found out and pushed them both off the cliff that fateful night. But that didn't explain how he had ended up drowning with them as well, or what Millicent was trying to tell me. I didn't have time to ponder all that right now, however. I had Tucker to deal with.

I walked over to the tiki lounge. Tucker was still sitting at the bar, his arm around a sickly woman who looked like she hadn't had a full meal or a shower in quite some time. The rest of the bar was filled with characters in the same state of affairs: tattered, stained clothes; gaunt, dirty faces; probably not a full set of teeth among the entire bunch. It seemed more like I was at a bar on skid row than a tropical island resort. Was this a moment from the past as well? I couldn't tell. I decided to try to talk to Tucker and see if he could hear me.

"What are you doing, Tucker?" I asked.

He put down the bottle of tequila he was holding, wiped his mouth, and looked at me through bleary eyes.

"What does it look like I'm doing, Red?" he asked with a rough chuckle. "I'm drinking. Why don't you sit down and join me?"

I was relieved to see he could hear me. That had to mean that we weren't somewhere in the past. Still, the situation wasn't good.

"This is what you've been doing here every day you disappear? Drinking?" I couldn't believe it. The rest of us had been working so hard to get to the lighthouse—getting shot at and attacked by a dragon—and here he was getting hammered. I had an overwhelming desire to knock him off his stool.

"You bet your beautiful ass I have," Tucker said, grabbing the bottle of tequila and finishing the bottle in one long swig.

I shook my head, then grabbed the flare gun out of the back pocket of my shorts, walked out from underneath the thatched hut, and shot it into the sky. The flare soared high above the resort, leaving a trail of bright light behind it. I hoped that the rest of the team was somewhere where they could see it, and they would get here fast.

I didn't want to go back into the lounge with all those grimy-looking people, but I couldn't leave Tucker in there alone. He wasn't lucid, and he was drinking—a very dangerous combination, as far as I was concerned.

I walked back in to find Tucker grabbing another bottle of tequila out of the well.

"Tucker, who are all these people?" I asked. "They look like they're in pretty bad shape."

"They're fine," he said with a wave of his hands.

I wasn't sure whether they were the astral bodies of sleeping people, the spirits of the dead, or something else. Either way, they were not the type of energies you'd want hanging around you while you were sleeping.

"Put the bottle down," I said. "It's time to go."

Tucker's smile faded and his eyes turned to slits. "You think you're so much better than me, don't you? The truth of the matter is, we're the same, Red. I use this to numb out," he said, lifting up his bottle. "And you use the future. You think you'll get a fancy job, or find a pill, that's going to take the pain of life away forever. At least this makes me feel better now. Your fix will never come. You're addicted to ghosts."

"What I'm doing isn't making me sick," I shot back.

"What are you talking about? You've been making yourself sick for years. But you keep striving, don't you? Keep looking for that magic pill. That magic job."

"Screw you, Tucker," I said, anger rising in me. "You don't know anything about me. Now, let's go!" I ripped the bottle of tequila out of his hand and impulsively threw it onto the floor.

The other patrons of the bar stopped what they were doing and shifted their attention toward me. I could feel the desperation in the air—feel them feeding on my anger—but I didn't care.

"I'm not going anywhere with you," Tucker said, glaring up at me.

"Why? Don't you see? These bottles aren't real!" I said, picking up a bottle of vodka out of the well and throwing it onto the ground. "None of this is real. We're dreaming. Do you understand? It's all an illusion! You think you're getting drunk, but you're not. They don't even stock alcohol at this bar in waking life. You've created these bottles with your imagination." I picked up another bottle and threw it to the ground, where it splintered into a thousand pieces.

"What are you doing?" the woman next to Tucker cried. "She's throwing it all away! Make her stop!"

"Leave it alone, Red," Tucker warned, slamming his fists on the bar and making everyone in the place jump, including me. "You don't want to make me angry right now."

I paused for a second, then went back to smashing bottles, one after another, onto the floor. The whole place smelled like booze, and glass sliced into my legs, but I didn't care. Tucker sat hunched over the bar, gritting his teeth and squeezing his hands into fists, and I knew I had only a few seconds before things erupted into violence, but I couldn't stop.

"Throw one more bottle on the ground. I dare you," he growled.

I took the last bottle from the shelf and a hushed silence fell over the bar. I saw the fear and rage in Tucker's eyes. I lifted my chin and released my grip on the bottle, and before the thing had even hit the ground, Tucker pounced.

The second his body collided with mine, I felt the wind go out of me. He knocked me backward, out of the bar, and we landed on the sand outside. Tucker's hands reached for my neck and I realized I'd taken this all too far. I was trying to get him to remember he was dreaming, not get strangled to death. The patrons rushed outside and circled us, some crying for him to stop, others egging him on. I ignored them. They weren't going to help me; I had to get out of this myself.

Tucker's hands squeezed tighter around my throat and hot pain shot up my neck. I had to somehow get through to him. But when I tried to scream at him to stop, nothing came out. His grip around my throat was too tight.

I clawed at Tucker's wrists, trying to pull his hands off me. I finally managed to loosen his grip around my neck, and I yelled the first thing that came to me, "Tucker! Remember!"

Instantly a bright light shot out of my hands and hit Tucker square in the face, lighting his whole body up like a light bulb. He fell back onto the ground next to me and lay there like he'd been hit by a stun gun.

I scrambled away from him and gulped for breath, my throat throbbing. I turned to look back at him, half expecting him to come after me, but instead he was sitting up and staring down into his hands, which were glowing bright. I had no idea what I had done. All I'd wanted was for him to remember that we were dreaming. Remember who he was—a good guy who was on my side.

Tucker looked up at me, blinking. Clarity had been restored to his eyes. "How did you do this?" he asked, holding out his palms. There I saw a map much like the one Millicent had showed me, glowing in the sun.

"I . . . I don't know," I stuttered as the map on his hands began to fade.

"I remember now," he said. "We're dreaming,"

"Yes." I let out a huge sigh of relief.

"This alcohol isn't even real," he continued. "I was getting drunk only because I believed it was real. But it's not. Here or on the earth plane. I've been feeling like I need to numb myself to deal with life, but"—he looked wonderingly down at his hands—"now I remember what I really came here to do."

"What's that?" I asked.

"I came here to help people," he said staring back at his palms. He was getting more information than he was able to relate to me. "And I can't do that if I'm drinking. What I need to do is become lucid there, just as we do here. I'm sure of it." He picked up a broken bottle from the ground next to him. "To think I tried to hurt you. Over nothing!"

I noticed the entities around us were now leaving the bar in droves. It was like they had lost interest now that Tucker wasn't drinking anymore and the drama was over. One of them, an unkempt man in a shabby, oversized suit, stood off to the side staring nervously out at the swimming cove. I knew that look well; I reluctantly followed his gaze, already knowing what I would see: a massive wave rising unnaturally high on the horizon.

"We don't have time for apologies, Tucker," I said, springing to my feet. "We've got to get out of here, now."

"Why?" he asked.

I pointed out to the horizon.

"Oh crap," he said as I helped him up. "Wait, Max. If we're dreaming, that wave really can't really hurt us, right? I mean, it's just an illusion. Just like the alcohol. Just like everything else here."

"It can't hurt us permanently, no," I said. "But dying here in the astral is just as painful as dying in real life."

"So what do we do?" he asked, rubbing his hands over his face. He appeared quite sober now. And why wouldn't he be? He hadn't really been drinking alcohol. He'd only been dreaming he was.

"Now," I said, "we run."

●●●

Tucker and I scrambled up the path toward the hotel and the great lawn at full speed, our feet smacking the cement loud and hard all the way up. Maybe, I thought, if we were able to get to higher ground, we might be able to avoid the wave that was now barreling straight toward the beach. As we ran out onto the great lawn we saw the rest of the team coming out of the north woods toward us. They'd seen my flare and followed it. Unfortunately.

"Go back!" I screamed at them, waving my arms. "Get to higher ground!"

I spun around to assess the situation. The water had already taken the beach and was in the process of crashing over the restaurant and lounge. We didn't have much time.

Seeing the wave rising up behind me, the group took no time in turning and running back the way they'd come. I could hear the trees breaking and buildings crumbling under the weight of the water surging up behind us. I looked back; it had swallowed up the entire resort. Part of me thought that maybe I should stop and face it, but that was crazy. Like Angelique had said, you can't fight a tidal wave. There was only one thing I could do.

I stopped running and shut my eyes.

"What are you doing?" Tucker asked, slowing down next to me. "Why are you stopping?"

Silently, I set my intention to wake up. When I felt the energy move through me, I snapped my fingers, and I felt the tug of the silver cord on my back pulling me backward. A few seconds later I woke up in my physical body, back in the lab. Everyone else was still asleep in their chairs.

I felt both overcome by relief and yet frustrated at the same time. I couldn't keep running from that wave—but what was the alternative? Even when it caught me it continued to haunt my dreams. What was I supposed to do?

I sighed, then reached over to the brass gong and pushed it over onto the floor.

25

"Tucker, why don't you start by sharing what happened with you in the astral today," Micah said. It was nighttime, and the seven of us were once again sitting in the great room for our debrief.

Tucker shook his head slowly. "Well," he said, looking up to the ceiling and pursing his lips together, "I've been telling you all that I was getting lost in the astral, but really, I knew what I was doing. I've been going in there and drinking down at the bar every day while the rest of you have been working so hard to get to the lighthouse."

It looked like he might break down, but then the moment passed. We all sat quietly as he gathered his thoughts.

"So you were lucid when this would happen?" Micah asked softly.

"Nah," Tucker answered, staring at the rug. "I didn't want to stay lucid, man. That's what drinking is about for me—checking out. And the truth is, it's easy to check out in a dream. The staying lucid part is what's hard. Both in there and out here. I tried to tell myself that because we were dreaming it didn't count. That drinking in the astral was actually a good thing, because there were none of the usual repercussions: no hangovers, no endangering myself or others. No consequences."

"But there were consequences, weren't there?" Micah asked.

"Yes," Tucker admitted. "I felt just as bad afterwards as I did when I was using. Coming back was like waking up from a nightmare. Maybe I didn't have a hangover or a DUI, but the guilt and the shame was just the same. So I'd tell myself I wouldn't do it again—but then the next day, the minute we got into the astral all I had to do was think about the bar and suddenly I'd disappear from wherever I was and appear at the bar with a drink in front of me. Once I was there, I forgot about everything else: the dream, the lighthouse, you guys, everything."

"And what do you think that means?" Micah asked, his tone calm and non-judgmental. "What do you think you're supposed to learn from this?"

Tucker shook his head back and forth slowly. "Coming to this island was supposed to be my chance to get sober, and I've been wasting it—or so I thought until today, when Max reminded me that I was dreaming. I can't remember all the details but I felt for the first time that there was something important I came here to do. I felt a divine presence—or whatever it is. The power of pure possibility. Pure grace. It was like nothing I'd ever felt." He looked at me, and a shadow crossed his face. "Thank you, Max. I'm so sorry that I hurt you in there."

I nodded my acceptance of his apology. Yes, he had hurt me, but the dream world was different than this world. Brad was right—in the astral, everything was symbolic. There wasn't much of a difference between thinking something and having it manifest before you. Your impulses realized themselves instantly, and you didn't always have the power to stop them—or at least none of our team did.

"So what is it you need to do then?" Micah asked.

"I need to recommit to the Lucidity Project as well as my twelve-step program. I haven't been taking either of them very seriously," Tucker said. "I think that's really the key to helping me remember what Max reminded me of today. I came here for a reason, and I intend to find out what that reason is."

Tucker looked sad, and yet his eyes were filled with hope. They were the eyes of a man who was ready to go to any length to change.

●●●

By the time I got back to my room it was almost ten o'clock, and Zoe was in bed reading *Ghost Hunting for Dummies*. She was wearing a frilly white baby doll top and giant black-rimmed glasses, and her hair was braided and wrapped around the top of her head, giving her the appearance of a nerdy but sexy milkmaid.

"Hi roomie," she said, looking up.

"Looks like you've found a new hobby," I said, nodding toward her book.

She grinned. "Listen to this," she said. "Ghosts exist in a state of confusion and often don't know what happened to them or even that they are dead."

"Yes, I get that part," I said. "What I really need to know, though, is how to get them to move on. Speaking of . . . any word from Frances?" Since I was so busy with the Lucidity Project I'd left my Facebook page up so Zoe could check to see if we'd gotten a response from Millicent's aunt.

"No," she said with a frown. "I can't believe she hasn't gotten back to us."

"Yeah, me either," I lied. The truth was, the message we'd sent her was pretty bizarre. I probably wouldn't have responded to it either. Not before, anyway. A lot had changed since I'd come to the island.

"You did get a message from Sofia, though," she said. "It seems urgent. Something about a promotion."

"Sofia?" In the past week I'd given very little thought to my best friend.

I ran over to the desk, sat down, and opened my laptop. Sofia was the first name in my list of messages. Her first lines read, "Earth to Max! You've been promoted! Where are you???"

Promoted? Was this a joke? I quickly clicked on the message and read the rest:

> I've been emailing and calling you all day. The new staff writer we hired is bailing on us for another show, so I convinced Evan to give you a shot. That means you need to be back in the writers' room by Wednesday. Wednesday, Max—as in, two days from now. So pull it together and get your ass back here ASAP!

I couldn't believe it. I'd been so wrapped up the Lucidity Project I hadn't checked my phone or messages all day and had almost missed the chance of a lifetime: a staff writing position on a prime-time television show. I reread the message, trying to get a hold of the thoughts swimming through my head.

"Everything okay?" said Zoe.

"Yeah . . . I got a promotion at work," I said, feeling more confused than happy.

"Is this good news?" Zoe asked hesitantly. "Because you kind of look like you're going to throw up."

"I feel like I'm going to throw up," I said, putting my head in my hands. A week ago this information would have sent me to the moon, but now I had a sour feeling in the pit of my stomach. Start on Wednesday? Today was Monday. That would mean I'd have to leave tomorrow. What about the Lucidity Project? What about Millicent Last's message?

"You know," Zoe said. "If you don't feel like going back home, there's a job opening in the kitchen. It's nothing fancy—just helping the chefs prepare meals and washing dishes—but then at least you could stay on the island."

Stay on the island? I lifted up my head and took a deep breath. "I think I need to take a walk."

"Good idea," Zoe said, getting out of bed. "I'll get my shoes. We can go talk it out, come back, make a pros and cons list—"

"No," I said, "I need to do this by myself."

She nodded her head in understanding, unfazed. "If you need to talk, I'm here," she said with a smile.

I gave Zoe a hug and headed out into the hallway, feeling nervous and edgy, like there was too much energy in my body. Before I even knew what I was doing, I found myself running down the hall, and then down the stairs to the main floor. A few people sitting on the porch turned to watch me as I raced out the front door, but I was too upset to care. Why was this job opportunity coming now? Why couldn't it have waited just a few more weeks, until I was done with the Lucidity Project? Now I was going to have to choose between the two most important things in my life right now—my dream job and the Lucidity Project. Whichever choice I made would affect my life forever. The pressure was just too much too handle.

It was only when my feet hit the cement path outside that I realized I was barefoot. I hesitated briefly, then took off again, toward the beach. *Am I overreacting?* I wondered. Maybe this job had manifested because of all the good work I was doing on myself; perhaps I'd already done everything I needed to do on the island, and this promotion was my reward. But if that was the case, why did I feel so conflicted?

A few minutes later, I found myself in front of Micah's house. I stood a few feet away from his door, wondering what the hell I was doing there. It was almost as if I had run there on autopilot.

I was just about to turn around and leave when the door opened. Micah stood there in grey sweatpants and a white T-shirt, his blond hair messy and out of place as usual.

"I got promoted to staff writer," was all I could say, trying to keep my voice from shaking. "They want me back to work on Wednesday."

A shadow fell over Micah's face. Suddenly I realized coming there was not a good idea. What kind of person runs over to their therapist's house at ten o'clock at night in their pajamas?

"I'm sorry," I said, backing up. "I shouldn't have come here. I know it's late."

I thought he was going to tell me to go back to my room, but instead he looked past me up into the night sky, sighed, and said, "No. In fact, you're right on time."

● ● ●

A few minutes later I was sitting on the old leather Chesterfield sofa in Micah's living room, feeling the roughness of his jute rug against my bare feet, which were still a little sandy from the running down the beach.

"What did you mean when you said I was right on time?" I asked as he set a cup of mint tea down in front of me.

"Often when we've started down a new path, we come to a crossroads—a junction in our lives where we have to make a choice between our old life and the new one that's trying to come forth. It's time for you to make that choice."

I sighed. Another cryptic answer. But for once I understood the gist of what he was saying. I needed to choose between my new job at the television show and the Lucidity Project. Not that I didn't know that already.

"I don't know what to do, Micah. Being a television writer has always been my dream. But you've done more for me in one week than anyone has in the past ten years. This is the first time in forever that I've had the energy to get up in the morning and make it through the day. My body is feeling stronger, and my mood is probably ten times better than it was when I got to the island. I want to stay here and work on the Lucidity Project, but if I do I'll lose this job. What should I do?"

Micah sighed. "I can't tell you what to do, you know that. I mean, don't get me wrong, I want to—but that's not the right thing to do."

"Okay, fine then, help me figure out what I think I should do, because right now I honestly don't know."

"Well," he said, "when I have to decide between two options I like to ask myself which one gives me power and which takes it away."

I frowned. "What do you mean?"

"Every decision we make either gives us power or takes it away," he said. "There is no in-between. And I'm not talking about external power. I'm talking about soul power. The power of your spirit. Your core essence."

I thought about my dream job. It would give me money, status, make me feel accomplished and successful. But the work itself was incredibly draining. Sitting in a room for upwards of ten hours a day trying to write a television show by committee was beyond stressful for a highly sensitive, easily overstimulated person like me.

"Okay, so maybe being a writers' assistant doesn't energize me," I admitted, "but this new job as a staff writer might. It's what I've always wanted."

"Something that drains your power now will never lead to more power in the future," Micah said, shaking his head.

"Yeah, well we don't all have the luxury of winning the lottery and being able to choose a job that makes us happy, Micah."

"I manifested my money by following my path and doing something that made me happy," Micah replied. "Not by doing something I thought *should* make me happy."

"So you're telling me to give up my dream?"

"I'm not telling you that—your own life is telling you," Micah said, standing up and facing me. "You're so good at staying lucid and reading cues in the astral. Now it's time to use those powers in the waking world."

"Like how?"

"Take a look at your life," Micah said. "You work at a job that you hate, so much so you wanted to end your life. You worry constantly about what people think about you, especially the people you call your friends. You live your whole life according to rules made by other people—and then you wonder why you're drained and miserable. Until you learn how to honor your authentic self you will continue to be unhappy, and continue to manifest circumstances that make you unhappy, even once you accomplish your so-called dream. The answer is staring you right in the face. Why don't you see it?"

I looked up at him, stunned into silence. What could I say? Every damn thing he'd said was true. No matter how much I wanted to, I didn't like my job, and I wasn't going to like this new job, either. During the past two years on the show I'd gotten even more run-down and depressed than I'd ever been before. Sitting in the writers' room all day long wasn't exhilarating for me, it was exhausting. And being promoted to staff writer would only mean more hours in that room, more stress, more responsibility—more of all the things that drained me. I thought my depression was keeping me from enjoying myself in the writer's room, but the truth was that I was depressed because I didn't belong there. Maybe that was part of why I had been unhappy for so long: I was always trying to fit myself into places where I didn't belong in the first place.

The tears came fast and hard and there was nothing I could do to stop them. Couldn't I have one conversation with Micah that didn't end with me crying?

"I thought you said you weren't going to tell me what you thought I should do," I said as a tear rolled down my cheek.

"I thought so too," he said with a sigh, and he sat back down next to me. I leaned against his shoulder and cried for the dream I'd held for so long, the one I'd convinced myself would solve all my problems and make me the person I'd always wanted to be: successful, confident, and, most of all, happy. It was like I was going through some kind of terrible breakup, but worse.

After a few minutes the tears subsided and I looked back up at Micah. "So what am I supposed to do now?"

"Go toward what is working," he said, wiping a tear off my face.

I sat and thought for a moment. "The only thing that's working in my life is what we're doing here," I finally said. "But I can't pay my bills by lucid dreaming all day."

Micah grinned. "Who says you can't?"

"I'm not like you, Micah. You've cut out a great niche for yourself here with this New Age guru thing, but you really believe in all of it. You really believe that I'd magically be able to make a living and become a happy person if I just had faith in the universe, or whatever it is you think is running the show. That's not who I am. I'm glass half empty. You're glass half full."

"You think I was always glass half full?" he asked, an amused look on his face.

"You're going to tell me you were just like me once? Yeah, right." I practically snorted.

"I was," he said. "Not in this life, of course, but the one before."

I cocked my head at him. Leave it to him to get all *woo woo* in the middle of a serious discussion. "Okay, Micah. Fine," I said. "Tell me about how you used to be just like me in your *past life*. Did you have to give up your dream of being a television writer to cavort with hippies on a Caribbean island, or did you just have an underlying sense of anger and depression that you couldn't quite get a handle on?"

"More the second one," he said, ignoring my sharp tone. "I also did a lot of cavorting—with alcohol mostly, but also with women. Like you, I forgot about my purpose here—my mission—and in the process, I hurt I lot of people deeply."

"Why are you telling me all this?" I asked, turning to face him on the couch. "You know that I have a hard time believing in past lives."

"I know you do. I'm telling you to remind you that people can change. You can make changes in this life or wait till the next one to do it, but putting them off will only prolong your own suffering, as well as the suffering of others."

"You're talking about the message I have for the world again, aren't you?"

"I am," he said, suddenly looking very sad.

"Why do you care so much about this message anyway, Micah?"

"Because," he said, touching my cheek softly, "I've come here to help you remember it."

He looked down at me sympathetically, the way a person might look at a young child while trying to explain the concept of death or divorce, something they couldn't possibly understand. I looked deep into his crystal blue eyes, as if I might possibly find what I was looking for there, and a sleepy spell seemed to come over us both, something wonderfully and habitually familiar that reminded me strangely of home. A burning magnetic energy flared in the space between us, and I leaned in closer to him, so that our lips were almost touching. Everything felt so natural, as if we had rehearsed this moment hundreds of times before.

"What do you mean, you've come here to help me remember?" I whispered.

The sound of my words had a sobering effect on Micah, and I watched as awareness sprang back into his eyes. He quickly untangled himself from me and shot up from the couch, the hand that had been touching my face now running through his messy hair.

"I mean," he said, "that's what I'm here to do. Help people remember who they are. I don't want you to make the same mistakes I made in the past."

"That's not what you meant," I said, staring up at him. My face felt red and flushed, and I was hyperaware of the space next to me where he had just been.

He took a deep breath. "I've told you everything I can right now, Ms. Dorigan. It's late. I think you should probably go."

His words stung, and anger flared up inside me. I wasn't sure exactly what had just happened, but I felt manipulated somehow. I stood up and took a step toward him. He stared back at me again with a sympathetic look in his eyes, as if he wanted to explain something to me I couldn't possibly understand.

"You know, for someone who's trying to help me, you sure are messing with my head," I said. I stood there for a few seconds, searching his face for something—anything—that would make me feel better, but I found nothing.

As I headed out the door I could have sworn I heard him say, "Old habits are hard to break."

●●●

Sofia was as confused as I expected her to be when I called her the next day and told her that not only would I not be taking the job as staff writer, I wouldn't be returning to *You Sexy Witch* next season at all.

"Max, don't get carried away by this rehab self-help crap," she said. "This same exact thing happened to a friend of mine. She went to rehab, got on their pink cloud of rainbows and unicorn farts, quit her job, and moved to India. It took her two months before she came to her senses and realized what she had done. She came home and immediately relapsed."

"I'm not going to relapse," I said with a big sigh.

"You can't know that for sure."

"Yes, I can," I said. "The truth is, I'm not in rehab. Not for alcohol addiction, anyway. I tried to kill myself a few weeks ago and I'm here getting help for my depression."

"What?" she asked.

"I'm sorry I lied to you," I said, trying not to choke on the words as they tumbled out of my mouth. "The truth is, I was too ashamed to tell you the truth."

"Oh my God, Max. I don't know what to say. What have you been depressed about? Not getting this job? Because now you have it!"

"No," I said, "I've had depression for most of my life. It's not about the job. It's never been about the job." I was tempted to go on, but I knew I wouldn't be able to explain my depression to Sofia, and I didn't really want to try.

"But maybe if you take this job it might help to alleviate some of that," she said.

"I thought so to," I said. "But that's just not the case."

"But you won't really know until you try," she argued. "You've been working so hard for so long for this. What was the point of schlepping scripts and coffee around for the past couple years if you're just going to throw it all away now?"

"I know it doesn't make sense," I said, my heart thumping in my chest. "I'm just working out some stuff here, and I've realized that as much as I want that job it's not what I'm supposed to do."

"Supposed to do?" Sophia sounded confused. "What are you talking about?"

"I don't know yet," I said. "But I'm not coming back until I find out."

26

"Today I want to talk about signs," Micah said.

The seven of us were sitting in our chairs in the lab, ready for another afternoon of dreamtime. Our last few attempts to get to the lighthouse had all been unsuccessful: If we went down to the beach, the tidal wave came and I had to wake us up. If we went into the west woods the soldiers attacked. If we went into the north woods to try to cut around through Mango Beach we lost lucidity. We seemed to be out of options. Now it was Friday and we were all pretty frustrated. We only had a little over a week left of the program and we were no closer to getting to the lighthouse than when we'd first gone into the astral.

"What kind of signs?" Tucker asked.

"The kind of signs that help guide you to where you're supposed to go," Micah answered.

"Like the map that appeared on my hands?" Tucker asked.

"That's right," Micah said. "But that was a very obvious sign; as we go through life, signs are usually a lot more subtle than that, and if we aren't paying attention we can miss them. The same goes for signs in the astral. That's why it's important to stay alert and lucid."

"But we're trying, and it's not working," Angelique said.

"The reason you're having such difficulty getting to the lighthouse is because you're taking a human approach," Micah said. "And the truth is, you're not human. You are spiritual beings having a human experience. On the astral plane, you're all spirit—so it's time to tap into your natural way of doing things, and that's sensing and feeling things out with your intuition and not letting yourself be limited by time, space, or physicality."

"But how?" Tucker asked.

"Pay attention to the signs," Micah said.

"So what, exactly, constitutes a sign?" I asked.

"Mysterious coincidences, repeated occurrences, symbols, synchronicities, sometimes even thoughts—anything that captures your attention or makes you curious, including those things that make you upset or fearful. These are signs meant to give you support or direction."

"Anything that makes us upset or fearful?" Dawn mumbled as she reached for her headset. "In that case, the entire astral plane must be one big sign."

●●●

Minutes later, the six of us were in the astral heading out onto the great lawn.

"So what are we looking for?" Angelique asked, adjusting the swords on her back. I wasn't sure why she'd brought them. They hadn't seemed to help her too much against her dragon.

"Like Micah said," Brad said. "Something that gets our attention."

"But everything looks the same as it always does when we come out here," said Angelique.

Angelique was right. The great lawn didn't look any different. Green grass, coconut trees, blue sky, even the black raven that always seemed to be out here was ahead of us, pecking at the grass. As we continued forward it took off and flew toward the east woods, then landed behind us a few yards away. I realized that it did that every time we came out onto the lawn. Maybe it meant something.

"What about that?" I said, nodding at the raven.

"The bird?" Jeremy said skeptically.

"The raven," I said.

"Max could be onto something. In many ancient cultures, the raven is an omen of magic and synchronicity," Brad said. "When you see a raven in your dreams it's supposed to be a signal to watch for clues."

"Yes, that's right," I said, my heart beginning to beat faster. "It's helped me out before. C'mon. Let's follow it."

Before Jeremy or anyone else could argue I took off after it across the green. The raven let out a loud caw and zigzagged up into the sky in front of me.

"This makes no sense, Max," Jeremy shouted after me. "It's flying in the opposite direction of the lighthouse."

I ignored him and kept running until the raven flew up and landed on a tree branch at the eastern edge of the great lawn.

The rest of the team caught up to me seconds later.

"What are we supposed to do over here?" Tucker asked, looking around.

Just then, ahead of us, a blindfolded woman stumbled barefoot out from behind a tree in the jungle. She looked to be in her mid-twenties and was wearing only a man's ratty T-shirt. She was dirty, her hair was matted, and she had scrapes and bruises on her arms and legs. She held her hands out as she slowly picked her way along.

"What the hell kind of sign is this?" Tucker asked.

"That's the woman I've been seeing in my visions," Jeremy said, stepping forward.

"Then you should be the one to go talk to her," Brad said.

"I've tried before. Many times," Jeremy said. "I can't seem to get through to her. She doesn't make sense when she talks. None of them ever make any sense."

"Like I've told you before," Brad said, "the dead often don't know they're dead. They're stuck in a dream—or, in this case, a nightmare."

"You don't understand," Jeremy said as he headed into the forest toward the woman. "This woman *isn't* dead. She's alive."

The rest of us followed a few steps behind, our feet making crunching sounds in the underbrush. The woman sensed us coming and dropped into a defensive crouch.

"Who's there?" she whispered, holding her hands out as if she were attempting to ward us off. My heart ached for her; she was obviously frightened to death. I reminded myself to stay lucid, and not to get lost in the drama of the situation.

"I'm a friend," Jeremy said, approaching cautiously. "We're here to help."

"What do you mean she's not dead?" Tucker whispered to the rest of us. "She looks like a ghost to me."

"Dead?" the young woman asked. She'd somehow overheard us talking. "I'm not dead yet! But he's going to come back. Please help me!"

"We want to help you," Jeremy said, taking her outstretched hands. "What's your name? Where are you?"

"Where am I?" She attempted to look around despite the blindfold, then shook her head. "I don't know. I can't see. He's going to come back. Please don't leave me. Please."

"Who's going to come back?" Jeremy asked. "Who are you with?"

The woman appeared confused and tried to look around again. When it was clear she wasn't going to answer, he tried another tactic.

"Let me help you take that blindfold off," Jeremy said.

"You can't take it off," she said, pulling away from him. "He put it there. I'll be in trouble if I take it off."

Jeremy looked over at us, lost for words. Brad motioned for him to continue.

Jeremy swallowed. "I'll put it back on in a second," he said. "I promise."

She bit her lip nervously, then nodded her assent. Jeremy let go of her hands and carefully untied the blindfold, but when he removed it, there was an identical one underneath it.

Dawn gasped.

Jeremy looked back at us, equally disturbed.

"Jeez," said Tucker. "What does that mean?"

"It means," Brad said, "that this woman is in serious trouble, and we must find a way to help her."

"I told you it wouldn't come off," the woman said sadly.

Jeremy took her hands again.

"How about your name? Can you tell us your name?" he asked urgently.

The woman touched her blindfold, then leaned over to Jeremy and whispered, "He's taken my name."

Jeremy looked up at us for help.

"You're up, Max," Brad said.

"What do you mean?" I asked. I didn't have any experience with this sort of thing.

"You need to help her remember who she is, just like you did with Tucker and Angelique." He put a hand on my shoulder. "That's what you're good at. Helping people remember who they are."

The raven had gotten my attention and led us here, so we were obviously here for a reason. I had no idea how to help this woman, but it couldn't hurt to try.

I approached Jeremy and the woman and softly said, "I'm a friend too."

Jeremy looked relieved as she let go of his hands and grasped on to mine. They were cold—deathly cold. From the look of her frail, undernourished body and the feel of her hands it was clear she was in terrible trouble. I shut my eyes and tried to imagine the map on her hands but nothing happened. I felt my heart sink.

I tried again to replicate what I had done with Tucker. Setting an intention, then commanding, "Remember!"

"Remember what?" she whispered.

I realized we were probably speaking to only part of this woman's personality—like Angelique's fragmented little girl self. And that gave me an idea. Perhaps if we asked this woman smaller questions, simpler questions, that might help her to remember. This part of her had to have its own memories, right? Maybe we could glean something from them.

"Okay," I said gently, "why don't we start out with an easier question. Just tell me the first things that come to your mind."

"O-okay," she stuttered, her hands fluttering in mine.

"Think back and tell me. What was your favorite thing to do when you were a little girl?"

Jeremy and the others stared at us, their bodies taut with anticipation.

"I . . . I liked to play in the forest behind my house," she said.

"Where was your house?" I asked.

"In . . . Texas!" she said, her face brightening. The memory seemed to lift her spirits.

"That's good," I said, looking over at Jeremy, who motioned for me to keep going. I turned back to the young woman.

"Do you remember where in Texas?" I asked.

The woman stopped for a moment and I could see her face strain as she tried to remember.

"No!" she finally cried out sadly. "He's taken everything. He's taken it all from me!"

"Okay, okay. Let me ask you another question." I rubbed her hands lightly, trying to soothe her as my next line of questioning came to me: "Who do you love more than anyone in the world?"

"My mother," she said. "I miss her so much."

"Do you remember that funny nickname she used to call you when you were a child? It always made you laugh."

"Mandy Pandy," she said right away, lighting up at the memory. "She used to call me Mandy Pandy."

"Amanda?" I asked.

"Yes, that's it!" she said, smiling. "My name is Amanda!" She let go of my hands and put them over her heart, as if that's where her name had resided all along.

I let out a deep sigh and looked back to the team, grateful to be a witness to this woman getting a piece of herself back. Apparently, there was more than one way to remember who you were. A map was not always necessary.

Just then Amanda jerked her head around as if she'd heard something in the forest and pulled her hands away. "Oh no. He's coming," she said, and her body flickered a little, the way Tucker had before he'd disappeared to the tiki bar.

"We're losing her. I think she's waking up," Brad said.

"What's your last name?" Jeremy asked quickly. He reached out to grab her, but she'd already begun to dematerialize, and he ended up grabbing nothing but air. "Where in Texas?" he demanded—but she flickered once more and then disappeared altogether.

"She's gone," I said. My heart sank at the thought of the horrors she must be waking up to.

We all stood there in the silence for a few moments, staring at the place where Amanda had been.

"Hey," Jeremy said, touching my shoulder.

I looked up.

"That was really good, Max," he said. "Really good. Now I have a name and a state."

"That's not a lot to go on," I said.

"Maybe not," Jeremy said. "But it's more than I've ever gotten from any of them before."

● ● ●

"So let me get this straight," Tucker said. "You've seen that woman before in your dreams?"

"Not just in my dreams," Jeremy said. "I get hallucinations sometimes—of people coming to me for help. I have ever since the war."

We were walking at a steady pace toward the military base, carefully making our way through the thick jungle while scanning the surrounding areas for anything out of the ordinary.

"So how do you know they're alive?" asked Tucker skeptically.

"Because they tell me they are," Jeremy said with a shrug.

"But how do they know how to find you?" Tucker asked.

"I don't know," Jeremy said, shaking his head.

"It's your gift," Brad said.

"Yeah," Dawn said. "It's like how spirits and other entities have always known how to seek me out. You're, like, a medium for the living."

"Maybe they're guided to you both by whatever it is that's helping us in here," I said.

"I honestly don't care how they find me," Jeremy said. "All that matters is that I help them. That's all."

As we came out of the jungle and into a grassy meadow, a rumbling sound arose from up ahead in the distance, followed by a bone-chilling chorus of shrieks. At first I thought it might be the dragon again, but the sound was different. I peered in the direction where the sound was coming from—and my mouth went dry. About a mile or two away, on a large, grassy hill beyond the jungle to the north, was what could only be described as an army of monsters—and they were headed straight for us. From here they looked like a pile of ants blanketing the hill, but of course they couldn't be ants. If we could see them from here they had to be huge. The size of gorillas, or even larger. My heart dropped into my stomach.

"What the hell are those?" Tucker started. We all took a few steps backward and huddled together as they continued to barrel down the hill toward us.

"Those are my demons," Dawn whispered, her pale face going even whiter than normal.

I thought of the creature Dawn had claimed to see on the stairs of the hotel the first day we'd arrived. I hadn't believed her then, but I knew better now. I'd seen the picture she'd drawn depicting a gruesome-looking monster with claws for hands and a face full of pointed, shark-like teeth—and now here was an army of them descending toward us at breakneck speed. Good God. No wonder she was such a nervous wreck all the time.

Dawn reached up and grasped at her neck for her crystal, then looked up at us, her voice trembling. "My crystal! It's gone! It's the only thing that could protect us and it's gone!"

"Dawn, remember, we're dreaming," I said quickly. How that made this situation any less frightening I didn't know. If we all lost lucidity, however, things would go downhill fast.

"We have to get out of here," Dawn said, panic rising in her voice.

"Dawn," Brad said, stepping forward and grabbing her shoulders. "Listen to me. You don't need that amulet. You have all the power you need inside yourself. Micah made up the stuff about it protecting you. Crystals aren't that strong."

"Brad's right," I said. "Whatever these things are, you need to face them, just like Angelique faced her dragon. In the end she defeated it on her own without weapons, without an amulet. Maybe if you face them, they'll finally leave you alone."

"Face them! Are you crazy? Let go of me," she screamed, pulling away from Brad. "Don't you see? If we don't get out of here, they're going to kill us all!" She attempted to run, and I grabbed her—but even as I did, I realized it didn't matter whether she was dreaming or not. Dawn was scared of these things even in the waking world. She yanked her wrists out of my grasp and took off across the meadow, back toward the resort.

"Dawn, wait!" I yelled after her as she disappeared into the jungle.

"We need to go after her," Brad said, already moving in that direction. We took off at a jog after him.

"Yeah, but what's the plan once we catch her?" Jeremy asked.

"Micah told us that many of us have come in here to face our fears. It's our job to help Dawn face hers," Brad answered.

"Are you crazy?" Tucker asked. "There's only six of us. Angelique's the only one with weapons, and even so, we'd need an army to defeat those things."

"You guys," I said, an idea suddenly coming to me. "We *do* have an army."

"What, the soldiers in the west woods?" Jeremy asked. "They try to kill us every time we go near them!"

"Maybe that means they'll try to kill the demons too," I said, hopping over a tree limb. "Our best bet for now is to lead the demons into the west woods. That'll at least buy us some time until we can get through to Dawn."

27

We caught up to Dawn on the great lawn.

"Head to the lighthouse. It's the only safe place!" I called out to her.

Just as I suspected, Dawn was lost to the dream and highly susceptible to suggestion. She paused for only a moment before turning and running up Dasheen Pass. I permitted myself a small smile; I was starting to get the hang of the astral plane.

Jeremy dropped back so he was running next to me. "You're sending her right into the soldiers," he said. "You know that, don't you?"

"Better that she get shot than ripped apart by whatever those things behind us are," Tucker said. "At least with a gunshot she'll go quick."

That wasn't exactly what I had planned. I was hoping that I could get the soldiers to protect us from Dawn's demons. But to do that, I had to get them to remember who they were: not bloodthirsty soldiers protecting themselves from Nazis, but spirits who'd been dead for over fifty years and needed to move on.

The five of us shot up Dasheen Pass after Dawn and started up the slow grade. I started to feel winded, and then reminded myself it was just an illusion: *Astral bodies can't get winded.* As soon as the thought entered my mind, my fatigue disappeared and I charged up the path in front of the group.

We caught up to Dawn at Devil's Bend, just as the first shots rang out. The soldiers were heading toward us from the south, per usual.

"Everyone this way! Dawn, you too!" I yelled bounding north through the forest.

Dawn, still panicked and completely lost in the dream, did as she was told. After running for a few more minutes, all six of us took cover behind a large banyan tree.

"Tucker, give me your shirt," I said. I didn't wait for him to comply; I grabbed at the bottom of his white tee and pulled it up over his head.

"If you want to see my body, Red, all you have to do is ask," Tucker said teasingly.

"What are you doing?" Jeremy asked. He did not look amused.

"Hold on," I said. I grabbed a large stick off the forest floor and quickly tied the shirt to the end of it. I had an idea but didn't have time to explain. The soldiers were getting too close. I could hear them moving slowly toward us.

I shot the end of the stick out from behind the large tree and began waving the shirt back and forth where the soldiers could see it.

"Truce!" I yelled out.

"Max, are you crazy?" Angelique hissed. "Now they know exactly where we are!"

"We have to play into their fantasy," I said. "A white flag is an international symbol of ceasefire, right? These men are gentlemen. Back in their time these gestures were honored."

"Hold your fire," one of the soldiers yelled. I took a deep breath and peeked my head around the tree, continuing to wave the flag back and forth in the air, and inhaled sharply. There were at least fifty men in uniform right on the other side of the tree, guns drawn.

One of the men stepped forward, his rifle pointed at my head. I recognized him as the man with the mustache who had shot us all the week before. His eyes were nervous and glazed over, lost to the nightmare. I knew if I made the wrong move he'd shoot me without a second thought.

"Keep your hands where I can see them," he said. He clearly didn't recognize us from any of the times before. I wondered who or what I looked like to him. I had to get him to see me for who I really was, not what his fear was turning me into.

"Please help us, sir," I said, trying to speak clearly. "There's an army of monsters chasing us. They'll be on us any second. You must tell your men to prepare for battle."

Everyone but Dawn—who was curled up in a ball at the base of the tree in some sort of catatonic state—slowly came out from behind the tree.

"Colonel, maybe it's the Nazis," said a blond soldier to the right of the man with the mustache.

"How do we know it's not a trick?" whispered another.

"What are you doing running through the woods in your undergarments, young lady?" the colonel asked, eying my outfit with suspicion.

"My undergarments?" I looked down at my white tank top and faded cut-off jean shorts. I hadn't bothered to wear long pants since we'd stopped heading into the west woods. I supposed my shorts and tank looked like women's undergarments to someone from the 1940s.

"It's the Nazis," the blond man said angrily. "They've defiled this poor woman."

A murmur rose among the rest of the soldiers.

I looked back at Jeremy and he nodded slightly at me to keep going.

"She's not lying, Colonel. Look there!" said the blond-haired man. We all turned to see a few of the demons climbing up the hill toward us. They were even more frightening than the drawing Dawn had made, and were all holding swords, spiky shields, battle axes, and other frightening objects whose sole purpose was to maim and kill. The minute they saw us they let out a series of terrible shrieks that made my blood run cold.

"Well, I'll be damned," said the colonel. "It is the Nazis, just like this young lady said."

I wasn't sure how the demons appeared to the soldiers. Perhaps in their confused state the demons looked like monsters in Nazi uniforms. I was just grateful for the fact that the soldiers were seeing me for who I really was: a young woman in need of assistance.

"Will you help us?" I asked again.

"Yes, ma'am, we will," the colonel said, all chivalry now. "You and your party stay here behind this tree."

"If you can spare some extra weapons, Colonel, we would appreciate it," Jeremy said, stepping forward and saluting. "Something to protect the women." He shot Angelique a sheepish look.

Angelique pulled her swords out from their sheaths. "Just for the boys, Colonel," she said. "Us women have brought our own weapons."

"I think that can be arranged," the colonel said glancing over at

Angelique with a confused look on his face. He nodded to a few men behind him, and they stepped forward and handed a few pistols and what looked like a bayonet to Jeremy. The things were ancient; I hoped the guys knew how to use them.

"Good luck to you," the colonel said, and, waving his men forward, took off toward the monsters screeching their way toward us.

Angelique was right, us ladies had brought our own weapons, but unfortunately I wasn't quite sure how to use mine. I retreated back to the tree, where Dawn was still curled up in a ball on the ground, looking catatonic, and kneeled down beside her. I didn't have much time to get through to her.

As the first of the soldiers and monsters collided, the team made a protective semicircle around Dawn and me. She put her hands over her ears to block out the noise of the battle and began to rock back and forth.

"Dawn," I said, touching her gently on the shoulder, trying to keep my voice from trembling. "It's Max. I'm here to help you."

She didn't respond—in fact, she seemed to not to be able to hear me at all.

"You're dreaming, Dawn. You just can't see it because you're letting the fear take over. You have to try and fight it." But it was no use; her eyes were filled with pure terror. I heard the monsters' snarls and shrieks draw closer, and my heart beat hard in my chest. If they got to us it wouldn't matter whether she was lucid or not.

"No! No!" Dawn screamed, tucking her head in between her knees and wrapping her arms around herself. "I don't have my crystal. It was the only thing keeping them away from me. Now we're all going to die!"

I needed to get Dawn to feel the power of the map on her hands, just like I'd done with Tucker, and Millicent had done with me—but I didn't know how to bring it back. What had happened with Tucker a few days earlier had been an accident, and I hadn't been able to do it with the blindfolded woman in the woods. I had to at least try, though.

"Brad was right," I said. "You don't need that crystal. You have something a million times stronger than any crystal inside of you, I promise. Look—I'll show you."

I dragged her balled fists away from her chest and slowly pulled on her fingers until her hands were flat. Her body was rigid, but she was too weak with fear to fight me. I concentrated all my energy on her hands, imagining the map appearing there, and said *"Remember"* over and over again. Soon I felt energy and light traveling down my arms and into Dawn. Her palms began to glow, and then the map appeared.

The minute Dawn got a glimpse of her palms I saw the recognition light up her eyes. She looked up at me, her face full of wonder.

"Oh God," she whispered. "I can't believe I could have forgotten this when it was right here all along."

The map grew more detailed and began to morph into different shapes. It was communicating to her nonverbally, just like mine had—about her past, her purpose on earth, and beyond that to infinity. All of who she was and had been and would ever be.

And then something even more strange happened: A wind rushed through the forest and into the hollow where we sat, whipping up leaves and underbrush. But this was no normal wind. It was so strong the banyan tree began to creak under its force.

The wind intensified, and I stood up and stepped back. Dawn stood as well—and then slowly began to lift off the ground. Jeremy grabbed my hand protectively and the five of us stood back to give Dawn room to do—whatever it was she was about to do.

As Dawn rose into the air, the glowing map spread from her hands to encompass her whole body. Her lavender hair whipping against her face, she extended her arms out at her sides, and ribbons of light and dark vapor swirled in circles around her body. Her lips moved as if she were reciting some sort of chant, but I couldn't hear anything over the wind. I expected her eyes to be completely vacant, trancelike, but when I got a glimpse of her face I could see that they were lucid and resolute—she wore a look of pure determination. She was fully participating in whatever it was that was happening.

The ground began to shake as if something were trying to come up through it. I looked around the tree at the battle happening mere feet away, and saw that the demons and soldiers were still carrying on, though they were having a difficult time fighting through the heavy winds and ground shaking beneath them..

I looked back at Dawn just in time to see her head shoot back. Beams of light and dark shot out of her eyes and mouth, and as they did, the demons nearby were ripped from where they stood and sent screeching up into the sky, where they disappeared into the dark clouds above. Then another bunch a few yards farther away were sucked up into the dark clouds as well, and then another, until all of them were gone and the soldiers were left awestruck, staring open-mouthed up into the sky.

Finally the beams emanating from Dawn erupted into an explosion of light, like a star bursting in the night sky, and Dawn dropped from the air and landed firmly on the ground.

Dawn turned to look at me and I saw that her eyes were blazing with purpose. The fear I'd come to associate so closely with her was gone, and something else had replaced it. It was almost like she was no longer Dawn. No, that wasn't right . . . she was more Dawn now than she ever had been. She was all of Dawn.

The colonel walked back toward us out of the jungle and approached Dawn, his soldiers following slowly behind him in silence.

"Thank you, ma'am," he said to Dawn with a respectful bow of his head. "We've been waiting a long time for that."

"So have I," Dawn said. Her lavender bangs were blown back and out of her face, and she stood so tall I barely recognized her.

The man looked tired. There were bags under his eyes and his face was weathered, but there was life in his eyes—something new and awakened coming forth. I knew that look well. It was the first glimmerings of lucidity.

"My name is Colonel Steven Carter," he said. "My men and I were ambushed here some time ago and we've been lost in these woods ever since. We can't seem to find our way back to our base. It's so very strange. I used to know this jungle like the back of my hand, but now . . ."

He looked around again, his eyes suspicious. Obviously, he still didn't understand that he was dead, but he knew something was wrong, especially after witnessing that demon firework show. He had been stuck here on the astral plane, swimming around in his fears and fantasies, for decades. But now the confusion was falling away. He was beginning to remember.

Dawn turned to us. "The lighthouse is going to have to wait."

It was an order, not a request. Probably the first Dawn had ever given in her life. My eyes fluttered to Jeremy, who I thought might be disappointed by this news, but he only nodded stoically, as did the rest of us. As much as we wanted to make it to the lighthouse, right now this was more important.

Dawn turned back to Colonel Carter. "Colonel, I know where your base is," she said. "It's just on the other side of these woods. Why don't you come with us and we'll take you there?"

A wave of relief came over the man's face. "That would be very kind of you, ma'am. We've been out here an awful long time."

"I know you have," she said. "Let's get you home."

●●●

As we reached the edge of the north woods I could see the brick buildings of the old base peeking through the jungle ahead of us, and as we got closer I noticed a bright light shining through the trees as well. When we stepped out of the jungle and onto the service road, I was shocked beyond belief to see it was the lighthouse.

Jeremy and Angelique saw it too, and together we ran to where it sat, right in front of the gate of the military base. How it had gotten from its place on the bluff to here? *When you're supposed to get somewhere on the astral plane, mountains will be moved for you*, I mused—*and I guess lighthouses as well.*

As the soldiers came out of the jungle behind us, some of them cried out in relief at the sight of the base.

"How did the lighthouse get here?" Tucker asked incredulously, running up next to us with Dawn and Brad.

We all gawked, mouths open, looking up at the tower's gleaming light.

"We're dreaming," Brad said with a shrug. "Anything can happen in here. Literally anything."

Jeremy shook his head. "I keep trying to think logically—work things out on my own the way I'm so used to the earth plane—but that's not the way things work here, is it?"

"Honestly Jeremy," I said, "I'm beginning to think that's not the way things work in waking life either."

"But why is the lighthouse here now?" Tucker asked.

"Because," Dawn said, turning back toward the soldiers, who were all staring up at the lighthouse as well. "We're ready now. It's time."

"Time for what?" Tucker asked from behind her, but she didn't answer. Her eyes were focused on Colonel Carter, who was making his way toward her through the crowd of soldiers.

"This is where we go now?" the colonel asked when he got closer. He nodded up at the lighthouse. His face was sweating in the afternoon heat, and his uniform was dirty from the battle. "This is the way home?"

"That's right," Dawn said.

"I don't remember this building being here before," he said, studying the lighthouse. "But of course we've been gone such a long time. I suppose a lot has changed."

"Yes," Dawn said. "More than you know."

Colonel Carter stood there quietly, and I realized he was waiting for one of us to go up to the lighthouse and open the door.

Dawn put her hand on Jeremy's arm. "Would you do the honors?"

"This is your show, Dawn," Jeremy said. "You've earned it."

"I already got what I was looking for," she said, smiling up at him. "Anything we get in there is just icing on the cake."

He looked around at the rest of the team and we nodded our consent. Yes. Jeremy had wanted to get to the lighthouse most of all. He deserved to be the first to see what was inside.

We watched in silence as Jeremy tentatively walked up the steps of the porch to the lighthouse, like he was taking part in a sacred ceremony—which, I realized, he was. He paused at the door for a second or two, took a deep breath, and opened the door.

28

A great golden light burst out of the lighthouse door the moment Jeremy opened it, enveloping everything around us so that I could barely see. I was instantly immersed in a feeling of loving warmth, like the light was alive and wanting me to come closer. My skin warmed at its touch, and it felt as if it was shining on my insides as well. I could tell everyone else was feeling it too, because a calm settled over the crowd, and as a group we began to make our way toward the door. All I wanted was to get as close as I could to the light—but not in a desperate way, I felt entirely at peace. And for some reason I felt sure that everything I'd ever wanted to know was held somewhere inside it.

I followed my friends up the porch steps and in through the door.

It took a few seconds for my eyes to adjust to the brightness when I walked inside; then the scene around me came into view. We were on a crowded city street flanked with skyscrapers and packed with people. Down the center of the street was a motorcade surrounded on all sides by WWII soldiers who were marching and waving, and crowds of people were cheering at them from all sides, waving American flags. A marching band was playing "When the Saints Go Marching In," and the sky around me was filled with flying strips of paper and confetti. We were in the middle of a ticker tape parade, and by the looks of the buildings around us, plus the old-timey cars and clothes, we were back in 1940s Manhattan.

The soldiers filed in quietly behind me, looking around in awe at the scene. I spotted Jeremy standing at a lamppost, watching the parade, and I made my way toward him, waving for the rest of the team to join us.

"What's going on?" Tucker asked as he approached. "What is this place?"

"I think we're in the higher astral plane," Brad said. "A bridge to the other side."

As we stood there, people began coming out of the crowd and approaching the soldiers lined up on the sidewalk next to us. A beautiful brunette in a yellow polka dot dress ran up to Colonel Carter, and he took her up his arms before burying his face in her hair and breaking down in tears. She, on the other hand, was calm and serene—not at all the way I'd assume a wife would be welcoming her husband home from war. Instead of tears, she gave him a warm smile, and then without a word took his hand gently and guided him into the parade.

I turned and looked where they were heading. A few blocks down, the parade disappeared into a bright tunnel—which I now saw was the source of the brilliant gold light.

"I don't understand what's going on," Tucker said. "Is this a flashback?"

"No," Brad said. "This must be the parade the soldiers would have been in if they hadn't been killed in the war. It's been duplicated here as a way to welcome them home to the spirit world—to make the transition easier. These people you see are the spirits of their loved ones, coming to take them to the other side."

All around us mothers, fathers, wives, and even children were stepping out of the parade to receive the lost soldiers for whom they'd been waiting for so long. They had all died in the years since the war, and now they had come here to guide the men home.

I looked into the light once again and was hit with a strong feeling of déjà-vu—a feeling that I had been there before. The place I had been to hadn't looked like this—there hadn't been soldiers or a ticker tape parade or a marching band or any of it—but I recognized that light. I was sure of it. I tried desperately to hold on to that feeling before it slipped away.

A big band was playing on a float ahead of us and people were dancing in the street. I couldn't help but want to follow after them and go toward the light.

I felt someone walk up and stand next to me. It was Jeremy.

"I think we've been here before, Jeremy," I said.

"Yes," he said. "But it was different somehow." He nodded toward the tunnel up ahead, and I knew all the answers were there.

As we walked with the parade toward the light, the atmosphere around us became brighter, filling with more peace and more love, if that were even possible—more powerful than anything I'd ever felt before. It had a magnetic feel, drawing us to it. I felt a warm pulsing sensation on my hands, and looked down: the map was back, glowing brightly on my palms.

And then I remembered: My message for the world was to remind people that we were more than our physical bodies by helping them remember who they really were before they incarnated here on earth. That had been the plan all along. I *had* been to this place before, not just once but many times. I just couldn't remember the details.

The reason I had been so depressed was because I had forgotten who I was, and what I came to the earth plane to learn and share. My depression was actually a gift—an attempt from some higher something to alert me to who I really was. But instead I had been too wrapped up in my ego desire of wanting to become a successful television writer. In listening to my ego desire instead of my soul desire, I was led to believe that if I found the right medication or had the right job, the right boyfriend, or the right friends, I would somehow find happiness. Without my depression, I never would have come to the island and found my true purpose. This insight may not rid me of my depression completely, but at least I understood part of its cause now.

This all came into my brain, into my being, at once, like a download, and I no longer worried about needing to remember the map on my hands. I would not be forgetting this information when I woke up. I had all the tools I needed now. I'd always had them; I'd just forgotten.

I looked next to me and realized I could barely see Jeremy now—only the outline of the light around his body—but I could feel him smiling. He squeezed my hand, and I was happy to know that I could still feel him. I was filled with a peace I believed would never end. The euphoria was almost too much to bear.

The energy around us intensified, so much so that my body began to thrum with a vibration that bordered on ecstasy. As we got closer and closer to the light, the vibrations amplified. I felt like a piece of glass next to a blaring speaker—like I might explode into a thousand pieces.

"Max," Jeremy said. I turned back to him and realized he wasn't speaking to me verbally. He was using his mind. We could communicate telepathically here. "My visions are a gift," he said. "That was always the plan. I remember that now."

"Yes," I said. Jeremy had gotten his download too—and so, I was sure, had the rest of the team. And the answer was the same for all of us: All these problems we'd come to the island to solve . . . they were actually gifts. These so-called "problems" were the impetus that had driven us to come together and search for meaning and truth, and ultimately remember more about our infinite selves.

"Don't forget, Max," Jeremy said. "We must never forget it." And then, as if to seal our pact, he leaned down and kissed me on the lips— gently at first, but then he wrapped his arms tightly around me and took me in deeper, until I felt our bodies begin to merge. Whatever was coming through him, it felt like magic—all sparkles and light, like I was drinking in his essence. I opened my eyes to see what was happening, and sure enough we were surrounded by even more light than before, so much so that Jeremy had disappeared altogether. It was like we were in the middle of a star, or the sun. We were part of the light.

I wanted so much to hang on to this feeling—stay here forever and never leave—but I knew that was impossible. The feeling was too intense and I couldn't hold it. Grayness descended, signaling that the dream was coming to an end.

No! I didn't want to go back, not yet. I tried to hold on to Jeremy, pushing myself into him and kissing him harder as his arms tightened around me—but the grayness continued to build, and the feeling of ecstasy began to fade away. Then I felt Jeremy slip away from me. I grasped for him desperately, but the pull was too strong. I felt the tug of my own silver cord, and I went flying backward, down into nothingness, until everything went dark.

● ● ●

I opened my eyes only a few seconds later to find I was back in the lab, in my recliner. I slowly sat up in my chair and surveyed the room. Next to me, Micah was just coming to. Taking off my headset, I looked over at Jeremy, who blinked his eyes and stared back at me, looking slightly stunned, as if all of him hadn't fully come back yet. A few seconds later, though, his eyes became clear, and he smiled at me. I smiled back, then looked down, feeling embarrassed, like I was twelve and I'd just had my first kiss—ever. And in a way, I supposed, I had.

"Holy crap!" Tucker yelled, making me jump and bringing me further into the present. "We did it! We made it to the lighthouse!"

I didn't have time to consider the repercussions of my kiss with Jeremy or what it meant. Everyone jumped to their feet, laughing and congratulating each other. Tucker picked Angelique up and spun her around. Jeremy came over and gave me a squeeze and a kiss on the forehead, and I relaxed a little about what had happened between the two of us. Angelique even gave me a hug.

"To think, the lighthouse could have come to us at any point all along," Angelique said, shaking her head.

"We didn't do all that running around for nothing, though," Brad said. "They say it's not the destination, it's the journey, right?"

It was a little cliché, but Brad was right. It couldn't and shouldn't have been any other way. When we had learned the lessons we needed to learn in the astral, that's when we'd been given the lighthouse. If it had shown up at the very beginning, we would have missed out on the entire adventure. I never would have seen the map on my hands, Angelique never would have found her missing piece, Dawn never would have conquered her demons—in truth, none of us would have done any of the work we needed to do in there. Getting to the lighthouse couldn't have been any other way.

Dawn turned to me, her eyes shining with victory. "Thank you, Max," she whispered as she stood on her toes to give me a hug. "What you can do for people is a real gift. Cherish it."

"I will," I said with a grateful nod. Behind Dawn I noticed Jeremy making a beeline for the door. I gave her another quick squeeze, then took off after him, catching up to him just outside the lab.

"Where are you going? Don't you want to stay and celebrate?" I asked. He stopped and turned to face me. I felt like a needy child trying to get a parent's attention.

"I don't have time to celebrate," Jeremy said sternly. "I have a girl to find."

"Amanda," I said. So much had happened since we'd seen her in the astral I'd almost forgotten about her.

"This is it—this is what I've been sent to this island to do," Jeremy said. "I can find this girl. I know I can."

"Yes, of course," I said, feeling a little selfish for wanting his attention when he was trying to save someone's life. "Do you need some help?"

"I will at some point, but right now I have to call my superiors and see if they can find out if there are any women named Amanda missing in Texas. I'll see you later, okay?"

He turned to go, but I caught his arm, feeling the need to address the kiss, though I wasn't sure how. "I'm sorry about what happened in there at the end," I said, looking down to avoid his gaze.

"I'm not," Jeremy said. I raised my eyes to his. He was smiling, but he was serious. I, meanwhile, wasn't sure how I felt. I was definitely attracted to Jeremy, but I'd been so involved with trying to get to the lighthouse and the drama with Millicent, I hadn't had time to think about it much. Then, of course, there was Micah.

"What about Micah?" I asked, heat rising in my cheeks. "What if he saw us?"

"Micah didn't see us," Jeremy said. "He wasn't even there."

"How do you know?" I asked. Micah always seemed to know what had happened in our sessions. He was obviously there watching even when no one could see him.

But Jeremy had other things on his mind at the moment. "You're getting too worked up about this. It could be a lot worse. You could have hooked up with Tucker."

I laughed, but sobered quickly. I knew he was making light of what had happened for me, but if he'd experienced anything close to what I had in there, then we were in trouble.

••

By the time I returned to the lab, everyone had left except for Micah, who had his bag over his shoulder. When he saw me, he put it back down on his chair.

"Congratulations," he said. Just one look at his face and I knew he had seen the kiss between Jeremy and me. For a therapist who was adept at reading people's feelings, he wasn't very good at hiding his own—at least, not from me.

I walked over to get my notebook but stopped short of my recliner and faced Micah.

"It was an accident," I said, trying not to sound too defensive. "What happened between Jeremy and me in there."

"I didn't say anything."

"I just meant that I didn't mean for it to happen."

"Yes, you did," he said. There was a hint of sadness in his voice. But why would that be? Anger bubbled up inside me. What did Micah possibly have to be upset about?

"Well, so what if I did?" I said, tilting up my chin. "Jeremy's the one making sure I don't get killed or hurt in there. Meanwhile, you sneak around in the shadows like a ghost!"

"You don't understand," he said. "You're in a very important place right now. I don't want to interfere with that. Neither does Jeremy."

One minute Micah seemed to be emotionally invested in me, and the next he was pushing me away. I knew he had feelings for me, so why was he trying to keep such a strange distance between us? And what did Jeremy have to do with any of it?

"How do you know what Jeremy wants?" I asked, holding his gaze. When he didn't answer I took a few steps closer to him. "You act like you're just my therapist, but we both know you're more than that. If you don't want me to have feelings for you, stop sending me mixed messages."

"I can't," he said. His eyes carried that sadness I seemed to be seeing more and more of lately. "I'm sorry."

"Why not?" I demanded.

He pursed his lips together, sighed and shook his head. "Because I made a promise," he finally said.

"A promise to who?"

"To you, Ms. Dorigan."

"What promise? I don't remember you making me any promises." But even as the words came out of my mouth I somehow knew they weren't true.

"No," he said, looking more forlorn than ever. "You don't."

"Why don't you tell me what's going on then? I thought I'd reach the lighthouse and come out feeling enlightened, with all my questions answered, but now I feel even more confused than before. Why did you bring me to the island, Micah? What do you want from me, *really*?"

"I want you to remember who you are," he said, his voice shaking.

"I know, I know," I said, throwing up my hands. "Everybody wants me to remember who I am. But didn't I just do that today? We made it to the lighthouse, if you haven't noticed."

I snatched my notebook off the recliner and spun on him, my voice heavy with anger. "You obviously know more than you're letting on. If that's the way you want to be, then fine. You can't hide it from me forever. I'm getting better in the astral, and sooner or later I will find out what you're keeping from me. I will."

"Good," Micah said with a sad smile. "I'm counting on it."

29

That night we didn't have a debrief. We needed time to process what we'd learned in the lighthouse—namely, that the things we'd come to the island to get rid of were actually gifts. While I didn't have the same euphoria about it as I did in the astral, I still was able to see my depression, while a difficult burden, was also pushing me toward where I needed to go. This meant I couldn't return home to LA the following week. I needed to learn more about my gift, and the best way to do that was to stay on the island. Zoe had mentioned that there was a job opening coming up in the kitchen, so I left a message with Dr. Luna and crossed my fingers that it hadn't been filled.

••

Micah and Jeremy didn't show at breakfast or for our mid-morning run the next day, and by the time I arrived for our session in the lab, I was anxious to find out what they'd been doing. Had Jeremy found something out about Amanda? Was Micah working with him? I was the one who'd figured out Amanda's name in the first place. Why weren't they involving the rest of us?

Just as I was about to get up and go find Jeremy, he walked into the room, followed by Micah. They both appeared a little tense.

"Did you find out anything about Amanda?" I asked, stepping toward Jeremy. "What's going on?"

He opened his mouth to answer, but before he could, Micah gently took me by the shoulders and guided me toward my chair, away from Jeremy. "Why don't we all take a seat?" he said. "We have a lot to cover today."

I sat down, a little taken aback by Micah's odd behavior. It was apparent he didn't want me talking to Jeremy—but why?

I eyed him suspiciously, then looked back at Jeremy, who was busy avoiding my gaze. Had the two of them had some sort of a chat since last night? Had they talked about the kiss? My face went hot with embarrassment.

If Micah noticed my concern, he didn't let on, and as soon as we all got settled, he launched into teaching mode.

"You've gotten to the lighthouse," he began, "and as you all know now, getting to a desired location in the astral is difficult . . . in the beginning, anyway. Understanding—as you do now—that working toward a goal in the astral is more than just mind over matter, should make things easier." He smiled. "As I've said before, there are various forces at work in our lives—and it's your job to decide what they are and whether you want to work with them or ignore them. Are you going to let them guide you, or do you want to be the one to lead the way? And that," he said, reaching down and pulling a stack of manila envelopes out of his bag, "brings us to Level 2."

Level 2? I had no idea there were levels to astral travel—and by the blank looks on everyone's faces, neither did anyone else. Per usual, Jeremy was the only one in the group that didn't appear surprised.

Micah handed the stack of envelopes to me. "Please take one and pass the rest down, but do not open them."

I took the first envelope and passed the stack to Angelique. The envelope was very light. It felt like there was barely anything in it— perhaps one piece of paper at the most.

"In each of these envelopes is a picture of a person, place, or thing that you are to locate in the astral," Micah said. "Consider this your target."

"Our target?" I snorted. "What are we, trying out for the CIA or something?"

"Hopefully!" Brad said brightly, and we all laughed.

"It's funny you should ask that," said Micah. "This is a procedure invented for the CIA. It's called remote viewing."

"Now you're talking!" Brad crowed, clapping his hands together. He looked so excited, I thought he was going to start dancing around the room.

"Does this mean we're going to be splitting up this time?" Dawn asked.

"No," Micah said. "As usual, this session will be a group effort. The pictures you hold are all identical. Your target is the same."

"Is this person, place, or thing on the island?" I asked.

"It could be anywhere in the world," Micah said.

"You mean we might have to leave the island?" Angelique asked, sitting up in her seat. "We had a hard enough time getting to the lighthouse. This seems very advanced."

"It is advanced, but I have faith you're up to the challenge," Micah said.

"So can we open the envelopes now?" Tucker asked.

"No," Micah said. "You won't be opening the envelopes until you come back from the astral."

"What do you mean?" Tucker asked. "How are we going to know where we need to go?"

"We have to do it psychically," Brad said eagerly, pushing his glasses up on his nose. "That's what remote viewing is all about. Psychically intuiting information."

"But not all of us are psychic," I said.

"Really?" Micah asked. "How did you help Dawn yesterday? Or Tucker and Angelique before that?"

"I was able to do those things because I was in the astral," I said. "Not here."

"What's the difference?" Micah asked—but before I could respond, he held his finger up. "Don't answer that. Now, if and when you do find your target today, I want you to take a mental picture of where you are and who and what is around you so that when you wake up you can write down or sketch everything that you saw. If you can, try to find out where you are—a city, a beach, a desert? Note landmarks; if you can get an address or a phone number, even better. Numbers of any kind are important, actually. Tomorrow we'll compare all your notes to the picture in the manila envelope and see how well you did."

And with that, he reached over and switched on the lucidity machine.

••

"So," Jeremy said once we were all in the astral, "anyone have any ideas on how to locate the target?"

"I've got one," Tucker said. "How about we just open these manila envelopes?"

I wondered how that would work in the astral. Of course the physical envelopes wouldn't actually be opened on the earth plane, but I didn't doubt that we could see what was inside.

"No," Jeremy said stepping forward. "Let's do as Micah said. This is an exercise to test our psychic abilities in the astral."

"Fine, fine," Tucker said, putting up his hands in surrender. "I'll tell you one thing though: my way's much easier."

"Why don't we try to do an intuitive group reading?" Brad said, picking his manila folder up from his lounge chair.

"What do you mean?" Tucker asked.

"I mean," Brad said, "that we try to psychically intuit what's in them." When no one moved he elaborated. "There's not much to it. You just put your hand on the envelope and see if you get any impressions. Pictures, feelings, anything."

"Couldn't hurt," Angelique said with a shrug.

Since our chairs were already occupied by our sleeping bodies—*So creepy*, I thought—we grabbed our envelopes and sat cross-legged on the floor in a circle.

"So for those of us who aren't psychic experts," Tucker said, "how does this work, exactly?"

"Just shut your eyes and see if you get any images or feelings, or hear any words. Like this," Brad said, shutting his eyes and putting a hand over his envelope.

We all sat and watched. After a few seconds he opened his eyes. "You don't expect me to do this all by myself, do you?"

We looked around at each other, then mirrored Brad and put our hands on our envelopes. I closed my eyes.

"This is weird," Tucker said after a few seconds.

"Concentrate!" Brad snapped.

I felt nothing at first—but I tried harder to concentrate and open my mind up. After a while a red pickup truck appeared in my mind's eye. It looked like it was driving on a road somewhere, but I couldn't see who was driving or where the road might be.

"Okay," Brad said after a few minutes had passed. "I got a blue freeway sign with the numbers 45 or 35. What about you guys?"

"I got a red pickup truck," I said.

"That's good," said Brad. "Anyone else?"

Dawn said she saw the numbers 2233. Angelique didn't see anything visually, but said she felt a deep sadness.

"I saw a six-pack of Budweiser on a table," Tucker said. "That *could* mean something . . . or it could just mean I really want a beer."

"Did anyone get water?" Brad asked. "Besides the sign, I just kept seeing a body of water. Like the ocean."

"Well, that does us a whole lot of good," said Angelique. "Those numbers could mean anything, and there's no red pickup truck or freeways on the island."

"There is an ocean though," Brad said. "Maybe we should go down to the beach. Unless any one has any better ideas."

Angelique shrugged. "Might as well."

We left the lab to make our way down to the beach. I took the opportunity to talk to Jeremy.

"Hey," I said, touching his shoulder. "Where have you been all day?"

He turned to look at me, his eyes glinting in the sun. "Working on trying to find out who Amanda is," he said.

I was kind of hurt that he hadn't asked for my help, but now was not the time or the place. "Any luck?" I asked, trying to keep my voice neutral so that he wouldn't be able to sense my unease.

"We're working on it," he answered, his eyes shifting away from mine.

I could swear he was trying to hide something from me. Was he uncomfortable about what had happened between us in the astral? He hadn't seemed to be right after it happened, but now it was like he was avoiding me. If it wasn't because of the kiss, then why?

We quickly made our way around the front of the hotel, past the pool, and down to the beach, which was peppered with people from the resort sunbathing and swimming on the earth plane.

"What now?" Angelique asked as we walked across the hot sand down to the shore.

"Maybe we should take the boat," Brad said, looking down toward the dock where the *Serendipity* was docked.

"And go where?" Angelique said.

"I don't know," he said. "But we're pretty sure our target isn't on the island, right?"

We all nodded. I looked back out at the ocean, wondering perhaps if there was another way, when I saw it, just about a mile out: a large, familiar swell rising up in the ocean. My stomach dropped.

"Oh no, not now," I heard myself say.

"What?" Angelique asked, turning toward me quizzically. I pointed at the horizon and we all became silent.

The water began to pull away from the shore like it was being drawn with a magnet back into the sea. From the swell and speed of the water, I could feel that this wave was going to be a big one.

I sighed and faced the group. "We can't outrun it, but I can wake us up again. Just give me a few seconds."

I began to shake out my hands, but Angelique caught my arm before I could get focused.

"What are you doing?" I snapped, already starting to panic.

"You can't keep running from it," she said quietly. "You have to face your demons, just like the rest of us did."

I looked around, and from the looks on everyone else's faces I could tell they agreed.

"But this isn't a demon," I said, looking back at the wave, which was rising steadily in the distance. "It's a tidal wave."

Dawn turned to me and said quietly, "Remember, Max, this isn't real. That's what you've been telling us all along, isn't it?"

"I know it's not real," I argued. I was still lucid; I knew that. "But I can't stop the pain it will cause, even if we're dreaming. And believe me, it's quite painful. Do you know how long it takes to drown?"

No one answered.

"Six minutes," I said. "Six minutes that feel like a thousand. Believe me. I've been through this so many times before. Too many. It's not worth it."

The wave charged toward us at an ungodly speed, rising higher and higher as it came. A few more minutes and it would be on top of us.

"It is worth it, Max," Angelique said, staring into my eyes. "I promise you, it is."

"But . . ." I tried to come up with some sort of argument, but Angelique was right. This was *my* demon, *my* dragon—the thing always waiting just beyond the horizon to take me down. As scared I was, I knew I had to face it. Micah's words echoed in my mind: *The cure for the pain is in the pain.* Yes, it was going to hurt, but I was going to have to do it anyway. I looked back out to sea. The wave was only about a half mile out and already taller than a skyscraper.

But what about the rest of the team? This wasn't their issue to face.

"Then the rest of you should wake yourselves up," I said. "I can teach you now, quickly, before it gets here."

No one spoke. Instead, Jeremy, who was standing on my left, took my hand and squeezed it tight in solidarity. Dawn took the other one and did the same. Angelique walked around to the back of me and I felt her hand, strong and determined, on my back. Then I felt more hands on me as Brad and Tucker too came and stood behind me for support, and together we all stood and waited for my wave.

Whatever happened to me would happen to all of us. I felt the warmth of all of their hands pressed against me, and as the wave barreled toward us I felt a cry rise up in my throat. How much they must care about me to stand here by my side—to not run away.

As the wave came closer, my heart pounded faster, my resolve weakened, and my body began to shake all over. The reality of the situation hit me all at once, and the small amount of courage I had managed to gather within me disappeared. As it did, I leaned back, almost involuntarily—but Tucker, Angelique and Brad pushed back supportively, and Jeremy and Dawn's hands tightened around my own. I couldn't run even if I wanted to. My friends were closing in around me, solidifying their grid of support. Despite this, my knees began to give out, and they all had to practically hold me up to keep me from falling to the ground.

Just then I heard a familiar cawing in the sky. Looking up I saw the raven flying toward us, and my heart flipped in relief. Maybe it had come to rescue us! It swooped down behind us and I heard what sounded like someone landing hard in the sand behind me, and then I felt yet another hand on the small of my back, warm and familiar. I looked back quickly and saw that it was Micah, a pair of great black feathered wings spread high behind him. If the rest of the group could see him, they didn't let on. I couldn't believe it. He was the raven that had been helping me all along.

For a second I felt a rush of relief, sure that Micah was going to stop the wave—but then I looked at him again, and he only smiled at me sadly—the smile of a friend watching someone they love about to do something terribly difficult. He was there to stand with me; that was all. My heart sank as I turned back to the wall of water that was now only a few yards away.

At the last second, instinctively, I thrust backward away from the wave and into the hands on my back. Tears poured from my eyes and my body shook uncontrollably, but my friends held to me tightly as the wall of water slammed down on us all.

30

The force of the water ripped me off my feet and tore the seven of us apart instantly. Then I was tumbling violently in the cold water, my heart thrumming with fear and dread. I flailed and struggled, trying to grab on to anything that might help me, but I found nothing.

The wave had knocked the breath out of me, and my lungs were starting to ache from lack of oxygen. I had to somehow get to the surface for air, but fighting against the powerful current proved hopeless. The terror was overwhelming; I wanted to scream, but I didn't dare let go of what little precious breath I had left.

Frantic, I opened my eyes. The salt stung but I kept them open. I was not going to die with my eyes closed. As more seconds passed without air, my lungs began to feel as though they were collapsing on themselves. The pain was beyond unbearable, but I held on, trying to stay upright as the water pushed me along.

Now that my eyes were open, I could see that I was traveling over the buildings of the retreat center. Leaves and pieces of wood shot by me as I tried again to swim to the surface of the water to get air, to no avail. And then, suddenly, I realized something: I was absolutely powerless. All I could do was pray for a miracle.

I had nothing else to lose at that point, so pray I did: *If anyone is out there*, I thought, *please help me!*

I repeated those words in my head, like a mantra, and as I did the force of the current softened and everything began to go in slow motion. I was still being carried along, but was no longer traveling at such a great speed.

Then, below me, out of the deep, I saw a figure swimming toward me. At first I thought it was a dolphin or a seal, but as it came closer I saw it was a woman—a woman with dark hair in a black evening gown. Millicent Last! My heart leapt with both fear and relief; was she here to save me or drown me?

She swam toward me with conviction, a look of determination on her face. When she got to me, she grabbed me quickly by both hands and thrust my palms in front of my face—where my map appeared once again. Then, with her beautiful, white face only inches from mine, she commanded, "Remember!"

Instantly it all came back to me: I was dreaming. Something incredibly powerful was helping me and I had to trust it. Millicent was part of that somehow; she was relaying a message from beyond— a message to remember who I really was, a power beyond measure, part of a greater something that could never ever be destroyed. I had forgotten that very important fact once again, which had made me lose perspective on reality. I had forgotten that if I wanted to, I could breathe.

I squeezed my eyes shut and took a deep breath—and instead of contracting in pain, my lungs opened and somehow drew the oxygen out of the water, like a fish. The pain dissipated and there I was, breathing underwater. And I saw in my mind's eye that everyone from the team was also remembering and taking a breath. I couldn't see them in the water around me, but I intuitively felt them nearby. It was as if we were all one consciousness. Just one of us remembering had helped us all.

Now we all were tumbling and falling, gliding, and whirling in the current, but it was no longer unpleasant. I knew now what I didn't understand before: I didn't need to fight the current; it was pushing and pulling me to exactly where I needed to be. Now, instead of fighting it, I could relax and enjoy the ride.

As I settled into this new state of being, the water became clearer, the salt stopped stinging my eyes, and I could better see the objects around me. Next to me, the lighthouse swiftly floated by, its light shining bright in the dark waters; then a palm tree came along, followed by the *Serendipity* and Angelique's dragon belt.

Out of the corner of my eye, I noticed another dark figure coming up fast behind me, and I turned to see who it was. *Micah.* He was using the current to propel him: one of his hands was outstretched in front of him, while the other was down at his side, giving him the appearance of a waterborne Superman. When he'd glided close enough, I reached out my hand, and he clasped it—and as he did, I felt a strong shift in the rendering of things, like something that had been broken was now being repaired.

Micah gazed searchingly into my eyes, as if he were waiting for something, and I gazed back. As usual, he gave up nothing; he just stared back at me as if he were waiting for something, his blond hair waving like seaweed in the water.

"What are you waiting for?" I asked him.

"For you, Ms. Dorigan," he said. "I'm waiting for you."

Before I could respond, one of the dirt bikes came at us fast in the current, and I was forced to let go of Micah's hand to avoid it and he was quickly pulled away by the current. I didn't understand what he meant, but I didn't let it bother me. I continued to feel a sense of peace as the water, which was now warm, carried me forward.

After a few more minutes of floating, the light above me began getting brighter, and I realized I was rising to the surface of the water. Part of me didn't want to leave the exhilarating flow of my oceanic adventure ride, but regardless, I could feel it was time for it to come to an end. I swam with the pull of the water, up toward the light.

As I broke through to the surface, I saw that I was now travelling over a dry, barren farmland as if I were riding high at the helm of a flash flood, or the crest of the wave like Poseidon. The sight was spectacular. Behind me the rest of the team began to surface in the water, but before I could call out to any of them, I felt myself being pulled up higher into the crest of the wave and began to feel fear creeping in again.

The wave got you this far, I reminded myself. *Why not take it all the way in?* With that thought I relaxed my body, and the wave crested, fell, and dropped me smoothly onto a patch of dry grass in front of an old, rundown farmhouse. I turned in time to see my friends also being tossed onto the grass in front of me, and then the water receding and evaporating off the dry grass, as if we'd just been caught in a summer storm and not a giant tsunami.

I lay there on the grass stunned, taking deep breaths of air, trying to comprehend all that had happened. I had faced my fear and it hadn't destroyed me. In fact, I'd come out on the other side more myself than I had been before. I'd taken something back by facing down that wave—something that could never be taken away from me again. I should be shaken to my core after that experience, but instead I felt invigorated. I was not alone—not here or in the waking world. I had finally faced my biggest nightmare, and instead of killing me it had carried me. I now knew for sure that a divine, loving power was at the reins, and all I had to do was surrender to it. There was some sort of plan for me—for everyone.

"You okay, Max?" asked Jeremy's voice. I turned my head and saw him next to me, getting to his feet. The rest of the team was still sprawled out on the lawn, soaking wet and in various stages of awe and confusion. Millicent and Micah were nowhere to be seen, although something told me they were both still with me—somewhere.

"Yes," I said as Jeremy helped me to my feet. "I think I'm more okay than I've ever been in my entire life. And I have all of you to thank for that." I looked around at my friends. "For staying with me and helping me face . . . what I came here to face. Thank you."

Everyone got to their feet and stood with me quietly for a few seconds. What I had experienced, they'd experienced too. How utterly and completely selfless of them to help me get here.

●●●

The tidal wave had come and gone, and yet the rickety white farmhouse in front of us remained perfectly intact, as was the equally dilapidated old barn behind it. The telephone poles, too, remained in place. I looked around at my friends. Our wet clothes and hair were the only evidence left that the wave had ever existed.

"Well, folks, I don't think we're in Kansas anymore," Tucker said. "Though on second thought"—he examined our rural surroundings—"I guess this could be Kansas!"

The house in front of us was the only one around for miles. The rest was dry farmland. But to the right of us I noticed a familiar pickup truck sitting in the driveway.

"It was your wave that got us here, Max," Angelique said, turning to me. "You have any idea where we are?"

"No," I said, turning back to the house. "But I know where our target is."

Brad's eyebrows raised. "Where?"

"Here," I said, nodding to the Chevy pickup truck in the driveway. "That's the red truck I saw in my vision."

Everyone turned and looked, their mouths wide open in shock.

"Well, I'll be damned," Tucker said. "How about that?"

"And I think those are the numbers I saw," Dawn added, pointing up at the house. "But I can't tell for sure. They keep moving all around."

I followed her pointer finger to the eaves above the porch, where four rusting metal numbers hung. I thought I made out the numbers 2233 before they started to morph and change.

"Well, I guess a tidal wave is one way to get us to our target," Tucker said, scratching his head. "But for future trips, Red, I'd prefer to use a boat."

"You and me both," I said with a sigh.

We headed up the creaky wooden steps to the porch. An old rotting floral sofa sat to the right of the door; next to it was a mason jar filled with brown liquid and cigarette butts.

Jeremy rapped twice on the door and called out, "Hello! Anyone home?"

"If there is, it's not like they can hear us," Tucker whispered. "We're in the astral."

"If they can't hear us then why are you whispering?" Angelique snapped at full volume.

"They might hear us if they're asleep and in the astral too," Brad said. "You never know. We don't know what we're dealing with here."

"Yeah," Angelique said with a note of sarcasm. "It's not like Micah would send us somewhere dangerous. Oh, wait . . ."

Jeremy didn't seem at all intimidated by what danger might lie ahead for us; he was already reaching forward to try the door. But it was locked.

"What now?" Dawn asked in a hushed tone.

Before anyone could answer, Jeremy took a step back and kicked the door hard with his foot. My heart jumped at the loud crack as the door slammed open, revealing a dark hall.

"Jeez, Jeremy," Angelique said. "We could have tried the back door before you decided to go all commando."

"We don't have time," Jeremy mumbled before charging into the house. The rest of us fell in behind him with a bit more caution. A few steps in and we could see the house was just as old and uncared for on the inside as it was on the outside. The walls were covered in floral paper that was yellowed and peeling. The wooden floor below us was worn and scratched. Ahead of us were stairs that went up to the second level, and to the right was the living room, where an old, rust-colored sofa sat in front of a flat-screen television—the only indication in the room that we were in the twenty-first century. Beyond the living room was the kitchen.

The whole place looked like it hadn't been cleaned in years. Clothes lay in piles in the corners. Food wrappers lay on the floor around the old sofa in the living room. In short, the place was disgusting. I was glad we were in the astral or I'd be afraid to touch anything for fear of germs.

"Where are we?" Tucker asked, looking around.

"I don't know," Brad said warily. "But this doesn't feel right."

Brad was right. Something dense and heavy hung in the air. I wanted to get out of there, but I knew we couldn't leave until we'd figured out where we were. That was the whole reason we were there.

Just then we heard a door shut upstairs and the sound of footsteps overhead. My heart jumped.

"Into the kitchen," Jeremy said, and we all shuffled back to the kitchen to hide.

It was filthy, with sticky, peeling linoleum floors and dishes piled high in the sink. As we all huddled in the back corner, next to an avocado-colored refrigerator, we heard footsteps coming down the stairs, then a huge burp. I looked up at Jeremy, who creased his brow. Whatever we were dealing with was human, at least. Slowly, all six of us crawled to the kitchen door to peek out.

Standing at the dining table inspecting his mail was an overweight man in his late forties, with a paunch and comb-over, wearing ratty jeans and a stained white T-shirt.

We relaxed a little bit at the sight of him. He hardly appeared to be a threat. Still, you never knew in the astral.

"Do any of you recognize this guy?" I whispered, looking around at the team. Everyone shook their heads no.

"What should we do?" Dawn whispered.

"I think we should try to talk to him if we can," Angelique said.

"What if he's dangerous?" Dawn asked.

"Are you kidding me?" Angelique asked. "He's got a beer gut and comb-over. I think the six of us can take him."

Before we could come to a consensus, the man turned and began to walk toward the kitchen. We quickly scooted back until we were pressed against the sink at the back of the tiny kitchen, but beyond crawling underneath it, there was no place we could go to hide—we were trapped. But when he walked in, he only coughed and nonchalantly grabbed a bag of Cheetos off the counter before heading back into the living room, plopping down on the couch, and turning on the TV. He hadn't noticed us at all.

I let go of the breath I'd been holding.

"Well, that solves that," Angelique said, standing up. "The guy's awake on the earth plane and can't see us. We're safe."

"For now," Dawn said.

Angelique ignored her and walked into the living room, where she stood in front of the TV. "He really can't see me," she said, leaning over and waving her hand in front of the man's face. "It's so weird."

Once we saw it was truly safe, the rest of us came out and joined Angelique by the couch.

"Who do you think this guy is?" Angelique asked.

"No idea," Tucker said. "But there's the beer I saw in my vision." He pointed to a six-pack of Budweiser sitting on a side table next to the couch.

We stood there and stared at the man as he shoved a handful of Cheetos into his mouth.

"It's our job to find out who he is," Jeremy said, "as well as *where* he is. So let's get to work. I don't think we have much time left before we wake up."

"I'm telling you, I don't like this guy, and I'm getting some bad vibes from this place," Brad said, "especially from over there." He eyed the door to the left of the kitchen. He walked over to it but stopped a few paces away, apparently afraid to open it.

Jeremy walked swiftly over to where Brad was standing and, with no hesitation at all, swung the door open, revealing stairs going down to what I assumed was a basement.

We all came over and looked down into the dark stairway hesitantly.

"Okay," Angelique said, putting a hand on her hip, "so who's going to volunteer to go down into the dark, creepy basement with the bad vibes?"

"We don't know how much time we have," Jeremy said. "I'll go. The rest of you split up and try to find an address or name. Something to indicate where we are."

"You should take at least one of us with you," I argued, laying a hand on his arm. Going down into a dark basement with bad energy on the astral plane could lead to nothing but trouble.

But the room began to dim, a sure sign that our time on the astral plane was coming to an end, and Jeremy shook his head. "We don't have much time!" he said, pulling his arm out of my grasp. "We've gone through a lot to get here. Let's not waste it. We may not be able to get back here again. Brad, you search upstairs. Dawn, you take this floor. Tucker, the backyard. Max, you try to get the license plate number of that truck, and Angelique, see if you can find a street sign outside," he called out.

Everything dimmed further as Jeremy disappeared down into the basement. If he was heading into any danger, at least it wouldn't be for long.

"Okay, let's move!" Angelique yelled, grabbing my hand and pulling me toward the front door. Behind me, I heard footsteps clomping on wood as Tucker, Brad, and Dawn scattered to their assigned places to search.

Once we were outside, Angelique took off running down the street and I headed straight to the back of the truck, where I fell to my knees, determined to get the number off the plate. To my dismay the letters and numbers were shifting and moving all around, just like they did when I looked at my watch—a good indication I was in the astral, but not too helpful in moments like these.

The scene around me dimmed again and I strained to decipher the license plate. It looked like it started with 4N6, but I couldn't be sure.

As I stared harder at the license plate, the grayness closed in around me, and then everything faded to black.

●●

"Welcome back, everyone," Micah said as I opened my eyes. He handed me a stack of white paper. I sleepily took one and passed the rest to Angelique before removing my headset.

"We're going to do something different this evening," Micah continued. "We'll have the debrief now, and then I'd like to invite you all to my place for dinner tonight. But right now, before we do anything else, I want you to write down everything you saw when you reached your target. Feel free to work together."

As soon as everyone got their papers, we got to work. I wrote down everything I could think of from the farmhouse, including the first three letters of the license plate on the red Chevy and all the details I could recall from inside and outside of the house.

After we were done writing separately, we brainstormed and drew a diagram of the house together. Well, Tucker drew it and the rest of us filled in the details. Dawn had found mail in the house addressed to a name that began with a J. With the moving text, she hadn't been able to read the exact name, but she thought it was something like John or James.

By the time we were done with the exercise we had the make and model of the truck figured out, as well as the first three numbers of the license plate (we thought), a partial address, and a crude sketch of the comb-over man and the outside of the farmhouse.

In typical fashion, Micah refused to answer any of our questions about the purpose of the exercise, or whether or not we'd actually made it to our intended target. All would be revealed, he insisted, the next day.

31

That night we all gathered together for a dinner in Micah's backyard around a farm table he had made himself out of salvaged wood. Bistro lights hung overhead like magical floating lanterns, and we had front-row seats to the sun setting behind the ocean on the beach. The air was as warm as the sky was pink. For dinner Micah served fresh red snapper with lemon butter sauce, spinach, and a mixed green salad with almonds and dried cherries. The food was light and delicious, and we ate it with great zeal—well, all of us except for Jeremy, who was once again a no-show. There was no doubt in my mind at this point that the man was avoiding me.

"So Micah," Tucker said as we scarfed down our food, "what was with the weird dude with the comb-over? Let me guess, he's your fraternal twin. You two were separated at birth and have only recently come to learn about each other. Obviously you got all the good genes."

Tucker grinned, but Micah's face went very somber at the mention of the man with the comb-over.

"More like Hannibal Lecter's twin," Angelique said. "Seriously, Micah. That guy was creepy. You could have sent us anywhere in the world: the Taj Mahal, Machu Picchu—"

"The Playboy Mansion," Tucker jumped in.

Angelique elbowed him.

"What?" He shrugged. "It's a very spiritual place. They have peacocks."

Angelique turned back to Micah. "So why there?"

"I'm afraid that's a question for tomorrow," Micah said with a smile, but it seemed uncharacteristically forced. "For tonight, no more talk of astral traveling or strange men with comb-overs."

"Fine," Angelique said, crossing her arms over her chest. "What do you want to talk about, then?"

"Ice cream," he said. "I would like to talk about ice cream."

••

After dessert, Angelique, Brad, Tucker, and Dawn headed down to the hot tub at the pool for a soak. I volunteered to stay behind and help Micah with the dishes.

Between the two of us, the kitchen didn't take long to clean. When we were done Micah offered me a cup of tea, and we went back out on the porch and sat together under the stars to drink it.

"I saw you in there today—shape-shift out of that raven," I said, taking a sip of my tea. "You've been in there helping me all along, but not the others. Why?"

"I thought I said we weren't going to be talking about astral travel any more tonight," he said.

"I know what you said," I said, looking at him expectantly.

Micah sighed. "The others have help too. I'm not the only one in there helping."

"Does this mean the tidal wave won't be in my dreams anymore?" I asked.

"There will still be waves," Micah said. "But hopefully now when they come, instead of scaring you, they'll help you to remember you're dreaming. And if you don't run from them, they'll get you where you need to go."

"Easier said than done," I said.

"That's why it's so important to breathe," he said with a smile.

I smiled back, feeling the importance of that first breath of trust I took underwater again. But that was in the astral plane—a place where pain could be ended in an instant, simply by waking up. It wasn't real life. If I had been asked to take that leap of faith here in the waking world, I didn't think I could have done it.

I looked around again at the twinkling stars and the ocean

sparkling in the distance, drinking in the chattering of birds in the trees, the symphony of crickets all around us, and the warmth of the balmy air on my skin. I never wanted to leave this place.

"I'm not going back to LA," I said.

"I know." Micah took a sip of his tea.

"Dr. Luna told you?" I asked, turning toward him.

"No."

"Do you think I should stay here?" I asked. I wanted to hear him say it—say that he wanted me to stay.

"Or wherever else you feel led to go."

"Where else would I go?"

"I imagine," Micah said, "the answer to that question will come very soon."

I sighed. "You're being awfully vague right now—and when I say vague I mean even more than usual, and that's a lot."

"I can't tell you what to do, Ms. Dorigan, you know that." Micah looked pained—a look that had appeared more and more in his eyes lately. It was like the closer we got the sadder he became.

I suddenly felt angry at him for that sadness, for not trusting me enough to tell me why it was there. He seemed to have no problem bossing me around when I'd first arrived on the island. Why couldn't he do it now?

"Micah," I said finally, searching his eyes, "just for one night can we not play teacher and student?"

He stared back at me, his eyes glittering in the darkness. "What do you want to play?" he asked, reaching up and tucking a piece of hair behind my ear. I was taken aback by the tone in his voice. It was one I had never heard from him before. I met his eyes, and saw that the sadness had been replaced by something else—something that looked like longing.

Footsteps sounded behind us, coming toward us in the house, and we both turned around just as Jeremy came through the back door. He stopped in his tracks when he saw us, and I heard him take in a breath as he surveyed in the scene—Micah and me just inches apart, sitting together on the settee under the stars.

"I didn't realize you were here, Max," he said, a little stiffly.

"We missed you at dinner," I said, moving away from Micah and into a less compromising position on the settee. I was glad it was dark outside, because my face was flushed with embarrassment. I had kissed Jeremy just yesterday. It had happened in a dream, that was true, but the line between reality and fantasy was a very fine one these days.

"If you wouldn't mind," Jeremy said, more formally than necessary, "I need to talk to Micah—alone."

"Not at all," I said, trying to keep my voice from shaking. "I was just about to leave anyway."

I turned back to Micah awkwardly, not knowing what to say, the feeling of our intimate moment still hanging in the air. "Thank you for dinner. I'll . . . see you tomorrow."

He nodded back at me, a silent good-bye.

Jeremy refused to look me in the eyes as I passed him on my way out, instead choosing to gaze at something far off on the horizon.

●●●

I woke early the next morning to the sound of the phone ringing.

Zoe turned over and tossed a pillow at the desk. When it missed its target, she crawled over, grabbed the receiver, and croaked, "This had better be good."

A few seconds later she tossed the phone at me and flopped back onto her bed. "It's for you."

"Hello?" I asked, still tangled up in sleep.

"Come to my room," Angelique said in a brusque voice. "Now."

Two minutes later I was in Angelique and Dawn's room. Brad and Tucker were already there. I'd managed to throw on my running clothes, which were the first thing I could find, but still felt a little discombobulated from being woken with such a start.

"What's going on?" I asked.

Angelique put her finger up to shush me as she barked into phone. "Well, if Jeremy shows up can you tell him to call me immediately? Tell him it's important." She slammed down the phone in a huff, turned to Brad, and ordered, "Show her."

Brad, who was sitting at the desk, turned his laptop around. On the screen a headline read: *Kidnapped Woman Rescued in Texas After Anonymous Tip.* I walked closer to the computer to get a better look.

Below the headline was a picture of the creepy man with the comb-over we'd seen in our astral session yesterday. Next to it was a picture of a girl with strawberry blond hair and freckles. My hand flew to my mouth. "That's the blindfolded girl we saw in the forest in the astral two days ago."

"Her name is Amanda Jenson. They found her last night after receiving an 'anonymous tip,'" said Brad, putting air quotes around his last two words. "It's all over the news. She was kidnapped six months ago by James Russell Conway, the comb-over man. He's had her chained up in the basement the whole time."

"Oh God," I said thinking back to the dark stairs going down to that basement. No wonder we'd gotten such a bad feeling about the place. Jeremy was the one who had checked the basement. Had he found Amanda down there and decided not to tell us? That would explain why he wasn't at dinner the night before, and his urgency to talk to Micah the previous evening. My mind reeled with all the possibilities.

"She was found just hours after we handed over all that information to Micah last night," Angelique said in an accusatory tone. She grabbed a manila folder off the desk next to her and shoved it into my hands.

I looked down at the folder. "This is the target from our session yesterday?"

Angelique nodded. I looked over at Dawn and Tucker, who stared back at me anxiously, then opened the folder and pulled out what was inside: a photograph of Amanda Jenson. It looked like a high school portrait, unnaturally posed with a grey background.

"Where'd you get this?" I asked them.

"Micah's house," Brad said. "I went over there as soon as I saw the news this morning. He wasn't there and his bed hadn't been slept in. I found the envelopes in the desk in his office."

"You just went in there and took them?" I asked.

"I'm not the only one around here being sneaky," Brad said defensively.

"What's that supposed to mean?" I said.

"It means Micah sent us into the astral yesterday with the intention of finding Amanda Jenson and giving the information we came back with to the FBI."

"So what's wrong with that?" I asked. "We probably saved that girl's life."

"That doesn't excuse the fact that Micah went behind our backs," Angelique said. She was practically snarling. "Why didn't he just tell us up front? He knows we would have been more than willing to help."

"What are you getting at, exactly?" I asked.

"I think it's possible that the Lucidity Project is some sort of secret government or military project," Angelique said.

"No way," I said, shaking my head. That would be crazy. Micah was a New Age, peace-loving, astral-traveling hippie. He wasn't the type of person to get involved with the military. They fought wars and killed people. Everything Micah was against. "We know Micah."

"Do we?" she asked. "Really? Then why have he and Jeremy been sneaking off together every night since we saw Amanda Jenson in the astral?"

"You think Jeremy's in on it too?" I asked.

"Of course Jeremy's in on it too. He's a sergeant in the army, Max. He started working with Micah way before the rest of did, and he's the one that went down into the basement yesterday, where it's obvious he found Amanda. So what is the Lucidity Project, really? Micah's been telling us it's a therapeutic program, but what if it's not? What if he's been working with the government all along and the Lucidity Project is some kind of program to train psychic spies for the government?"

"That's crazy," I said.

"Is it?" she asked. "We don't know who Micah works for. We don't know where his money really comes from. We don't know anything!"

"But we know Micah," I said, "and he wouldn't do this."

"Get real, Max," Angelique said. "You've known him for less than a month. And then there's Jeremy. He said the army sent him here to help him get better, but what if that's just his cover? For all we know the entire institute is run by the government."

I didn't want to believe anything Angelique was saying, but some part of me thought she might be right.

"I feel like I should remind all of you," Brad said, "that when we first started trying to guess what the Lucidity Project was, I intuited that it had something to do with the government. The rest of you didn't believe me, but I think this is what I was picking up on."

Yes, I remembered him saying that that first night at dinner. Back when I didn't believe in psychics. So much had changed.

Before I could say anything else, the phone rang. Angelique answered it on the first ring.

"Hello?" she asked. "Yes, Micah," she said coldly. "We are all here. Except for Jeremy. I assume that's because he's with you. Yes . . . okay, good-bye."

She hung up the phone as we all stared at her expectantly.

"Micah wants us up in the great room. Now."

●●●

Micah was waiting for us in the great room, along with a very official-looking older man in khaki slacks and a button-down shirt. He had salt-and-pepper hair and deep frown lines. Suddenly Angelique and Brad's "secret government project" theory didn't seem so farfetched.

"Please have a seat," Micah said as we came in.

"We saw the news this morning," Angelique said, ignoring his request. "Who are you?" she asked the other man. "FBI? CIA?"

"U.S. Military," the man said with a calm smile, not bothered in the slightest.

"I knew it," she said, turning to all of us as if she'd caught the man in a lie. "Didn't I tell you?"

"What's going on, Micah?" I said, coming up behind Angelique.

"Have a seat," he said, putting a hand on my back. "We're going to answer your questions in a second."

When we were settled, Micah continued. "This is Major Skip Keller. He's an intelligence officer in the U.S. Military. As you've seen, the work you did in your session yesterday led to the rescue of Amanda Jenson. She disappeared six months ago while walking to work."

"So you've been working with the government this whole time? Why didn't you tell us?" I asked, still trying to wrap my head around what was going on.

"In the past when we told our remote viewers they were looking for kidnapped civilians they became very anxious and weren't able to complete the task," Major Keller said. "After failing, and knowing people's lives were at stake, many of them took it very hard."

"I thought you said we were the first ones to take part in the Lucidity Project?" Dawn asked carefully.

"You are," Micah said. "Major Keller is talking about the research he's done on his own projects."

"And what projects are those?" Angelique demanded.

"Have any of you heard of Project Stargate?" Major Keller asked.

"Project Stargate," Brad said, almost falling off his chair. "I thought that was terminated in 1995?"

"What's Project Stargate?" I asked.

Brad looked at me like I'd just asked who the president of the United States was. "Only the biggest research program of psychic phenomena in government history. It was supposedly terminated in 1995 for failing to produce any useful intelligence information but that was lie."

"That's right. The truth is," Major Keller said, "Project Stargate was never terminated. Only the name was changed. It's now called Project Star Game, and as you probably guessed, Jeremy here is one of our newest recruits."

We all turned to Jeremy, who held his head high.

"So what, you're like a spy?" Angelique asked. "You've been spying on us?"

"No," Jeremy said. "I'm a guinea pig, really. My mission was to come here and find out if the Lucidity Project was something we could use for Project Star Game."

"What was all that stuff you told us about having PTSD?" Angelique asked, eyes narrow. "Was that even true?"

"Yes," he said. "Everything I've told you about how I came to the island was true. My PTSD. My dreams and visions. All of it."

"That's how we became aware of Jeremy's gift in the first place," Major Keller said.

"When I told my psychiatrist at the base about my visions, I figured she'd think I'd completely lost it and put me on more meds—but instead she introduced me to Major Keller, who suggested I come here. Not only to develop my gift but to see if the Lucidity Project was something we could use at Project Star Game." He rubbed the back of his neck. "After Max got Amanda's name, and the fact that she was from Texas, I told Major Keller, and with that small bit of information he was able to track down a missing persons report for an Amanda Jenson from Waco, Texas. When he sent me her picture, I was shocked to see she was the same girl we'd seen in the astral. Major Keller suggested we do a blind remote viewing exercise in the astral to attempt to find her location."

"What if we hadn't found her?" I asked.

"Then we wouldn't be having this conversation right now," Jeremy said. Then he smiled. "But we *did* find her."

"And what do you get out of all this?" Angelique asked, turning to Micah, her tone less angry now.

"I get the opportunity to help people on a very large scale," he answered, placing his hands in his pockets.

It was hard to stay mad at Jeremy or Micah for what they'd hidden from us. Their motives had been to help people. Yes, we had been misled, but with good intentions: to save a woman's life without traumatizing us in the process.

"So what now?" Brad asked. "Are you leaving the island?"

"Yes," Jeremy said.

Angelique shifted in her seat. "You can't leave," she said, her voice soft now. "We've just gotten started here. We have so much more to do."

"That's true. That's why I'm hoping you'll come with me." He looked back at the major, who was standing, stern-faced, behind him.

"You want us to leave the island?" Dawn asked. "To go where?"

"We have a top-notch training center in Virginia up in the Blue Ridge Mountains dedicated to this kind of work," Major Keller said.

"You want us to join the military?" I asked, incredulous.

"No," the major said. "You'd be brought on as civilian contractors, not subject to all the rules and regulations of military life."

"Well, you can count me in," Tucker said, slapping his hands together. "When do we leave?"

Brad shook his head. "I've read quite a few of the books that previous viewers from Project Stargate wrote about their experience at your so-called top-notch facilities and they all said the same thing—that they were treated abysmally," he said. "Locked away. Ridiculed. Ostracized. Overworked. Underpaid. Completely unappreciated."

"Project Stargate was mishandled in many aspects and that's why we're going a different way this time around," Major Keller said. "We have state-of-the-art modern facilities and equipment, excellent nutritional chefs on site to cook all your meals. People like you are no longer hidden away; in fact, they're treated like rock stars. You've got to realize people with psychic abilities are much more accepted these days, even revered. They have their own reality shows, talk shows. They write books and travel the world sharing their gifts. It's very different than it was in the seventies and eighties. These days, with the resources we have available, you can help a lot of people and make a lot of money doing it."

He had Brad's attention. "How much money exactly?" he queried.

"Starting salary is a $150,000," Major Keller said. "Full benefits plus bonuses, and one month off a year with pay."

Angelique looked over at me, eyebrows raised. Brad got quiet, then turned to the rest of us and shrugged. "That's a pretty good deal for a bunch of kids," he said. "Half of us never even went to college."

He got that right. I wouldn't even make that much as a staff writer at *You Sexy Witch*.

"How long do we have to decide?" Dawn asked.

"Well . . ." Major Keller paused. "We have a new project that's quite urgent. After seeing what you were able to do with the Amanda Jenson case, we'd like to get you to our facilities in Virginia as soon as possible. As in, tonight."

"Tonight?" I asked. "What if we need more time?"

"I can't guarantee we'll be able to take you on later if you change your mind," he said. "And if we do, you'll be put in a different group. From what I understand, the six of you have gotten very close. You don't want to split up now after all this time together, do you?" He didn't wait for an answer. "The ship sets sail tonight at six," he said. "If you want to come, you need to be on it."

"What ship?" asked Brad.

"That ship," Major Keller said, nodding out toward the ocean. We all turned to the windows to see where he was pointing. Way to the right, out past the cove, was a huge naval ship. We'd been so involved talking about secret psychic spies, we hadn't noticed it at all.

"So, you just happened to be in the neighborhood when all this went down?" Angelique asked, her eyes narrowing in suspicion at the major.

"Let's just say we have quite an interest in what you all are doing over here. Now," Major Keller continued, loosening his tie, "It's not every day I make it out to a tropical island in the Caribbean." He turned to Micah. "I hear you make a mean green smoothie on this island."

"We certainly do," said Micah. "Why don't I show you around, and we'll give the team some time to talk."

The major agreed. As they turned to leave, Micah's eyes met mine for a brief instant—giving nothing away, as usual. Then he walked out the door.

"Look, I know this is a lot for everyone to take in," Jeremy said as soon as they'd left. "And I don't expect you all to just drop everything and do this just because I want you to."

"You can say that again, Jeremy," Angelique said. "How are we supposed to trust you after you hid something like this from us?"

"I didn't want to keep this from you, believe me. My intentions were good," Jeremy said. "You know they were. That's why none of you could sense what was going on, except maybe for Brad."

Brad smiled smugly at Jeremy's compliment.

"I'm here to help people, just like the rest of you," Jeremy continued. "The truth is that Project Star Game is bigger than me. Bigger than us. Whatever your politics, whatever your feelings about the military, they have quite a lot of resources to help us help others on a massive level. There are a lot of other people like Amanda Jenson out there and they need our help. So, what do you say?"

"Like I said, I'm in, man," Tucker said, smacking Jeremy's hand.

"Me too," Brad said, adjusting his glasses. "But I want my money up front."

"I'll see what I can do." Jeremy said, smiling, and then he turned to Angelique. "What do you say, Ange? You ready to get off this island or what?"

Angelique crossed her arms across her chest—and then let out a resolute sigh. "You know I am. But if you keep something big like that from me again, I'll break both your legs."

Jeremy laughed and turned to Dawn, who peered up at him from beneath her lavender bangs.

"Dawn? How about you?"

I thought there was no way Dawn would do something as

adventurous as join the military as a psychic spy, but that was the old Dawn. The new one looked up and said quite confidently, "I'm in."

All eyes fell on me. I stood staring back, like a proverbial deer in the headlights.

"Max?" Jeremy said. "What about you? Are you with us?"

"I can't believe that the rest of you have agreed to do this without finding out any information besides salary and a few minor details," I said, trying to buy myself some time.

"Honestly," Angelique said, "I'm really just going with my gut on this one. It feels like this is—"

"Going to be totally kickass!" Tucker crowed.

"I was going to say, the next right step," Angelique said. "I've been on this island for two whole years and it's been incredible. But I'm ready to leave. And now I have someplace to go. And on top of that I'll be paid to work on the Lucidity Project? Are you kidding me? It's kind of a no-brainer."

"Well, not for me, it's not," I said. "Three weeks ago I was a writers' assistant on a television show with a serious depression problem. Now I'm supposed to be a psychic spy? I just got used to the idea of giving up my old life in LA to stay on the island."

Jeremy took in a tense breath, as if he was about to argue with me.

"Jeremy," Angelique said gently, putting a hand on his shoulder. "You know this is a big commitment to ask of any of us."

"But we're supposed to stay together," Jeremy said, passion in his voice. "I may not be as intuitive as the rest of you, but that I know."

I had just last night decided I would stay on the island instead of going back to LA. Why did everyone have to leave now? I shook my head. "I'm sorry. I only just found some relief from my depression, and I found it here. I can't risk that now by leaving. I just can't." Tears pouring down my cheeks, I turned and bolted out of the room.

32

Twenty minutes later, I found myself panting at the top of the bluff. The lighthouse stood before me, but that wasn't where I was heading. Something was drawing me over to the cliff. Perhaps it was just habit; after all, we ran to the cliff every day. And every day, instead of jumping off along with the rest of the team, I chose the safer way, down the sandy path to the beach below. Was that what I was doing now by not leaving with them? Choosing the safer way?

I jogged over to the edge and stared down at the calm sea below, which was so clear you could see down to the very bottom in places. *If only I could jump*, I thought. If I had the courage to do that, maybe this decision wouldn't be so hard. But even as I thought that, a familiar feeling of vertigo twisted its way through my insides, and I had to take a few steps back.

My heart sank. *I'm not even brave enough to jump off this stupid cliff. How can anyone possibly expect me to survive the military?* No, I needed to stay here on the island. This was the best place for me now.

"You finally gonna do it?" a familiar voice called out.

I turned to see Micah jogging up behind me, significantly less out of breath than I was.

I inched toward the edge, looked back down at the water, and once again felt faint. "I can't," I said, stepping back, defeated. "How'd you know I was here?"

"I saw you crying and running dramatically into the woods," he said, that old smirk back on his face. "I thought you might need some-one to talk to."

I wanted to be mad at him for all that he had kept from me, but I couldn't for some reason. "I guess I know the secret you were keeping from me now. Working on a top-secret government project—I never would have guessed that one." I shook my head in disbelief.

"I didn't want to keep it from you," he said, "but that's the thing about top-secret government projects: you can't tell anyone about them."

"I'm not even upset about that part," I said, waving him off. "I understand why you did what you did. I'm just not sure what I'm sup-posed to do now. The whole team has decided to leave with Jeremy, which seems crazy to me. How could they agree to change their whole lives in just a few minutes? Even Dawn is going. I wish I had that kind of courage, but I don't. My depression just lifted for the first time in years. If I leave, it could come back. I can't risk that."

Micah frowned. "So basically the only thing holding you back is fear."

"Common sense too," I said. "Up until just a couple weeks ago I was completely unstable. Can you imagine me in the military? They kill people, Micah. Honestly, it surprises me that you even agreed to work with them. Aren't you trying to change the world?"

"What better place to start but the United States Military?" He smiled. "It's not perfect. Believe me, I know that. But at least they're trying to avoid casualties—and looking for better methods than the ones they have in place. And that's why they need people like you and the team in there to help change that." He looked out at the ocean. "The truth is, Ms. Dorigan, we're entering a new age, and people who can see the light need to shine that light on the places that need the most transformation. It's part of our evolutionary process. It's messy; it's uncomfortable; and there will be missteps along the way, and failures as well—many of them. But does that mean we shouldn't do it?"

"If you're so interested in helping the military, why don't you go with the team?" I said, sounding a little more confrontational than I intended. I didn't want to say what I was really thinking: that maybe if he went, I'd feel safer going too.

"Because it's not what I'm supposed to do," he answered with a shrug. "It's not part of my purpose here."

"What is your purpose here, exactly?" I asked, crossing my arms. Everyone seemed to know what they were supposed to be doing except for me.

"I'm here to help you."

I waited, expecting more—but he didn't continue.

"Your purpose here on earth is to help *me*," I reiterated in disbelief.

"Not just you. Others too," he answered, as if it were an afterthought, "with my research on the island. At least for right now."

"Well, you can't help us if we're not here," I said.

"You can help yourself now," he said. "All of you can."

I took in a breath. "You think I should go with them."

"It doesn't matter what I think. This decision is up to you."

I looked back down at the ocean below and the urge to jump off hit me once again. What if I just did it? It's not like it would solve anything, but it would feel so good to just let go and jump. I knew I wouldn't get hurt. The rest of the team managed to make the jump every day. I inched a little closer to the cliff—and noticed the jagged rocks jutting out from the cliff's base. If I didn't jump out far enough, I would hit them and break my neck.

Any courage I'd had dissipated and was quickly replaced by tremendous vertigo. My stomach dropped, and everything in front of me began to fade from view. I stumbled back and Micah rushed forward and grabbed me to keep me from falling over. He stood there, solid as a rock, holding me steady as I got my bearings. After the feeling passed, I looked up into his eyes, which appeared even paler than usual. No, I wasn't ready to leave this island quite yet.

"I'm staying here," I said, pulling away from him.

"Ms. Dorigan—"

"You can't talk me out of it, Micah. This is where I'm safe. My depression is gone for now, but it could be back tomorrow. If here is where I'm happy, here is where I should stay. Don't you want me to be happy?"

"Of course," he said, his eyebrows cinched together as he looked down at the ground in front of his feet. "But . . ."

"But what?"

My words hung in the air as I waited for his answer. He tilted his head and looked up like he was listening for something, then nodded sharply.

"But nothing. You're right," he said, looking back at me. "You need to trust your own process."

I took a deep breath. "It's settled, then."

I held his gaze, daring him to try to argue with me further, but he didn't. Yes, it would be different here on the island without the rest of the team, the people who had quickly become my closest friends in the world. But there would be others. I didn't have to join some secret government program to help people. I could do that right here. Give back to others what I had learned myself, what I was still learning. Micah was the key to all of that, wasn't he? I knew I had experienced only a fraction of what was possible on this island.

I peeked back over the bluff to the water in the cove below. "One day I'm going to come up here and jump off this stupid cliff."

"I know you will," Micah said. "And I wouldn't be surprised if it's sooner than you think."

••

After our talk I stayed behind while Micah headed back to the resort. I was afraid if I went back and faced the team they might convince me to go with them, or at the very least make me feel incredibly guilty. I couldn't risk it. Instead I spent the rest of the day swimming and eating mangos at Mango Beach, then fell into a restless sleep in the shade of one of the trees.

At five thirty I came down off the mountain to see off the people I'd spent every day with since I'd arrived on the island—the people who knew more about me than anyone else in the world, and who I may never see again.

I found them heading down the dock with Major Keller, wheeling their belongings behind them. At the end of the dock a shiny blue speedboat waited to take them out to the naval ship that was still sitting about a mile off shore.

"Wait up!" I called out as I ran down the dock toward them—then realized my mistake as soon as I saw everyone turn back toward me with expectant looks.

"I . . . I'm just coming to see you off," I clarified as I approached.

"Girl, you got me all worked up," Brad said, throwing his bags down dramatically. He was all set for military life, dressed in a pair of camo pants and tight grey T-shirt.

"I'm sorry," I said. "I just didn't want you to leave before I got a chance to say good-bye."

"You sure we can't convince you to come with us?" Major Keller asked. He had on a pair of aviator sunglasses and looked even more intimidating than he had earlier that day, if that was possible.

I swallowed. "I'm sure."

The group's energy quickly deflated. Jeremy made what sounded like a grunt, then turned and tossed his suitcase into the boat with a loud thud.

"Well, we can't make you do anything you don't want to do," Major Keller said, as if he were longing for the good old days when the military had more power to steamroll people. He lifted his sunglasses, gave me a quick wink, and climbed down into the boat.

"I guess this is it then," Brad said, and he wrapped me in a big hug, only to pull away a few seconds later. "That's all you get," he said. "I can't let those tough military boys see me cry. I'm in the army now."

I nodded and wiped a tear out of my eye as he boarded the boat.

"I'm going to miss you, Red," Tucker said, stepping forward and cupping my face in both of his hands. He looked sincerely into my eyes. "Not just for all you've done for me, but also because you have an amazing ass."

I playfully pushed him away. He bowed dramatically and then turned and swung down the ladder to the boat.

After that it was just Angelique, Dawn, and me standing on the dock facing each other.

"This will be good for you," I said to Angelique, trying to sound upbeat. "To get off the island and try a new adventure."

"Yeah," she said, not sounding too convinced. "And good luck on your new adventure as well. You deserve to be happy, Max. You really do."

All I could do was nod a yes. If I tried to say anything else, I was sure to start crying once again. Luckily, Dawn saved me by coming up and giving me a hug. I felt in awe of her as she pulled away and stood before us, shoulders down and back, head held high, big blue-grey eyes in clear view. I couldn't believe this was the same person I'd come to the island with less than a month ago.

"I'm really going to miss you guys," I choked out. There was no use trying to fight the tears.

"Don't spend too much time crying about it," Dawn said as she turned away. "We'll be seeing each other again soon."

"How do you know that?" I called after her. "From what Major Keller said it sounds like you guys are going to be gone for a long time."

"Time has nothing to do with it," Dawn called back.

"Angelique, let's go!" Jeremy yelled as he helped Dawn into the boat. It was clear from the impatient look on his face that he didn't plan to come back to say good-bye. My heart sank as I stared after him.

"He'll get over it," Angelique said, reaching down to squeeze my hand.

"Will he?" I asked, looking hard at him, hoping he would at least give me a wave, a look, something. I had no idea when I would see him, any of them, again. What if they were put into covert ops and had to go undercover or something? Did people really do that, or had I watched too many movies? The whole thing felt so surreal. But what else was new? This island never ceased to surprise me.

I snapped out of it and met Angelique's eyes. "You know where to find me," I said, then pulled her in for a hug. We squeezed each other tightly before she let go and headed for the boat.

The next thing I knew, Jeremy was making his way toward me. He didn't try to hide the anger in his eyes as he approached, and part of me wondered if he weren't going to physically try to carry me off with him. Instead he stopped a few feet in front of me and said honestly, "I'm not going to lie: I think you're making a big mistake."

"I know that, Jeremy, and I'm sorry."

"Come here, then," he said, and he wrapped me in his big arms. A knot stuck in my throat as he kissed me softly on the side of the cheek, then let go and walked back to the boat.

I was left with a dizziness akin to the vertigo I'd just experienced on the cliff. I couldn't bear to watch that boat take my new friends away, so I headed back to the hotel before it even left the dock.

As I walked back to the hotel, my emotions churned inside of me. Had I made the wrong decision? *No*, I told myself, *I'm just upset that everyone is leaving*. I belonged here on the island with Micah, and nothing was going to take my happiness away from me. Nothing.

●●●

As I was walked down the cement path back toward my room, I saw Zoe running toward me from the hotel. She was wearing her thin, white dress and having a difficult time trying to run in flip-flops.

"Max!" she called out when she saw me.

"You missed the boat. They just left," I said, assuming she had gotten caught up with something and forgotten to say good-bye to the team. "You might be able to make it down to the beach in time to wave from the shore."

"No," she said, shaking her head, trying to catch her breath. "I said my good-byes at lunch." There was a look on her face I had never seen before.

"What's going on?" I asked. Had they sent Zoe after me to try and change my mind? That didn't make sense. She was coming from the direction of the hotel, not the beach.

"You have a message from Frances Duncan!" she gasped, her large eyes looking bigger than ever. "You need to read it right away."

I made a mad dash for my room, and two minutes later I was at my desk in front of my laptop. The message was still up on my Facebook page where Zoe had left it.

Dear Ms. Dorigan, it began.

> I'm sorry it's taken me so long to get back to you. I'm in my nineties and do not check my Facebook account very often. What a strange message to receive, yet I have to admit, I'm quite intrigued. It's not every day someone emails you to say they're seeing your dead aunt's ghost. I myself was not a believer in the supernatural until I was well into my sixties, but I'll get to that story in a minute.

Yes, Millicent Last was my mother's sister. Her death was quite tragic and it deeply affected the whole family. From what my mother told me, however, Millicent had had quite a difficult time of it before she died. She struggled with depression, and had even spent time in an institution. They didn't have the resources back then that they have today to help such unfortunates. Their methods back then were quite barbaric, and the poor thing suffered greatly.

Of course it didn't help that Millicent chose a philandering alcoholic for a husband, who had no doubt married her for her money—Roald Last, a somewhat successful stage actor. According to my mother, Aunt Millie was extremely unhappy in the marriage, and it seemed to fuel her depression. Roald was a heavy drinker and the two had very public spats that embarrassed the family to no end.

There were also rumors Millie was having an affair with Roald's brother Charlie, but that was never proven.

That fateful night on New Year's Eve there was a big party at the Avalon, the resort in the Caribbean you mentioned which I guess is now called The Theta Institute. I have little recollection because I was a young child at the time, but according to what my mother told me later, sometime after midnight Roald, Charlie, and Millie all went up to the lighthouse, perhaps to watch the storm. From what I understand, they'd all been drinking heavily. We don't really know what happened after that except that all three of them ended up in the ocean that night. Apparently they had been swept off the bluff during the storm. Of course there were rumors that Roald pushed Charlie and Millie off the cliff after finding them together at the lighthouse, but it was never proven, and in the family it was always referred to as an accident.

After my mother died I didn't give the matter much more thought. Then, about twenty-five years ago, a man contacted me to tell us a very strange story. He said that from the time that his son could talk he insisted his name was Roald. The boy had repeated night terrors of drowning in a stormy sea, and he told his parents he wanted to go to an island to find and help people he had hurt. Finally, one day, when he got old enough, he was able to explain to his parents that he had lived before as another man—an actor. He'd done something very bad and it was important that he find as much out about his former self as he could so he could make things right. His parents, who were from California and quite open-minded, began to suspect he was suffering from some sort of past-life trauma.

Roald isn't the most common name in the world, and it didn't take too long for them to track me down.

We weren't quite sure what to make of the story at first, but the family insisted on flying out from California to meet us. I don't know why I agreed to the meeting—the boy just seemed so sincere, and of course I was curious. I remained skeptical until the boy arrived and mentioned a doll Roald had given me when I was very young. He told me things that had been kept private within our family—things that only my mother and I knew. He refused to discuss the mystery around how Roald, Millicent and Charles had died that night, and when I attempted to press him, he became agitated. With his parents there, I couldn't be too persistent, and I had to let it go.

By the time the boy left I was absolutely convinced he was the reincarnation of my Uncle Roald. You couldn't coach a child to act the way this one had. And even if you could, what would be the point? The parents wanted nothing from me. In fact, after that day I never heard from any of them again.

Like I said before, that was over twenty years ago, and that boy is now no doubt a man. Since you seem to be so open-minded regarding the supernatural, I suggest that you contact him. His name is Micah McMoneagle. I'm sure he shouldn't be too hard to track down—not in this day and age, and with a name like that! I hope you can get more out of him than we did.

Sincerely,
Frances Marjorie Duncan

My eyes shot over to Zoe, who was still standing wide-eyed at the foot of her bed. My mind felt like it had been shocked with a cattle prod. Micah had been Millicent Last's husband in a past life? I had to grasp the desk to keep myself from falling out of my chair.

"Do you think Micah did it?" asked Zoe, bringing me back to the present moment. "Killed Millicent in his past life, I mean. Maybe that's what Millicent's been trying to tell you. Maybe she's been trying to warn you against him all along!"

"No . . ." I said, staring numbly at the screen. My mind was swimming in a sea of shock and confusion. Up until now I'd been on the fence about past lives, but after everything that had happened, I knew that what Frances had written was true. Micah had been Roald Last in a past life, and Millicent had been his wife. As for Micah's guilt in Millicent's death, I didn't know. It seemed totally out of character for him—but you could be a totally different person in a past life, couldn't you? I remembered the conversation Micah and I had had where he'd admitted that he'd been a scoundrel in his past life. Why hadn't he just told me then that he believed he had once been Roald?

There was only one way to find out. I stood up slowly from the desk and walked toward the door, still feeling stunned. There was so much apprehension in my body I found it difficult to move.

"Where are you going?" Zoe asked.

"To Micah's," I said. "He's the only one who knows the truth."

"I'll come with you," she said, taking a step toward me.

"No," I said. "This is between Micah and me. I have to go by myself."

33

I found Micah standing at his kitchen sink, washing dishes. He didn't seem at all surprised by my intrusion, or the fact that I'd come into his house unannounced. When he turned around to face me, his face was passive. It was almost as if he'd expected me.

"Millicent Last was your wife in a past life," I said, trying to keep my voice from shaking. "But you've known that all along."

"How did you find out?" he asked, turning off the water.

"Zoe and I tracked down her niece, Frances Duncan."

"Ah," he said, nodding as if he had just been let in on some secret plan. He appeared quite pleased, considering the situation. "Frances, yes. That makes sense."

"No, Micah," I countered. "None of this makes sense. None of it."

"Not yet," he said, drying his hands off on a dishtowel. "But it will."

I didn't wait for him to elaborate. "This is the secret you've been hiding from me all along. Why didn't you just tell me?"

"It was something you needed to discover yourself—when you were ready."

"More lies! More secrets!" I yelled at him. "You've lied to me this whole time, about everything. It's like I don't know you at all."

"That's not true." His voice soft and steady.

"Frances said there were rumors that Roald Last pushed his brother and Millicent off that cliff. Maybe this whole time Millicent has been warning me against you. Warning me to stay away from you. Trying to scare me so I'd get off this island."

"Is that what you really think?"

I had no idea what I thought. From what Frances had said in her message, Roald had been an alcoholic and a philanderer. Micah was neither of those things. How much did he have in common with his past self? I needed to know more. I needed his side of the story.

"What happened that night, Micah?"

"Are you sure you're ready to know?"

"Yes," I said.

"Then I think you should hear it from Millicent," he said. "She's been trying to get you to a place where she could show you all along. You weren't ready before, but now you are."

His demeanor baffled me. Instead of appearing upset that I'd found out this dark secret, he looked relieved. Why?

I followed him into the living room, and he nodded me toward the couch, then walked over to the lucidity machine and flipped on a few buttons.

My mouth dropped open. "You want me to go into the astral with you right now? You must be crazy."

"Millicent wants to show you what happened herself."

"Oh really? That's what *she* wants?"

"Yes," he said. "She wants it very much."

"Prove it," I said.

Before the words were even out of my mouth, one of the pairs of headsets shot off the lucidity machine by itself and into my hands. My fingers instinctively closed around them, and I looked up at Micah in utter shock.

"Why is she haunting me?" I whispered. "She should be haunting you."

"She does," he said. "Every day."

●●●

I had become quite adept at astral travel at this point, and it didn't take me long to make the transition to the other side. It was like the astral plane was a radio station frequency, and I knew exactly how to tune into it. As soon as the vibrations started, I forced my eyes open. Micah was already standing by the front door, waiting for me. I slowly rose and went to him.

"Are you ready?" he asked, putting his hand on my shoulder. I shrugged it off. There was a deep knot of dread down in the pit of my stomach, some part of me that didn't want to see whatever it was Micah was about to show me. I had a brief thought that I should wake myself up and leave the island immediately, but that would mean going back to the life I had in Los Angeles—a life that felt wrong on every level now. There was no going back. Forward was the only way. Reluctantly, I nodded yes.

Micah opened the front door, but instead of stepping out onto his front porch, we found ourselves entering the great room at the top of the hotel. I recognized it by the two tall arched windows overlooking the great lawn and the carved marble fireplace, but those were the only parts of the room that were the same. In the place of the more contemporary furniture that was usually there, the room was now decorated as a Victorian-era drawing room. The walls were grey and adorned with oil paintings of men and women stiffly posed in frilly clothing. The wood floors were covered in Persian rugs and topped with myriad sofas and settees, including a red Victorian sofa—the same red Victorian sofa Micah had in his office.

Micah walked across the room toward the bar in the corner, which in present day was filled with bottled waters and herbal tea, and began to fix himself a cocktail.

I was about to tell him this was no time for a drink when he turned back around and I saw he was a different man—the man with the purple hat I'd seen in my dreams. *Roald Last!*

I took in a breath and realized that when I'd seen the man in the purple hat in my dreams before, it must have been Micah in disguise. He knew how to shapeshift into a raven in the astral—why not into the image of his former self? Micah was the one who had come to me in the hospital. And later he'd been the one to save me from the dragon. It had been Micah all along.

I heard talking behind me, and I turned to see that there was a crowd of people coming into the room. They were quite animated and dressed in 1920s fashions: drop waist dresses for the women, and preppy jackets and slacks for the men. A butler in a black jacket and bowtie walked around offering cocktails to the lively bunch.

The door opened again, and Millicent stormed in. She was dressed to the nines in a beautiful chartreuse dress and pearls, looking healthy and very much alive. Her makeup had been done but it was clear by the dark tears running down her cheeks she'd been crying; her eyes burned with rage as she headed straight for her husband, the man with the purple hat.

In her hand was something white and lacy.

"Cheater!" she screamed at him. "Lying, no-good snake!" With that she threw the lacey thing in her hand at Roald. As it landed on the ground in front of him I could see it was a woman's slip.

The people in the room froze with horrified looks on their faces. These weren't the types accustomed to public altercations.

Roald grabbed Millicent roughly by the arm and marched her out the door into the hall. I followed them into the next room, a small, private office. Once there and out of the sight of his guests, Roald threw Millicent to the floor. She landed hard on her hands and knees.

"How dare you embarrass me in front of my friends!" he hissed at her, keeping his voice low.

"Your friends. Ha!" she yelled back. "The only reason they're here is for the free vacation and booze. If it weren't for my family's money and estate they wouldn't even be here, and neither would you!"

"Keep your voice down!" he spat.

"I will not!" she said even louder. "Why do you insist on hurting me again and again? I don't understand why you just can't love me. Is it really that hard?"

With that, she collapsed at his feet in tears. He stood stock-still for a second, seeming to contemplate his next move. I could tell by the cool look on his face that yes, it was hard for him to love her.

Roald sighed, seeming annoyed that he had to put in such an effort to placate his wife this evening. But he plastered on a smile, then leaned down and gently tilted Millicent's face up toward his with the tips of his fingers.

"Of course not, darling. I do love you. And I know you love me too, don't you?" he asked her.

"Yes," she said, sniffing back her tears. "Yes, I do."

"That's right," he said, his voice sounding plastic. He was the kind of man who could easily use his charm to manipulate others, a talent Micah had clearly carried over into his present life as well. "That's a good girl. Why don't you go up to bed? I'll have Alice bring you some tea."

"Why?" she sobbed, jerking her head away from his hand. "So you can be with your *mistress*? You can't get rid of me that easily, dear husband. If you so much as glance at that woman tonight, I will humiliate you beyond your wildest dreams."

The smile on Roald's face disappeared and rage entered his eyes. "You do," he said as he jabbed his finger down at her, "and I will have you committed again. This time for good. I will lock you up and throw away the key. Do you hear me?"

"It's going to be hard to lock me up if I file for divorce, which I plan to do as soon as we get home!" she screamed back.

"Go right ahead," he said, laughing. "You know full well that if you divorce me your mother will cut you off without a cent. Face it, darling. You're stuck with me and there's nothing you can do about it."

Millicent sat there on the floor looking helpless. I could see this was a game they'd been playing for a very long time, and yet both failed to recognize it was one that neither of them could win. The only thing Millicent could do was walk away—leave this life and start a new one of her own. That seemed to be what was being asked of her.

A new hope and knowing began to rise within me. Perhaps if Millicent left Roald, her soul would finally be at peace. Maybe that's what I had been brought here to do: help her change her past. She couldn't really change it, of course, but she could play it out differently here in the astral, just as Angelique had done in vanquishing her dragon, and I had done in facing my wave.

She must understand she's supposed to leave now, I thought—but when I looked down at Millicent's horrified face, I could see she was nowhere near that realization.

I knelt down next to her. "Can't you see this relationship is destroying you?" I whispered. "Why don't you just leave?"

To my surprise, Millicent broke eye contact with Roald and jerked her head toward me, anger in her eyes. "Yes," she answered, her voice full of spite. "Why didn't I?"

"I . . . I honestly don't know," I stammered. I thought I had been watching a replay of the past, and wasn't aware that she could see or hear me. But clearly she could.

"Well, maybe this will help you," she said.

As if on cue a door quietly opened and an older woman entered. I recognized her as Millicent's mother from the photograph Zoe and I had found in the library. She looked to be in her fifties, with grey hair pulled back in a bun. She wore a long black dress with a brooch at the collar, and everything on her face was pinched, from her forehead to the tip of her chin.

Millicent looked up, tears trickling down her face. "Mama!" she cried. "He's done it again. He's brought a woman to the island this time. She's staying here at the hotel for the New Year!"

The older woman bent over and I moved out of the way, thinking she was going to comfort her daughter, but instead she reared back and slapped Millicent hard across the face. The younger woman's head spun back and hit the wall behind her. I stood there stunned at the cruelty that had just erupted from this dignified-looking older woman.

"You wicked girl!" the older woman whispered. "You are just bound and determined to give this family as many scandals as possible. All these people have come all the way from New York to have a good time, and this is how you behave? This is no way to treat our guests."

"Matilda . . ." Roald said, stepping toward the older woman. "I can handle this."

"Oh yes, you've been handling it just fine so far," she snapped back.

Roald's pale blue eyes showed no emotion. "I'm going to go back to see what I can salvage of the party." He shot Millicent a reproachful look, as if they were both children and she'd just gotten him into trouble, then left the room.

"Mama, please," Millicent whimpered. She was huddled against the wall in a self-protective crouch, as if she expected to be hit again. "You must let me divorce him now. You must."

"I'm not going to talk about this again, Millicent. No one in our family has ever gotten a divorce, and no one ever will. You and Roald have done quite well scandalizing us all without one. Why must you only think of yourself?"

"Because I can't take any more," Millicent cried.

"You knew what you were getting into when you married Roald. I tried to warn you against it—we all did. An actor, for goodness' sake . . . what did you expect? Now you're stuck with him, so instead of acting like a spoiled child, maybe you should try a little harder to please him. You have two eyes. Use them to look the other way."

As Matilda spoke I noticed there was something familiar about her. Not the way she looked, or her mannerisms, but her essence. I took a step closer to see what I was sensing and her face briefly shifted into another face I knew well—Sofia's. Then it quickly morphed back into Matilda's stern visage. *What was going on?* It didn't make sense.

Before I could explore things further, the room around me began to spin, swirling into a blur of colors and lights. This only lasted a few seconds, and when the spinning stopped I was in the middle of a huge party in the ballroom of the main hotel—the same party where Micah had saved me from Millicent in my dream.

Ahead of me, Millicent was making her way through the crowd of revelers ringing in the New Year. She was wearing the same black beaded gown that I usually saw her in, only it wasn't torn to shreds and soaking wet, and her body was healthy and fully intact. This was the night she was going to die. Chills went through my body at the realization.

I didn't have much time. I needed to get Millicent to leave the island as soon as possible. Perhaps if she were allowed to play out a different ending, one where she was able to go to Los Angeles and start a new life with Charles, she'd be able to find some peace and perhaps even reincarnate like Roald.

The situation was not promising, however. Millicent was having a hard time walking straight, and the angry haze of alcohol clung to her as she moved like a dark cloud through the party. She was heading toward a large column near the back of the room; as I got closer I saw Roald was just behind it, standing close to a blond girl in a cream-colored silk dress. He didn't seem to notice Millicent as we approached, but instead whispered something in the blonde's ear as he ran a hand down the side of her body. The girl looked up at him with a coy finger in her mouth and let out a playful giggle, then whispered something back. He looked down at her like a wolf stalking his prey, then grabbed her by the hand and pulled her out of the room.

Millicent, who had been standing just feet away watching the whole thing, dropped her shoulders, then slowly turned back around and walked past me out of the ballroom. There was no fight left in her.

Her face appeared gaunt, her spirit broken, as if the core of her being had been fractured. I scurried after her out of the party and into the dark foyer.

She stopped in front of one of the large French windows at the front of the hotel and stared out into the violent storm raging outside. Lightning flashed across the sky, followed immediately by the roar of thunder. The lights in the ballroom dimmed for a few seconds and screams erupted from the ballroom—but as the lights went back up, the screams turned to giggles, and the party continued on as if nothing had happened.

I was trying to think up something to say. How could I convince Millicent that she had the freedom to do things differently here? From what I understood about ghosts, they were stuck in the past and didn't understand that they were dead—not fully, anyway. Still, there had to be a way to get through to her. But how?

"Looks like things around here haven't changed a bit since I've been away," said a voice behind us before I had a chance to speak. I turned to see that it was Roald's brother, Charles, looking quite charming in a white tuxedo. His eyes were fixed on Millicent. "Aren't you tired of it, Millie?"

"Yes," Millicent said, turning to face him. "I am."

He came closer and placed his hands on her shoulders.

There was something so familiar about Charles, and it wasn't the fact that he looked so much like Roald. I stared hard, and for just a moment his face morphed into Jeremy's.

I couldn't believe it. Jeremy was Micah's brother in a past life? Sofia was Millicent's mother? How could this be?

"You need to get out of here," Charles said.

"Yes," Millicent said, her eyes glazed over with a faraway look. "I do."

"I'm heading to California in the morning."

Millicent's eyes came into focus. "To live with the spiritualists?" she asked, biting her lip. "But you'll be an outcast!"

"I don't care," he said. "I can't be myself with these people and neither can you. It's killing you. It's killing both of us."

"Please don't leave me, Charles." Millicent's voice was growing desperate.

"I can't live this lie anymore. My visions are demanding I go to Los Angeles. There's people there I need to help. And you are supposed to come with me."

"You know I can't do that," she said. "This is the only life I've ever known."

Charles shut his mouth and nodded reluctantly. "Well then, I guess this is good-bye. I can't wait for you any longer."

"No, please don't leave me," she cried, grabbing at him. "I'll die here if you do."

"You'll die here anyway," he said. He turned on his heels and stormed out of the room.

A single tear rolled down Millicent's beautiful face and she turned back to the window. As if on cue, Roald and the blond woman from the party ran out into the drive in front of the hotel, got into a car parked there, and drove off wildly toward the great lawn.

"I have nothing now," Millicent said.

I walked up next to her. "Charles is right," I said, hoping she could still see and hear me. "You have to get out of here, tonight, or you're going to die. Literally. Do you understand? Do you remember?"

Millicent didn't respond at first—only stared out the window watching the storm, which was now so intense the trees outside looked like they were about snap in two. Branches and debris blew across the grounds, and the French windows shook so hard I thought they might shatter.

"It's true. I should have gone to Los Angeles with Charles." Millicent's voice was heavy with regret. "There was quite an exciting life waiting there for me there. But I didn't go, did I, Max?"

I started at the sound of my name leaving her lips. So she did understand that this scene she was taking part in was some sort of reenactment, and not a recording of the past as I had previously thought. So why was she reliving it? And why did she need me to be a part of it?

"You can still leave," I said, hope rising in my voice. "Let's go find Charles. You can leave with him in the morning and play it out differently this time."

"But that's not what I'm here to do," she said. "I'm not here to change the past."

"Then what are you here to do?" I asked.

"I'm here to help you remember it." She reached up slowly and touched her finger to my temple, and in an instant everything came rushing back to me. Growing up in New York in the early 1900s with Matilda as my mother—an uptight woman who cared for nothing but social mores. Rebelling against it all at nineteen and marrying Roald; battling through our marriage and my depression; my dreams to be a writer; my affair with Charles; my desire to get out from underneath my family's thumb and go out on my own. My body lit up with chills as it all rushed back in at once.

"We've all been trying so hard to help you remember what happened so you can do things differently in this life," Millicent said, her face suddenly becoming quite serene. "Tell me, Max. Do you remember now?"

"Yes," I whispered as tears began to fall down my face.

"What do you remember?" she asked, a tinge of hope brightening her dark eyes.

"I remember"—I paused, incredulous at the words about to leave my mouth—"that I was you."

Millicent shut her eyes, and a wave of relief washed over her face. When she opened them again, her jaw was set and determined.

"Well then, I guess you know what happens now," she said, reaching out and offering me her hand.

I looked down at it for a second, not quite understanding what was going on. When I saw the conciliatory look on her face I realized she was making me an offering: to show me what happened in my past life in full detail. There would be no do-over scenario, no plotting an escape to Los Angeles with Charles. That wasn't how it had happened. If I wanted to rewrite my story, I would have to do it in present day, as Maxine Dorigan. But to do that, I had to know what happened so that I wouldn't repeat it—so that I could move forward.

I placed my hand in Millicent's, and instantly felt my astral body being pulled towards her, sucked into to her. Her consciousness began to overtake my own. Reflexively I fought it, but my attempts were futile.

Just relax, Millicent thought as I faded into the background. *It will all be over soon.*

34

As I stepped out from underneath the porch awning and made my way toward the stables, the rain fell hard against my skin and the wind was so strong I could barely stay on my feet. My dress grew heavier as it absorbed the water, and the dark charcoal I used for eyeliner stung my eyes, blurring my sight. Between the wind, rain and darkness I could barely see. But I wasn't even thinking at this point; I just knew I must get up to the bluff before the alcohol wore off and I lost my nerve—before the numbness subsided and I changed my mind. I didn't have much time. Roald would pay for what he'd done to me. He would pay dearly.

Numbly, I saddled up my horse, Lady, in her stall, and then climbed on, tearing my dress in the process. Lady was jumpy, but I wasn't bothered. I was a strong rider, and despite her nerves I easily guided her out of the stables. Horses and high society—the two activities my mother had made sure I exceeded at. *Oh mother, if you could see me now.*

Together, Lady and I flew across the great lawn to the road that led up to the lighthouse. I rode like a bat out of hell through the rain and wind, kicking Lady hard in the ribs and edging her onward. It was as if the storm were on my side, pushing me toward the lighthouse. The faster I got there, the sooner Roald would pay.

We made it to the top of the cliff in record time. As we came around to the front of the lighthouse, I saw Roald's car parked there, and the soft light of a candle emanating from a window—one of Roald's signature moves. I jumped off Lady and made my way through the wind and rain up to the door, my Mary Janes pounding against the wooden steps of the porch.

The door opened without hesitation—and why wouldn't it? Roald wouldn't expect anyone else to come up here in this weather, least of all broken little me.

I found the two of them on the floor of the front room, moving under a pile of blankets in the candlelight. Myrna screamed when she saw me. I imagine I was quite a sight, standing there soaking wet in my black dress and eyeliner dripping down my face. Roald looked up, a little afraid—until he saw it was me.

"Get out, you bitch!" he shouted, as if I was the one in the wrong.

I did as I was told: walked back out the door, down the porch steps, and out into the rain. Nothing that Roald said mattered. I hadn't come up here to try to get him back. I'd come up here to punish him, and punish him I would.

I turned and walked back out to the porch, then down the steps and out into the rain. I took a few steps out onto the grass, and the winds picked up faster, pushing me forward on my feet, as if urging me to run.

Behind me I saw lights coming up the road behind the cliff. As a car pulled up, I saw that Charles was behind the wheel. He must have seen me leave the hotel and followed me up here.

I didn't have much time. I turned and bolted toward the cliff. Each time my feet hit the soft, muddy grass I was one step closer to nothing-ness—to peace. Soon it would all be over.

Behind me I heard Charles's voice calling out for me to stop, but it only spurred me on faster. Then I heard Roald's voice as well, which was surprising, but did not give me pause. Not on this night.

I had planned to just keep on running straight off the cliff, but as I neared the drop I stopped short and took a moment to look down at the rough waves crashing onto the rocks below in the usually calm cove. *That's where I need to land,* I thought. *Just hit my head on one of those rocks and it would all be over quickly.* All I had to do was lean forward and fall straight down. The rest would be done for me.

And so I fell.

The very second my feet left the cliff an agonizing jolt of regret struck me, and I knew I had made a terrible mistake. As if in slow motion, my life flashed before my eyes; not the life I had lived, but the life I could have lived—should have lived. I saw myself moving to Los Angeles with Charles and Alice and becoming one of the head members of the spiritualist center in Hollywood. I saw myself bonding with other intuitives and learning to stop relying on others for approval. I saw the people we would have helped, and what a huge sensation the book I would have written would have been—the message I'd come to share with the world.

I fell, and I knew: If I had gone with Charles to LA, I would have gotten to experience the type of freedom I'd been dreaming about my whole life. I would have been happy—truly, honestly, wildly happy, living the life I was born to live.

But that was not to be.

I hit the rough water hard, at an awkward angle, and heard a horrific snap—the sound of a bone breaking. An agonizing pain shot up my leg. Instead of hitting my head on a rock, as I had hoped, I'd landed on my leg, snapping it like a twig. Horror overcame me as I realized that instead of dying a relatively quick and painless death it would be a slow and painful one now—very, very painful. Frantically I flailed my arms and legs, attempting to get up to the surface of the water, but the waves were immense. Massive. They looked just like . . . like giant tidal waves. Just as I was able to come up for air, another huge wave crashed down, pulling me under and dragging me closer to the jagged rocks below the cliff.

I was able to come up for only a few seconds, long enough to call out for help, before another wave crashed down on top of me and I went tumbling again, head over heels.

Roald and Charles had probably thought I'd died in the fall but now, after hearing my screams, they both stood teetering at the edge of the cliff.

The water brought me to the surface once again, just long enough to see Charles—and then Roald—jump. And why wouldn't they? We'd jumped off this cliff together a hundred times before, only that was during the sunny days of summer while the waters were calm and serene.

We would all die now. And their blood would be on my hands. Regret engulfed me. *Why didn't I just stay quiet?*

Another wave crashed over me, pushing me down. In the darkness I couldn't figure out which way was up. I gasped for air but instead inhaled water; my lungs revolted, and pain tore through my chest. As I coughed and sputtered, taking in even more water, another wave crashed down and slammed me into a rock. I tried to let out a scream and my lungs filled with water. I couldn't breathe! The pain was excruciating, but knowing that Charles and Roald were sharing my fate was too much to bear.

Another wave blasted me backward, and I heard a crack—and then everything went black.

35

When I came to I was surrounded by a gray mist so thick I could see nothing else. All I knew was that I was no longer in the water. My shin ached with pain, as did my head, but it was a dull throb, not the piercing pain I'd felt before.

After a few seconds the grayness cleared and I saw I was sitting in a small rowboat in the middle of the cove, only a few hundred yards from Mango Beach. It looked to be morning, and the water was calm. I turned and, to my immense relief, saw that Roald and Charles were sitting in the boat behind me. They were wet and shivering, still in their tuxedos from the night before, and I was still in my evening gown, which was now in tatters. Roald stared straight ahead and looked white as a ghost, while Charles had his head in his hands. Hardly the attitudes I would expect from men who had just had their lives spared.

"Boys, don't look so blue," I said. "We've been saved! I don't know how, but look at us! It's a miracle!"

Gratitude and relief swept through me. As soon as we got to shore I would do everything that I'd seen in my vision: leave the island and travel to Los Angeles with Charles, take whatever job I could get, and be wholly grateful for this second chance at life! A new day was dawning, and it was time to grab it by both hands.

I looked at the oars of our little boat; they lay listless in the water. Both Charles and Roald were still sitting there, practically catatonic. By golly then, I'd row us all to shore. I scooted back and reached for the oars—and my hands went right through them.

Roald said something but I couldn't hear. I ignored him, too busy concentrating on the oars. Why couldn't I get a hold of them? I reached for them again and the same thing happened. It was absolutely impossible. Impossible unless . . .

Unless the three of us had died in the storm. Unless I really had killed us all.

I looked back at Charles, who still held his head in his hands. I'd cut his life short. He hadn't been able to fulfill his life's destiny of using his gifts to help the world—because of me.

Roald made his way toward me in the boat. I still couldn't hear him very well, but a few words came through. "We'll try again," it sounded like. In his eyes was a warmth and kindness I hadn't seen from him for so long.

"I'm so sorry," he said, reaching out and putting his hand on my face. "I failed you."

How had he failed me? Our deaths were on my hands, not his. I was the one who had played the victim. I was supposed to have left him, not killed myself! If I had left the island instead of jumping off that cliff, we'd all have lived and gone on to do what we had come to earth to accomplish. The self-hatred and despair I felt at this realization was so great, it was enough to span lifetimes.

Roald pointed ahead to Mango Beach, where I now saw there was a group of lighted beings waiting for us. As the boat glided gently toward the shore I began to recognize the faces: there was Alice and my mother, and then there were others that felt familiar even though I didn't recognize them. A beautiful dark-haired woman with long black hair and star tattoos along her neck; a young black man with glasses, dressed in gingham shorts; another athletic-looking young man in a baseball cap and shirt with no sleeves. They smiled at me kindly, but I couldn't place them.

I began to remember the plans I had made when I'd been in this realm before—the time just before I began my life as Millicent. I had come to earth wanting to learn about independence, courage, and inner strength. The soul that was Roald had agreed to partner with me to teach me those things. He had been acting out his side of our contract so I could gather up the courage to go out on my own, and I had failed. My heart felt like it was going to break in two with regret as more memories of my mission began to come back to me.

"I forgot," I cried as the lighted beings came forward and helped us out of the boat. "I forgot it all. Everything we planned!"

"We can try again." I felt Roald's hand on my back. He was still trying to comfort me.

"I couldn't save them," Charles said softly behind us as he stumbled out of the boat. "I tried, but I couldn't."

"It's not your fault, Charles," I said, but he didn't seem to hear me.

The lighted beings surrounded the three of us, and I realized they had been with us along our whole journey. Some, I suddenly realized, had even incarnated with us, and parts of them were still on earth.

"We must go back," I said to the beings as they moved closer, intensifying their light. The effect was calming, like I was being bathed in warm bliss. "Please let us go back and try again."

"We weren't supposed to be done this soon," Charles said, shaking his head, and he looked at me with confusion in his eyes. But then the light surrounded him and I couldn't see him anymore.

"This wasn't how this was supposed to turn out," I said to Roald.

The beings came even closer to us now. The light emanating from them was composed of pure love and it warmed my entire body. But still I resisted. I knew they were trying to ease our pain, but to do that they would have to make us forget—and I didn't want to forget.

I reached out and pulled Roald closer to me so that his face was only inches from my own. He was almost completely enveloped by the light now, and I knew I only had a few seconds before we would forget completely.

"Roald," I said, cupping his face in my hands. "Promise you'll go back with me and try again."

"I promise," he answered. The light was so bright now, his eyes were all I could see, but even so I could read his determination.

"If I forget, you must find me and make me remember. We'll find Charles and we'll complete our missions on earth."

"I'll find you," Roald said. "I promise I will find you, and I'll make this right if it's the last thing I do."

He pulled me to him, and I felt his lips on mine.

The light beamed brighter, and I had no choice but to surrender to it. I relaxed, and the light and I became one.

●●●

I awoke in Micah's living room overcome by a sense of peace I had never felt before—that is, until the full impact of everything that had happened in my past life hit me. Namely, the crushing realization that after coming back to earth as Maxine Dorigan, I'd almost forgotten what I had come here to do . . . *again*. I pulled off my headset and tried to get up from the couch but couldn't manage it. Instead, I slid onto the floor.

"Oh God," I said, covering my face with my hands. "You knew the whole time that I was Millicent. I wasn't being haunted by a ghost. I was haunting myself!"

Micah sat down on the floor next to me and pulled me into him. I fell against his warm chest as I tried to recall everything that had just occurred.

"You were trying to help yourself remember your past life," he said. "That's all."

"It doesn't make sense," I said, shaking my head, still trying to put all of the pieces of the puzzle together. "If I was Millicent, then who was it who attacked me at the lighthouse when I first arrived?"

"Don't you see?" Micah said. "You attacked yourself."

"That's impossible," I said, pulling away from him. "I saw Millicent with my own eyes. I felt her. She was corporeal!"

"When Angelique and Jeremy found you outside the lighthouse that night, they said you were the one hitting yourself with a rock. There was no one else there."

My mouth hung open in disbelief. Could that really be true?

"When one ignores an urgent need of the soul, it will do whatever is necessary to get your attention," said Micah. "The part of you that remembered was angry that you'd killed yourself in your last life and even angrier that not only had you forgotten you'd come back to make things right, you were also repeating all your same old patterns."

"I forgot it all," I said. "But you didn't. You remembered everything."

"Yes," he said. "I did."

I felt as if I were in a dream and had all of a sudden become lucid. I could do anything now. Anything I wanted.

"We've been given another chance," I said, grabbing onto Micah's hand. "We've been given another chance to do it right."

"To do it differently," he said. "Remember, this is a different life."

"How did you remember you were Roald? How did you remember me? Have you known your whole life?" So many questions came to my mind at once. How could he have remembered so much of it, and I, nothing at all?

"Most people who remember their past lives, remember it is as if it's a story they were told once—it has no real emotional charge for them," Micah said. "But I came into this life remembering almost everything. It started with night terrors as a toddler: dreams of drowning at sea, dreams of a man in a purple hat who was cruel to his wife. And as I got older, I began having dreams about the pact you and I had made—to find each other in this life and help each other remember our past. That's when I got interested in lucid dreaming and astral travel, which in turn led me to Stanford and eventually to creating the Lucidity Project."

"But how did you find me?" I asked.

"The same way you found Amanda Jenson," he said. "I was led to you on the astral plane. A few days before you came to the island I dreamt I was in a hospital elevator, and when the elevator doors opened, Millicent ran in. She didn't recognize me, and within a few seconds her face changed into yours. I had found you at last, and I sent Dr. Luna to go and get you."

"Why didn't you just come and get me yourself?"

"I knew you would probably have a strong aversion to me after what happened between us in our last life."

He was right. I thought back to the day we first met on the island. My dislike of him had been so strong I could hardly stand to be in the same room with him. I might not have recognized Micah cognitively, but my soul had recognized him.

I sat there, amazed and exhausted, my senses opening to a new world. It was that exhilarating feeling of lucidity, realizing all my limitations were just illusions of my own mind. There was no question of what I needed to do now to pursue my life purpose. Micah was on his path—he needed no help from me—but there was a group of people who did need my help: Jeremy, Brad, Tucker, Angelique, and Dawn. I'd refused to go with Charles to Los Angeles in my past life. I couldn't make that same mistake again.

"I'm supposed to go with Jeremy and the others," I said, looking up at Micah.

Micah nodded, a look of relief on his face. He had known this all along as well.

Then the tears came. I didn't want to leave Micah. We'd just found each other again, after all this time.

"Maybe you can come with me," I said, looking up at him hopefully. But the words sounded wrong as soon as they left my mouth, and he shook his head no.

"I'm supposed to stay here. This is your chance to go off on your own."

Micah was right. And I knew there was nothing more to be said. Perhaps he and I would be together again sometime in the future, but right now it was time to do what we'd come to earth to do. And I knew that the next right step for me was to join Project Star Game.

Micah was already up and moving toward the French doors. "We'll need to move quickly if we want to catch up with them," he said. I followed him out to the back patio, where we had a perfect view of the ocean. The naval ship was nowhere to be seen.

"They're gone," I said. "Can we catch up to them in the Serendipity?"

"It's not here," Micah said. "One of the cooks took it to St. Lucia for the evening. But the ship didn't leave too long ago, and it's heading north along this side of the island; if we head up through Dasheen Pass, we might be able to catch them as they go around the lighthouse."

"But that's over two miles away," I said.

"Well," Micah said, "I guess it's a good thing you have on your running shoes."

Two minutes later I was on the back of Micah's dirt bike heading fifty miles an hour back to my room. He screeched to a halt at the front of the hotel, where Dr. Luna and Ida were sitting and drinking iced tea on the porch.

I jumped off the bike and flew up the stairs.

"Looking for this?" Dr. Luna asked, holding up my backpack.

I stopped running and stared for a moment, and she stood up and handed it to me. A note pinned to the outside said, "Just in case you change your mind. Love, Angelique." I opened the bag to find that she'd packed the most important of my belongings in it.

"Thank you," I said to Dr. Luna, giving her a hug. "For everything."

"We'll hold de rest of your tings for you until you come back," Ida said.

"I don't know if I'm coming back," I said, kissing her on the cheek.

"Oh, you'll be back," she said with a wink. "Everyone always comes back."

I nodded gratefully to them both before running back down to Micah and jumping on the back of his bike. We tore off across the great lawn and up Dasheen Pass, but were only able to make it about a fourth of the way up before the road got too steep, at which point Micah killed the motor.

"We'll have to go on foot from here."

I nodded. I'd been doing this run almost every day since I'd gotten to the island. I was ready. I tightened my backpack around my shoulders and charged up the path.

As we flew through the jungle, I noticed that there was no hint of fatigue anywhere in my body. The feeling was so odd I had to do a reality check with my watch, just to make sure I wasn't dreaming.

As we rounded Devil's Bend I gritted my teeth and went even faster. A few minutes later we ran out through the clearing to the bluff and my heart soared. I could see the naval ship ahead of me, still about a mile out, with the sun setting behind it.

"It's almost gone!" I yelled, running toward the cliff.

"You don't have time to get down to Mango Beach to swim out to it," Micah said as he caught up with me at the cliff's edge. "You're going to have to jump."

"What?" I asked. It wasn't like the thought hadn't crossed my mind, but still. I'd spent the last few weeks afraid to jump off this cliff. And after learning that I'd died falling off this cliff in my past life, it made total sense. I couldn't do it!

"Here," he said, reaching into the bag he'd been carrying and pulling out a flare gun. "Once you land in the water, shoot off a flare and start swimming as fast as you can toward the ship. They'll have to send someone out for you."

I gave him a blank stare.

He grabbed my shoulder. "If you take the time to take the path down to the beach, by the time you swim out far enough, the ship will be past the cove and won't see you. You can do this, Ms. Dorigan."

I looked down at the ocean, so far below me, and the familiar feeling of vertigo returned. "I can't, Micah. I can't!" I cried, panic screaming through my body. "Just shoot off the flare from here and maybe they'll wait."

"Are you willing to take that chance?" he asked.

I looked out at the ship and then again down at the ocean. Micah was right. If we shot off the flare from land, they wouldn't know what we were signaling and wouldn't be required to stop. Jumping into the water and shooting off the flare from there was the only way.

"Okay, I'll do it," I said. My body started to tremble. I knew I needed to make the jump quickly, before I completely lost my wits and passed out. "I have to take a running start," I said, and took a few steps back from the ledge.

Micah grabbed my face and looked deep into my eyes. "Remember you came here with a message. You have to promise me you're going to get that message out into the world."

"I will," I said. "I promise."

"Don't worry about how to do it. Just wait for guidance and it will come."

"It's already come," I said. "I know this sounds crazy, but I think I'm supposed to write a book about my experience here on the island. I'm beginning to think my message isn't something I can sum up in a few sentences. It's a whole story, you know? This story."

He nodded, relief in his face, then kissed me lightly on the cheek and took a few steps back to give me room. I glanced back at those pale blue eyes I'd probably been looking at for lifetimes, then took a deep breath, launched into a full sprint toward the edge of the cliff. . . and jumped.

About the Author

© Bruce Glidewell

Abbey Campbell Cook studied creative writing at UC Berkeley. She now writes (and sometimes sings and dances) about her ongoing quest for spiritual and physical wellness on her blog, *Adventures in Woo Woo Land*, which often includes pictures of Channing Tatum in his underwear (Ryan Gosling, too, if you're lucky). *The Lucidity Project* is her first novel.

SELECTED TITLES FROM SHE WRITES PRESS

She Writes Press is an independent publishing company
founded to serve women writers everywhere.
Visit us at www.shewritespress.com.

How to Grow an Addict by J.A. Wright
$16.95, 978-1-63152-991-7
Raised by an abusive father, a detached mother, and a loving aunt
and uncle, Randall Grange is built for addiction. By twenty-three, she
knows that together, pills and booze have the power to cure just about
any problem she could possibly have . . . right?

Beautiful Garbage by Jill DiDonato
$16.95, 978-1-938314-01-8
Talented but troubled young artist Jodi Plum leaves suburbia for the
excitement of the city—and is soon swept up in the sexual politics and
downtown art scene of 1980s New York.

Cleans Up Nicely by Linda Dahl
$16.95, 978-1-938314-38-4
The story of one gifted young woman's path from self-destruction to
self-knowledge, set in mid-1970s Manhattan.

Wishful Thinking by Kamy Wicoff
$16.95, 978-1-63152-976-4
A divorced mother of two gets an app on her phone that lets her be in
more than one place at the same time, and quickly goes from zero to
hero in her personal and professional life—but at what cost?

The Black Velvet Coat by Jill G. Hall
$16.95, 978-1-63152-009-9
When the current owner of a black velvet coat—a San Francisco artist
in search of inspiration—and the original owner, a 1960s heiress who
fled her affluent life fifty years earlier, cross paths, their lives are forever changed . . . for the better.

The Wiregrass by Pam Webber
$16.95, 978-1-63152-943-6
A story about a summer of discontent, change, and dangerous myster-
ies in a small Southern Wiregrass town.